The Mason List

A Novel By:

S. D. Hendrickson

For more information, visit **www.sdhendrickson.com.**

Author Photo: Courtesy of Andrew Lam Photography

ISBN 978-1505641790

For John,

my own dark-haired boy,

who believed I could write a novel before I typed the words.

Chapter 1

Today, 8:15 p.m.

I see the bloodstains around my nails. I scrub and scrub at the dark places. I scratch until my skin turns red with fresh, oxygen-infused spurts from my own body. Grabbing a paper towel, I wrap my fingers to hide the marks. A set of haunting eyes stare back from the mirror with a jagged, swollen cut above the right one.

I fight the urge to drive a fist right into the reflection. I need to hear the crisp smash of the glass. I need to feel the release if only for a moment before the waves crash down again in my heart.

Leaving the hospital bathroom, I walk down the hall, hearing the soles of my shoes squeak. A nurse stares as she passes by, pushing an empty wheelchair. I know what she is thinking. Her pudgy legs can't walk fast enough back to the station to tell the others. *I saw that girl.* The sneer of her intruding smile makes me want to scream in her face.

Trailing aimlessly past the rooms, I search for a vacant space away from the crowds. I knew these halls very well. Better than I ever wanted to know them. On a lone bench, I collapse far away from everyone else. I can't stand to see any of them. I am so incredibly tired of the stupid thoughts that should stay inside their stupid brains.

I hurt. I hurt so damn bad, and nothing will make it better. Tucking my knees to my chest, I curl into a tiny ball. I squeeze tight, feeling the bones crush into my lungs. Tighter and tighter, feeling the pain. I can't breathe. I try to draw in a gasp of air, but nothing can escape through the pressure. The endless, suffocating pressure.

This is what it felt like for him as time ticked by in the distance. Struggling. Gasping. My feet dangle from my legs, exposing my gray shoes covered in dried blood, just like my hands. His blood. My blood. Her blood. Who the hell even knows anymore. I yank them off and jump from the bench.

Throwing the first one, I see the stained glass vibrate and the gray canvas fall to the ground. I beat the second one over and over again, begging the multicolored panels to crack. Picking up the small potted plant, I toss it up, making contact. A violent explosion sends shards in every direction. A sliver of relief sparks the cells of my skin.

I collapse onto the cold floor, feeling the cuts from the daggers of glass. I let the tears fall down my cheeks as I choke on my own spit. The bile rises up, and vomit trickles down my neck into a pool around my head. The world spins around much like a Tilt-A-Whirl. I feel nothing inside my cold, numb body.

"Is she dead, Momma?" I hear the tiny voice of an angel.

"No, baby."

A soft hand brushes the hair away from my forehead. I feel a towel dab at my cheek and across the trail of stench seeping into the neck of my shirt. Opening my eyes, I look into the face of a beauty queen. A smaller version with silky blonde hair touches my hand.

"She's got blood on her clothes, Momma."

I saw the blood. It was everywhere. The body so still. The flesh covered in red, like someone dumped a bucket of paint all over it; the skin hanging off in clumps.

I can't handle the images. So I fall…deeper and deeper. The world spins in perfect rhythm beneath the halls of the hospital that transform into the sting of the meadow sun. Turning and spinning as the girl screams. She screams and screams, echoing shrill and loud in my head.

"Alex, stop…"

The voices turn to whispers. The voices try to take me away. I fight. I scream. I hit and I kick them away. The arms wrap over my body like a cage. The screams turn to sobs. Every face blurs into a rain cloud of tears. The beauty queen tells me it will be okay very soon. I feel a pinch in my arm.

The lights blink on and off.

On and off.

On and off.

The angel, with blue eyes, leans over close to my face. She is beautiful with a halo of light behind her long, glossy hair. The wallpaper crackles, and the lights dim. Her blonde hair turns to black. The face of the angel turns into one so familiar. His blue eyes smile. He pushes the strands of dark hair off his forehead, just like a hundred other times. The angel was the boy, or the boy was the angel. It hurt to breathe. A voice whispers in the distance.

I need to tell you something.

My throat scratches on the words. I dry heave against the shoulder of the beauty queen. The blue eyes fizzle into nothing. He was gone.

Wait. Come back.

I beg his sweet face. My lips taste heavy. I reach toward the wall. I reach to where his face disappeared. My fingers grasp at nothing until the world grows black from the ashes in the wind. I let the breeze take me away to a place that is happy—a place that existed before my life dissolved into this pain.

Chapter 2

When I was six...

Sitting high in the tree, I watched the sky full of large, cotton candy-shaped clouds, twisting and changing into the shapes of dragons and dinosaurs. My arm reached out and grabbed a piece of the white fluff, seeing it dissolve into an iridescent fairy dust in the palm of my small hand. I sprinkled it over my entire body. The fairy magic transformed me into a red bird sitting on a limb. I lifted my wings out into the wind, feeling it toss my crimson feathers around and against my skin.

"Alex Tanner! You get down from that tree!" My mother yelled up to where I sat perched on the branch. I opened my eyes to the blinding sun and scanned the rooftops of the houses scattered below my dangling feet. My gaze stopped on my mother, who was standing on the porch looking very unhappy. Her red hair glowed against the garden backdrop. I would be in trouble again.

"Aw, Momma, it's not that high," I protested as my feet slipped a little on the bark. I made my way down from the oak, careful not to rip my pink fluffy princess dress with sparkling jewels. I liked the jewels; they were the best part. The jewels had to stay on there. With a dramatic jump to save my dress, I landed with a solid thud on my butt in the flower garden.

We lived in Dallas in Snow White's cottage. I knew it wasn't really her house, but it was close to the one in my stories. We had a flower garden on the south side of the house with lots of trees, surrounded by a white fence covered in green ivy. My mother didn't like it when I climbed high into the branches of the trees. She said it was dangerous. I climbed up there anyway.

"Alex, I've told you not to go up there. You have enough to do in the yard without falling out of a tree." My mother, Anna Tanner, glanced down with a stern look that needed a little more anger to be convincing. I knew she couldn't be mad at me for long.

"I know, Momma, but it's so cool seeing everything from up there. I can see the top of our house. And guess what!" I could barely contain myself as I giggled up at her. "I could see into Mr. Wilson's yard. He was outside sweeping his porch in just pink shorts and white socks."

I saw the disapproving shake of her red head. She tried to hide a laugh at the thought of mean, old Mr. Wilson in pink shorts. He really didn't like us very much.

"Come on, Alex. Let's leave Mr. Wilson alone." I followed on her heels up the path to the porch. I heard a scramble and turned to see a furry blur coming from one of the bushes. The brown streak went around my legs and came to a halt on the porch steps. Slobber dripped off a pink tongue surrounded by a face caked in mud.

"Digger, you got dirty," I giggled as my arms went around his little body. Digger slimed my face with mud and drool. He was a little curly mutt picked from a cage of other mutts at the dog pound two years ago. From the day we brought him home, Digger never left my side.

If I were outside, he was lurking under the bushes, pouncing on bugs, or chasing me around the trees. Everyone who met Digger loved him. Well, everyone but Mr. Wilson. One area of the fence had a hole just big enough for Digger to wiggle into Mr. Wilson's yard. He didn't find it funny that Digger was named for his worst habit: digging in roses.

"Put Digger down. We have to clean you up. It's time for your lessons." Momma didn't like my spending the whole summer up in a tree like a monkey.

"Aw, rats! Can we color, please?" I begged, looking up at her tall frame with pleading eyes. I wrapped my arms around her waist, leaving dirty handprints on the back of her white T-shirt. It wasn't nice; but I knew one hug from me, and she would change her mind. My mother looked down at my freckled face, and I smiled back, exposing my missing front tooth. I knew that would seal the deal.

"Okay, Alex." She sighed, shaking her head. "You can color today, but you aren't getting out of practicing your letters tomorrow, deal?" I nodded with excitement. My mother stuck out her hand to shake in agreement.

"Deal!" I said, bouncing off into the house. "Come on, Digger." I scooped him up in my arms as I went inside to wash off the mud. The rest of the afternoon, I scattered drawings all across the wooden kitchen table. I had aliens in three shades of green and purple spotted giraffes with two heads.

My mother stopped by to check on my pictures. She rested a hand on each shoulder, laughing at my colorful characters and agreed it was the scariest space creature she'd ever seen. The afternoon faded into evening, and I heard the front door open. I took off in a sprint to find my father.

"Daddy!" I jumped into his arms as he carried me to the living room couch.

"Okay, Pumpkin, what do you have for me tonight? Another picture for my office?" He smiled as we settled down on the couch. He had called me Pumpkin since I was a baby because my hair was the color of an orange jacko'-lantern. As I described my picture, he smiled in a way that made his face really happy. My father, Henry Tanner, always liked my pictures.

I didn't understand what my father did at work every day. My mother said he made sure grocery stores had all the items they needed, like broccoli. My eyes always crinkled up in confusion at the details. Why would my father buy everyone broccoli?

Sitting me down, my father grabbed my mother for a lingering hug, and then slipped an arm around her waist. He kissed her on the lips. I knew my father and mother loved each other very much. He always looked at her the way the prince did when he danced with Snow White.

That night, after two stories and a glass of milk, my father gave me a big kiss right on the top of my head. "Good night, Pumpkin."

"Night, Daddy."

Turning off the light, my mother whispered next to my cheek, "I love you, Alex, more than all the leaves on the trees."

"Love you too, Momma," I said over a muffled yawn.

With the sheets pulled up tight, little Digger jumped on the bed to get settled in for the night. The little brown ball of fur stretched out at the foot of my bed, covering the tips of my toes. I drifted off to sleep, dreaming of flying horses.

Chapter 3

Today, 8:42 pm.

Beep.

The happy place disappears; the happy place with my mother. The words slice through as my first thought in the headache-induced confusion. She failed to haunt my dreams for some time now.

Beep.

I will my eyes to open. Something nags in the back of my thoughts just beneath the banging noise in my head. It was Saturday. No, it wasn't Saturday. I drove from Dallas on Saturday. I try hard to remember the day.

Beep.

My hand feels around for the bedside alarm buttons to kill the incessant beeping. The more I tug, the more my wrist feels caught. The realization hurt my chest more than the pain in my head. I am not in my bed. I am tied to a hospital bed.

Beep.

Panic kicks in as I struggle to move. The slits of my pale-blue eyes move just enough to take in my surroundings. The lights glow with halos around each bulb. The beauty queen stares back at me. I want to scream at the sight of her face.

Beep.

"Alex, can you hear me? Just try to be still. I'm sorry. I tried to keep them from usin' the restraints, but they were afraid you'd do somethin' again."

Beep.

"Make it stop. Please…please!" I can't stand it anymore. The sound jabs at me. It jabs in my brain like a knife. I pull at the band on my wrists. I try to kick free. I yank with every muscle, feeling the joints pull in my hands.

"Alex, please don't make it worse."

Beep. Beep. Beep.

I scream. I feel the images again, those terrible pictures searing through my gut. They hurt my mind. They hurt my heart. A needle goes into a bag dangling above my head. The sounds become lost in a gentle swoosh, lulling me back down into the depths of my dreams, back to the where it all began.

Chapter 4

When I was eight...

Sitting in my tree, I watched the people in our yard. Anger burned deep inside of me. They were all just vultures, digging and tossing our stuff around without a care in the world. I had the perfect view as they picked apart everything in their sight. None of them were concerned that it was my whole life sitting out on the lawn. It was just another sale to them. It meant nothing to the vultures—no memories or stories.

I watched two men secure our couch to the back of a truck. Their hands fiddled with the ropes, making them so tight that the fabric split open and stuffing blew out across the grass. A man and his wife knocked our table against the trailer, and the leg fell off in the street. They had the nerve to ask my father for a discount because it was damaged before it even left our house. My sad father just handed back a few dollars to the mean couple who broke our table.

I hated the vultures. *I hated them all!*

"Pumpkin?" my father called. "I need you to come down from there and help put the rest of the stuff back in the house." Without a word, I climbed down into the garden and followed him to the front yard.

I shoved a yellow vase into a box with some old glasses and carried it back into the living room. Dropping the cardboard on the hardwood, I heard the glasses bang against each other. I picked the box up and dropped it a little harder, feeling the prickly anticipation for the sound. The vase vibrated a little harder this time. I continued with another try, putting my strength into the throw. A crackling smash came from inside of the box.

Feeling the warm tingle of satisfaction, I looked around the room. The house was empty. According to the foreclosure notice, we had until tomorrow morning to be out of the only place I had ever called home. It was hard to grasp how much our lives had changed in a year.

My mother had something called ovarian cancer. The doctors were hopeful at first, but the cancer had quickly spread to the other places in her body. She had spent weeks at a time in the hospital while my father alternated between work and sitting at her bedside. I had stayed with mean, old Mr. Wilson and his wife. The happy days were over; no more mornings playing in the garden and no more laughing afternoons drawing with my mother.

For months, I cried myself to sleep every night, clutching little Digger. I had just wanted it to be normal again. I wanted my bedtime story. I wanted my mother. I was incredibly sad. I didn't think our lives could get any worse, but then my father came home carrying a box. I knew from his sagging shoulders something bad happened at work. My father said his company had let him go. They'd used some excuse about a bad economy, but we knew the truth. He had missed too many days sitting at the hospital. My father had cried and cried that night. I didn't know what to do as the big tears rolled down his cheeks. *Parents don't cry.*

The bills had piled up everywhere: pink ones and blue ones and eventually red ones. Some were from hospitals or doctors. Some came from the little plastic cards. They all wanted money as my father struggled to find another job.

Maybe he was a little too honest in the interviews. They were always sympathetic with his situation, but he was never picked. My father took odd jobs, but it just wasn't enough money. The bank ordered us to leave the house by the end of May. We could no longer pay for our pretty little cottage and my garden. I was losing both my mother and my home.

I had cried for days and refused to come out of my room, losing my temper more than once, smashing doll china like the Mad Hatter destroying high tea. The meltdowns became farther apart as I slowly came to acceptance. With every breath, I felt the fear and uncertainty of our future. With every breath, I felt a hard, ridged coat form over my heart.

My father looked for us a new place to live and a place to take care of my mother. The treatments had stopped working months ago. It was time to just keep her from feeling pain. He found a hospital west of Fort Worth in a town called Arlis that took charity hospice cases. My father wanted us to live there too. I hated the idea of moving. I hated leaving my home. I hated the bank; it was cruel, like the evil queen who attacked Snow White.

As we packed the house for the move, my father handed over two small boxes. He struggled to look me in the eye as he told me to choose only the things that were most important to me. I stared back, wanting to scream in his face. His sad eyes had stopped every word from flowing out of my mouth. Instead of yelling, I bit down on my lip until I tasted blood. I bit down hard, feeling the coat squeeze around my heart. I needed that coat to block out how dark I felt inside. It would keep the tears away. I may have only been eight, but I felt the reality of the outside world like someone twice my age. No more daydreams up in the trees. It was time to be strong. I needed it, and my father needed it too.

Without a word, I had followed my father's instructions and only packed items I needed for the trip. All the jeweled dresses and crowns stayed in the closet; this Arlis town was no place for a laughing princess.

"Hey, Pumpkin, can you get those blankets and pillows out? We can stretch those out in your room tonight."

"Okay," I muttered, snapping back to reality. My tongue traced the familiar cut that still remained on my bottom lip. I watched my father pile the remaining items up in the living room. The creases on his forehead seemed ingrained on his skin. Today had been hard on him too. We were leaving with only few boxes and a little money, which only existed because we sold everything in our house.

I got the blankets from the garage and laid them out on the carpet in my room. My little white bed had sold this afternoon. The new owner seemed like a nice little girl. Maybe she would love it as much as me.

I wrapped up in the blanket while my head rested against the pillow. Digger bounced out from some hiding place deep in the house. His tongue licked my nose and eyes. I pulled him close in a bear hug. It would be my last night with Digger. He was staying with Mr. Wilson. My father had rented a room at an extended-stay motel in stupid Arlis. I had begged my father to let me take Digger, but the stupid motel said no pets.

I squeezed my dog tighter as my father walked into my bedroom. He sat down on the floor next to me. "You okay, Pumpkin?"

"Can't we just sneak him in the room?"

"I'm sorry, but it's better for him to stay with the Wilsons than the motel taking him away."

"I know." My throat hurt on the words as the tears burned in my eyes. The coat around my heart got thicker, and I cried no tears for Digger.

"It'll be okay. You'll like Arlis," my father said as he tried to pull together a smile.

"How do you know? You've never been there!" I snapped back. In the weak moment, I struggled to contain my anger. I hurt too much tonight.

"Alexandra! You need to change your attitude about this." I felt myself cringe; he never got upset with me. I didn't want to make this worse for him.

"I'm sorry, Dad. I didn't mean that. I know you're right. It will be good there." The words didn't calm the storm I felt inside, but it made my father's face relax a little. I said the words he needed to hear. I said the words to comfort my father.

I blocked out his voice as he continued to talk about that stupid town and that stupid motel and that stupid hospital. I bit my lip until I tasted the salty blood in my mouth. I squeezed my eyes shut, begging the darkness to carry me away.

By the time I woke the next morning, my father had the old SUV loaded with our belongings. The back had boxes packed to the ceiling. The Wilsons stood outside talking to my father. I saw Mr. Wilson pat my father on the shoulder as they nodded about something I couldn't hear. I carried Digger over to his new home. Mrs. Wilson smiled down as I handed over the ball of fur.

"We promise to take good care of him," she said, trying to reassure me. I muttered *thanks* and climbed in the truck. I saw the tears in my father's eyes as we backed out of the driveway. Mine were completely dry as I pressed my nose against the glass to look one last time. The coat around my heart got even tighter, seeing our little cottage with the garden fade into the distance.

Chapter 5

When I was eight...

From the hospital room window, I peeked through the closed curtain and watched three children on the red-and-yellow playground. They seemed happy. A boy joined in for a game of tag. He chased a girl around the green hedges.

"You should go down there, Alex." I heard a faint voice come from the bed. My mother was in a deep sleep most of the time. I preferred it when she was out because I knew she didn't feel the pain. Those wishes came laced with selfishness. I liked to sit in silence. It was easier than a forced conversation with a dying person, even if she were my mother. I really didn't know what to say anymore. The days just seemed better when her skeleton face didn't speak. Shame filled my chest. I stopped the terrible thoughts and buried them with a crooked smile.

"It's ok, Mom. Do you want me to get you a drink?" I left the window to sit in the chair next to her bed. Her skeleton hand patted my arm. I felt a shudder and focused on her bald head instead.

"Maybe a little sip." She looked so pale, and I saw the strain on her face as she tried to speak. "I worry about you, honey."

"Why?"

"You should be doing something, I don't know—" Her voice cracked. A faint cough interrupted, and then she continued, "Fun. You're like a little grownup now. I miss my little Alex in the trees."

"I'm okay. Really. Besides, you were right. It was dangerous climbing up in the trees." Fleeting images of our garden flashed through my mind. I wondered if my mother understood the trees were gone from our lives forever.

I pulled the blanket up around her shoulders and kissed her cheek. My throat fought back a gag. Her skin used to smell like the roses in our backyard. Now her skin stunk like moldy bread.

"Mom, I'll see if…" My words trailed off as I watched her eyelids close. I sighed with relief and settled back in the windowsill. Silence.

It didn't take long for the Tanners to get into a routine. We arrived in Arlis at the end of May. Over the last few weeks, we shuffled between the nasty motel and the hospital. My father and I took turns sitting beside my mother's bed. He would leave some afternoons to search for a job but got the same reaction in Arlis and the surrounding Palo Pinto County. Not a single person wanted him.

I studied the cheap, fake pink-and-blue bouquet in the corner vase. My father bought the flowers last week in the half-price bin at Dollar General by the extended-stay motel. I wrinkled my nose at the mere thought of the "suite" we called home. *Suite, my foot!* It was filthy, and a strange animal lived in the bathroom. Each morning, I studied the small pile of poop left in the corner by the brown-stained tub. I had it narrowed down to a rat, a wall possum, or a snake. I assumed a snake could poop too.

My clothes always smelled musty from the odd fumes that seeped through the walls from our neighbor on the right side. I didn't like him. He scared me. I wanted to tell my father how much he scared me, but I knew there was nothing we could do about it. Every night, that man stood on the balcony. His eyes followed each of my steps to our apartment. From the base of his throat, an evil tattoo glared like a second pair of eyes. My father turned the lock on the door, but I knew that two-headed monster stayed just on the other side of the old wood.

As soon as we settled in each night, I struggled to sleep with the banging and yelling from the neighbor under our bed. The words came through muddled except for a few snippets that sounded like "pig-faced bitch." My father just turned up the volume on the television louder to drown out the noise.

Sometimes I watched our downstairs neighbors. He was a skinny man for having such a loud voice. I thought the woman was rather pretty and nothing like a pig-faced bitch. Once, I watched them from the front window until I coughed. The walls had black mold from rain coming in through holes in the glass.

I hated that place. Although hate didn't come close to describing my feelings for our new home. I needed a word stronger and bigger than just *hate*.

"Hey. How are my girls?" I turned to see my father walk back in the room. He gave me a little squeeze. Something seemed off. I'd gotten pretty good at reading my father over the last year. He leaned over to kiss my mother on her forehead. The sleeping corpse never responded.

"Dad, is something wrong?" I had to ask even though I was afraid of the answer. Given our recent luck, it was inevitable our life would just get worse.

"No, Pumpkin, everything is fine." I saw by the tilt of his eyes that my father was lying. We sat for a couple of hours as the sun faded into the sky. My mother never woke up after our little talk. My father and I left for the night. The soles of my shoes squeaked on the floor. They hurt my feet, and I needed new ones. My toes seemed to double over at the front just to fit inside.

My father and I crossed the parking lot. I saw the Bronco under the streetlight. The old truck sat packed to the roof, just like the day we arrived in Arlis.

"Dad!" I gasped, looking at the truck and then back to his devastated face.

"I couldn't pay the weekly rate last week so the manager let it slide. When I didn't have the money today, they made me pack everything up in the car." My father stood on the hot pavement staring at the ground like he failed all of us.

My stomach lurched as the reality twisted inside my body. *I'm homeless.* The Tanners literally were homeless without even an option for a place to go. I knew a flood of tears wanted to flow in ugly streams down my cheeks. I pursed my lips and bit down hard on the lower one. I no longer allowed tears. Not since we lost our home. Not since we had to travel to Arlis. Not since I left Digger.

I settled in the passenger side of the Bronco. My eyes felt as vacant as the deserted parking lot. I cranked down the window with the manual turn knob. I needed air. I couldn't breathe.

"Wait, Alex. We can't put them down until all the cars are gone."

I wanted to scream. I couldn't hold back the words. Turning to unload a gut full of hate, I stopped cold. Tears gathered in the corners of my father's eyes. One rolled over the edge. His face tilted toward the driver's side window to hide the fact that he sat crying in our old car. A sob cracked in his throat, turning into a terrible sound, like a wounded animal. I pretended not to see the breakdown. Resting my head back against the seat, I stared at the stains on the cloth ceiling of the Bronco.

Over the next few nights, I curled up in the passenger seat and rested against the hot window until it was safe to roll it down. We visited my mother during the day. I sneaked into the hospital bathroom to wash up. Some nights, I just dabbed off my arms and legs in the sink.

My father left every morning to find anything to bring in money. He tried to walk as much as possible to keep from using the last of our gas. Even if he found something, I knew it would be a few weeks without money unless someone paid cash. I sat in grateful silence each day that my mother was too weak to catch on to what was happening right under her hospital room window.

On the *eighteenth* night of sleeping in the Bronco, my father and I sat in the front seat watching the sun set. I took a bite of my pimento-cheese sandwich from the vending machine. Halfway through it, I noticed mold growing on the underside of the bread. My stomach fought back a gag as I hid the rest of the sandwich in a napkin. I didn't want to upset my father. The hot air in the car couldn't handle another one of his breakdowns.

I'm not sure what he picked from the machine tonight. My father said he ate a sandwich while I was washing off in the bathroom. I think he was lying. My stomach rumbled trying to digest the molded bread. I was afraid. The coins would eventually run out and so would the supply of spoiled food.

I fluffed my pillow against the glass and did my best to block out the sticky heat. Two cars stayed in the corner of the lot. I wanted to yell, "Go home to your stupid house."

The Bronco had developed a lingering smell of dirty socks and bologna. Each morning, we killed roaches that scattered across our seats. I think the nasty bugs lived in the boxes we stored in the back part of the car. They came out at night looking for food. I felt the bugs; their tiny legs pricking my skin as they stepped down my arm and across my stomach while I slept. My father insisted they didn't have teeth.

I took a deep breath watching the parking lot. The air pulled sharp through my nose, but it felt so hot. Every breath was like sucking in the fumes of a hair dryer. I fought the urge to fling open the door and run down the street with my feet pounding against the cement. I would run until my shoes filled with blood from my curled-up toes.

A man walked out the side doors to the last car. *Finally!* I could get a cool breeze through the window. He stopped dead in his tracks and stared in our direction. Noticing the jet-black hair, I recognized him as one of the people who took care of my mother. Dr. Mason fixated on the Bronco. He continued to stare with a worried look on his face.

No, no, no! He was coming over. He would see us—the creepy homeless people living in the parking lot. I wanted to slide into the floor and put the pillow over my face. *Go away*! I screamed in my head while my dad rolled down the window for Dr. Mason.

"Hey, Henry. How ya holdin' up tonight?" I saw Dr. Mason's eyes glance to the back of the Bronco. Even in the low light of the dark parking lot, I knew the doctor had a good idea of our current problem. Old boxes packed to the ceiling. Clothes draped over the headrest, drying from today's hand washing in the shower. And the smell. I knew the exact stench that escaped like a giant cloud of death when the door opened.

"Doing okay, Dr. Mason. Did you need something? Has something changed with Anna?" I heard my father trying to keep his voice steady. At this point, I wasn't sure if the tremor came from the fear that something had happened with my mother or just plain embarrassment of getting caught in the parking lot.

"No news. Everythin' seems to be holdin' steady at the moment." Dr. Mason looked over in my direction, and I quickly dropped my eyes to the floor. I wished my mind possessed magical powers to dissolve my body into the carpet floorboard, but I was no longer the child who believed in fairy dust.

"I saw you leavin' and thought maybe you'd like to stay in the room with Anna tonight. I think it'd be big enough to pull in a couple of cots." I looked back up in surprise but only saw kindness in his expression.

My father glanced at me with a strained face as he tried to hold it together. He asked for my reassurance. I wrinkled my nose and tilted up in defiance. I was so tired of being his strength. Slowly, I nodded back at my father and gripped the pillow tight in my hands. *Fine!*

"Sure," my father said with a smile. "I think that would be a nice change to stay overnight. Could do Anna some good."

Dr. Mason walked back to the hospital while we gathered a few items from the back. I looked over the parking lot and took in the reality of the moment. Shame pumped through my body with each beat of my heart. I hated charity. I hated depending on others. I hated being homeless. I hated people knowing we had nothing.

Every fiber of my being wanted to scream as I followed my father back through the sliding doors of the hospital. Each tennis shoe clomp on the tile took us down a path of no return. The stomping made the tight shoes hurt worse. I didn't care. Until tonight, it had been our secret, and now everyone would know.

Since my mom got sick, a little piece of my life disappeared every day, yet we still survived on our own. Tonight was different. It was the first step into the bottom of the barrel. We needed so much more than just a cot for the night. Dr. Mason had to know this about our life.

I watched one of the hospital staff wedge two small cots between the bed and window. It was a tight fit. Dr. Mason came in with some blankets, pillows, and a few towels.

"You know where the bathroom is with the shower. It's shared with these six rooms on this wing. You'd be fine takin' showers in the evenin's. The patients usually have 'em in the mornin'." He looked at my father and nodded a good-bye. My father looked at me.

"Alex. It won't be like this forever. I promise. We will be okay. It's just going to take some time."

His words were meant to comfort me, but his eyes begged for reassurance again. Everything about our relationship seemed reversed and twisted. I gritted my fingers into the palms of my hands. I needed composure. When did I stop being the child and become the rock for my father? I nodded in agreement. It completely sucked. At the time I should have been getting a bedtime story, I was lying to my father so he didn't have another breakdown.

I settled on the cot and focused on the ceiling as I tried to drift off to sleep. I heard the monitors tracking the remaining signs of life coming from my mother. I smelled the hospital. It always had a rotten stench that infested your nose and wouldn't leave; a mix of bad food, urine, and cleanser intended to wipe away the stench. To me, it was the smell of death.

After tossing around for an hour, I got up to use the restroom. I heard people moaning deathly groans from their beds. I shoved my hands on each side of my head to block out the awful sounds.

I needed something to release this feeling. I would never be able sleep with this twisted aggravation circling through my thoughts on the brink of eruption. Two crystal glass dishes the size of my hand sat on the decorative table by the elevator. I slipped the cold objects under my shirt and sneaked to the small balcony at the end of the hall. The sticky air caused sweat to bead up on my forehead. With a large swing, the first glass item hit the pavement below. *Smash!* The air rushed in my lungs. I could breathe. I launched the second one, feeling the anticipation build as I waited for the crashing sound. *Smash!*

I slipped through the balcony door and dragged my aching feet back to the room. The small sliver of release disappeared into the moans of the patients. My heart felt like the inside of a dark, clouded thunderstorm. Our fate was now in the hands of Dr. Mason. My mother just kept hanging on. Our lives remained stuck in this limbo. It would never get better as long as she continued to drag on and on. I wish she would just let go. *I wish she would just die!*

I pulled the blanket over my head to block out the awful thoughts and bit my lip until I tasted the salty blood.

Chapter 6

When I was eight...

I peeked through the slit in the curtains that blocked the sunshine from flowing across the hospital room. The start of a new day remained hidden beneath the thick drapes. My father left earlier. I stayed in the room staring at the clouds in the distance. The white puffs filled the sky without a single flying horse. I wondered if God was watching me right now. My father always talked about God watching over us. It was just something I couldn't understand. I didn't feel like I was being watched by anyone accept maybe the nurses lurking around the corners.

A knock on the door rattled my attention away from the window. I turned around to see a lady standing in the doorway. She had a stern expression on her face, surrounded by beautiful blonde hair. My eyes trailed down her tiny figure at the expensive dress suit made of tan silk, accented with a strand of pearls just visible under the collar.

"Hello, you must be Alexandra. I'm Eva Lynn Mason. Is your father here?"

I don't know if I were more startled by her sudden appearance or the fact that she called me Alexandra. I felt self-conscious in my crinkled-up shirt and jeans. I often just slept in my clothes and never bothered to change. Sometimes I wore the same thing for days so I didn't have to wash it out in the sink. I knew I smelled, but it didn't matter when my home was our car. It smelled too.

"Now, young lady. You really should speak when someone asks you a question. Do you know where your father is? I brought both of you lunch."

Mesmerized by her strong Texas drawl, I had failed to notice the large container in her hands. I finally spoke up and said, "I'm Alex. He's not here."

"Well, Alexandra," she said with a stressed emphasis, pulling out each syllable. Every word took twice as long when they left her flawless mouth. "I guess I will just have to wait until he returns, and please call me Mrs. Mason." She turned and sat the container on the table by my sleeping mother who was oblivious to everything.

While I contemplated Dr. Mason's other half, something in the hallway caught my attention. It was a boy. He leaned against the wall, just staring at the floor as if to say, *I would rather be anywhere but here.* The boy looked about the same age as me, but it was hard to tell. He was really tall, but so was I. He looked over to where I stood in the doorway.

I froze as he stared at me. The boy had blue eyes outlined with thick, black eyelashes. Blue eyes so bright and clear, like sunshine on a cloudless day. His black hair was a little shaggy and fell across his face almost covering the left eye. His hand went up and smoothed the hair to the side. His face took on a mischievous grin as the hair fell back in place over his blue eye.

"Don't just stand out in the hallway taking up space. Be useful, Jessup. Go to your father's office and bring back some plates."

I watched Mrs. Mason with fascination. I'd never met anyone like her. So elegant, yet she held a commanding presence that ate up the whole room.

"Okay, Mother," he paused and then looked at me, "You wanna come too? It ain't very far."

"Jessup, please speak correctly." Mrs. Mason struck again, but the look on her face was more effective than her words. She had just the right authority in her stare that made you want to never be on her bad side.

"Yes, ma'am," he answered as he disappeared through the door. I stood there a second and then took off behind him. We walked side by side past a few rooms before he said anything.

"Don't worry about Mother. She's not too bad most of the time." I looked over at him, and he glanced back. "Want some Skittles?" He pulled a half-eaten package out of his pocket and tilted the bag up to his lips.

I watched as he chewed the large wad of candy in his mouth. I'd never seen someone with eyes that color of blue against such tan skin. *He must spend hours running through the sun*, I thought. As I studied his face, I was fascinated by how very different he looked from my ivory skin and faint red lashes.

"Why're you starin' at me?" He wrinkled his eyes at me. Heat filled my cheeks, burning as red as my hair.

"No Skittles. Um, so, um, your name is Jessup?" I grasped for something to help recover from my embarrassment.

"No. Well, yes. I guess you ain't from 'round Arlis. Most people's heard of the Jessups here. We own Sprayberry. It's a ranch, ya know. The kind with like oil and cattle and stuff." I nodded along like those were normal things to just own. "We've got horses, and it's really big. Like, you can ride for hours before you get to the other side."

I nodded as he kept talking and crunching at the same time. "Mother named me after 'em. She was Eva Lynn Jessup before she married my dad. Family legacy thing. At least, that's what she tells me, anyway. I think it's stupid." He kicked a wadded-up piece of paper across the floor.

I tried to process everything he had just told me about the Masons and the Jessups. They must be pretty rich to have a ranch like he had described. I tried to think of something to say back; it felt a little weird talking to a strange boy. I talked mostly to my father the last few months.

Jess pushed a few strands of shaggy hair off his forehead. I looked down at his jeans with holes in the knees and a faded-out T-shirt. Instead of sneakers, Jess wore one very expensive pair of cowboy boots. He looked a little sloppy, but it was in the rich-kid kind of way.

"So your first name is Jessup, and your family's last name is Jessup. That kind of sucks having it the same, I guess."

"Hey, that's not nice." He bumped my shoulder, catching me off-guard. I looked at him in surprise as he raised his eyebrows and smiled. I didn't answer, so he just kept talking. "No one but Mother calls me Jessup. I'm really just plain old Jess. "

"Nice to meet you. I guess I'm just plain old Alex."

I felt those blue eyes looking me over. They slide from my hair to the ratty, gray canvas shoes. My little toe poked through a hole on the left one between the fabric and white plastic. He noticed but didn't say much. Jess just shrugged and said, "I think you look like an Alex."

I felt the heat flood my cheeks. Was that an insult? I rubbed my sweaty palms across my thrift-store jeans. I knew they were boy jeans because they were the only ones that fit my long legs. My red hair was bobbed at my chin. Without my mother, it had been awhile since my long hair held braids or bows. My father cut it off before the move to make it easier to manage. His fingers just couldn't get the twisting into something that even resembled a braid. With the chin-length crop, I had the hair of Orphan Annie—just without the curls.

I felt sad again, and so much older than eight. After moving around, sitting in hospitals, and taking care of my father, I grew up far beyond my age. It's strange how the reality of a situation could appear out of nowhere and just slap you in the face. I was a poor, homeless girl with ugly hair and ugly shoes. I looked back up at Jess. At least my eyes had no tears left to further embarrass me.

"Let's just get the plates and go back. I'm sure she's waiting." My tone was a little sharper than I'd intended. Something changed on Jess's face, like I'd just yelled at him.

"Hey, what'd I do? I thought we were talkin'." He studied me for a moment, trying to figure it out. "What'd I say, Alex?"

We really didn't know each other. Maybe Jess didn't intend to be mean. I tried to give him a smile, but it felt foreign on my face. I didn't want to offend this boy. We needed the Masons right now. It was an irritating thought. As much as I hated the charity, I had to at least appear grateful until we could get back on our own. Making Jess mad might just get us kicked out of the hospital.

"It's okay. Let's just get the stuff and go back to the room," I finally said with a shrug. I fought the urge to turn my eyes to the floor. I just didn't know how to do this anymore. I had to work harder to have a normal conversation with someone my own age.

Jess looked me over again without a word. The blue eyes scanned every dirty, grimy piece of me. An odd feeling spread through my chest as we stood facing each other. I was pretty sure he could see inside of me. Silent and watching, those clear-blue eyes reflected how dark I felt. The anger, the shame, and the complete lack of hope. His eyebrows wrinkled into a frown while the wheels under his shaggy mop came to an internal conclusion.

"Stay here." He flashed a quick smile and disappeared. I stood in the hall as Jess went into his father's office and came back with the plates. I looked into his wide grin and twinkling blue eyes.

"Come on…race ya!" He took off running down the hall. I paused, and then I ran after him. It felt crazy and strange. Our shoes pounded against the tile floor like a pack of animals. My feet hurt in the tight canvas, but I didn't care. I had a burning need to catch him. Jess brushed too close to a cart of supplies, and it tipped over. The crash echoed through the hall. I accidentally kicked a nurse as I jumped over bedpans and containers covering the floor.

"I'm sorry!" I yelled back while trying to gain speed. Jess reached the doorway before I did. Running fast, I couldn't slow down as I plowed right into Jess. We tumbled to the ground, laughing and out of breath.

"You might be some fun after all," he said, smiling into my face.

"Yeah, well, that wasn't fair. I could have beaten you." The words come out in short gasps while I sucked in air from running. "You had a head start and threw the cart at me."

"Whatever makes ya feel better, *Alex*," he taunted back.

"Ahem." We turned to see the very upset nurse I'd collided with just moments earlier. Her arms were crossed, a deep scowl on her face.

"Where's your mother, Mr. Mason? I'm sure she would love to know that you're up to trouble again."

We looked at each other a little longer. A giggle escaped my lips, and we both busted out laughing. As the sound echoed in my ears, I realized it had been a very long time since I'd felt like a real kid.

"*Now,* Mr. Mason. And your friend needs to come too."

Jess turned, and I followed him into the room with the nurse behind us. Mrs. Mason had the food set out in a proper lunch display, despite the fact that it was in a hospital room. My father was back, and they appeared deep in discussion. Next to my mother's bed, a bouquet of fresh yellow flowers sat in a crystal vase. *Just another gift from the Masons*, I presumed. The thick curtains were open. As sunlight flowed through the window, the sickness faded into the ugly walls of the room.

Our life had transformed into a different scene from twenty-four hours ago. These Masons didn't just come into your life slowly; they arrived with the force of a hurricane. I glanced over at the boy with bright-blue eyes, and he smiled at me. I felt the corners of my lips creep up on the sides. His happy face was more contagious than any infectious, nasty bit of cancer.

In just a few short minutes, Jess Mason had made me truly smile from the inside out.

Chapter 7

When I was eight...

"Ever use one of these?"

"No." I looked back a little hesitantly. "I don't know if we should do it, Jess."

"Come on, Alex. You know ya want to."

I stared into a scheming set of blue eyes. I'd seen water guns, but nothing like the double-barrel, turbo, twenty-foot slingers Jess pulled from his large duffle bag. He walked to the sliding doors leading out behind the hospital. Looking back over his shoulder, I got his ornery grin. "You comin'?"

That seemed to be the way Jess handled things. He just assumed I would follow behind, and well, I always did. "Wait. I'm coming."

Every day for the last two weeks, Mrs. Mason brought us food. She delivered baskets of casseroles and foil-wrapped hamburgers and even a pie with fluffy meringue. I wasn't sure if she actually made the food or scared some poor soul into sending us handouts. Mrs. Mason was a little over the top, but I didn't care. Every time she came, Jess always arrived with her. It was hard not to be pulled into the contagious world of Jess. With each visit, he gave me a few hours to be a kid again.

My mother continued to get worse and eventually slipped into a coma. Most afternoons, Jess and I were sequestered in a corner of the waiting room. We played board games and watched television. Jess liked to talk. He carried most of the conversations while I said little. He had an accent as thick as pancake syrup. When he got excited, he slurred all his words together, making it hard to understand.

"Alex, you're goin' on this side of the buildin', and I'll get on the other side by the bushes. The tree in the center is the safe zone. Make sense?" He handed me a Super Soaker he filled up from a faucet behind the hospital.

"Yeah, I guess so. No leaving this area, right?" I asked. From that exact angle, no one could see what we were doing with the water guns.

"Nope." He shook his head back and forth, making his shaggy black hair swing over his eyes. Jess grinned with a smirk, "Go!"

We spent the next ten or so minutes running around, taking wild shots and diving behind bushes. Jess was much better than me. I took a few hits to the back, soaking my gray T-shirt to the skin. My shots were not as well aimed. Jess had a few splattered water spots across one leg of his jeans.

Jess ran out of the fight zone toward the hospital side entrance. I followed after him inside the building just in time to see the elevator door slide shut with Jess inside. I glanced around, looking for the staircase. Sprinting up the steps two at a time, I reached the top just as the elevator doors opened. I shot in rapid-fire motion, hitting Jess in the face and chest. The water in my gun flowed down like a waterfall against the walls, soaking the carpet. Jess pushed every button on the panel to get the door to close, but I dove on my stomach across the metal grate just before they slid shut.

"I've got you! Surrender!" I pumped every remaining drop onto his face. The heavy stream hit his skin and overflowed into the control panel. Sirens blared. Red lights blinked. The elevator came to a screeching halt in emergency mode.

"What did you do?" I glared at him.

"What did *I* do?" He yelled back at me over the sirens.

"I was just following you! I knew you would get us in trouble. You broke the buttons!"

"*You* shot water in the controls!"

We stood on opposite ends of the elevator, staring each other down. His hand uncurled with a red knob clasped inside.

"What is that, Jess?"

"I don't know. It sort of just fell off. Please don't get mad at me." Jess looked pathetic with his hair plastered to his forehead, water dripping down his cheeks. "I didn't do it on purpose."

"You always act like this, don't you?" I sat down on the floor, my wet clothes causing me to shiver. The siren pulsated in the background, making it much harder to think and talk in the elevator.

"Oh, come on, Alex. I'm really sorry," Jess pleaded. "I should have left those at home. I just wanted you to play with 'em. You said you ain't ever used one before."

"I don't want to talk to you right now." I glared at him. "You have nothing to lose. I'm the one who will be in so much trouble."

"You think I don't ever get in trouble? Well, I do!"

"*Sure* you do," I shot back.

"They're gonna have me scoopin' poop again. I hate poop."

"Poop?"

"Yep. Poop."

"I don't understand."

"Horse poop. Cow poop. Dog poop. He'll make me clean all of it. Gets all over me."

I secretly laughed at the idea of Jess with poop smeared all over him. *Serves him right!* Water gun in a hospital would be a big deal to my father. He would ground me until I could drive.

"You want a Skittle?" Jess pulled a bag from his pocket. I glared *no*, as he shoved a few handfuls in his mouth. I swear that boy ate nothing but Skittles.

The minutes ticked by as Jess crunched next to me. I did my best to ignore him. The sirens stopped, but the elevator didn't move. He was driving me crazy chomping on his dang candy.

"Why do you come here?" I asked.

"What'd ya mean?" He looked up.

"Here at the hospital. Why?" I'd contemplated the idea for some time. Our whole family situation had me thinking terrible things.

"I don't know." He shrugged.

"You don't know why you come here every day?"

Jess shrugged again. "It's fun to hang out here."

"Your mother doesn't make you?"

"Why would she do that?" He looked confused.

"Forget it," I shot back. He didn't seem to know what I was talking about, and it was time to end the questions. I went back to angry silence.

"You think she makes me hang out with you, don't ya?"

"You have your whole ranch and everything. You talk about it all the time. But you come here. I just don't understand why you don't stay home."

Jess watched me like he was trying to figure out what to do next. His lips twisted around before answering. "I'm the only kid at the ranch, so I like comin' up here. I like hangin' out with you. I think you're pretty cool. I mean, for a girl."

My cheeks burned red. "Oh."

"You wish I didn't come?"

"I don't know," I mumbled.

"You don't know? Maybe I just won't come anymore since you don't like me."

"No, wait. That's not what I meant." It was difficult letting someone get this close to me, letting him see how far my broken life had spiraled. Letting him know I would crumble back into the deep darkness if his visits stopped.

"I don't want you to stop coming."

"So ya *dooo* like me?" His blue eyes shot open, lifting his dark eyebrows. "I knew ya did."

"Don't make a big deal out of it." I felt the red flush on my cheeks.

"Okay," he said, cramming another handful of rainbow dots in his mouth. He crunched with that silly grin.

"Jess, I think we are moving!"

We jumped up and waited for the doors to open. Stepping out in the lobby, we faced a crowd of people. Each set of eyes stared at the water dripping from our clothes and the large orange guns in our hands. I took a quick tally and saw my father, the Masons, the maintenance crew, three firemen, and an assortment of hospital staff.

This was bad.

I took a step sideways to be shoulder to shoulder with Jess. It felt much better to be closer to him. I needed reassurance from the boy who was my only friend. Jess winked at me with a half smile. Glancing back toward the crowd, I avoided the disappointed look on my father's face but found another one that seemed worse. I was right about her. Mrs. Mason was definitely scary when she was angry. Maybe Jess wasn't kidding when he talked about getting in trouble.

This would be bad for both of us.

Chapter 8

When I was eight...

My father and I sat on a bench in the garden area outside the hospital. As the August heat exploded like steam off the cement, I braced for the same old speech.

Over the last week, I received different versions of the same lecture. I wanted to crawl under the bench to avoid it again. He used the same sad tactic every time with pathetic, glossy eyes. "Alex, you need to be spending the last few days with your mother instead of running up and down the halls destroying things." His words made me feel horrible. I felt sad for him. I felt sad for my mother. I felt sad for the little girl who used to be me.

Mrs. Mason continued to bring food, but I never saw her *or* Jess. She left the food at the nurse's station. Dr. Mason stopped by each day and talked to my father about my mother's impending death. I wanted to ask about Jess, but I was afraid it would remind him of the incident with the water guns. The *problems* my father wanted to rehash.

"Dad, you know I am really, really, *really* sorry."

"I know. But that's not what I want to talk to you about. Staying in the hospital has become a problem."

"Like, what kind of problem?"

"We can't stay here anymore, Pumpkin."

I bit down on my lip to stop the sudden gasp. The doors slid open, and my stomach fell to the bottom of an elevator shaft. Our car no longer was an option, and now the hospital kicked us out too.

"I…I don't understand. Where are we going to live?"

He smiled. "Sprayberry."

The next day, we drove down a dirt road with the old Bronco packed full. This Sprayberry place was out in the middle of No-wheres-ville. My only experience with a ranch came from Jess's constant ramblings. I missed his stories. I missed his smiling face. But even if I were tortured, I would *never* tell Jess how much I missed him the past week.

Sprayberry Ranch had a small, vacant farmhouse on the north end of the property. The Masons said we could stay for free if my father would do the repair work. When things got better, we could pay rent. The Masons didn't want us to worry about any of that for now. I wanted to scream, but I knew we had nowhere else to go.

"Pretty cool, isn't it?" My father asked as we pulled up the driveway to the little farmhouse. The sun sparkled across the tall grass, and I spotted a few red cows in the distance. I imagined the worst, but to my surprise, it was decent. I don't know why I expected anything less from the Masons.

Our new home was a simple, one-story house, covered with faded gray siding, blue shutters, and a wooden porch. My father took a quick look around the outside of the old place. He smiled at my frowning face.

"Well, not too bad. A few rotten boards will need to be replaced along the sides around the roof, but it shouldn't leak. Just needs a good cleaning and painting as far as I can tell. Come on." He put his arm across my back. "Let's see the inside. I think you'll like it."

We walked through the small living room with hardwood floors, shiny from a recent coat of lacquer. Old, pink paper covered the kitchen walls. I slid my hand across the countertop with mud-colored stains bigger than my palm. Wandering down the short hallway, I found two bedrooms and a bathroom.

"The one on the right is yours," my father called from the living room. He found his old, cheery attitude again the moment we turned into the driveway.

The room caught me by surprise. Driving out to the ranch, I didn't think about furniture. The bedroom had a large, white bed with a matching dresser and mirror. It wasn't elaborate, but I could tell it was meant for a girl. It was meant for me.

A fluffy, purple bedspread covered the mattress. I didn't see a price tag, but it smelled brand new. Absently, I pulled open one of the drawers and found a few clothing items. I saw my father watching from the doorway.

"Mrs. Mason asked if you had any new school clothes. I told her we hadn't gone shopping yet. She asked for your sizes. Said she could get some for you since we wouldn't have time to shop before school starts next week."

Yeah, right! I yelled in my head. It's more like we didn't have the money. It was just another item to add to the growing list of debts we owed these Masons.

I said nothing and pushed open the closet to find that it held more clothes hanging neatly on hangers. As my fingers thumbed through new jeans and shorts, I studied the choice of outfits picked by Mrs. Mason. She had purchased a few plain shirts resembling those I'd worn around the hospital. However, most of the items had sparkles or flowers or were stamped with a fancy logo.

In the back, I found two nice dresses, suitable for Easter or maybe Christmas. I frowned, letting my fingers touch the fabric. This Alex didn't wear such clothes. On the floor, my eyes scanned two new pairs of canvas tennis shoes, a pair of sandals, and a pair of shiny leather dress flats. I now had fancy shoes to go with the fancy dresses to wear to nonexistent fancy parties.

I let out a deep breath through my lips. It was all very frustrating. Sitting down on the floor, I slipped off my tight, ragged gray shoes. I stuck my foot into a pair of the new canvas ones. My toes wiggled at the tip with plenty of room to spare. My feet let out a sigh of relief and sucked in a big gulp of freedom. If only my heart could feel the same way.

Outside I heard a rumbling noise in the yard. I laced the other shoe and stood up beside the bedroom window, seeing Jess on his four-wheeler. My chest jumped as I watched him. It took everything in me not to go running down the hall and out the front door. Instead, I walked slowly to the front porch, trying to play it cool. I stood by my father and waited for Jess to talk first.

"Hey, Alex."

"Hi," I said, feeling my lips smile.

Jess didn't look any different than when I saw him at the hospital. He wore the same old, roughed-up jeans and T-shirt with the exception of the boots. Today's pair was old and caked with mud.

"Hey, Mr. Tanner. Y'all moved in?"

"We're getting there," my father said back. "You want to come in?"

"Well, ummm. I was wonderin' if I could give Alex a tour. Show her all the good spots." He flashed one of his big grins that made you doubt he could ever cause any problems. My father looked at me and back at Jess.

"I guess so, but you two need to try a little bit harder not to get in trouble." He gave us both the typical stern-parent look.

"I promise, Dad." I squeezed a quick hug around his waist and walked over to the four-wheeler.

"I like your shoes."

"Um, thanks." I felt the heat burning on my cheeks. My brand-new, gray canvas shoes felt like blood money.

"You gettin' on or what?"

"Sure," I muttered, glancing at the seat, then back at Jess. "How do you do this?"

"Here, let me help ya." Jess pulled me on the extra space toward the back. "Your arms go here." He put my hands on his waist in a tight grip. "Now just hang on!"

Jess tapped the gas, and we started out at a slow speed toward the ranch. The wheels hit a few holes, and I bounced up from the seat. As we reached the clearing away from my father's view, Jess punched the gas and the vehicle lurched forward. I screamed, but my voice disappeared in the fast wind as it whipped across my face. The grass and trees flew by in a blur.

He would kill me! My first day at the ranch, and Jess would kill me out in the meadow with his stupid four-wheeler. I yelled at him to stop, but I couldn't even hear my own words. My fingers dug into the fabric of his shirt for a tighter grip.

We zipped around the ranch for what seemed like an eternity. In the distance, a large building came in to focus. Jess slowed down at the driveway entrance. My eyes grew large at what had to be the Masons' house.

I'd never seen an actual plantation, only on television. We traveled up the tree-lined driveway leading to the large, white column structure with a wraparound porch. I thought back to that afternoon when I'd watched *Gone with the Wind*. I knew without a doubt this was a house that would make Scarlett herself jealous.

As we approached the front yard, the giant white house with black shutters took shape in front of me. I counted six massive white columns starting at the ground and extending to the roof. The poles were so large it would take three of me with outstretched arms to circle around one of them.

The lower level boasted a full wraparound porch covered with chairs and tables assembled into a fancy sitting area fit for a tea party with princesses. The second floor also had a full wraparound balcony with black iron guardrails. The Masons had two whole balconies on a single house.

The landscaped yard held bushes shaped in fancy designs, resembling the botanical garden from last year's school field trip. The Masons literally had their own park. The whole place made my old secret garden look like a tangled-up bird's nest.

Jess circled around the yard to the back of the house. The dirty four-wheeler looked out of place on the manicured lawn. I expected someone to pop out from behind a bush to yell at us for driving on the grass.

"You live here?" The question came out half-stupid as I muttered against his ear. I hoped the sound of the motor drowned it out.

"Yeah." I felt his shoulders shrug.

Jess parked next to an outdoor gazebo that could hold at least fifty people for a garden party. The white structure overlooked an extravagant inground swimming pool with a ten-foot waterfall flowing from a rock ledge. Two fountains shot up from the deep-blue water on each side of the wavy shape. It was bigger than any motel pool I'd seen as a kid.

"You can swim in the pool if ya want after school. I like jumpin' from the top of 'em rocks. Almost as much fun as the pond," Jess said rather matter-of-factly. "You swim?"

"No." The thought of being in that deep water made my teeth bite into my lip. I hated swimming.

"Let's go. I'll show you the really fun stuff." Jess maneuvered around a few hedges and then punched the gas to take off through the tall grass. The wind slapped across my face, my hair flailing out to the sides. He slowed down again when we reached the barns.

"We've got lots of horses. You ever been on one?" he asked as I studied the expensive looking stables.

"No." I shook my head.

"It's okay. I can teach ya. You think the four-wheeler is fun, wait 'til you ride a horse out here." Jess laughed and punched the gas again. I grabbed his shirt as we shot off into the depths of the ranch. I wasn't so sure about the horse-riding thing.

The wind blew in my face as we bounced along the meadow. It was beautiful and so carefree being out in the wide open space. I knew why Jess loved it so much. Driving out on the ranch, the weight lifted in the breeze. For a moment in time, I felt free.

Jess alternated between a dirt path and plowing straight through the tall grass. We passed a group of red cows who watched us with bored eyes. I'd never seen one so close, but the furry heads didn't seem unfriendly. Jess circled over a pond dam and came to a stop next to the water.

"You like fishin'?" He asked, pointing at the murky pool. "There's some pretty good ones in there."

"No. I mean, I've never been. I might like it, I guess." It was my general answer to all his questions that day. I'd never done any of this stuff.

"It's really fun. We'll have to come back when it starts gettin' cooler this fall." I couldn't see his face, but I knew he was grinning with excitement. His words stumbled over each other like pancake syrup again.

"How did your family get Sprayberry?"

"It was my grandfather's dad's ranch first. The Jessups have sold red Angus for a long, long time. You see all of those out there?" He turned a little sideways and pointed to the other side of the ranch.

I'd lived in Texas my whole life. I may have never gone fishing or swam in a fancy pool, but I knew what an oil well pump looked like even from a distance.

"It was just cattle until they found the oil. My uncle Frank still sells 'em—the cattle. My grandfather just lived here and got rich."

"Your uncle and grandfather both live here?" I said, interrupting.

"No. Just Uncle Frank. My grandfather's dead. House was his first, then mother made it even bigger. Anyway, he crashed one of his planes with my grandma in it. Happened right after I was born. He'd learned to fly and wasn't so good, I guess." He chuckled and glanced back at me over his shoulder.

I wrinkled up my nose at his morbid joke. I realized what his story implied. Did he say his grandfather owned *planes*—as in, plural?

"When my grandfather found the oil, he kept buyin' and buyin' stuff. Made my uncle Frank mad. After he died, all of this was my mother's and Uncle Frank's. He's an old grouch. Never been married, and I think he hates kids. Or maybe just me. He lives in a house off over there. That's who I've been helpin' for bein' grounded for the elevator thing."

"Uncle Frank...Jessup?" I asked. It was interesting to know another *Jessup* existed besides Jess.

"Yep, he's got me scoopin' horse manure out of the stalls at five in the mornin'. I gotta do that 'til school starts. I hate poop."

"I know. You told me."

"Well, I still hate it." He turned back to face the front.

"I'm really sorry."

"Nah...not your fault. We better get back. Don't want to make your dad mad at me the first day."

He punched the gas, and I fumbled to grab his shirt. It was a lot of information to process for one day. The ranch itself was enough to overload my mind. It was positively paradise. I counted off more items to add to what my father and I owed these Masons: a house, school clothes, furniture, and this place called Sprayberry.

Chapter 9

When I was eight...

The day finally arrived, and my secret, terrible wish came true. My mother, Anna Tanner, passed in her sleep a mere three days after we moved to the ranch. She was now a skeleton in a box, her body waiting to be laid in the ground—waiting for the bugs to slither through the cracks and devour her skin and bones.

"The Lord is my Shepherd, I shall not want…He leads me beside still waters…"

Reverend Cooper read Psalm 23, his voice carried among the small gathering next to the closed casket. Over and over again, my eyes followed the same silver leaf pattern etched on the right side of the box. I heard very few of the reverend's words. In all aspects, my mother's funeral represented the finality of the worst years of my life.

"Even though I walk through the valley of the shadow of death, I will fear no evil, for you are with me."

I lifted my eyes up to scan the group. Only a handful of people came to the funeral. My parents didn't have any family left in Texas. No parents or siblings. No Uncle Franks. The Masons had guided my father through the preparations for the simple service. I had no idea how much this kind of production would cost our family. I no longer asked who paid for our expenses. In the cemetery, I mentally added the funeral to my growing debt to the Masons.

"And now, please join me in sending God's child Anna, a loving wife and mother, back into His loving arms." The reverend's voice carried a soothing tone.

I stood beside my father as they lowered my mother into the deep hole. The place with the bugs. I imagined them waiting, six feet down, for the fancy box with silver leaves. Sitting in the dirt. Mouths open. Teeth bared.

My father let go of my hand. He walked slowly to edge of the hole. His strong fingers crushed the delicate, yellow flower his hand. His body shook from the tears running down his cheeks. I felt a presence at my side and looked over to see Jess. He reached out and slipped his fingers into mine. Feeling his hand squeeze tight, a warmth spread through the coldness in my chest.

"And from the great story that began in Genesis, 'Dust thou art, and unto dust thou shalt return.'" The Revered took a handful of fresh soil, and it trickled through his fingers down into the hole that held the casket. "Ashes to ashes and dust to dust. Amen."

My father released the crushed petals of the rose. I watched the yellow pieces float in the air and then disappear down into the darkness to their final resting place. My father turned and walked back to where I stood with Jess. His face wore a sadness I'd never seen in all our struggles. Mrs. Mason reached out with a handful of tissues. He blotted his eyes and sniffled into the white paper.

"Come on, let's go home." My father placed an arm around my shoulders, and Jess gave my hand one last squeeze. With dry eyes, I walked out of the cemetery wearing one of my fancy new dresses and shiny leather shoes, courtesy of the Masons.

The Tanners were not alone the night of the funeral. The Masons and a few others in the community came by to bring food and offer their condolences. A man named Mr. Buckley discussed a job opportunity for my father at the hardware store in Arlis. Mr. Buckley wanted to retire. If all was well the next few months, my father would be the overseeing manager of Buckley's Hardware on the Main Street Square in Arlis.

The adults' voices trickled out into dark while I sat with my arms draped over the railing of the front porch. My eyes watched the clear sky. Jess sat a foot away with his legs dangling over the ledge, bumping the side of the wooden porch.

The night sounds of the meadow felt good compared to the sadness that filled the inside of our new house. My mind retraced the moments of the last twenty-four hours. I'd lost my mother today. Yet, the sadness didn't come as it should from such an event. I think something was actually broken inside of me.

"So it looks like you're stayin' here," Jess said, interrupting the silence of my broken thoughts.

"Yeah…you mind?"

"Nope, I think it's gonna be fun havin' someone else 'round here." His eyebrows furrowed together as he laughed in a way that meant only one thing.

"Hey, you can't get me in trouble anymore." I bumped him with my shoulder. A smile formed on the corner of my lips just thinking of being here with him.

"Nah…no trouble." He laughed quietly. "We just can't get caught. By the way, the hardware store is haunted."

"What?"

"It is. I promise. I heard it from Gunther talkin' at the feed store when I was there with Uncle Frank. You'll be fine. Just don't be there at night. Might see an ax go flyin' through the air."

"That's not true."

"I guess you can stay there one night and find out." He gave me a wink. I rolled my eyes, and then a faint glow caught my attention.

"What was that?" I craned my neck, peering out in the darkness.

"A shootin' star. You ain't never see one before?"

"No. Like one of those just fell from the sky?"

"Sort of. You have to make a wish now." He grinned back at me.

I focused off in the distance, trying to conjure up something that would make me feel better.

"Now tell me what it is," his syrupy voice pleaded.

"I don't think wishes work that way."

"Oh, come on. *Please*, Alex."

"Tell me yours first."

"I didn't make a wish."

"You did too. I saw your eyes closed. Must have been a big wish."

I startled him. Jess blinked back at me for a moment with a rare loss of words, "I…um, can't tell ya."

"Will you tell me if it comes true?"

"Yeah, I promise." He grinned. "There's pictures up there, you know. I'll teach you to find 'em."

"Pictures?"

"Yeah. Like that one's the Big Dipper," he said, pointing above us. "It's a big ice-cream scoop."

I looked across the Texas sky, listening to Jess tell me about his pictures. In all my nights in Dallas, I'd never seen so many sparkling dots winking back at me. It was beautiful and mysterious, a never-ending blanket wrapping the world up tight and cozy for the night.

"Hey, Jess, why don't you have other people over to the ranch?" I asked casually. I'd pondered the thought for some time.

"You really wanna know?"

"Yeah."

"Most people want to be around us because they think we're rich," Jess answered with a flat tone.

"You are rich."

"I know. It's just not always fun havin' everyone tryin' to be your friend because of it." Jess looked serious with the thought. "You don't know what it's like bein' here in Arlis. But you're goin' to find out real soon."

"I'm sure you know about us. Your parents have paid for everything for my dad and me." I didn't intend the sneer in my tone, yet that's what happened when I finally said those words out loud. It was a truth that haunted me for weeks.

"I know." He looked right at me with his blue eyes. "Actually, I knew that the first day we met. My family pays for the hospice ward too. That's why y'all moved to Arlis. Because of us."

He caught me off-guard. I remembered my father's revelation of being accepted into the hospice ward in Arlis. *The life-saving moment*, according to him. I didn't realize it was also funded by the Masons. In reality, I should have put that piece of the puzzle together before tonight. My stomach tightened up, and I looked back at Jess with wide eyes, hatred burning on my lips. I despised their stupid charity.

"And that's why, Alex. I know you're different than the others. I knew it from the first day in the hallway. You hate the fact that my family's rich." He smiled back smugly.

Chapter 10

Today, 9:37 p.m.

It takes everything in my body to fight to the surface. Every time I try, the warmth of invisibility pulls me back down into the comfort of the past. It feels good there—deep in the meadow sunshine, seeing his blue eyes. Letting go, I finally emerge in the cold chambers of the hospital. I watch the beauty queen pour a glass of water. She carries it with a tight grip over to the side of the bed.

"Drink this."

The restraints hold my wrist in their tight jaws. She pushes the straw up to my lips while I take a sip. The liquid tastes cool as it rinses the grit off my teeth. Pushing the hair back from my forehead, she looks at the cut.

"You need stitches in that. If you want, I can take care of it."

My eyes grow wide at the mere thought of her offer. When I fail to respond, she pulls up a chair next to the bed. Faint black smears rest just below her perfect blue eyes. I follow the outline of her face down to her blue scrubs. She has a pin close to the top with tiny kittens playing with tiny balls of yarn.

"Are…" The sound crackles in my throat. "Are you working today?"

"I was this mornin'."

"And now?" I squint in her direction, feeling the painful glow of the florescent lights.

“Well, I was leavin’ when I found you in the hall. So I stayed. Thought you needed some company.”

Blinking back at her odd statement, I lift my hand up to rub the tension behind my eyes. The restraints keep my fingers in place. An IV snakes out from the tape in the center of my left hand.

“I want them off,” I beg to her.

“Try to be still.” She smiles, though something resembling sadness lingers in the hollow depths of her lips. “I’ll turn off the lights.”

The room slips into darkness, except for the faint glow of the moon. It was daylight when I came to the hospital. The warm summer day had become night. The world kept turning even when I wanted it to stop.

I hurt. I hurt so deep inside. Two tears roll over my cheeks, soaking into the fabric of the pillow. With my hands in the cuffs, I can’t even wipe them away. I feel the soft fabric of a tissue dab at the corners. The blonde face stares down at me, the dark smudges appearing more prominent under each of her lashes. In that moment, I knew the beauty queen was crying too.

Chapter 11

When I was ten...

After we dropped my mother in the ground, life had continued on without her. The Tanners traveled on a path across Sprayberry paved with Mason dollars. The closer we got, the more indebted we became to the family. My father took everything they offered without batting an eyelash.

On the other hand, I let myself be pulled in by Jess. The broken, leftover shell of a girl felt bright and shiny whenever he stepped in a room. One look into those blue eyes, and I did whatever his scheming mind conjured up for us. We did everything together and couldn't be closer if our legs were bound tight with an actual rope.

Just like when Mrs. Mason took us to the annual Arlis Fair. We laughed and ate our way through the whole place. I looked down at the photo strip clasped in my hand. One of the clubs had an old-timey photo booth. As we walked past, I saw the costumes hanging from the rack. Jess refused until he saw the sword dangling from a hook. He couldn't say no to being a pirate.

Out of the corner of my eye, I saw Jess staring at his feet. He was still mad about the Tilt-A-Whirl.

"I can't believe you puked on my boots," he muttered. "They're my favorites."

"I told you not to make me eat your corn dog after I had mine and a funnel cake. I couldn't help it." I glared at him. He would not blame this on me.

"I'm not seein' corn dogs on 'em. They're stained blue from all your cotton candy. You ate three bags!" Jess crossed his arms and wrinkled up his eyebrows.

"You made me go on the Tilt-A-Whirl. I told you I felt sick. But *nooo!*" My voice grew louder. "You just had to ride it. *Again!*"

"Well, you made us take those *stupid* pictures and…"

"Enough, you two." Mrs. Mason cut Jess off as she intervened from the front of the Escalade. "Jessup, you have new boots at the house. I told you to stop wearing those anyway."

"Ahh, Mother. The new ones ain't broken in. I just got these the way I like 'em,"

"I said enough! No more talking the rest of the way home. It's been a very, *very* long evening."

"Yes, ma'am," we answered in unison.

I saw Mrs. Mason's eyes in the rear-view mirror. She gave that look; the one that terrified me. Mrs. Mason got agitated every so often with us. The previous week, Jess and I had a burping contest in the living room. She walked in as we bickered over who could get the furthest in the alphabet. Mrs. Mason gave me the cold stare of unladylike death at the mere thought of me belching. Good thing she didn't see one of our spitting contests. Goopy, hacked-up loogies. Jess was still better. He could hit a tree at six feet. My best was still only three.

I turned my gaze out the window at the flashing red, blue, and yellow bulbs. It had been a magical night with carnival rides and games amidst all the smells. *Cotton candy.* My stomach lurched at the thought of it. The strong odor of sticky sweet vomit still lingered against the expensive leather of the Escalade.

Arlis held a large town fair every fall. Local business and clubs lined the streets around the town square with concession booths and games. For us kids, we waited all year for the carnival rides to arrive from Dallas. Mrs. Mason worked the Arlis Women's Auxiliary booth most of the evening. My father had stopped by briefly to check on me before heading home from the hardware store. It had been two years since he took the job.

Mr. Buckley stayed true to his promise and retired. After six months, he put my father in charge of the complete management side of the business. He was excited to be getting things back in order for our lives. Money was still tight because of all the hospital bills and credit card debt we owed. Collection companies called frequently.

We settled into a routine of me going to school and then home to Sprayberry. I stayed clear of most students. I'm not sure how they knew about my life with the Masons, but word spread through the ears and mouths of the town residents and on to their children. In a place such as this, my presence was pegged as just a little different than everyone else's. I was seen as poor but spent all my time with Jess Mason. In Arlis, that bit of information was very intriguing amongst those who liked to gossip.

My hair grew back rather fast, and I learned to create two long braids down my shoulders all by myself. Mrs. Mason attempted to convert my style to resemble a girl and less like a tomboy. She visibly cringed every time I arrived at the house with Jess after school. I usually had on overalls or stained-up jeans. Sometimes I wore a baseball cap on top of my head.

The outfits she bought were just not practical for what Jess had planned during the afternoons on the ranch. Most evenings, I returned to the farmhouse covered in dirt from riding four-wheelers and fishing. I'd avoided horseback riding. I knew it was only a matter of time before Jess would stop taking no for an answer.

Our parents limited us to only one sleepover a week or else that boy would stay every night. Sometimes we camped outside in a little red tent that my father set up in the front yard. Lying side by side, we stuck our head out the front flap to see the stars. Jess taught me all the pictures in the sky.

When I spent the night at his house, Jess and I stayed in the Masons' theater room in sleeping bags. I'd never imagined an entire room just for watching movies. He kept a secret stash of every kind of candy imaginable. I watched him eat gummy bears together with Snickers, knowing he did it just to hear me squeal. Jess let me pick the movies because I insisted on watching the gory, horror kind that most girls hated.

Spending time with Jess made the days pass with bursts of happiness. Those days kept me from falling completely into a black hole. The years of anger and sadness crept into my pale skin like a stain that refused to go away. I think that's why the idea of Jess felt so appealing. He was like sunlight to my dreary cloud.

The Escalade came to a stop in front of the old farmhouse. I unlocked the door and stepped out in the driveway. "Thank you, Mrs. Mason, for taking me to the carnival."

It was tough hearing those words come from my lips. It was a reoccurring statement just with an interchangeable last word. Tonight's food, games, and ride tickets had all been courtesy of the Masons.

"You're welcome, Alexandra. Tell your father hello." She smiled from the front seat, her strong drawl holding each word.

"Yes, ma'am."

I looked over at Jess before shutting the door. I saw the sticky, blue goo all over the front of his boots and up the legs of his Wranglers. His blue eyes watched me from his seat. *Dang it!* I would be angry, too, if he puked all over me. I still wasn't sure how it ended up all on his feet and none on my gray shoes.

"I'm sorry about your boots, Jess." I smiled a weak grin.

"Ahh, it's okay. I got some other ones." He shrugged. "See ya tomorrow?"

"Yeah." I nodded back and shut the door. Right before it slammed, I saw Jess pull a red package from his pocket. *You had to be kidding me!* How could he still eat with that sickening, sweet smell of cotton candy in the car? I just shook my head and walked to the front door.

"Hey, Pumpkin. You have fun at the carnival?" I heard my father from the kitchen as I shut the door.

"Yeah, it was good. Here's a picture." I handed him the photo strip and looked around at the tiny white packages on the counter. "What's all of that?"

"Looks like you two had fun." He smiled and handed it back. "Well, this is a steer. I'm trying to get all of it to fit into the freezer."

"A steer? Like hamburger and steak and stuff? Where did it come from?" I don't know why I asked. I surveyed the beggar's loot sparkling like pirate booty with the Sprayberry logo stamped in red. I knew exactly who sent the little packages on the counter. We didn't have the money for that large amount of meat.

"Well, the ranch was butchering some for the year, and they included us on the list. We *do* live on a cattle ranch, you know." My father smiled down at me and nodded his head. "Should last us a long time, I would think."

"How much did *that* cost us?"

"Well, we are tenants on the ranch. They just included us too." I knew he didn't understand what I was implying.

"You mean they *gave* it to us. Just like everything else." The words came out more sarcastic than he deserved, but I was tired of pretending all the time. We depended completely on this family.

"Alex, it's not like that." He wasn't angry yet, but I knew I was pushing it.

"Then how is it, Dad? Why do the Masons keep helping us and why do you just let them?" I saw my father contemplating what to say. I thought it would make him angry. Maybe I wanted it to make him angry. Let him see how I felt for a change.

The Masons did everything. Something new or useful every time we turned around. Hundred-dollar bills handed out like tissues to wipe away the grime.

They gave us the perfect tree every Christmas, stocked with a pile of big presents and small presents covered in expensive, thick paper. I got a new bike last month just because I mentioned one day I used to ride around our old neighborhood in Dallas. In the spring, Mrs. Mason dolled me up in a special Easter dress—a grotesque pile of pink ruffles mailed all the way from some fancy shop in New York City.

The old Bronco stalled out in month seven at the ranch. The Masons replaced it with a brand-new Ford double-cab in a color called Oxford White. It was so clear it sparkled like it was painted in diamonds. The charity list went on and on, making my head dizzy.

"It's not that easy to explain, Alex." He set the white package down on the counter and looked up into the anger growing on my face. I couldn't hide it.

"Then try. I want to understand," I said with an even tone. I had him cornered, and I felt some triumph knowing I may finally have an answer to the million-Mason-dollar question.

"Wow!" His hand went up to rub his forehead. It was something he did out of stress. "Sometimes I feel like I'm talking to a sixteen-year-old instead of my little Pumpkin."

Whose fault is that? I wanted to yell in his face, but stayed calm instead. "I will be eleven in a few weeks, Dad."

"Okay, well, I guess I can try. The way I see, sometimes bad things happen in life. You want the bad part to be taken away. You plead or sometimes pray for a miracle. I don't know, Pumpkin. I asked so very hard, but it didn't happen for us. I didn't understand." His eyes got a little sad.

"But you know, not all miracles come in the form you ask or even in the way you think they should. It was hard at first for me to understand it, but once I did"—he smiled again—"things just made sense."

"I don't understand."

"Well, your mother. It was not good with her. Then everything just seemed to get worse. So I prayed for a miracle. I wanted it so bad. It wasn't just about losing your mother. I needed her to be healed because I thought everything would be fixed if she was healed. I didn't know how to do life by myself without her. But no matter how much I asked, it just didn't seem to happen." He paused, shaking his head for a second.

"Things got worse. We lost everything. I felt like a failure toward my family. I was angry some, just like you are. I kept asking, and my words just seemed to evaporate into thin air. It was day after day of defeat."

"It took moving to the ranch house to see what I'd been missing. One morning, I woke up to the sun shining through the window, and I knew. Life is a much bigger picture than just what concerns me. I know we got that miracle I asked for. We got the Masons at the very lowest point in our lives. They stepped in out of the blue and got us back on track. I have an eternal level of gratitude toward that family. You should too."

Stunned! The letters of the word repeated over and over through the crevices of my brain. My father gave an answer far beyond what I ever could fathom regarding the Masons. Not only did he willingly accept this fate; he embraced it.

"So this miracle to have my mother healed was replaced by the Masons? The miracle was them?" I wasn't buying this miracle nonsense. The Tanners just gave up and let the Masons take over their lives. It was frustrating.

I wanted clarity or something that would make me understand why we became reliant on charity. Instead, my father babbled some garbage about miracles that opened up the second line of questions. I didn't grasp the Masons' role in our lives.

Why would they continue to bail out this poor family over and over again? Did it make them feel powerful over others? Something they could hold over gutter trash like me? Something they could brag about with their other rich friends?

"Look, Pumpkin. The Masons are nice folks. I know Mrs. Mason can be a little harsh at times, but they have good hearts. Actually, they have really big hearts if you would just look at it that way. You even have one of them as your best friend. I don't question why. It's not something that is in our control. They came into our lives when we needed them the most. Don't worry about *why* they were our miracle. You need to just be thankful they *were* the miracle and not be angry. Your mother wouldn't like to see you this way."

"Well, I guess it's good she's *dead!*" The internal thoughts accidentally slipped out into real words.

"Alexandra!"

I stared back at his face, feeling the impact of my sudden outburst. I didn't want to talk about it anymore. I'd caused this to happen tonight. I ruined the amazing evening of the carnival with my ever-present struggle over this deep-rooted, grown-up issue. I may have sounded sixteen, but all I really wanted to be was ten going on eleven.

Turning on my heels, I stomped to my bedroom and slammed the door. A little better, but it wasn't enough. Opening my closet, I looked around with wild eyes and saw the latest pair of dress sandals, courtesy of Mrs. Mason. I grasped the toe and beat the little shoe into the wood floor. *Come on, break!*

"Pumpkin, what are you doing in there?"

My shoulders froze, waiting for the door to swing open. I stood up with my arms held high above my head, gripping a patent leather shoe as if it were a weapon. I felt the thud of my heart with each breath. He could not see me crack. I set the shoe carefully back in the closet and threw a shirt over the wood floor damage—something I would need to fix later.

"I'm sorry," I said, cracking open the door.

He didn't believe me. The reality of being a father and not a mother registered with sadness as he watched through the four-inch slit, not sure if he should extend comfort or punishment. "I know, but I think we should talk about it some more. I don't think you understand."

I saw the look of failure in the creases around his eyes. He was worried that I was on the brink of a destructive meltdown. Maybe I was. Instead, I took on the role of comforter to the broken man in front of me. Back to being sixteen.

"I *do* understand, Dad. I'm really sorry for saying that. It won't happen again. And I'm glad we have the Masons." He looked back at my face, and the reassurance seemed to help. "I'm going to bed now. I'm kind of sick from all the cotton candy."

"Okay. Good night." My father reached through the opening and patted the top of my head like I was three.

I shut the door tight. This wasn't over. He could think whatever he wanted. I would not sit idle and let our debts go unaccounted for to the Masons. I would pay them all back; I just didn't know when or how; I just knew it would happen. Someday, I would repay every so-called miracle. I would not be a product of charity.

Pulling out a piece of notebook paper, I drew columns down the page with a ruler. I numbered in the left corner and tried to picture the first day I met the Masons and every item that was delivered.

I turned the pencil over and applied the eraser. This list needed to go back even further than the first day in Arlis. I wrote number one as MOMMA'S HOSPITAL BILLS. As Jess had pointed out when we first came to the ranch, the Mason-funded hospice wing was the reason for us even moving to Arlis. My fingers cramped as I printed in tiny letters down the first column. I sat back, reflecting on each item.

I glanced at the filmstrip from the carnival, our laughing faces side by side. My friendship with Jess was a difficult thing for me when it came to the Masons. It was the one thing that had my feelings completely divided. My eyes shifted back, contemplating the items. It needed to be called something. I guess it was pretty simple. I printed the name in large letters across the top of the page for THE MASON LIST.

Chapter 12

When I was ten...

The next Saturday after the carnival, Jess showed up at the farmhouse. He said today was the day for horse riding and refused to take no for answer.

"Are you sure I can touch them?" I looked at the two horses and shuddered. I was a tall girl, but these beasts towered over my head.

"They're really nice. You just have to give 'em a chance," Jess said over his shoulder as he tied the lead rope to the fence. "Here's some carrots. Feed 'em to Blue Bonnet."

"Which one is Blue Bonnet?" I looked back and forth between the two tan horses. Maybe they had name tags like a dog.

"That one's BB," Jess said, walking to the other horse. I was surprised he could even stand up straight with all the excitement. Once we got here, he'd switched over to pancake-syrup talk, slurring every syllable into Texas gibberish. I knew my riding horses meant the world to him.

"I think BB is bigger than the other one. Maybe I should get the smaller one." It was only a few inches but a few inches seemed a little less terrifying at the moment.

"No, you don't want to ride Clive. You need BB. Here, take the carrots and feed her one. Like this."

My eyes grew wide as I watched Jess shove the carrot into Clive's mouth. I didn't know horses had such big teeth. Jess moved his hand up

Clive's neck to scratch behind his pointed ears. I knew Jess loved his horses. He desperately wanted to share his pretty animals with me.

Looking at BB's silky hair, I reached up to touch her neck. She lunged forward, and I screamed. BB knocked the carrot from my hand to the ground. Her big teeth scooped it up. The horse chewed with her big brown eyes fixed on me.

"What are y'all doin' back there?"

"I'm not going up. I can't even feed the carrots right."

"You're goin' up. Stop chickenin' out! You said you would do it!"

We stared at each other for a few moments. I took a deep breath and offered a compromise. "Fine, but I'm only sitting on her. No walking. Just sitting tied to the fence. Promise?" I needed a firm understanding with that boy before I ever got on top of his horse. I knew how he worked.

"Promise," he said with a grin.

After several attempts to boost me up, Jess finally got my behind on top of BB. Jess climbed up on Clive. He leaned over and untied them both from the fence.

"Hey! What are you doing?" BB followed along behind Clive. My fingers trembled, clenching the rein in one hand and the saddle in the other.

"You'll be fine! We can just go down the fence row!" Jess yelled back.

"You promised!" I was so angry but too scared to say anything else. I managed a few deep breaths and let them out slowly through my mouth. Each step jarred me sideways a little in the saddle. My thighs clung to the horse.

We traveled at a steady pace in a single line down the fence. Maybe Jess was right. I was doing okay. I wasn't upside down on my head. Feeling brave, I glanced around the fence. It was a different experience than a four-wheeler. So peaceful and quiet.

I released my tightly clenched hand from the saddle and patted BB's neck. Her hair felt really soft against my palm. I calmly stroked her until suddenly, a loud yapping came from my right. One of the cattle dogs chased a small orange cat around the stables and then through the grass directly toward us. I felt BB move faster, and then like a flick of a switch, she broke off from the fencerow and out toward the meadow.

I screamed and yelled. I grabbed a hold of anything my hands could grasp as I bounced along on top of BB. My screams got lost in the wind and the barns faded from view. The trees and grass flew by in a blur as the horse continued to gain speed. In the distance, I saw a fallen tree directly in our path. I panicked and felt the horse go airborne. She cleared the massive tree trunk, but I couldn't stay in the saddle.

I hit the ground with a hard slam that sent my body rolling for several feet. Everything hurt, and I couldn't catch my breath. I wanted to scream, but nothing came out. I thrashed around on my back, trying to breathe. I heard the sound of pounding hooves.

No! BB was coming back to trample me. As I tried to move away, I saw Jess ride up on Clive. He jumped off and ran toward me.

"A…lex…ah…are you okay?" He was out of breath, and his words came out in spats. Leaning over, his black hair flopped into his blue eyes. "I don't know…what…happened."

"I'm… going to… kill you!" I tried to rise up and throw a swing at Jess. My left foot gave out, and I crashed back onto the ground.

"Alex, you have to calm down."

"This is all your fault!"

"No, Alex. Be still."

"Jess!" I snapped with anger.

"There's a snake." His voice remained steady while his blue eyes darted to the left again. I looked over my shoulder to see the tan and dark-brown shape about a yard from my hand. The tail rattled just a little, sending prickly fear down my spine.

"What do I do?" I whispered through clenched teeth.

"I wish I had my gun," Jess whispered back. "It'll take too long to go get it."

Since moving to the ranch, I had listened to numerous tall tales involving rattlers. Right in that terrifying moment, I recalled the photographs Davey Rawlins had brought to school of his uncle's foot half-rotted off from a snake bite. Davey said it struck his Uncle Skeeter straight through his boot.

The images spread fear through my body. It would hurt as the snake sunk the sharp fangs into my skin. The venom would burn as it ate away the tissue, and then my hand would gradually fall off. Very simple.

"Alex, you listenin'?" His voice sounded like a hiss. Beads of perspiration dripped down the front of my pale, clammy face. I saw his eyes move to the snake, then back to me.

"I'm gonna move in slowly to the left. Then I'll toss a rock over in the other direction as a distraction, then pull you real hard. You gotta push off with your good foot. We only got one shot at this."

"It might bite me," I whispered.

"Yep."

"But…"

"Let's go," he whispered, giving me no time to think anymore.

Jess tossed a baseball-sized stone in the opposite direction and then yanked my arm, pulling me up from the ground. In the dusty air, the sound of rattles played like background music. His body held me up, dragging me along to keep the weight off my throbbing ankle. For several yards, we stumbled through sage bushes and vines cursed with thorns. The sharp spikes dug into the legs of my denim jeans.

"Are you sure it's gone?" I peered through the grass for signs of the scaly body.

"I think he went the other way when I threw the rock."

"You think?"

"No. I'm sure." Jess lowered us both to the ground. The muscles in my legs felt like Jell-O.

"That was really scary."

"I know. I ain't ever been that close to one without a gun." I watched his grungy fingers push the hair off his forehead.

"You saved my hand from rotting off."

"Your hand was gonna rot off?" His eyebrows scrunched up in a frown.

"Never mind. I just wanted to say thank you."

Jess looked at me for a moment, then shrugged. "It's no big deal. Friends have each other's backs. I'll always have your back, and you'll always have mine."

"Always? That's, like, forever. How do you know we will be friends forever?"

"I just do."

"You do?" I looked over at him in disbelief. He had no control over the future. I knew firsthand how life changed faster than the flash of a hummingbird wing. One moment you're playing Barbies, and the next your mother is dying while you eat moldy sandwiches.

"If you don't believe me, then we should swear on it. Then it ain't gonna change."

"I don't think swearing will make a difference."

"All right. A blood pact." His famous grin widened across his face.

"Are you crazy?" Maybe that rattler got in a strike and the venom was eating away at his brain.

"Nah, that's what they used to do. You know, Cowboys and Indians and stuff."

Jess pulled a small pocketknife from the left side of his Wranglers. He flipped out a blade roughly three inches in length. With a quick slice, red bubbled from the small opening in his palm.

"Stick out your hand." Jess grabbed my right hand in a tight grasp.

"I am not letting you cut me on purpose."

"Just a nick. Then we seal it with a shake. Trust me."

"Trust you. *Really*." I rolled my eyes. This boy was so unbelievable.

"I won't hurt ya."

"Okay. But I'm not watching."

With my head turned to the right, I let Jess Mason slice across the lines of my hand. The pain was the same as a paper cut. I unclenched my eyes to see a streak the color of deep crimson run to my pinky finger. Jess wiped the knife across the knee of his jeans, then snapped it shut.

"Okay. You ready?"

I nodded in agreement. Jess mashed the inside of my palm in a tight handshake, mixing the blood and dirt together.

"I promise we always will be friends and have each other's backs. No matter what. Even when we have no teeth and no hair."

"No teeth or hair? I will never have no teeth or hair."

"Alex! Just swear, okay?"

I watched the serious blue eyes of a ten-year-old boy waiting for my answer. Forever was a very long time to promise loyalty. I smiled as I thought about the last two years. I had numerous issues with the Mason family, but I'd never felt anything like I did when I was with Jess.

I saw the picture he painted with Jess bald and toothless, except I had long red hair and perfect white teeth. It was a fantasy that would never happen in the reality of our world, yet I looked into his grinning face and longed for it to be true. Maybe the act of speaking words sworn in blood could cement this pact into cosmic existence.

"I promise we will always be friends and have each other's backs, no matter what." I gave his hand a little squeeze to seal the deal. Dabbing my hand against my denim jeans, the cut left dark traces on the fabric.

"Now that I've got your complete, sworn trust,"—Jess arched his eyebrows up with a mischievous smile—"I'm gonna help you get up."

"Why do you need my trust?"

"Because we gotta get you up there." Jess motioned to Clive.

"Oh, no! No. I am *not* doing it." There was no way I would get back up on one of those things.

"We don't got no choice. You can't walk back, and we can't just sit, because the rattler's over there."

"I thought you said it's gone."

"Well, I didn't kill it, you know." A sharp, prickly feeling radiated down my spine at the thoughts of one very not-dead rattlesnake. Jess was right. I didn't have a choice.

With my ankle, it took some effort to get up on the horse. Jess climbed up behind me. I held a tight grasp on the saddle while he handled the reins. It was a completely different experience with someone else in control of the horse. We slowly trotted back to the barn.

"Alex, I'm really sorry. I didn't think any of this would happen. I should've had Uncle Frank out there with us."

"Um, that may have been scarier than BB and the rattlesnake combined."

"I know." His voice came with a burst of laugher behind my ear. "He's my uncle, but he's just plain scary sometimes. I turned 'round the other day in the barn and he's just standin' there. Watchin' me. Cigarette hangin' from his lips. I don't know how long he'd been there. He spit on the ground and said, 'Boy, you better hurry it up, or I'm turnin' the lights out and leavin' you in here in the dark with the rats 'cause you ain't goin' home 'til it's done.' Then he used that gross bandana 'round his neck to wipe his nose. That thing ain't ever been washed. Every day. Same ol' snot."

"*Eeew*. Have you ever thought Uncle Frank looks like that guy from *City Slickers*?"

"*City Slickers*? Like the old dude with the gold?"

"That's the one."

"You're right." He giggled. "You wanna sneak in his house? See if he's hidin' gold under the floorboards?"

"I bet he has shrunken heads or something."

"Maybe I'll just tie you up in there one night. See if they come alive. They might bite you." His fingers pinched my sides. "Eat your toes for supper."

"Jessup Mason!" I gasped at him. He laughed so hard I felt his body shaking the horse. "Stop it. We're gonna fall off."

"Okay, I'm sorry."

"You think BB will come back?"

"She'll find her way back. Hope it's fast, though, before Uncle Frank finds out." He stayed quiet for about twenty seconds and then asked sweetly, "*Sooo*, you willin' to try horse ridin' again?"

"I don't know." The sway of riding on Clive was nice but not enough to try it again alone. "Maybe I should stick to just petting animals."

"You can pet BB. I won't try to make ya ride her again."

"I was thinking more about one of the dogs in the barn."

"You like dogs?"

"Yeah, I used to have one of my own. Before we came to Arlis. His name was Digger."

"Why didn't ya bring it?"

"He couldn't come with us. Dad didn't know where we were staying, so I left him with our neighbor."

"We should go get him now. Why haven't you?"

"I asked my dad about Digger after we got moved into the ranch house. He said Digger got sick or something. He died not long after we left. I guess it was the truth. Our neighbor didn't like him much. He probably just didn't take care of him and Digger got ran over." I shrugged. "I thought about it some. Not knowing the truth. But I figured he was dead either way."

"Why didn't ya tell me your dog died?"

"I don't know," I muttered.

"I'd be real sad if I lost BB and Clive."

The loss of Digger was a story that should bring a child to tears. I spat out the words in a flat tone, knowing it was easier to feel nothing than something. Digger was from another time and another place that existed before Arlis. "I don't cry, Jess."

"Not even when you're by yourself?"

"No."

"Oh." His voice seemed strange. Sitting in front of Jess, I couldn't see his face to read what he was really thinking. "I'm sorry 'bout Digger."

"It's okay. He had nothing to do with here anyway."

Picturing his mangled and bloody body, I bit down hard on my lip and tasted the metallic salt on my tongue. Digger was in the ground now, the same as my mother. Deep down in the dirt with the bugs.

Jess and I rode the rest of the way, hearing only the sounds of the meadow and an occasional snort from Clive. Deep thoughts circled around in my mind. I trusted Jess. My trust let him cut my hand to seal our friendship in blood. I really wanted to mean it as much as that blue-eyed boy. I wanted to find a way to keep him forever, but the idea of forever just felt impossible.

We returned to the stables, and Jess called his father. Dr. Mason looked over my ankle and determined it was a bad sprain. After two days of searching, Uncle Frank found Blue Bonnet and turned five shades of red, yelling at Jess. He got a list of chores a mile long to remind him of the responsibilities when having a horse since he'd apparently forgotten. I promised Jess to help after my ankle could stand the pressure. After all, we swore in blood.

A week after the horse incident, my ankle held enough weight to help Jess out in the barns. I was getting ready when a faint knock echoed off the wooden door in the living room. I found Jess on the other side.

"I thought I would meet you at the barn," I said, confused.

"I know. But I got a surprise for you." He got all fidgety with excitement, making the words slur together He handed over a box with a lid on top. "Open it."

I pulled the flaps back and peered inside the present. A set of green eyes stared back from an orange, furry face.

"You got me a kitten?" I said, pulling the little body from the box.

"I found her this mornin' out in one of the sheds. I know she's not a dog, but I kind of liked her."

"She's really mine?" I asked, rubbing the soft fur against my check. I heard a small purr come from deep in the little kitten's throat.

"If you want her. I, um, thought maybe you'd forgive me. I'm sorry I got you hurt."

"I wasn't really mad at you."

"No?"

"No." I smiled, rubbing the orange fur on my cheek again. "She's really awesome. Thank you, Jess. I really mean it. What's her name?"

"I thought 'bout Carrot since, you know, she's got your orange hair."

"I don't have *orange* hair!"

"Whatever," he said back with a wicked grin. "*Pumpkin*."

"I'm going to choke you, Jess Mason!"

"You can kill me down in the stables. Come on. We gotta go. Get your ugly shoes on." Jess laughed straight in my face. I stared at him a few minutes, trying to give the worst possible glare to that dang boy. I would knock him in the head one of these days.

I handed the little orange ball of fur over and walked back to my bedroom. *Carrot.* It was a stupid name, but I liked it. *Typical Jess.* I laughed to myself. Sweet with a gift, and then ornery with the delivery.

Carrot wasn't the only thing that came from our horse-riding incident. Mrs. Mason said I needed real lessons if I planned to ride at the ranch. I worked with a trainer twice a week. It was a little difficult the first few classes since I refused to get on a horse. As the weeks passed, I learned to not be afraid and formed a level of control that could have stopped Blue Bonnet on that wild afternoon racing across the meadow. I convinced my father I was truly thankful to the Masons' for the lessons. Deep down, the contempt remained, as it was just another item penciled onto the never-ending Mason List.

Chapter 13

Today, 10:35 p.m.

The meadow fades away in my dreams. I wake again on the soft pillow. The warmth seeps into my skin, flooding me with comfort. I reach up to scratch my nose, but my wrist holds tight in the restraint. The damn thing still has me captive.

"Your dad should be back soon with the doctor."

I jerk, realizing my head is cradled in the lap of the beauty queen. "You're still here?"

"Yes."

"Why?"

"Your dad asked me to stay."

"Oh."

Her fingers brush through my red hair like I am a child. The motion feels soothing, even if I am dead on the inside.

"He wants me to help clean you up when they take these off." She smiles again. "Would you be okay with that?"

"I…I…don't know."

"They're bringin' you some clothes. I can help rinse you off in the shower and put 'em on."

"They?"

"I don't know. Your dad didn't say."

I forgot my clothes were still the same. The same white shirt and jeans caked in dirt and vomit and blood. The red liquid soaked into everything and dried a solid black. The images flash again—vivid pictures captured in my head forever. My fingers twitch into a fist, and my teeth bite down hard into my skin. I can't breathe. I want to curl into a ball, but the ankle clasps make my body thrash against the mattress.

"Take a deep breath, Alex. It's okay. Breathe in. Breathe out. It's goin' to be okay."

"No…"

"You have to be calm when the doctor comes, or he won't take them off."

"I want…I want"—the air comes in jagged gulps—"to see Dr. Mason."

"Breathe." She rubs a hand against my arm. "Breathe."

I cry. I cry ugly tears that shake my whole body. Nothing in my life will ever feel as painful as today. I feel alone. I feel hollow. The beauty queen curls her small body around my tall frame as I cry snotty tears into her pretty hair. At this rate, they would keep me all night. My eyes close, and my thoughts swirl back to the memories of the last time I slept in the Arlis hospital.

Chapter 14

When I was twelve...

I was bored out of my mind after a brutal two days stuck in the farmhouse. The sky had drizzled freezing rain all night, which turned into snow toward morning. "Storm of the century," according to every resident who purchased shovels and chains from the hardware store.

The living room held six new drawings from the last two days of confinement. I was officially out of ideas and needed something else to occupy my time. Jess called a little after lunch. He wanted to pick me up on his four-wheeler to go back to his house and watch movies. As it turned out, Jess promised his mother he would stay at my house until the snow stopped blowing—double cover for his stupid idea. If only he'd told me of his little plan, I would have dressed better.

My skin turned to ice as we bounced deep into the meadow on his four-wheeler. Jess punched the gas, hitting another drift. My arms clenched tighter around his waist in a vice grip. I wore only a small jacket and pair of fancy gloves that were Christmas presents from the Masons. Without layers, the frigid air slapped me in the face. I buried my frozen nose into Jess's back to keep my eyes from freezing shut.

"Where are we going?" I shouted the words over the sound of the four-wheeler.

"We're almost there," he yelled over his shoulder. "It'll be warm in the house."

"What house?" I pulled my face free to look around the area. Over the last four years, Jess dragged me all over Sprayberry into every nook and cranny except Uncle Frank's place. Nobody ventured inside the spook house except the man himself.

"Up there." Jess motioned to the trees.

Peering through the thick snow, I saw the outline of what resembled the wooden boards of a tree house. "You decided today was the best time to take me here? In a blizzard?"

"I know, right? It's gonna be so cool."

"Are you insane?" My breath formed each word in the cold air. "We have to go back. It's snowing harder."

"Come on." He jumped out of the seat and stomped through the snow to the tall oak.

"Jess…we can't."

He met my protest with a giant snowball, which smacked me in the chest. I formed one of my own and ran through the tall drifts to shove it down the back of his shirt. Jess spun around and put me in a headlock. His free arm grabbed a wad of ice, twisting it against my neck.

"Mercy!" I screamed.

"You goin' up?"

"Yes! Okay! Yes! Now let me go!"

He loosened his arms. "I promise. We won't stay long."

"You drive me crazy."

"I know." Jess grinned as the snow gathered on his long eyelashes.

As we reached the back side of the tree, I saw a ladder built into the trunk, leading up to a landing platform. "You go first, and I'll come up behind to make sure you don't slip."

I felt nervous, climbing the tree that towered about three times higher than mine in Dallas. My gloves stuck to the icy rungs while I took each step with Jess right behind me. We stopped at the landing platform, about forty feet off the ground. Jess reached around to unlatch the door.

It felt warmer inside the house without the wind pelting us with snow. In all the years living on the ranch, today marked the first time Jess ever brought me to his secret tree house. Two large windows sat on the back side, flooding the house with light. A Texas Rangers banner covered one wall while the other side was lined with hooks, holding various ropes and gadgets from the ranch. In the corner, a shotgun leaned against a metal tub filled with old toys.

"How often do you come out here?" I asked, looking at a shelf of jars that circled just below the ceiling.

"I don't know."

"You build it?"

"Not really. The Jessups haven't always owned the whole ranch. I found the house and showed it to my dad. We fixed it up. That's why you can still use it. Mother hates the whole thing."

"That sounds about right." I pointed up toward the shelf. "So why all the jars?"

"Spider collection."

"You serious?"

"Yeah, but that was a few years ago. They're all empty now." Jess pulled me by the arm over to the window. "Come on, you need to see this."

The view from the tree house left me speechless. A whimsical display of snow coated the sky, swirling down in the air. Instantly, I knew why someone picked this tree for the house. The tall oak rested on a small hill, with a view that went for miles and miles.

Jess pulled out a large blanket to wrap around us while we watched the snow. The musty fabric blocked out very little of the cold air. Shivering, I scooted as close as I could to him, trying to get warm.

"You were right. It's amazing," I said, hypnotized by the millions of sparkling flakes. "I haven't been up in a tree since back home."

"Before you came here?"

"Yeah."

"What was it like back then?"

"The end was a lot like what you saw, I guess. But, it was different before she got sick. We still had our house."

"What'd you do for fun?"

A smile crept over the corners of my lips with the memories of another time, another place. "We had this garden. I spent a lot of time climbing the trees, and I wore princess dresses."

"You're lyin'. *You*…in a princess dress?"

"It's true. I had several of them covered in jewels. I had a crown and wand too. Sometimes, I even liked to pretend that I was fairy princess with magical powers."

"That's 'bout the funniest thing you've ever said." Jess busted out laughing.

"What? You don't think I could wear a tiara?" I moved my fingers into a makeshift crown right on top of my head.

He laughed even harder. I liked to watch Jess when he got twisted up half-silly. His face got lost in the moment, so carefree with nothing holding him back. I watched until it became contagious. My lips busted open in a gush of laugher, making me fall over backward against the hard boards. Jess peered down at me with a funny smile.

"What?" I asked, rolling my eyes.

"I like it when you laugh like that. You sound happy." He shrugged. "Makes me wish I'd known you back then."

"Oh," I whispered, imagining the sad idea of the impossible. Jess without the tragedy of death. Jess without the Masons paying for my very existence.

My laughter faded into a frown. Sitting up, I looked out the window. The storm got worse as we sat in the house. A stab of fear traveled through my skin, seeing the meadow lost under the mounds of thick snow.

"Jess, we probably should go."

"Crap, it's startin' to look bad."

I wanted to say that it looked *bad* when we arrived, but that was beside the point. We rushed down the ladder, only to find the four-wheeler wedged in a snow pile under the trees. Jess tried to go forward, but the rubber tires spun under the drift. The whole machine vibrated as the motor grinded with a strange noise.

We climbed off and tried to dig it out. My numb fingers hurt under the wet gloves. "Do you have anything up in the house we could put under the tires?"

"I don't think so," Jess muttered. His eyebrows scrunched up as he stared at the four-wheeler. "This ain't workin'. I think we should just stay up there. It'll be worse to get the four-wheeler goin' and get stranded. I think somethin's wrong with the motor."

"How are we going to stay warm? It's not much better in the house." My voice betrayed what I was feeling. The cold air slapped me in the face. The once-magical flakes turned into chaotic weapons.

Panic crept into my thoughts. Jess and I both had lied. My father thought I went to the Masons. His parents assumed Jess sat tucked away at the farmhouse. They had no idea where to even look. Horrible thoughts of our frozen bodies spun through my mind—our faces black with oozing parts that burst in the snow. We would die.

I felt sick to my stomach. Taking in a deep breath, my lungs hurt feeling the bitter air. Jess came over and placed a hand on each of my shoulders. His black hair fell out of his stocking hat and froze to his forehead.

"It's goin' to be okay. I promise." The bright eyes lacked his ever-present confidence. "I got an idea that might buy us some time. That old tub up there is metal. We could build a fire in it."

"The tree house will just fill with smoke," I muttered, feeling another chilly blast hit my backside. The storm continued to attack from all directions.

"We could crack the windows?"

"I…guess."

"See, we got a plan." He grinned, trying to look positive.

Jess and I used an old rope to pull the limbs to the platform. He dumped the toy trucks out of the tub and broke the branches down to fit inside it. I cracked the two windows while he dug around for a package of matches. We tore up an old box, trying to get the wet limbs to catch fire. After what felt like the hundredth try with the matches, a few embers burned in the old toy bin.

I pulled off my gloves, holding my hands over the fire. It wasn't a body-warming heat, but it was better than nothing at all. My lungs burned from the black cloud that hovered in the house. Staring into the flames, the fire lulled Jess into a trance. I wanted to ask how long he thought it would take for them to find us, but his slumped shoulders told me the answer. This was really bad.

The boy, normally full of endless smiles and words, said nothing as time ticked by in the house. Our fire burned lower, and daylight faded. Jess added more sticks to the bin. Smoke billowed out around us as we huddled together under the musty blanket.

"What kind of spiders?" I asked, hearing my voice against the quiet.

"Huh?"

"In the jars. What kind did you have?"

"Oh, brown ones," he muttered.

"Were they poisonous?"

"I don't know. I had to catch bugs for 'em. They ate too much. Most just shriveled up and died."

"Oh." I paused, glancing over at his sad face. "Can I ask you something?"

"Sure?" His blue eyes never even looked in my direction.

"Why haven't you brought me out here before?"

"I don't know." His shoulders shrugged next to me. "It's always been, like, my place. My thinkin' spot away from everyone."

"You've never talked about it."

"I don't know how to explain it without soundin' like some boy with a fort and a NO GIRLS ALLOWED sign."

"You didn't show me because I was a girl?" I shook my head, trying not to smirk.

"You think it's funny?"

"No, I think it sounds nice having your own place. But why'd you finally show it to me?"

He contemplated the question for a moment. "I was sittin' in the house and wanted to escape. Every time I want to get away, I think of this place. I always come up in the summer. I'd never been in the snow, and I wanted you to see it too. I wanted you to see my favorite place."

He shared his favorite place with me. The admission burned in my chest—a painful combination of friendship and the Masons always giving something to me. I wasn't sure what to say back to him. "You don't have to share everything with me."

"I know, but I want to." His sincere blue eyes spoke more than the words.

"What were you escaping by coming to the tree house?"

"It's before you came to live here," he said quietly.

"You were, like, eight."

"I know, it's stupid." He paused, letting out a deep breath. "Parents wanted their kids to be friends with me, you know, to have a way in with my family. They were always just droppin' in at the house. They'd act stupid. All of it just to have connections with my parents. I hated it. I'd leave when they came over and sneak out here. It lasted for a while, then y'all came to Sprayberry."

"What difference did that make?"

"Everything." The embarrassment reflected bright on his cheeks in the light of the flames. "You're different from all of 'em. I didn't need to hide out anymore. I had you."

"Oh," I whispered, hearing his answer that wasn't really an answer. This wasn't news about his family. I had lived in Arlis long enough to witness the dynamics. People wanted to use the Masons. With power came the great burden to distinguish real friendships from those who wanted to coattail on another's pot of gold, or in their case, oil.

I didn't see my family any different than the others. Yet, Jess saw me as the opposite; I was his savior when, in fact, his family was ours. The idea required more thought at a later time when I wasn't stranded in a snowstorm.

I watched the flames jump around in the metal bin until my sleepy head fell against Jess's shoulder. My nose tucked close to his hair that still smelled like soap, despite the smoke in the tiny room. In the moment, I was cold but felt safe next to him. Sometimes, I just pretended his last name wasn't Mason.

"*Jess!*" I screamed, jerking awake. A log exploded in the fire, causing it to shift and knock over the metal bin. He threw the blanket off as the flames spread up the fabric.

"Come on!" Jess grabbed my hand and pulled me up. "We gotta get to the hatch!" The room filled with smoke, and the old boards soaked up the flames. "Don't let go of my hand. I'm gonna slide around the outside wall."

I followed Jess blindly as we scooted through the haze to the exit. Something exploded, sending a wave of flames in our direction. I doubled over coughing as the heat scorched my face. Jess pushed me through the door, and I hit the landing platform on my stomach. I rolled over and screamed as Jess struggled to get through the hatch with his coat sleeve on fire.

"*Go!*" Jess pleaded as he beat his glowing arm against the landing floor. "I'll be right behind you!"

"No…I'm not going!"

"*Now!*" Jess shoved me off toward the ladder.

I slipped down the steps, desperately watching for Jess. At that angle, I couldn't see the top of the platform. Jumping the last ten feet, I fell backward into a drift. The whole house burned bright in the cold air with Jess still on the platform. I pulled myself out of the snow and climbed back up the steps. Orange glowing boards fell all around me. Something struck the back of my head, knocking me down in the snow. The pain radiated down my spine, and then everything went black.

My body moved slowly through the snow. Ice caked around the waistband of my jeans. Opening my eyes, the flames burned hot in the distance. It hurt to move my head. Jess struggled to take another step; his hands pulling under my armpits, dragging me away from the tree house.

"Don't—you're hurt," I muttered.

"Nah…just a little." His sweet face gritted up in pain. "Let's…g-get further a-away."

Everything went out of focus. For a moment, I didn't see anything but darkness. Feeling around my head, I located the knot just on the backside. I looked back up at Jess, smelling the scorched flesh. The image of his burning body stayed seared in my mind. Turning to the side, I saw something awful.

Jess made it a few more steps before sinking down in the snow. Crawling up beside him, I took a good look at his arm. My stomach lurched seeing the bloody, oozy mess mixed with melted fabric. I stared back into his sad, blue eyes.

"Maybe we should put snow on it."

"Okay," he mumbled.

I patted a handful of white fluff into the charred arm. I was afraid to push too hard. What if I knocked off part of his skin? The idea caused bile to form in the back of my throat. Taking another clump, I added a new layer, seeing the blood darken the ice. "Feel any better?"

"Yeah." He half-smiled as a tear trickled out of his eye. The water froze on his cheek. My chest hurt, seeing him cringe in pain each time I touched his arm. I stopped packing the burn with snow. Jess needed a doctor.

"I don't know what else to do."

"It's almost numb now," he muttered. "It shouldn't be long now. They'll see the fire and come lookin'."

Scooting closer to his side, I wrapped my arms around his shaking body. We clung together in the snow, waiting to be rescued. The smell of his burned skin lingered in the air.

It wasn't long before two beams of light headed in our direction. The big four-wheel-drive truck barely stopped before both of our fathers came running toward us out on the meadow.

The burns and the head injury landed us both in the hospital. Jess would need to see a specialist in Dallas. They held me overnight for observation for a concussion. Dr. Mason arranged for us to share a room in side-by-side beds. Once again, I slept in the Arlis hospital, but this time as a patient.

That night scared me. It scared me in ways I didn't want to think about as I watched my friend stare up at the ceiling. I knew he was still in pain.

"I'm really sorry," he whispered softly.

"It's okay."

"No, it's not. I do stupid stuff sometimes. I get caught up in the moment and I…I know we joke 'round, but you're my best friend." The blue eyes glistened in the dim room as he rolled over to face me. "You wouldn't wake up after you got hit. I kept shakin' you, and you just laid there. The boards were fallin' everywhere…and I was scared. I don't know what I'd do if somethin' happened to you."

An odd pain stabbed me in the chest. I sucked in a deep breath. Every time I closed my eyes, I pictured his body covered in fire. I pictured the orange flames eating up his skin. I pictured a life without Jess. The image hurt. It hurt deep inside my chest in a way nothing else could reach me.

"I would cry," I whispered.

"What?" His voice cracked like it often did these days.

"I would cry for you, Jess."

Chapter 15

Today, 10:52 p.m.

The hospital still has the same wallpaper. I notice this as I open my eyes. The dim moonlight illuminates a man sitting in the chair, his hand resting across a knee.

"Dad?"

"Hey."

Wiggling my hand, I move it free of the restraints. I lift it up to see ugly red marks across the blue stars inked into the skin on my wrist. Bruises speckle the rest of my arm, disappearing under my sleeve. I hurt in every possible way a body could hurt. I hurt from my skin to my soul.

"What time is it?"

"A little before eleven."

"What's happening? I want the truth."

"You need to get cleaned up, and we can talk." His face constricts on the words.

"Stop it."

"Alex, you broke the stained glass window in the chapel with a plant. You need to take it easy. I know you're upset."

"*Upset?* You think I'm *upset?* You of all people should understand I'm not just *upset!*" Panic grips my skin. I can't breathe. Tucking my knees close, I grab on tight.

"Pumpkin, it will be okay."

"Stop lying to me."

He rubs his tired eyes. "I'm not lying. I just don't have an answer, so it's the only thing I know to say."

"So you don't know?"

"No," he mutters. My father stands up from the chair. He sits down next to me on the bed, pulling me against his shoulder. "I would tell you if I did. I won't keep it from you."

"Promise?" Two tears slip down my cheeks upon hearing that word. Those two syllables represent something powerful in my world, the very one that spins in a perilous orbit.

"I promise, Pumpkin."

Chapter 16

When I was fourteen...

Arlis. "Not big enough to spit on," according to those passing through the hole-in-the-wall Texas town. It didn't take long for me to know exactly what Jess meant when I arrived at Sprayberry. Arlis was not a wealthy place, which made the Masons stand out as local royalty among the gossipmongers and coattailers.

My involvement with the family became fodder of many dinner-table discussions. The snippets of our legendary scandal caught my ear through the years. "How'd those con-artist Tanners wiggle their way in with the Masons? You know they pay for everything. Bought the dad another new truck just last year."

For Jess and me, those wild days at Sprayberry made the rest disappear into oblivion. A bubble built by children destined to burst, but we lived every moment happy and together. That worked until one summer. In a few weeks, high school would start, bringing the full world of Arlis right to my doorstep. It was an understatement to say I was worried. Those thoughts plagued my subconscious as I sat sketching poolside at the Masons.

"When are you getting your ass in the pool?" Natalie demanded from the cool, blue water. I looked up at my only other friend besides Jess. She'd spent the last hour floating around on a reclining raft in his pool while I sketched in my notepad.

"Um, maybe later. I want to finish this, and then I'll jump in before we head back."

"Good luck, Nat. She's not gettin' in unless you push her."

Hearing his deep voice from the white lounge chair, I tilted my eyes up long enough for a nonverbal *shut up!* Jess winked back.

"Jerk," I mouthed at him.

I met Natalie when she moved to town during seventh grade. The school-board members, who graduated high school with Moses, thought junior high students still needed a jungle gym. This just drove some kids to hang out behind the bus barn smoking whatever they could rustle up, and the rest to stand around with petty stares of social-ranking popularity.

One lunch period, while trying to escape the courtyard of fake smiles, I found a girl kicking the crap out of the Dr Pepper machine with her laced-up Dr. Martens. She wore a black, ruffled skirt and a tight, Nine Inch Nails T-shirt. As I watched the strange girl, she turned and gave me a twisted smile that screamed, "Back the hell up!"

That was the day I met Natalie, the most unique person I'd ever seen. She came to Arlis kicking and screaming louder than me with a family-forced move, courtesy of her grandfather's dementia. I understood and accepted the fellow outsider to this place. Despise plus despise equaled a match made in despicable heaven.

Hearing a splash, I glanced up again over my paper. Jess slipped in the deep end and surfaced close to Natalie. He slicked the dark hair back off his forehead. Swimming up to the raft, he grinned close to her face. "You wanna play volleyball?"

Seeing Natalie's hateful snarl, I chuckled to myself. Those two basically tolerated each other because of me. I don't think Jess disliked Natalie; he just didn't understand her harsh personality or love of black clothing. On the other hand, Natalie saw Jess as the spoiled rich kid.

Jess assembled the net across a corner section of the pool. Natalie reluctantly climbed off the raft to play with him. Sitting under the large umbrella-covered table, I focused again on my sketch, adding a few more lines of shadows around the windows. I had to admit, the architecture of Mason Manor was very interesting to reconstruct on paper. Jess *hated* the nickname I gave the house. I used it as much as possible just to grate on his nerves.

"Alexandra, would you care for some lemonade?" I looked up to see Mrs. Mason standing over me. Her drawn-out words practically turned the last one into four.

"Yes, ma'am."

She handed over a glass with her perfectly manicured fingers. Mrs. Mason's eyes paused briefly on my Rangers baseball cap. I thought the blue canvas looked nice with my red braids sticking out on each side. She apparently thought otherwise.

"What are you working on, dear?" She smiled, the sun reflecting off her glossed lips.

"Um, some drawings." I noted her carefully selected outfit. The crisp white pants and gold dress sandals complemented the yellow sleeveless sweater top.

"Do you mind if I have a look?" Reluctantly, I handed over the paper. I didn't like someone seeing my work. Even if it was just a building, the picture was a little part of the person I was inside. Mrs. Mason scanned over the drawing. "Very nice, Alexandra."

"Hey, Al, show her your book. She's really good."

I glared at him.

Taking a deep breath, I opened my backpack. Thanks to Jess and his big mouth, I really didn't have a choice except to show her my drawing pad. A flush of nausea shot in my stomach mixed with the pretty lemonade.

Mrs. Mason thumbed through the pictures of animals and buildings and flowers from the meadow. She paused on the sketch of Jess perched on Clive's saddle. The entire picture was gray-and-white pencil except a few highlighted points. I added bright-blue watercolor to Jess's eyes and the blue bonnets in the background.

"Your sketches are very good, Alexandra. Did you ever take lessons?"

"No, ma'am. Not formal ones." Feeling the judgment, I absently chewed on my bottom lip.

"Hmmm, I see. Well, carry on, dear." Handing back the sketch pad, she walked toward the house. "Jessup, you really should put on sunscreen."

"Yes, ma'am." Jess agreed to her motherly request even though he never burned. The sun just turned his skin into dark caramel.

Jess and Natalie climbed out of the pool to get some lemonade. They each took one of the decorative poolside cups, accented with a lemon wedge in the top corner.

"Stop dripping all over my stuff!" I spat at Jess, pulling my sketchbook away.

"Maybe you should just get in the pool." He grinned, taunting me. Bending down, he scooped me up from the chair. I kicked my feet in every direction and tried to elbow his chest. Walking over to the edge of the pool, his arms held me in a vice grip, making my clothes wet.

"Don't you dare!"

"What'd ya think, Nat?"

Natalie just nodded her dyed-black head in agreement.

"What? You two are agreeing on things together now!"

I twisted around trying to get free, but Jess gripped harder into my skin. He'd spent the entire summer training with the high school football team. I couldn't beat him anymore. His toned-up body got stronger every day.

"Okay, let's do this." His voice cracked with a laugh. "One, two…and three!"

I flew in the air and then landed in the cold, blue water. Thrashing around, panic climbed from my chest into my throat. My toes fought against the cement bottom until I stood upright in the shallow end.

"You asshole!" I surfaced, coughing up water. "I hate both of you!"

Jess landed with a cannonball next to me, sending another splash over my head. I wiped the spray from my eyes. "I'll get you back. You better watch it."

He laughed, getting close to my face. "What're you gonna do 'bout it?"

"Take you down."

"*Really.*"

"*Yes,*" I taunted right back into his blue eyes.

"Like this?"

I screamed as he dunked me under the water and pulled me back out again. I got in a few good punches to his side. He just laughed in my ear as he carried me to the side of the pool. Jess dumped me next to Natalie on the cement.

"You really should wear a suit. I can see through your shirt."

"Then stop looking, *jerk!*"

Crossing my arms over my tank top, I turned to Natalie. She seemed bored, flicking her purple toes in the water.

"We still on for tonight?" Jess climbed up next to us on the side of the pool. "I lifted the keys this mornin' to the Jeep."

"You want to come with us?" I invited Natalie, knowing she would say no.

"Where are you going?"

"We're sneakin' out drivin' tonight," he said in that syrupy voice. "Maybe out toward Nickel Creek."

"That's lame."

Ignoring her stupid comment, he turned a sweet smile over to me. "I'll be over 'round eleven-thirty. Your dad should be asleep then, right?"

"Yeah, I think so." My stomach did a little flip-flop at the prospect of sneaking out of the house. However, it was just too tempting not to go driving with Jess.

I heard the phone ring after dinner. My father answered, and I knew immediately from the tone of his voice, he was discussing something with Mrs. Mason. My body tensed up, hearing the phone click back in the cradle.

"Hey, Pumpkin? You in the kitchen?" My father yelled from the living room. I'd just finished putting away the dishes in the cabinet.

"Yeah," I said back a little hesitantly.

He leaned against the doorjamb. "I just had an interesting discussion with Mrs. Mason."

"Um, you did?"

"So I guess she looked at some of your sketches this afternoon."

I didn't see that one coming. I knew something flashed on her face as she looked through the pictures. Anger festered under my skin.

"Well, Mrs. Mason talked to a friend over in Fort Worth and found some fancy instructor who'd like to see some copies of your work. If he finds you promising—her words," he chuckled, "this instructor would like you to come over two Saturdays a month to work one-on-one."

You had to be kidding me! Her interceding involvement in our life would never stop. I'm sure this *fancy* instructor, who only took a student based on an audition, would be extremely expensive.

"Isn't that exciting?" He smiled while the silent screams stayed inside my body

"No, I don't think it's a good idea."

"Are you sure?" His smile fell just a little. "If you're worried about the money, Mrs. Mason said she'd handle the cost."

Of course she would. I shook my head, knowing this couldn't happen. We had to draw the line somewhere.

"Dad, I don't want them paying for it."

"But I want you have these kinds of opportunities. You're good, Pumpkin. I'm proud of you."

He always wanted the best for me, and I didn't want to crush my father. A snarl formed in my throat. He was going to guilt me in to letting the Masons pay for it. *Fine!*

"Okay, I'll do it," I muttered. Taking a deep breath, I let it out slowly. I wished I felt differently, but I just couldn't.

After finishing in the kitchen, I went back to my room to wait for Jess. I pulled out my list, penciling in the new entry. Most of the columns were full on the front side. The large, blank backside waited for more of the inevitable charity that came from the family. I chewed on my bottom lip as I absorbed the magnitude of the debt. Shaking my head, I tucked the paper away in the drawer. No one had ever seen the list. I'm not sure how I would explain the columns of items if anyone every stumbled across the hidden paper.

Climbing under the covers, I pulled Carrot up next to my face. A deep purr vibrated through her entire orange body. She was my favorite present from that crazy boy. I thought about Jess coming by later. This wasn't the first time we had sneaked out after dark. Sometimes, we took the four-wheeler to his thinking spot on the meadow.

After the tree-house fire, Uncle Frank removed the charred boards. He cut down the tree, leaving just a smidge of its former glory overlooking the meadow. Jess carved our names into the stump as a reminder of the night we almost lost each other.

JESS + ALEX

The letters etched in time, forever. Jess loved the place before the fire, and now it became a place he shared with me. His place became our place.

A light tapping sound pulled me from a foggy haze. The side-table clock glowed a quarter until twelve. I stumbled from the bed over to the window and lifted the glass panel.

"Hey, you ready?" Jess whispered, his pink lips grinning in the moonlight.

"Yeah," I mouthed the words. Jumping through the window, I followed his silent footsteps down the road to where he parked the Jeep just out of sight from the house. Jess wore a navy shirt with his Wranglers that made his body blend in with the hot night.

We drove down the dirt road toward Nickel Bridge. On a Saturday night, the old metal contraption would be full of drunk high school kids hanging off the rails, laughing and smoking. Their truck gates folded out like tailgate minibars.

Jess had the Jeep cruising about seventy-five down the dirt road. He weaved around another washed-out hole in the ruts. I clenched the door brace tight in one hand and the bottom of the seat with the other. The Jeep skidded through a curve, making me scream.

"Hey, sorry! I was just testing it out."

His hand went up to the radio dial and flipped through some stations. The Jeep didn't get many channels.

"I like that song," I said, reaching over to stop him.

"I'm the one drivin'." He swatted my fingers away, settling on a station with a George Strait song.

"I don't want to listen to country all night."

"Don't be hatin' on George. He's just a guy with a guitar."

"*Exactly*," I snarled. Jess grinned back at me, singing along to the swaying words. I rolled my eyes. "You're a dork."

"It just feels wrong, you know. A little like blasphemy, listenin' to anythin' else when you're drivin' out here with the dust kickin' up and the wind in your face. Don't you feel it?"

I gave him a *whatever* glance. Living in Arlis or even Texas made me feel conflicted. Some of those feelings came from my over-all attitude toward the Masons, but some of it came from my inner desire to know what else was out there.

I had a poster of Paris taped to the wall of my bedroom. A mesmerizing picture of the Eiffel Tower lit up at night with the city in full swing around it. Sometimes, I closed my eyes tight and imagined I was part of that world. I sat on the bench at the bottom of the photo, watching the beautiful and exotic place that always smelled like pastries. In this fictitious world of my poster, I was independent and self-reliant while the favors of others never existed. It was a dream that ended in reality when I opened my eyes. My beautiful picture hung on the wall of a house owned by someone else, in a town that never heard of petits fours.

Jess commented once on my print of the Eiffel Tower. "You know there's a Paris, Texas." I followed with a sharp whack to his arm.

Jess never mentioned his secret dreams for the future. The die-hard country boy would seem out of place in a city with a tower. I tried to picture his boyish grin all over the globe, but the puzzle piece only seemed to fit in one place: Sprayberry.

The Jeep bounced down the road as the hot air blasted me in the face. Watching the grass fly by, the moment lulled me into a sleepy trance. This was nice. Everything else faded into the distance, even George Strait and his pathetic love song.

"Stand up."

Hearing his deep voice, I opened my eyes long enough to shake my head no. He motioned again with his hand pointing up to the clear sky.

"Come on, I'll drive nice."

I looked at his sweet smile that I knew so well. Just another one of his 527 ideas of fun that would probably get me killed. Jess slowed his foot on the accelerator to a reasonable pace.

"You promise?"

"Yes."

I took a deep breath and took my seat belt off. Balancing against the door, I climbed to a standing position on the dash. My fingers grasped the roll bar at the top. Strands of my red hair whipped around my face in every direction. Wedging a thigh against the window, I lifted my hands high above my head. The darkness engulfed my body, and I felt wrapped in a cocoon from everything else in the world. My palms pushed back against the rushing breeze. A slight smile curved across my lips as my head dipped back.

It was a magical sensation of flying high above the ground. For the first time since coming to Arlis, I finally had *that* moment. It was the freedom I once knew so long ago, sitting in the garden tree. One by one, the cells in my body jumped to life.

I hung from the top of the Jeep until Jess parked in a field area on the outskirts of the bridge. Seclusion was a big draw for the weekend parties, and the abandoned bridge had the perfect cover nestled down a small ravine. Jess grabbed a box out of the back, but I couldn't see the contents in the dark. I followed him down the gravel side, sliding a few times. My knee came down on a large rock, ripping a layer of skin from my leg.

"You okay?" Jess reached out and wrapped his arm around my waist to keep us steady.

"Yeah," I said, holding tight against his arm.

It was an impressive drop off the side that would make me scared to death to experience it drunk. We made our way to the center of the bridge and sat with our feet dangling over the edge. Jess pulled something out of the box, making my skin crawl.

"Are you crazy? You swore no more firecrackers. They'll put it together if we get caught out here."

"They're just little ones." He grinned.

Back in June, Jess and I sneaked out to the north side of the ranch with homemade bottle rockets. The Landrys had a group of round bales across the dirt road. The air and grass held the dryness from a record-breaking drought. After the third shot, the hay burst into flames like an explosion in a desert. Jess and I ran back to the house. Two kids were no match for a fire of that size. We kept silent as the arson rumors circled through the lines of

Arlis gossip. We agreed there was no point to confess when it didn't change the fact the hay was gone. Jess and I swore never to shoot off fireworks again.

"Jess, I still feel bad about the Landrys."

"I know, but we ain't gonna hurt anythin' tonight. Here, hold this." I held the small tube as he lit the match and touched the end. "Hurry up and throw it."

I threw the fireball forward and watched the explosion a few yards below the bridge. The pink sparkles illuminated the creek before falling into water.

"See, it's all in the water, so stop worrin'. I'm not gonna burn somethin' up."

His smug grin made me laugh. "Yeah, okay…give me another one."

I tossed a second stick off the bridge. It sizzled white, all the way down to the creek bed. Everything was quiet except the bang of the firecrackers. I looked at this fourteen-year-old boy. Jess was older now. He looked older and definitely sounded older. My best friend was changing right before my eyes.

"Jess, are you going to come out here with everyone—you know, on Fridays after the game?"

"Maybe, I guess. If that's where everybody's headed." I felt his shoulders shrug against mine.

"You planning to do a lot of stuff with the football team?"

"Maybe, I don't know."

I still couldn't believe he caved into the whole football thing. I had an interesting summer watching Jess become friends with the people he'd always hated. It wasn't long ago that he ran away to a tree house to avoid the superficial families who tried to associate themselves with the Masons.

"You gonna come watch me play?"

"If you insist."

I got a whack to the arm on that one. This sucked. I wasn't sure how I felt about everything at this point. I wasn't sure where I fit into his new life.

"You could've been a cheerleader, you know. Could've rode the bus to the games with me."

"You really see *me,* dancing around, showing my ass at the games?"

"I just think you should make some new friends beside Natalie. She's all…you know."

"Dark and dreary, like me," I replied.

I never thought it possible, but Jess Mason might be on the verge of becoming a snob. Looking down at my fingers, I knew some of her influence affected my choices, but they were mostly harmless. My nails were painted in her favorite shade of crimson black.

"No, you ain't like her. She's just a little too—I don't know. It's like she's dressin' up for Halloween every day."

"So you're calling Natalie a freak. Stop it, Jess," I spat. "I like her because she's nice to me."

"I didn't mean it like that. I like Natalie. Most of the time, anyway. But I got a little afraid today that the pool might turn black from her hair." He laughed.

"Really? A hair joke? Maybe I should just dye mine black too."

"Yeah, maybe you should," he taunted back.

I didn't reply, but I pulled my ponytail holder off my wrist to tie back my hair.

"You should leave it down. You never do," Jess said, looking over at me.

"What's with your dumb hair obsession tonight? You're being more annoying than usual." I wrinkled up my nose as I pulled it back anyway. He rolled his eyes and dropped another red explosion off the bridge.

"Al, I just think next year, you should be lookin' at all your options. There's other people out there. Some of 'em might be nice if you gave 'em a chance."

"Like who? Ashley Cartwright? *That's* not happening." My temper edged up by the second. Jess was close to getting himself shoved off Nickel Bridge.

"Ashley's not that bad if you took time to get to know her."

Picturing her blonde, curly hair, I threw up a little in my mouth. "No, I'm pretty sure she's all bad. You've always thought the same thing too. When did you start drinking the Ashley Kool-Aid?"

I got up and walked down the bridge. It was too hot, and I'd decided I'd had enough of his thoughts. I had wanted this to be fun tonight. My gray tennis shoes drew up dust as I stomped down the dirt path. I had a deep fear about the way things were changing. I knew Jess spent time with other people over the summer. Practicing with the team as a freshman was a big deal, and it brought attention from certain people like Ashley. I just didn't get it.

"Al, wait." He caught up in only few steps and grabbed my arm.

"What, Jess? You want to change how I walk now too?"

"What's gotten into you?"

"Into me? What about you? You're just…just…" I looked down at the ground. Now that I had the floor, I didn't know what I even wanted to say.

"I'm what?" He stood in front of me, but I refused to look at his annoying face.

I knew it would be different in high school. The magnitude of the difference scared the crap out of me. I couldn't lose Jess even if he *were* a Mason.

"Al, look at me. Are you worried? You shouldn't be. I'll still be me."

"It's already changed," I mumbled. "Everything is already different with you."

"I know. I get what you're sayin'. It's just, playin' football has made things different. For the first time, people notice me for *me*. It's got nothin' to do with my family. It just feels different, and I like it. But that's not gonna change us."

"But it already has, Jess."

"No, it hasn't." He pulled me against his chest with a tight hug, crushing the air from my lungs. My nose buried deep against his shoulder. I pulled in a deep breath, smelling his familiar soap. His arms squeezed tight around my back, and I heard his voice next to my ear. "We'll still be us."

"Promise?" I felt vulnerable asking, like an exposed wound. High school would be a big deal. All joking aside, I needed to hear Jess promise. It was something that was always a constant with us. If Jess looked at me and promised, it would ease the fear in my gut.

He let me go and peered into my face with his familiar sweet smile. "I'll always promise. You, me, and Sprayberry and burin' shit down."

"You promised not to burn anymore shit down."

"I know. I'm keepin' that promise too." Grabbing my hand, he pulled me toward our spot on the bridge. "No more fightin'."

Settling next to him, I let my gray canvas shoes dangle over the edge. I watched as Jess dropped the remaining fireworks into the water. Tonight felt like the end of an era in some ways. It was only a matter of time before his promise wore thin, like when the teenage boy got a driver's license and an interest in girls like Ashley. Despite his grand speech, my chest carried a heavy feeling that wouldn't lift. I was afraid of losing him, even though he really wasn't mine to keep.

"Wait." I grabbed his arm to stop the next firework. I pointed up at the shooting star. It flashed through the sky, leaving a trail of dust. Alone in the middle of the night, the moment felt magical, like our very own show.

"What'd you wish for?" his deep voice asked next to me.

"I can't tell you."

"Will you tell me if it comes true?" He grinned.

"Only if you tell me yours."

"Maybe I didn't make a wish."

"But I know you always do, Jess." I smirked at him. His pink lips puckered up for a moment in thought, and the bright eyes became a little serious. The seemed a darker blue tonight. "What's wrong?"

"Nothin'," he said, shaking his head, making the dark hair flop across his forehead. "You ready to head back?"

"Sure, but I'm driving."

"Can I trust you with my stolen Jeep?"

"You're going to say that after the drive out here?" I reached over and pulled the key chain from his pocket. Jess twisted me back against the dirty bridge. His body pinned me down as he bent my arm sideways to pull the keys away.

"Mercy, okay, *mercy*!"

Laughing down in my face, he handed them back. "Go get it started."

"You play dirty, you know."

"I know." He winked and then rolled off the top of me.

I climbed up the embankment, excited for the open road. Firing up the ignition, the radio blasted a twangy song I recognized by Tim McGraw. I shuddered, hearing something about girls being rain. I worked the dial, trying to find something else the old Jeep could play on the ancient speakers.

"What are you doin'?" Jess asked, getting in the passenger side. His hand reached over for the dial.

"Ah, no, you stay on your side of the car."

"You're not drivin' if you make me listen to that angry-girl shit again."

"Shut up. Okay…this is good," I said, smiling sweetly back at him.

The drums pounded. I slung my head back and forth to the hard beat of the Foo Fighters. The music had the power to open up every bit of reserve, letting me belt out the first line. I pulled the Jeep off the embankment and peeled out on the dirt road to home.

"Geez, you sound terrible. You need to just stick to drawin' stuff."

"You really want to provoke the driver?"

"What the hell is this?"

"*My Hero*."

"What? You said I'm your hero?"

"Shut up. It's the Foo Fighters."

"Your Kung Foo music is gonna wake up half the countryside."

"It's Foo Fighters!" I shouted over Dave Grohl's gravelly voice. Turning toward Jess, I caught him swinging his arms around in karate chops. His hands twisted and slapped through the air just to piss me off.

"I hate you sometimes, Jess Mason."

"I know." He grinned. Shaking my head, I turned back to face the road. A pair of glassy eyes reflected back in the headlights.

I screamed. Yanking the steering wheel to the right, I swerved, trying to avoid the deer. The back tires fishtailed on the gravel to the left. My fingers dug hard into the wheel, pulling it back straight, but the unstable dirt pushed the Jeep off the road.

The hood went through the barbed-wire fence. The metal spikes grated into the paint, bursting apart as they came in contact with the glass. The Jeep flew through the Johnson grass and slammed into a tree.

The impact propelled my body forward, only to be yanked back by the seat belt. I couldn't breathe; my lungs crushed from the shoulder strap. Coughing and gasping, I panicked. "*Jess…Jess!*"

I couldn't remember if he had fastened his seat belt. Dust floated in a light mist around the Jeep. My terrified eyes found Jess strapped into the passenger side. The electric guitar crackled through the speakers with the pounding drums. My heart accelerated with the sound of the Foo Fighters still screaming in the car. I couldn't breathe.

Jess reached down and turned off the blaring radio. The Jeep went eerie silent in the dark night. I couldn't speak as I watched Jess's lips say words I couldn't hear. Slowly, his voice came into focus, "It's okay. It's gonna be okay."

My white knuckles were still clenching the wheel. He reached over and pulled them away. "Are you hurt?"

"I…I…don't think…so," I mumbled back. One minute we were arguing about music, and then we almost…I couldn't even process the thought. I almost killed Jess.

"Okay…let's…umm…just get out," Jess said, unlatching his shoulder trap.

My hands were shaking, and I couldn't work the buckle. I couldn't breathe. My chest hurt from the bruise forming across my body.

"I got it." Jess came over to the driver side, setting me free.

Swinging my legs down, I climbed out into the grass. My knees gave out. He slipped an arm around my waist as we staggered to the front to see the damage. It was a tough old car made of solid metal, but the impact smashed all the way through the bumper and into the hood. The top was buckled up like a crunched can.

"It's bad," I muttered.

"I know, but I think I can get it backed out of here." He turned and looked at me with a frown. "You sure you're okay?"

"I guess."

"Okay, then let's go."

Jess walked with me to the passenger side. Crawling up in the seat, he latched the seat belt across my shoulder. I moaned, feeling the band cut into my throbbing chest.

"You sure?" The blue eyes stared into mine.

"Yes," I whispered. "I just want to go home."

"Okay. I'll get you there. Hold on." Jess jumped in the driver seat. He fired up the ignition, putting the Jeep in reverse, but the tires spun with each touch to the pedal.

"It's stuck, isn't it?"

"No, I'll get us out…just gonna take a bit."

Jess floored the gas, making the car shake. He eased up and tried again. The Jeep lurched sideways, spinning away from the tree. We pulled out on the road and headed toward the old farmhouse. Jess drove slowly. The cab rocked back and forth from the frame damage. The movement nauseated me. I sucked in another gulp of painful air.

"It's after three," I said quietly. "What are we going to do?"

"Well, I'm gonna drop you off and then try to get this thing back in the barn."

"We have to tell somebody," I pleaded. I figured we needed to wake somebody up when we got back to the ranch.

"We ain't tellin' anyone anythin' tonight."

"They have to know what I did."

"You didn't do anythin'."

"Jess, they will know. The Jeep's messed up bad."

"Yeah, I know. They're gonna find out, but it ain't gonna be like this."

"What are you saying?"

"I've got this, Alex. You're not involved. You weren't here."

"You're not taking the blame for this."

"Yes, I am. I'm gonna keep the keys. They won't notice the front if I park it just right. Then tomorrow, I'll take it out on the meadow." I saw him swallow hard and grit his jaw.

"And what? Run it into a tree? No, Jess! This is crazy! Just let me tell them what happened."

"Your dad will kill you, and then he'll kill me for takin' you out here. It won't be as bad if they think I did it on the ranch durin' the day. But if they find out we ran through the Nelson's fence in the middle of the night? Ain't either us gonna live through that one. So just let me fix it, okay?

"I don't like this." The nausea rolled around in the pit of my stomach. The Jeep crashed once and we survived, but Jess was going to crash it again on purpose. My stomach twisted, spinning bile up into my throat, "Oh, crap. I'm gonna be sick."

Leaning over the side, I puked as we rounded one of the curves. Bits of vomit flew out past the door in the darkness.

"Want me to stop?"

"No, just go." I waved my hand forward. "I just want to go home."

We reached my house, and I climbed down from the Jeep. It took every bit of control not to cry out in pain. Jess followed me down the road to the farmhouse. Reaching down, he tried to help me up in the window, but I grabbed Jess in a fierce hug. His arms circled around my bruised body. He felt solid; he felt safe. The hot summer night made my skin sweaty, but I didn't care. I clung to Jess, refusing to let go.

"I'm okay," he whispered in my ear.

"I almost killed you."

"Then I guess we're even."

"That's not funny." I squeezed harder, my fingers digging into his skin.

"Nothin' is gonna happen to me," he whispered. "I'm invincible."

Chapter 17

Today, 11:08 p.m.

The beauty queen enters the hospital room, carrying two towels and a bottle of fancy shampoo. My father uses her arrival as an excuse to walk toward the door. My hands shake, seeing him leave.

"Where are you going?"

"I'm going to get you some food."

"I'm not hungry."

"You need to eat. All I've seen you do is throw up the last six hours." His sad eyes glance toward me and back to her. "I won't go very far."

As he leaves, I look at the blonde in the corner. She smiles faintly as her lips sparkle with a light coat of gloss. "You ready for a shower?"

I shrug and glance down at my pants. Chills shoot up on my arms at the sight of the stains. I want those jeans burned in a trash can. I slide off the bed, feeling my wobbly legs collapse. She wraps an arm around my lanky body. I could crush her in one swoop, but she holds on with a tight grasp. Without a word, I let the beauty queen take me to the shower. I lean against the sink while she turns on the water and sets up the little handheld nozzle.

"Can you do this by yourself, or do you want me to help?" Her mascara-coated lashes blink in my direction, waiting for a response. She must have applied new makeup when she got the shampoo. "I do this all the time. I mean, the hospital stuff…seeing people naked."

I should care about this strange course of events, but I'm too tired to think straight. "I…I…don't want to keep you here. Don't you need to go home?"

"It's okay, really."

I nod back in submission. She smiles again, this time almost apologetically. I cringe, feeling her hands unbutton the front of my blue plaid shirt. Every moment of today was a page right out of a chapter from hell.

A tan bra covers my chest. The fabric is marked in black stains that had soaked through my shirt. A tear rolls down my cheek and lands next to one of the spots. She pauses for a moment, glancing up with something that resembles compassion.

"I'm a little dizzy," I mutter, turning my head away.

"It's the drugs they gave you."

"Are they safe? I mean…um…I think they gave me a lot."

She stops for a moment and looks me in the eye. "Yeah."

"Okay." I swallow hard, trying to keep my stomach in check. She moves to the front of my jeans. I hold onto her shoulders as I step out of the disgusting pants. I smell rancid. It wafts up, making me dry heave.

"You need a pan, Alex?"

"No." I take a deep breath, closing my eyes. Her fingers slip my stained bra off my shoulders. My white boy shorts follow over my thighs. Standing naked and vulnerable in front of this woman, I open my eyes to see her calm face. I swallow the bile back down my throat.

"Let's get you in."

I sit on the built-in seat used for old people. She soaks my skin with the spray wand. I scrub my arms and legs as a dark trail disappears into the drain. The beauty queen lathers up shampoo and rubs it into my scalp. The floor fills with foamy dried blood.

"The little girl earlier," I ask as a distraction, "is she your daughter?"

"Yeah, that's Corrie. She's four."

"Did she go home?"

"Yeah, my mother stopped by to get me after my shift. Corrie stays with her when I'm at work."

"That's nice. Where…um…is her father?"

Her fingers pause for a moment before she answers. "He didn't want her."

"Must be hard."

"I don't complain much. I can't imagine my life without Corrie. I guess the hard part is rememberin' what it was like before she existed."

"I guess life works that way, doesn't it?" I mutter.

"Yeah, it does." Her eyes catch mine. "Come on. Let's get you out." She turns off the water and wraps one of the towels around my red hair. Taking the other one, the beauty queen dabs the soft fabric down my skin. Yes, today was a page right out of a chapter from hell.

Chapter 18

When I was sixteen...

The jingle of the door caught me by surprise. My stomach automatically tightened at the sight of her. Ashley Cartwright walked through the front door of Jeeter's, followed by two of her *Ashley-bots.* It was a cliché, really, when you looked at the facts. However, clichés only become notorious in the world for a reason. It was just too damn common of a story. Unfortunately, it was currently mine.

"Look at Ashley," Natalie said, her eyes shifting toward the counter. "She went home after school and got slutted up for a Coke. No one's even here but us."

I knew exactly what she was trying to do in Jeeter's. The day or the moment wasn't clear in my mind when everything started with Ashley. Ever since I moved to Arlis, she'd looked down her perky nose at me. It didn't matter much back in those days. I had Jess and the ranch. He didn't like her, so I wasn't forced to spend much time in her presence.

As life evolved, it all became a different playing field in high school. I'd fretted about the changes that would come as we grew older. I wish I'd known just how hazardous it would get the next few years. Who knew Jess would become the football star, love the popularity, and start dating my mortal enemy? I really could just kill him sometimes. I pictured my hands around his throat, choking out his lust for Ashley.

"I guess I need to go help them." I slid out of the booth.

"I can do it."

"No, it's my turn." I let out a sigh and walked toward the counter. The words of Kenny Chesney played on the jukebox, announcing my impending doom.

Ashley stood at the front of the group, wearing tiny pieces of raveling denim she called a skirt with a tight, blue tank top that forced you to look at her breasts. Flowing blonde layers she had modeled after Jessica Simpson's hair surrounded her perfect skin. With the cowboy boots, Ashley could be an ad for that new country line-dancing bar on Highway 37. I wondered if Mrs. Mason had seen her lately. She would definitely not approve of this outfit.

I self-consciously smoothed my hands over my uniform, trying to dust off the splatters of ice cream. The afternoons on the ranch ended quite some time ago. These days, Jess went to football practice while I made milkshakes at Jeeter's after school.

Old man Jeeter had opened the place almost sixty years ago. His granddaughter Caroline now owned the restaurant, which sat conveniently down the block from the hardware store. My father picked me up after he closed the shop. Caroline always made sure we had something wrapped in foil to take home for dinner. She was the doting, fussy type and about my father's age. He said it was my imagination, but I think she liked him.

"What can I get you, Ashley?" I plastered the fake, service-worker smile on my lips and glanced back at Lila and Katie Rae. I never could tell where they stood toward me. Obviously, they were her Ashley-bots, always following along silently in the background, doing what they were told.

"I don't know." Her glossy lips pursed in contemplation. She wasn't friendly but wasn't hateful. Hopefully, it would be a good day. The thought didn't release the tight knot in my abdomen.

Jess and Ashley had known each other their whole lives. Somewhere along the way, he went from hating her to dating her. I couldn't blame him, really. She was sexy, and sometimes he was just a stupid boy.

Ashley's family owned the tag agency. In some twisted way, the fact that her parents slapped a date stamp on the back of every Arlis truck made her feel special. She was involved in every organization at school, including cheerleading. While every guy wanted to date Ashley, every girl either wanted to be her or was afraid of her, or a little of both.

Ashley wasn't necessarily an aggressive, mean person, unless you attempted to take away something she thought was hers. This caused most people to tread lightly because she assumed most things were hers. I guess this also explained why she developed a major issue with me. She thought Jess belonged to her, and I should vanish from the face of the earth.

"Have you decided?" I really didn't want to poke the bear with a stick, but two songs had played on the jukebox since she came to the counter. Ashley didn't answer. She briefly lifted her long eyelashes, caked in mascara, and then looked back at the menu. My fingers clenched into my palms. She was doing this on purpose.

I never knew how an encounter would go with Ashley. With Jess around, she was civil and sometimes over-the-top with gooey compliments. The selfish bitch would sneak around the corner when everyone else was out of sight. Often, it was little jabs whispered in my ear while walking past her in the hall, like "loser" or "homeless skank." If she had some free rein, her words turned into long, drawn-out barbs about me stinking up a room.

About a month ago, Ashley crossed into hostile after coming to a dinner hosted by the Masons. I knew something would happen the moment the words left his lips. Jess had the guests laughing at one of our ranch stories. I had watched the fake smile on her face change to a menacing look in my direction. Ashley didn't like attention focused on me when it involved Jess.

The next day, I opened my locker to find my jacket and backpack soaked in something that smelled like rotten garlic juice. I threw away my clothes, but my locker still carried the faint odor. Every time I smelled it, I hated her a little more. The lingering scent haunted me until she got me with the eggs.

A few weeks ago, I returned home to find the farmhouse pelted with sticky, cracked yokes. Not just a quick, drive-by fling, but roughly ten dozen eggs, baking in the hot sun to a curdled mess. I frantically scrubbed every piece of wood on the front of our house, praying to finish before my father returned from work.

With each shell picked from the ground, a deep hatred burned through my skin. I went absolutely nuts when I saw the lipstick prints on some of the mangled pieces. My blonde tormentor planted a signature kiss on the eggs before destroying my porch. I carried the shells behind the shed and beat them into splinters with a hammer. Maybe I couldn't destroy her, but I could at least kill the evidence.

"Ashley?" I prompted her menacing face. I would not stand here all day, waiting on her twisted mind to figure out her order.

"Since you are so impatient, I need one scoop…not two, of the low-fat vanilla yogurt…slightly blended, with low-fat milk." She turned her piercing eyes from the board to focus at me.

Good grief! Just say small yogurt milkshake.

I rang up Lila and Katie Rae's orders. Turning my back to use the mixer, I felt their eyes watching my every move. It was difficult to do my job knowing she was just a few feet away. Finishing the orders, I handed the cups to each of them. Ashley peered down at the shake, then slanted her eyes at me.

"I said one scoop, not two. That's two."

"You watched me make it. There's just one," I said, keeping my tone even.

Ashley smiled at me, never breaking eye contact as she tilted the cup sideways. I watched half of the white contents splatter to the floor.

"There. One scoop. All fixed. No need to thank me." Ashley's perfect nose pointed up as she grinned. Turning to leave, she stepped over the sloppy mess. "Come on, girls."

Ahh! I wanted to scream in her smug, flawless face. I wanted to put my hands around her throat. I pictured Ashley's happy-hater eyes popping from her skull as my fingers tightened.

"That's some seriously, twisted shit you got with her." Natalie came up behind me with towels. "You need to squash that bitch."

From my angle on the floor, I only saw the laces of her black combat boots. "Like how? You act like she's a spider I can just step on."

"For starters, tell your BBF that his perfect girlfriend is bat-shit crazy."

"I can't do that. This has nothing to do with him."

"Sure it doesn't."

"Ashley has never liked me." I scrubbed the ice cream splatter off the benches by the counter.

"She didn't like you in seventh grade. She put a bull's-eye on your ass four months ago when she pulled your horny friend in the backseat of her Mustang."

"Don't say that about Jess. It's not his fault."

"Don't defend him for being a dumbass."

Natalie knew about Ashley's increasing torment, but I refused to tell Jess. What would I say? "The most popular girl in school, who just so happens to be your girlfriend, is harassing me for not having any money and living at your ranch." He would just try to take care of it, and I didn't want that from him. This was personal. She purposely targeted the worst area of my life. School would be out soon for the summer. I just needed to stay clear of her and let the tension die down between us. Maybe Ashley Cartwright would just forget about me.

Chapter 19

When I was sixteen…

I was wrong. By the end of summer, my life was the same, if not worse. I kept up a good face for Jess, but I felt a deep strain on the inside of my gut. He had a beautiful girlfriend, and I had a scary bitch, haunting me like a red stain on Mrs. Mason's carpet.

"Alex, you okay?" Jess asked as I sat next to him in the meadow. He was taking a break from cutting hay.

"Yes," I muttered. I watched him take a bite of the hamburger I had brought him from Jeeter's. Over the summer, I didn't spend much time with Jess. He worked long hours at the ranch around his football practice schedule.

"Sure? You ain't sayin' much."

"I'm fine."

My black nail polish-tipped finger flicked a fire ant from my knee. The tightly woven strings of bracelets on my wrist seemed to constrict into my sweaty skin. I'd become good with the intricate braids and painted designs on top of the macramé threads.

"Skeeter Rawlins came into Jeeter's this morning, bragging about his meatloaf," I said, trying to get his attention elsewhere.

"Meatloaf?" Jess laughed.

"You know how everyone was talking about Sara Beth Nelson baking cookies in her car? Well, Skeeter apparently tried to top that with a pan of meatloaf on the dash of his truck."

"Gross. I guess he ate it?"

"What do you think? I had to listen to every detail about how it was a little dry and chewy on top, but still gooey in the middle from all the eggs and ketchup."

"Really? I'm eatin' here."

"How do you think I felt? I swear I saw a piece of raw meat still caked in his dirty beard."

"Geez, you can be real nasty sometimes." His nostrils flared in disgust. "I guess it doesn't surprise me. I heard he went fishin' and got down to the pond with his Marlboros but no lighter. Skeeter decided it wouldn't be much different if he just chewed 'em up and ate 'em."

"No way he ate cigarettes."

"Why would he make up somethin' that stupid?"

"I don't know," I muttered.

Jess took a drink of his Dr Pepper. I went back to picking at the strands on my wrist. He chewed for a few minutes. The hot sun baked more freckles into my pale skin.

"I want to talk to you 'bout somethin'."

"Okay?" I asked, hesitant at the direction this was going.

"I'm gettin' a back-to-school campin' trip together over Labor Day weekend. That's our off week with football, so everybody should be free. I want you to go with us."

"Us?"

"Buzz, Gentry, and Ashley. Maybe a few of the girls. Thought you and Natalie could come too."

"You want me to do *what?*" My throat tightened. The bubbles burned in my nose. Just last week, Ashley had dumped a bag of trash in the cab of my father's truck while I was at Jeeter's. Now Jess wanted me to spend the whole damn weekend with her.

"Al, look at me. Don't do this. It'll be fun."

I watched Jess take another bite of the burger. The cheese dripped over his bottom lip as he licked it back into his mouth. He continued to chew while staring at me, waiting for an answer.

"I'm starting to regret that I brought you lunch."

"Come on. You're gonna have to talk to me. What's your hang-up with Ashley?"

"It's nothing. We are just different people." I pictured her perfect fake smile and gagged.

"She's not that bad. You should spend some time with her. She's a fun person."

Fun for you! We didn't discuss that part of his life, but I was fully aware of his sex-capades. The whole damn school heard plenty from Ashley. I hoped for the sake of public sanitary purposes that most of the stories were just inflated gossip.

I watched Jess cram the rest of the burger into his mouth. Leaning against the tractor tire, he wore a fitted white T-shirt and old pair of Wranglers. His shaggy black hair was pushed back off his forehead with a University of Texas cap. Almost a decade older now from when we first met, but he still had the same deep-blue eyes. Those same pink lips turned into a frown. I squinted back with a mean stare.

"You're goin' to have to do better than that. Either you talk to me, or you're goin' to Possum Kingdom with us."

"There's nothing to say, and I am not going camping." I gritted my teeth in aggravation.

"You need to give her a chance. Spend some time with her."

He had to be kidding me! Give her a chance, my ass! Just knock me in the head, tie me to a rock, and throw me in the freaking lake. I'd rather spend the weekend dead instead of being in a cabin with *her*.

I took a deep breath, inhaling through my nose, trying to calm my patience. I cared about Jess and hated seeing him with such a terrible person. It was my fault that his kind heart was currently being held captive by the devil's sister. I should have told him months ago about her dark side, but now it was past the point of no return.

"Al, please do this for me. You don't have to get in the lake. I know you hate it. Please…just say yes." He wrinkled his eyebrows up at me. "I don't feel like I see you as much lately."

"Don't tell me you miss me. I see you all the time."

"You know that's not true. It used to be just us. Now there's school, and football, and you're at Jeeter's, and I help Frank."

I frowned at his words. I wish it were just those things keeping us apart. Why was growing up so tough? I missed being those carefree kids running through the meadow.

"Please say you'll do this." Jess put a palm on each side of my face; his thumbs rested on the corners of my lips, forcing a smile. He moved my head up and down. "See, I knew I'd get you to say yes."

"Gross! Get your cow manure hands off my face. I can see it under your nails." I glared at him, batting his hands away.

Everything was just too complicated. Come clean about Ashley, or go camping. "Fine! I'll go, but I'm doing this for you and only you."

"I knew I'd talk you into it."

"I hate you sometimes."

He gave me one of those irritating grins. The things I do for this boy. Shaking my head, I stood up. "I gotta go back to work."

"Stay and ride a couple of rounds with me."

I looked up at the old tractor that lacked an air-conditioned cab. "Why are you driving that one?"

"The new one already needed some hydraulic part. I kinda like the old one. It's nice, once you get goin'."

"Fine. I'll go, but just a couple of rounds. I have to change before I go back to town. Thanks to *you*, I'm covered in *sweat*."

"Stop complainin." Jess climbed up to the cab and leaned down to pull me up beside him.

"I'm not complaining." His fingers clung to my wrists as the soles on my gray canvas shoes slipped up the worn steps.

"It's hot." His voiced pitched high to mock me. "I'm sweatin'. I don't want to go campin'."

"I'm going to hit you."

"Shut up and sit down."

"Fine!" I hissed, despising the fact I had to touch him.

The cab didn't have room for two people. It was really just one seat with a small fender ledge over the tire. I plopped down on the hot metal, feeling it burn through my jeans. Jess fired the tractor up, and we rolled forward. The breeze picked up as we made the first curve.

"You wanna drive?"

"Is that your apology for being an ass?"

"Stop shootin' off your mouth and get over here." Jess pulled me from the ledge into his lap. My fingers grabbed the steering wheel as my shoulders relaxed into his chest. It was hot and sticky being pressed against him. The sweat of his body seeped through the back of my shirt.

"This is different than driving a car."

"Yeah, it takes a little body movement to turn the wheel. It's got some power-steerin' issues."

I made the turn a little wide and tried to line back up in the row. My palms fought the wheel to stay in a straight line. Tractor driving was hard, but fun. The wind kicked up, putting a breeze across my hot cheeks.

"Al, you smell like hamburgers."

"Hamburgers? Geez, Jess. You smell like sweaty gym socks washed in horse shit."

"You must like it too, or you wouldn't be sittin' here." He laughed in my ear. "You know you want some of it." He smeared his hands over my arms and across the top of my legs.

"Stop it, jackass!"

I heard the laugher building in his voice. This was bad. "Seriously, Jess. Don't go there." His fingers dug into the side of my ribs and tickled their way up under my armpits.

"Quit," I screamed, but his fingers moved down across my stomach. I fought back, but his hands kept finding more places to grab my body. Finally, I elbowed him hard in the gut. "*Stop!*"

"I'm sorry." Jess released his hands, letting me slide back to my place on the ledge. "It's just too much fun, making you look mad."

"I am mad at you!" I spat back.

"I know." He continued to laugh. "Your face is gettin' all red and angry-lookin'."

My eyes narrowed, shooting death rays at his white, smiling teeth. I clung to the ledge, hoping to keep myself as far away as I could from Jess. I inhaled deeply, trying to calm my anger. The smell of freshly cut grass filled my nose as we rounded the field for another pass through the meadow.

"I'm sorry. Don't be mad. Come here."

"No," I huffed.

"Come on. I'm really sorry." His blue eyes pleaded, trying to win me over.

I let Jess put an arm around my waist. He pulled me back down into his lap. I fell against his chest, feeling his heart beat fast through the sweaty shirt. The pounding slowed down to a steady rhythm as he held me close to his body. This time, his fingers stayed in place across my rib cage.

"Are you still mad at me?"

"No," I muttered. I never could stay mad at him for long. His sweet face never allowed it.

"I like it when you ride with me. You haven't been out all summer."

"I know," I said, letting out a deep breath.

"I know you like it too."

"I guess."

"You guess?" He chuckled next to my ear.

"Yes."

Ashley wouldn't have had the same answer if she drove out to Sprayberry. Riding on the tractor with Jess just might get my house burned down, or rather, the *Mason's* farmhouse.

His arm tightened around my waist as we bounced over some ruts. The burn scars popped out from his skin, shining through the dirt and bits of grass. His flesh singed forever from our afternoon in the snow. I touched the biggest gash next to his elbow. Hair didn't even grow over most of the places. They looked painful, but I knew he didn't feel a thing. My fingers traced along his skin until the jagged lines ended by his wrist.

"You know," he spoke close to my cheek, "I don't really mind it much when Frank has me cuttin' grass. It's kind of peaceful, don't you think?"

I shrugged against his chest. As long as *she* stayed in my life, there would be no peace. I wish there were another way around this Ashley situation. I needed to stop being the victim and find a solution—one that didn't involve Jess.

"It's one of my favorite things 'bout this place," he said in that syrupy voice. "I like it better, though, when I'm out here with you."

"Would you be quiet? It's not *peaceful* with your constant blabbing in my ear."

"You know you like me blabbin' in your ear." He smirked next to my cheek.

I rolled my eyes, even though a grin stayed on my lips. That boy drove me crazy sometimes.

We traveled up and down the meadow with the tractor rocking us back and forth in a clunky rhythm. Leaning my head back against his shoulder, I listened to Jess hum one of his dirt road songs. I wanted that peace he talked about so fondly. Closing my eyes, I did my best to enjoy the rest of the rare, Ashley-free afternoon with Jess.

Chapter 20

When I was sixteen...

I sat alone under a tree and watched the boat return with the rest of the group. It had been a nice, quiet few hours while everyone else played on Possum Kingdom Lake. Jess, Ashley, Lila, and I had left yesterday in his Ford truck, pulling the boat. Gentry Jones followed behind in his Tahoe with another one of the players, Buzz Farland, and Katie Rae.

Natalie had flat-out refused to even consider the trip. I pleaded and then threatened with every piece of dirt I could muster. She gave me a deadpan stare and said, "I would rather stick my hand in the deep fryer at Jeeter's than be in literal hell for the weekend. I'm not sure you deserve to be first in our class if you're that stupid to go too."

The two-story cabin had full-size and bunk beds spread out in the different rooms. I opted for a small, twin bed off the second-story landing. It was not in a bedroom, but I would rather be there than stuck in a closed-off room with one of the Ashley-bots.

As for the guys, I didn't know much about Gentry since he moved to Arlis at the end of last year. Jess befriended the outsider the first day he stepped in school.

As for Buzz, he was really Bobby. Jess said the nickname went back to the time he showed up in kindergarten with bloody, mangy spots missing from his hair. His dad got drunk and tried to use the dog clippers. Mrs. Mason took Bobby to the barber and got the spots evened out, but it was too late. Arlis officially dubbed him Buzz.

"Hey, watcha workin' on?"

Startled, I looked up over my drawing pad to see Gentry's green eyes. "Umm…just a picture of the shoreline."

The broad-shouldered boy sat down next to me. Gentry had the body of a dump truck with tree limbs as legs. He played defense for the football team. By some armchair coaches, Gentry *was* the defense, like a cement wall that blocked while Jess ran the ball.

"Can I see?"

"Okay," I muttered, handing over the notepad. I watched him study the picture. His short, buzzed-off hair suited his wide face. Anything longer would just look silly.

"You're good. I've seen some of your others in Jess's room."

"Thanks," I mumbled, feeling a little sick. I didn't think about people looking at those drawings. I'm sure Ashley loved seeing the watercolors tacked on the wall of his room.

"So we're goin' back out to see some cliffs on the north side. You should come."

I looked at Ashley out on the dock in a tiny bikini that sculpted her butt and barely covered anything on her chest. A daunting feeling flooded my nerves. I committed to the trip, so I needed to just get out there. It wasn't like we would be alone together.

"Okay." I smiled. "I'll put my stuff away and be down in a sec."

Jess gave me a surprised look when I boarded the boat, but he didn't say anything. I knew he would be intrigued with my decision to join the rest of the group. Keeping my tank and shorts on, I didn't even look at Ashley.

A silhouette of cliffs outlined the distant view long before we reached the shore. This was a bad decision on my part. I wasn't really thinking about the intent to jump from the cliffs when Gentry suggested the boat ride to see them.

Jess leaned over and whispered in my ear, "You don't have to go up."

I made eye contact with Ashley as he said the words. Her lips clipped on a cryptic smile. I took a deep breath and muttered, "I'm okay."

Jess anchored his boat off a small inlet on the rocky backside of the cliff. Everyone climbed out and started the hike to the top. Last to leave, I dropped my clothes and stepped out in my black, modest, two-piece suit. I slipped and crawled over the jagged incline of rocks. Jess lagged back, pulling me over some of the larger ones. I swatted him away.

Reaching the summit, my eyes took in the jaw-dropping, forty-or-so-foot ledge that overlooked the dark lagoon. *Shit!* The word circled over and over through my head. I never would have made the climb if I'd seen this view from the boat.

The guys rushed for the first jump, leaving me with the girls. Katie Rae went next, followed by Lila. They squealed all the way down into the water. Ashley extended a nonverbal, middle-finger challenge before propelling off in the distance.

Last to go, I peered over the edge. The water was like a black pit into hell. Panic spread through my chest. There was no way I could jump. My body wouldn't allow my descent into a bottomless pool. Backing away from the crumbling edge, I hid from view. My stomach twisted up, and my skin got clammy.

"Alex?" Jess yelled.

I couldn't speak, or I would throw up. This was bad. I could never face any of them. If I didn't jump, Ashley would make me pay. Her imaginary taunts rang loud in my ears.

"Aaaaaa-lex!" I heard Jess's deep, funny voice. When I didn't reply again, he shouted back, "Seriously Al, are you okay?"

I put a single palm in the air with a thumbs-up sign. Closing my eyes, I pictured myself anywhere but on top of a damn cliff. I hoped they would just go away in the water and forget about me. The hot sun burned my skin, but I stayed in the circled-up position. A little bit later, I heard a scrapping sound alongside the rock path. His sweaty face came into view.

"Hey, you still up here?"

"Where do you think I went?" I mumbled.

He reached the top of the cliff and crawled over next to me on the ground. His concerned blue eyes stared into mine. I glanced away. My stomach rolled over again, and I bit down hard on my lip.

"Hey, stop that. You're gonna bite a hole through it one of these days."

I let go, tasting salty blood on my tongue.

"Look at me," he said softly. "It's okay. You don't have to jump. I can get you back down the trail. But, if you wanna jump, I'll help you."

"You gonna just toss me over?"

"Thought 'bout it, but I'm afraid you'd hate me. Can't have you hatin' me anymore than you already do on this trip."

"I don't hate you."

"Yes, you do." He grinned. Reaching up to my face, Jess tucked a piece of red hair behind my ear. His eyes trailed down my neck and over my skin to the red scar on my rib cage. I thought the color would fade, but it was still a nasty, feisty red a year later.

Reaching down, Jess touched the three-inch gash just below my bikini top. A mark made by a fishing lure right into my gut. It hurt like hell that afternoon when he hooked me. It hurt even worse when he clicked the reel and wedged it under my skin. I screamed even louder as he worked it free from my stomach. The lure left a nasty, pond-water-infected gash. I had needed stitches and a shot. Instead, Jess had talked me in to supergluing it shut.

"I did a shitty job fixin' that up." His fingers felt cool on my bare skin as he touched the mark.

"Yeah, I think that every time I take a shower."

"You think about me naked in the shower?" His smiled, trying not to laugh.

"Don't be gross."

"You're the one who said it." Jess gave my ribs a quick pinch, his blue eyes getting that ornery look in them.

"Stop it," I warned.

Giggles drifted up from the black water, getting my attention. I pictured her face, feeling my stomach clench again. I knew what needed to happen.

"What's this plan of yours to get me to jump?"

"I'll jump with you."

"You actually think that will work."

"Come on." Jess stood up, grabbing my hand. With our fingers still intertwined, I saw everyone floating in the dark pool below the cliff. They cheered as we came into view. Our shuffling feet bounced a few pebbles off the side of the ledge. I felt Ashley's vicious stare all the way up, forty feet in the air. My stomach clenched again. Backing away from Jess, I bent over, dry heaving.

"Al, let's just go back down the trail."

"No!" I gasped, looking up and still doubled over at the waist.

"I'm not doin' somethin' that purposely terrifies the crap out of you."

"I have to do this."

"No, you don't. I wanted you to have fun, and you're not havin' fun. No one cares if you jump or not."

"I care. I'm doing this for me." I gathered myself up and told the angry bile in my stomach to be quiet. *Deep breath in through my nose; deep breath out through my mouth.* I chanted it over and over in my head.

"I'm better. Let's do this."

His troubled blue eyes stared intently at my face. I saw Jess weighing my decision, like it was his to make in the situation. A full minute passed before he caved in to me.

"You're 'bout as stubborn as hell sometimes. Okay, if this is what you really want, then I'll help. You'll just have to trust me. Can you do that?"

"Yes," I nodded without hesitating.

"It's gonna be deep when we hit the water. I'll find you and pull you to shore."

"Okay."

Jess put my hands on each of his shoulders and then slipped his arms around my waist. These days, he stood taller than my five-foot, nine-inch body. I watched sweat trickle down his neck. Taking a deep breath, I nodded *ready*.

"Look at me and forget 'bout everythin' down there. You got this," he said, trying to reassure me.

I tried to push the water and Ashley far from the racing thoughts in my mind. I trusted Jess. He would get me through this without getting hurt. It was all in my head. My eyes locked with his blue ones.

"I'm gonna count to three, then push off the side."

"Okay." I swallowed the bile back in my throat. My fingers dug into his sweaty skin.

Everything went silent except for his voice and the pounding of my heart.

"One."

Pound.

"Two."

Pound.

"Three."

Pound.

"Jump!"

He crushed me against his chest. My feet lifted up in the air as we pushed off the ledge. The descent seemed to go for ten minutes, when in reality, it probably wasn't even ten seconds. My stomach lurched into my throat, and my breath was gone. I screamed as we plunged into the water, knocking us apart. The impact pushed me deep in the black water.

Jess found my hand and pulled me to the surface. I heard loud cheers around me. My nose burned from not pinching it. I gasped for air, trying to stay above water. Jess pulled me around to his back and locked my arms around his neck.

"Th-thank you," I said, trying to catch my breath.

"How's it possible you never took swimmin' lessons?"

"I don't know." I did know. I hated the water and the Masons paying for it.

I clung to his back; my bikini-clad body pressed tight against his skin. I raised my hand to high-five Gentry as we passed. My eyes drifted over to Ashley. She wasn't smiling like everyone else in the water. Her eyes shot an icy warning in my direction.

Later that evening, Jess and the boys went back out on the lake, leaving me at the campfire with the girls. I wanted to beg them to take me on the boat, but it wasn't the best idea. Given Ashley's current temperament, I didn't know if it were better staying with her or leaving with Jess.

In the shadows of the fire, I kept my attention on a long string dangling off the leg of my cutoffs. Ashley acted like I wasn't here; at least, she did for a while.

"That's enough with Buzz. You were hangin' all over him today." She glared at Katie Rae. "He will think you're willin' to follow through with it."

"He's nice and he pays attention to me." Katie Rae paused, seeing the irritation on Ashley's face. "I just want Buzz to ask me to homecoming."

"The same way you got Evan Wiley to Spring Fling last year?"

"It didn't happen. You…you know that." She flushed, stumbling over her words. Spring Fling earned Katie Rae a reputation for extracurricular car activities that spread through the halls of Arlis High School.

"I know *what*, exactly?" Ashley's nose snarled a little.

"Nothin'." Katie Rae slipped a glance toward me, then back to Ashley.

Heat flooded my checks with the implication I was eavesdropping. Pulling out a bag of Doritos, I pretended to be somewhere else, but the details lingered in my mind. I had ammunition if I could figure out how to use it. I think that blonde bitch hooked up with Evan while she was with Jess.

"Ashley, I know you don't like Buzz, but he's really sweet. The other day he bought…"

"Stop boring me with the details of your trailer trash."

"He's gettin' a scholarship. Scouts have already come to the games."

"It's jucco, Katie Rae. Know the difference. Anything less than D1 will get you livin' in a single-wide, eatin' beanie weenies out of can."

"I'm not marrin' him. It's just homecoming."

"I'm sorry. I guess I wasn't thinkin' clearly." She turned with a sly smile, acknowledging my presence for the first time. "Not everyone can be me and have Jess Mason."

"I know. You're just the cutest couple," Katie Rae squealed. "He's goin' to be so cute in a suit. I bet your dress will—"

"Enough fawnin' all over me," she spat, cutting her off. "Shut it down with Buzz. I better see you far away from him the rest of the trip."

"Okay," she muttered in submission. I popped a Dorito in my mouth, watching the sad show.

"So, girls," she purred in an odd voice. "Let's play a game while the boys are gone. You in, Alex?"

I swallowed the chip, feeling it scrape down my throat. Her attention moved to me.

"Why not." I met her stare, holding my ground. I popped another Dorito. Her eyes blinked in disgust, tracing over my old T-shirt and cutoffs. I crunched on the chip, pretending not to care.

Ashley went to the cabin and returned with four cups of vodka, each with a splash of Sprite. Jess had sneaked a few cases of beer in with the rest of the supplies, but I didn't know anyone had brought hard liquor on the trip. I wasn't much of a drinker. Sometimes, Jess brought beer when we went fishing. This would be my first experience with something stronger.

"Okay, girls, the game is, Never Have I Ever. There's only one rule. You make a true statement about yourself, on something you have never done. If someone else has done this statement, that person takes a drink."

We all nodded in agreement. I swallowed hard, wishing I had gone on the boat.

"Alex, you start." The cool eyes of Ashley flashed at me.

"Okay." I looked over and said the first thing I could find different from us. "I have never been a cheerleader."

I watched all three of them take a sip. We went around the circle. Katie Rae rattled off something about eating sushi. My cup stayed clasped in my hand. Ashley was next.

"I have never worn clothes from Goodwill." Her gaze locked with mine as my fingers dug into the side of my red Solo cup. Was she serious? I lifted the rim to my lips and took a swig, feeling the burn of the vodka all the way to my belly button.

"It's your turn, Lila," Ashley said without even looking at her. Lila's eyes flickered over to me and back to Ashley.

"Um, okay." Her voiced held a tremor. "I have never had sex with Jess Mason."

Ashley's sculpted eyebrows arched up at me as she took a sip. Her eyelashes batted in my direction. *What the hell?* Did she think I would drink to that one?

"Alex?"

I jumped. "What?"

"It's your turn to go."

"Right," I muttered. "I have never…had a speeding ticket."

Lila drank to that one. Katie Rae followed with a comment about Sea World. I took another sip based on the trip two summers ago with the Masons. The next question was about Disney World. I took another swallow, for another Mason family trip that included me.

Ashley stared straight at me on her turn. "I have never thrown myself at Jess and got rejected."

My stomach tightened, the alcohol swirling. Did she think her calculated, planted question would pull some deep confession out of me?

"Alex?"

"Huh." Her lipstick glowed in the flames. Everyone's fingers held in place on the plastic cups. The buzz grew stronger between my ears.

"It's your turn again, unless…there's somethin' you want to tell us. We can keep a secret, you know. If you want to talk about it?"

"I'm fine."

Her evil smile watched me fidget. This game would be dirty in the lowdown, female-backstabbing kind of way. We continued to play over the next hour. I took swig after swig from her pointed questions. The faces across the campfire blurred into the night. The three Witches of Eastwick haunted me through the hazy view of the flames. The sneers and laughs floated in a satanic feeling as the vodka circled through my bloodstream.

"I have never lived in a car that smelled like dirty diapers. What's that sayin'? I've never slept where I shit." Her glossy lips pursed in a cryptic smile.

My eyes blinked a few times in a dead stare across the flames. At this point, the liquor had my brain feeling numb. I held the cup up in her direction for a toast, then kicked it back for a swallow. The vodka rolled into my stomach. I was too drunk for the ultimate slam to even hurt.

By the time Jess returned, I could barely hold myself up straight. Two bags of Doritos were empty, and my fingers were all orange. I wiped the stains across my stomach and giggled, seeing the marks.

"I ate chips," I muttered, his blue eyes staring me. I tried to stand up but tripped toward the campfire. Jess caught my arm before I hit the flames. Sitting me back down, he lifted my cup for a sniff. His frowning face bobbed around like a balloon, then floated away.

"What the hell did you do to her?"

"Nothin' she didn't want to do."

He went over to Ashley. Their voices got louder, but I couldn't hear the words. Gentry put an arm under my legs and picked me up.

"I can take her back to the cabin," he said, looking over at Jess.

The rest of the conversation floated in and out in jumbled pieces. I willed my brain to focus on the words. I think Jess was angry at Ashley. A laugh bubbled out of my lips. Everything just felt funny. As Gentry carried me up the stairs, I muttered incoherent words against his shoulder. I felt like a twig in his tree-trunk arms. My hand gripped his shoulder, feeling the solid muscle.

"They's right. You's are cement."

He laughed at me. "You sound like someone from the Old West when you're drunk."

"No, I's don't…not," I babbled back. "Hey, I's gots a question. Jess mad at Ash-a-lee?"

"Yeah, a little. You were drinkin' vodka and the rest of 'em were drinkin' plain Sprite."

"What's? Not fairs," I slurred.

"No, not really, I guess. You were the only one who was playin' a drinkin' game." He sat me down on my bed and smiled. His green eyes split from two to four. "You goin' to be okay up here by yourself?"

"I's sure. Fine." My fingers waved around trying to touch his face to make it be still. His cheek felt soft in the dim light. His shoulders were hard, and his cheek was nice. Gentry captured my hand to place it back on the bed.

"Okay. Well, I'll let you go to sleep. Night, Alex."

"Thanks, Gentry. You's nice." My eyes slid closed, and everything went black.

Sometime later, I regained consciousness, but it was still dark. The moon cast shadows across the second-floor landing. My mouth felt dry, and my tongue was scratchy. The inside of my stomach rolled around, scorched and angry.

"You okay?" A faint voice came from the floor.

I struggled to sit straight and keep my brain from spinning. Every cell of my body still felt drunk. I guess I *was* still drunk. It took a moment for the heap on the floor to come into focus. The faint light from the window reflected back two blue eyes.

"Jess?"

"Yeah," he whispered.

"Why are you here?"

"I was worried about you." He scooted up to sit beside me on the twin bed. I felt his hand in the center of my back right between my shoulder blades. The pressure felt soothing as Jess talked low against my spinning head. "Are you okay?"

"Yeah."

"What happened down there?"

"Nothing."

The spinning question took too much effort to keep my head up. I collapsed backward, bouncing with the impact. The contents of my stomach sloshed around up to my throat. I needed to keep still, or I would be very sick.

The bed shifted with his weight. Jess stretched out beside me on the twin bed. I relaxed next to his warm body. As I slipped back to unconsciousness, I heard a few faint words against my cheek.

"I'm sorry I made you come."

The next morning, Jess was gone. I felt all levels of hell from my head to my stomach to my feet. I puked one last time and slid my brown sunglasses in place. The pounding in my forehead practically vibrated the lenses. I had no intentions of seeing or talking to a single person. I dreaded the car ride back to Arlis. If Ashley knew where Jess stayed last night, she would be royally pissed on the ride home.

"Hey, Alex, you wanna ride with us?" I looked at Gentry standing by his Tahoe. I glanced quickly over to Jess's truck. His face held a twisted frown that broadcasted the level of his frustration. Ashley caught my attention as she jerked Katie Rae inside the cab. I guess that was her tyrannical move to keep Katie Rae away from Buzz and score a second win by keeping me out of the truck. Grabbing my duffle bag, I walked over to the Tahoe. I wanted no part of her drama this morning.

Jess watched me climb in the backseat. After this trip, he would make me talk. Maybe it was time to put a stop to Ashley Cartwright the only way I knew would work. I needed to tell Jess the truth. My stomach felt sicker just thinking about it.

Chapter 21

When I was sixteen...

Two days after the trip, Natalie and I sat in a booth at Jeeter's working on chemistry equations. She kept an irritated look in my direction, showing off her new haircut. While I was on the camping trip from hell, Natalie got a black, chin-length bob with fire-engine red highlights.

"Pay attention," she grumbled.

"What?"

"I'm starting to think you're the dumbass, not him."

I couldn't focus. My mind stayed a complete, warped mess. Once I got back to Arlis, I tried to delay the inevitable as long as possible. I avoided every attempt Jess made to get us alone to talk. I half-expected him to show up at midnight, tapping on my bedroom window, giving no opportunity for me to yell back with my father down the hall.

Hearing the bell tingle, I glanced up to see my favorite person walk through the door. My body physically shuddered at the mere presence of her smug face. The slits of the snake's eyes settled on our back booth. She wore a tight, white tank top and pink shorts. Her shiny blonde hair stood high on top of her head in a perky ponytail and matching pink bow. Ashley's tan legs walked at a determined pace back to the booth, stopping in front of me.

"I thought I would find you *here*." A sneering smile formed on her lips.

"Can I help you with something? We're fresh out of vodka."

"That's more your thing, not mine. I just came to give you a little bit of advice."

She rested a hand on the booth ledge, right behind my head. I heard the fake nails click against the metal. Ashley leaned in close to my face.

"You need to understand somethin'," she said in low voice. "Everyone just feels *sorry* for you. You should hear them when you're not around. Especially Jess." She smirked at his name. "You humiliated him on the trip after he felt *obligated* to bring you. We all know why he drags you around everywhere. Dr. Mason found you like some nasty, abandoned puppy livin' in your car. Eatin' leftover *trash*."

Ashley leaned in a little closer, to the point I smelled her strawberry lip gloss. "You should stop embarrassin' yourself and stop embarrassin' Jess. The Masons don't mind givin' to charity, but no one wants to see it hangin' around them every day."

My heart beat fast, like the time I drank three cans of Red Bull.

"I'm glad we agree." She smirked with an evil grin on her shiny lips. "Oh, and no need to thank me for the advice. Consider it a donation to a needy cause."

The next few moments flashed in slow motion. I'm not sure what triggered the first step. Ashley turned to walk away. My arm slithered out and grabbed her bouncy ponytail. The hair felt silky in my fingers. I yanked hard, pulling her backward toward the booth.

"You…you," she growled, "*bitch!*"

My fingers stayed in a tight grasp, but Ashley pivoted around, slapping me across the jaw. I jumped from my seat and dove at that smug face. We tumbled into a table, knocking it over on the floor. I slapped her back hard against her pretty cheek, hoping it left a hand-sized bruise.

Charging forward, Ashley slammed my body against the booth divider. For a moment, I couldn't breathe. I curled my fingers into a tight fist. With my full body weight, I hurled a punch aimed at the center of her face. Blood sprayed down the white tank top as I made contact with her nose.

The sound of hitting her flesh gave me satisfaction chills. It felt good; better than a box of crystal tea glasses smashing into a stained glass window.

Blood covered my fist, but I swung at her again. Ashley ducked and grabbed onto my legs. I lost my balance, falling down on the cement floor. She yanked a chuck of my red hair. Digging my nails into her arm, I scratched long, bloody marks in her skin until she let go.

I pinned her small body to the floor. Her flawless skin was caked in blood. Tears ran down her cheeks, smearing mascara under those long, stupid lashes. She blinked at me, begging for mercy. I didn't care. I smiled an evil grin at her bleeding face.

Pulling back, I punched her square in the nose a second time. She tried to jab me in the neck, but I hit her again in the side. I continued to punch anything I could reach with my fists. Suddenly, my body lifted from the floor, sliding away from Ashley.

"Let me *go!*"

"That's enough, Alex," Caroline said.

As the room came back into focus, I realized Caroline had one side of my body and Natalie held the other. It took both of them to stop me from beating every bit of stuffing out of Ashley.

"Natalie, go get some ice and towels," she said. "And give some to Mr. Landry."

Shit, it's Wednesday. Mr. Landry always got a banana split on Wednesday. The older man bent down next to Ashley. She was completely covered in blood. The tight, white tank top was now cherry red, her hair yanked down and pulled in every direction. Even from ten feet away, the bloody claw marks glowed from her perfect skin.

Reaching up, I touched my throbbing face, checking for damage. Sticky blood caked my fingertips from my busted lip. I looked around at the rest of the diner. Tables and chairs were tossed everywhere. The floor was a mess of blood-coated straws and hair.

My father walked in the door, making the bell tingle. Someone had already called him. *I hated Arlis!* The emotions played transparent across his face: shock to horror to disappointment. He didn't utter a single word in my direction as he gave a lengthy apology to Caroline. He finally spoke, only to order me to the truck.

The drive home was painfully quiet. His hands squeezed the steering wheel in a tight grasp as we drove in silence. My heart beat out of control, waiting for him to calm down.

"Alexandra," my full name came out of his clenched jaw. "I need you to tell me what happened. You're still grounded, but I need to understand why you did this."

Absolutely, under no circumstance, could I tell my father why this happened. I just shrugged from my side of the truck.

"You need to talk to me. Why did you attack Ashley today?"

What had come over me? Why was today different? My mind tried to rationalize, but I knew it was plain simple. I flat-out had enough of Ashley Cartwright. I should be given an award for keeping my temper in check all these months. Unfortunately, my father could never find out the truth. No child wants a parent to know they have been bullied for being poor and homeless.

"Is it Jess? I know those two have been pretty close lately. Did you get jealous?"

"No, Dad! It wasn't about him. I can't believe you even asked that."

"I know you're very attached to Jess. And he's um…*important* to you. I'm not your mother, but you can talk to me about it."

I panicked. The feeling came like an explosion from my stomach and spread to the rest of my body. This scenario failed to cross my mind before my father's pointed questions. He just asked what every person would speculate at school. If they didn't immediately jump to that conclusion, the sniveling gossips would tell them it was the truth. The lies would fill the hallways. Everyone would think I attacked Ashley because of my insane jealousy over Jess. *Shit! Shit! Shit!*

"Alex?"

"This has nothing to do with him!"

"Don't get that tone, Alex. I just don't know what to think. I'm trying to understand why, but you aren't giving me any explanation."

"She's just a bad person," I muttered, trying to keep my voice steady.

"There's not enough bad in her that would justify you doing something like this. I don't know what to say. Did I not do something you needed? I know it's hard just having me. I let you run wild on the ranch with that boy. I'm not saying he's a bad boy, but it made you a little tougher than others. It's not an excuse, though. Girls don't beat up other girls in restaurants. Do you understand?"

"Yes, sir," I muttered.

I tuned out the rest of the car ride as my father droned on and on. He seemed to ignore the wounds across my *own* body from the fight. My stomach hurt. I didn't want to go to school tomorrow. The whispers would circle around every corner.

Later that evening, Jess slammed through the door without even knocking. I sat on the living room couch, trying to put an ice pack on my eye and lip at the same time with my swollen right hand.

"What the hell were you thinkin'?"

"I'm not doing this right now. Go home. I'm grounded anyway," I said, muffled under the ice pack. The cold stung against my lip.

"Alex, you broke her damn nose!" His hands flung around with every angry word.

"I figured," I muttered. "Why are you here and not at her house?"

"Because we're no longer together!"

"I don't understand," I said, taking the ice pack down.

"How could I continue to date someone who treated you this way for months, *Alex?*"

"How do you know what happened?"

"How do you think? Natalie called me and decided I should know 'bout Ashley since you were *never* gonna tell me. I could just…" I watched his fingers clench into a fist and then release. He paced around for a second and then sank down on the couch next to me.

"I just don't get it. Why didn't you tell me? I even asked you," Jess said, looking directly at me with his stormy eyes. "If you'd just told me, I'd taken care of it without you goin' all Fight Club at Jeeter's."

"I don't need you to *fix* things for me!" I spat, feeling the anger burn.

"Alex, it's not fixin' things if it stops you from beatin' the shit out of someone, or you gettin' hurt. It should've never happened. You should've told me. You just let me date her while she was tormentin' you."

Jess leaned back against the couch cushion, staring at the ceiling. He let out a deep breath. His lungs pulled in air over and over again, making the couch shake. In all these years, I'd never seen this boy so angry. After a few minutes, his body seemed to relax. Jess turned to look at me, his blue eyes filled with concern.

"You don't really believe what Ashley said, do you?"

My eyes flittered up and then back down. "No, I just…" I took a deep breath. "I don't know what to say." The words left me. It was the same reason I had never said anything to Jess to begin with. "You don't understand. I know you try, but it didn't happen to you."

"What don't I understand?" he said back softly.

"Moving here, living here. All of it," I muttered through my swollen lip.

"I'm glad you moved here. I wish it was under different circumstances, but I'm glad you came. It's not somethin' you should ever doubt."

"You're not ever embarrassed? Always having me around and people knowing why?" I kept a steady gaze on the carpet. It was too difficult to watch his expression.

"Al, you were dealt a bad hand. I wasn't. It's not somethin' either of us could control. But you and I bein' friends? We chose it. At least I did, and it wasn't because you lived in one of our houses on the ranch. I know my parents have done things for y'all. But honestly, I don't even think about it."

I pondered his words around for a moment. My life consisted of taking handouts from the Masons. At one point, my very existence depended on what they were willing to give us. I had a secret, time-consuming habit of focusing on a list I planned to pay back in the future. Jess, on the other hand, never even thought about why I was here.

I was right. He didn't comprehend the magnitude of Ashley's words or the circumstances that defined me. It wasn't his fault. Like Jess said, I was dealt a bad hand and life had been pretty much perfect for him.

"I'm sorry for not saying anything." I looked at him, squinting through my bad eye. "I know it involved you, but the things she did were about me. I thought I could take care of it. I just wanted to do something on my own for a change. Do you get that?"

"I guess, but you beat her up, Alex."

"I know," I said, rolling my eyes. "I know."

"I could kill you right now." He smiled weakly, shaking his head.

"And…I'm sorry about you breaking up. I know she was your girlfriend, and you liked her. You saw the good parts of her." I wasn't sure she had good parts, but something made that boy date her.

"Ashley and I weren't exactly…in a real relationship."

"It was just sex?"

I startled him when I said it. Jess refused to look at me and stared into the blank television. I heard him mutter, "Somethin' like that."

I regretted saying it. My skin felt hot with embarrassment. I really didn't want to talk about Jess having sex with Ashley any more than he wanted to discuss it. My conscious still held an unspoken obligation.

"There's something you should know. I…um…I think Ashley cheated on you. I heard Katie Rae on the camping trip."

"Evan Wiley?"

"You knew?"

"I had a pretty good idea. She got pissed when I took you to the Rangers game. Shit, I should have ended it back then. I really wish I never hooked up with her. It was stupid."

"Stop it. This is not your fault."

"But it is my fault. I knew she was a bitch, but I was just tryin' not to…I don't know." His voice went deeply quiet. "This is killin' me, Al. You matter more to me than anyone else. You know that, right?"

"I know," I muttered, feeling the heat on my cheeks.

"It bothers me to think she did those things to you. It's like I just let it happen. Like I let Ashley hurt you. I even tried to make you be friends with her." He let out a deep breath and gritted his jaw. "Just promise me you won't do somethin' like this again. You have to tell me."

"I…I promise." I nodded, feeling my head get dizzy.

During the fight, I think Ashley got a good punch in somewhere around my ear. I rubbed my forehead. "I feel like hell."

"You look like hell. Have you seen a mirror?"

"Briefly."

My head hurt, but I had the satisfaction of knowing Ashley was sitting this very moment with a broken nose. Everyone wanted me to feel guilty about the fight, but redemption clouded any remorse. I fumbled the ice packs trying to get them over my eye and busted lip. My knuckles didn't move very well when I clenched them.

"Here, let me help you." Jess scooted over and put his arm around my shoulder. He held the large bag against my eye. I put one over my right hand and then held the other up to my lip.

My head rested against his chest. Jess must have come straight from football practice. His hair was still a little wet, and he smelled like ivory soap. I closed my eyes, letting myself relax. The throbbing in my face numbed under the packs. Feeling his body move up and down with each breath, I felt calmer than I had in months.

"I never said thank you for the other night. You know, staying with me," I muttered.

"I was worried about you. You were covered in cheesy Doritos, babblin' shit."

"Ugh, no more Doritos. I've never felt that sick before."

"You snore, by the way, when you're drunk."

"No, I don't."

"You do, like a pig snortin' gravel."

"That's not funny."

My father walked in the door. Seeing his eyes move from me then over to Jess, I panicked. Finding us both on the couch together just affirmed his questions from the car.

"Hey, Mr. Tanner," Jess said as I moved quickly to the other cushion. Before today, our friendship had never been an issue with my father.

"I guess you heard about Alex."

"Yeah, she's promised not to do it again."

I shot a nonverbal *shut up*. Less talking he did, the better with my dad right now.

"Well, I have some news. I just talked to Frank. He's got a list for you. Should be Thanksgiving by the time it's done. Every spare moment outside school and Jeeter's, you'll be on the ranch doing whatever Frank tells you to do. Understand?"

"Yes, sir," I mumbled.

"I can help you some," Jess offered, looking over at me.

"I don't think Alex needs your help on this one. Unless there's some reason you think she does?"

"No, Jess." I glared at him.

Despite my father being worried, he let Jess stay for dinner. Every mouthful of chili burned the cracks in my busted lip. Jess got increasingly quiet as the meal progressed. We chatted about the new horse Uncle Frank purchased over the weekend. Even that wasn't enough to pull out his usual pancake-syrup voice of excitement.

After dinner, I walked him out on the porch. Jess sat down on the top step expecting me to join him. I lowered my aching body down next to him, knowing my father expected me to come immediately back inside the house. Jess watched the dark sky, silent and weary. Sometimes, I wondered what really went on under that shaggy mop of hair. I thought I knew this boy so well, and then sometimes he was a complete mystery.

"Are you okay, Jess?"

He turned at the sound of my voice. His eyes seemed dark in the dim light, instead of the usual vibrant blue. Jess reached up to touch my swollen lip. "Guess I'm gonna have to look at that ugly face every time you talk now."

"Don't touch it. You'll just make it worse."

"I don't think that's possible." His fingertips traced around the puffiness, then slipped down behind my neck. He pulled me close to his side, leaving his arm wrapped around my shoulders. The warmth of his body felt comforting. He went back to silent and brooding.

"You can talk to me, Jess."

"I know," he said, letting out a deep breath. "I really messed everythin' up with you."

"You didn't mess up anything. The bruises will go away, and then it's like it never happened."

"But I can't help but feeling like it's my fault. And it's all because I thought… it was easier."

"Easier? That doesn't make sense. Easier than what? Being without her?"

"No, it's not that. Just let it go."

My father opened the door, causing me to jump. "It's getting late. You need to go home, Jess."

"Yes, sir."

I waited until I heard the knob click. "I'm sorry, but things might be a little, um, weird for a while. He thinks I did it because of you. I can't tell him the truth. It would hurt him to know."

"That ain't the truth? But I thought you were defendin' my honor?" He smiled, but it never reached his eyes.

"Very funny."

"All right, I'm leavin'." He stood up and stretched. "Pick you up in the mornin'?"

"My dad's taking me to school. I can't go anywhere with you for a while."

"Damn, he really is pissed."

"It's easier to blame you than to think his daughter beat the shit out of Ashley Cartwright for no apparent reason. He has to see her parents tomorrow, you know. There's only one building between the stores."

"Shit, I didn't think 'bout that."

"I know. This place sucks."

"It's gonna be okay tomorrow." He gave me a quick squeeze around the shoulders. "Night, Alex."

"Night, Jess."

The pipes fired up on his truck, but the dirt cloud trailed off in the opposite direction of home. Without even asking, I knew Jess drove out toward the old, burned-up stump, his thinking spot.

School was difficult. Everyone talked, just like I predicted. The rumors circulated, just like I knew they would about me. Conversations stopped whenever I rounded a corner in the hallway. My skin pricked up, hearing the whispers. All of it served as a different type of torment than the verbal assaults from Ashley.

A few days after the fight, I found a box sitting on the porch with a note. Lifting the lid, I stared at a pink set of boxing gloves. I opened the card to identify the sender of such an odd gift. A smile spread across my still, swollen lips. I guess everyone didn't hate me.

HEY SLUGGER

WOULD YOU BE MY DATE TO HOMECOMING?

GENTRY

Chapter 22

When I was sixteen...

On the back of the closet door, a store-bought mirror reflected the image of a person who seemed like a stranger. My glossy lips pursed into a frown as I turned to see the back of my creation. The pale-blue silk swirled into a flowing pool around my feet. I felt weird and out of place. Homecoming dances were not my thing.

Earlier this afternoon, I let an enthusiastic cosmetic worker apply a whole face worth of makeup. She decked out my eyelids in sparkly gold and blue shadow, then outlined her work with a very itchy, dark-brown pencil. This left my hair as the biggest self-styling obstacle. I liked wearing it up and rarely wore it down. It just was more practical. However, homecoming wasn't about being practical, which I hated. I finally settled on curling my long red hair into loose ringlets.

"What do you think, Carrot?"

The little orange ball of fur sat watching me in fascination. I scratched the purring chin with my bare nails. In honor of tonight, I scraped off the black paint. My bracelets were gone too. I had to cut the braided strands after the fight because they were soaked in Ashley's blood.

I took one more look in the mirror, making sure my chest stayed crushed under the strapless top. The last thing I needed was a wardrobe malfunction to add to my current notoriety. As I entered the living room, my father looked surprise. I noticed the camera gripped tightly in his hand.

"Really, Dad? Pictures?"

"I want to document the one time I know you purposely dressed this way. You look very beautiful."

"You can take one picture. That's it."

"I also get two when your date gets here."

"Dad! No, please don't."

Despite being grounded, my father agreed homecoming was technically a school activity, which gave the needed permission to attend the dance with Gentry. I think he was slightly relieved to see another boy in the picture besides Jess. After the fight, my father watched our interactions a little closer every time my childhood friend walked into the farmhouse. It was total nonsense, but what teenager could reason with her father.

I heard a knock at the front door. The butterflies fluttered through my chest as I pulled open the creaky, wooden frame. Gentry stood on the front porch, looking a little anxious. My eyes traced his jacket and tie all the way down to his shiny black cowboy boots. He looked cute tonight, like I-wanted-to-kiss-him kind of cute. I blushed at the thought.

"Alex, you look really awesome," he said, flashing a big smile. "I mean, that dress is hot!"

"My dad is standing here." I opened the door a little wider.

"Right," he muttered. "Hi, Mr. Tanner."

"Hello, Gentry." They shook hands while I gave my father eye daggers not to mention the camera. "I'm going to get a few pictures if you don't mind standing by the fireplace."

At least two dozen pictures later, I followed Gentry out the door. I still didn't know much about him. We talked a few times on the phone. He was an easygoing guy who had moved to Arlis from El Paso. Gentry's favorite food was barbecue ribs, and he thought the football team would make the playoffs. He planned to enlist with the Marines immediately after graduation. I figured this explained his buzzed, blond hair.

As we approached the entrance to the school gym, I heard music floating out into the parking lot. My stomach flipped around knowing the stares and whispers would come as soon as I got in the room. I clung to Gentry's arm as he navigated through the crowed entryway.

"You wanna dance?"

I nodded yes.

Gentry and I two-stepped the first dance. We spent more time laughing instead of dancing. His tree-trunk legs didn't shuffle very well across the floor. Slow songs were a little more our speed. My fingers clung to his broad shoulders while his hands stayed in place around my waist. Staring into his green eyes, I decided I might actually like Gentry Jones. He was a sweet guy. I imagined what it would feel like, letting him kiss me, letting his hands touch my body. I think I wanted that with him.

"You wanna get somethin' to drink?"

"Sure." I blushed, feeling like he could read my thoughts.

As we walked toward the refreshment table, I kept my eyes downcast to avoid their stares. People were intrigued with the fact that I came with Gentry. It just made the rumors about me a little more interesting.

Amidst the finger foods and very nonalcoholic punch, I found Jess looking annoyed with his equally enthusiastic date. When Jess told me that Natalie agreed to go to homecoming, I had to put my hand over my mouth to keep from laughing in his face. He claimed the options were limited this late in the game. She said he deserved one favor for breaking up with Ashley.

"Well, hello to the cutest couple in the room." I smiled at both of them.

Jess looked nice tonight. His normal shaggy hair was slicked back with gel, and the black jacket made his dark lashes stand out around his blue eyes.

"Dance with me. *Now!*" he hissed. Jess laced his fingers through mine, tugging my arm out toward the dance floor.

"Sorry, Natalie," I said over my shoulder. She frowned back.

Jess pulled me to a secluded area in the corner, which blocked at least a few people from gawking at us. I placed my arms loosely around his shoulders, leaving some space. The soft music intro changed to the slow sway of a guitar. I recognized the song by Gary Allan. Jess had played it all summer on repeat, driving me insane.

I glanced up to find him watching me with an amused grin. "What?"

Jess shook his head a little and laughed. "I didn't know if you'd go through with it. You know…the dress and all the makeup stuff."

"I know. I want to claw my eyes out. They won't stop itching."

"Hmmm." His lips puckered up. "I'm confused. You're not any taller."

"What are you talking about?"

Jess let go of my waist and forced my body into a spin. He pulled the hem of my dress up close to my knees, exposing the gray canvas shoes.

"Stop!" I yanked it out of his hand. He smiled just to torment me. "You're terrible, you know. The heels pinched my toes. I didn't think anyone would notice since it was so long."

"I'm sorry, Al." Jess put his arm around my waist, pulling me close to his chest. He leaned into my ear. "Are you wearin' perfume too?"

"Really? You're going to do this?"

"I'm not tryin' to make you mad."

"*Suuure.*"

"I'm bein' serious. You look pretty tonight." He reached up, running a finger through my hair. "But I always think you look pretty."

"Shh…don't say that." My face got red. "People will hear you."

"I like your hair like this too." He fiddled with a curl, then dropped it, giving me a smirk.

"Fine. Thank you. You look nice too," I answered, rolling my eyes.

He smiled sweetly and put his hand back on my waist. The music played around us. My dress swooshed against his cowboy boots as we slowly rotated to the sound of the grave voice on the speakers.

"You havin' fun?" he whispered in my ear.

"Yeah."

"I just want you to be happy tonight."

"I told you. I'm good."

It was a convincing statement that was about 75 percent truthful. Ashley remained exposed, but the Arlis grapevine kept the story rolling, even if it were the wrong story. Right now, people watched Jess and I talking. They noted exactly where he put his hand on my back. They calculated just how long I gazed into those blue eyes. Everyone waited to see if his lips touched my body. I frowned, feeling the anger fester. It was none of their damn business.

"Al, what's wrong?" His boots stopped moving.

"It's fine."

"You don't look fine. Screw 'em, Alex. Screw every single one of 'em." His hand left my waist and gestured toward the people just a few steps away. "I was the one who brought 'em into our lives. I'll take 'em out. I'll even quit football. We don't need anyone else."

"Jess…" I slipped my hands on each side of his warm cheeks, looking into his troubled eyes.

"Yeah."

"You're getting all worked up again."

His hands wrapped around mine as they cupped his face. "I just want you to be okay."

"I know." I smiled at him. "So dance with me."

"You hate this song."

"But I know you like it."

Jess pulled my hands up around his neck. His boots started to move again, swaying slowly to the music. Even though I knew people were watching, I rested my head against his shoulder. Jess wrapped his arms around my back, holding me tight against his chest. I tucked my nose close to his neck.

"I like dancing with you," he whispered next to my cheek.

"Me too."

I relaxed against his body, and it felt good. I closed my eyes and pulled in a deep breath, smelling the familiar cologne coming from somewhere around his neck. Dancing in the corner with my best friend, the stares and whispers faded away. I let myself enjoy the moment with him—a moment free from the problems circulating around us.

When the song ended, I felt sad. I wanted to dance with him again, but I knew I should get back to Gentry. Natalie may have scared him right out the door.

"Well…that's my cue, I guess." Jess stepped away but left his hands on my waist.

"You, um, want to dance again later?"

"No, it's okay. Go find your date."

"Okay, but, um, would you do something for me?"

"Sure." He grinned.

"Dance with Natalie, please?"

"She just had to get her lip pierced before homecomin'. I'm glad she got all freaky just for me."

"Be nice."

"Fine, I will for you."

In the shadows, he looked like a sullen boy who was being punished. I pulled his hands from my waist and gave them a little squeeze. "Thank you for dancing with me. It made me feel happy, Jess."

"If anyone says anything tonight." He glanced back toward the floor. "If they…"

"I will find you. I promise."

"Okay."

Jess disappeared into the crowd as I left in search of my blond-haired date. To my right, a group of people ogled, like a line of paparazzi taking down notes. I noticed Katie Rae with them. She leaned over and kissed Buzz full on the mouth. I was surprised to see them together. However, Ashley didn't come tonight since she was still recovering from nose surgery.

Gentry came up from behind and slipped an arm around my waist. Leaning over, he whispered something funny in my ear. His breath felt warm on my neck. I blushed at the way it made my skin tingle. Gentry pulled me out on the floor for another dance. I smiled, feeling happy.

After a ride home in his Tahoe, Gentry walked me up the wooden porch steps of my quiet house. I wondered if my dad were asleep or secretly peering out one of the curtains. Leave it to good old Henry to pop out with his camera.

"You're a lot of fun, Alex," he said, bringing my attention back to the porch.

"You have some, um, mean moves out there."

"I never claimed to be a good dancer when I asked you to go."

"No, I guess you didn't," I said back quietly as we stood facing each other. The butterflies circled through my stomach. It was a little overwhelming processing all this girl stuff.

In the shadows, I saw his green eyes get a little nervous. I knew it was the pinnacle moment of the evening, if he would just go for it. I took a deep breath and smiled, trying to let him know it was okay, even though I was nervous too.

Gentry leaned forward, slightly bumping my nose. His pink lips tasted salty from the platefuls of chips consumed at the party. He kissed the way he did most other things. It was very nice and sweet. Gentry turned the slight peck into a deeper kiss, using his lips to pull open mine. He was definitely much better at this than dancing.

After Gentry left, I tiptoed through the dark house to my bedroom, trying not to wake up my father. I was surprised he wasn't sitting in the living room waiting for me. Flipping on the lamp, I slapped a hand over my mouth to keep from screaming.

"What are you doing here?" I whispered, seeing Jess sitting on my bed.

"I was…just makin' sure you got home."

"Shhh…"

"Sorry," he whispered. Jess had his tie off and the white shirt unbuttoned at the throat. He grinned at me as I came over to stand in front of him.

"You need to go. My dad will kill you if he comes in here."

"Okay." He stumbled a little getting off the bed.

"Have you been drinking?"

"Just a little." He grinned close to my face. I smelled beer on each word that left his pink lips.

"Did you drive here?"

"No, I, um, parked about half mile away on the four-wheeler."

"Okay."

As I walked Jess to the window, his arm went around my back, holding on to me. He leaned over to my ear and whispered, "Did you kiss him?"

"That's none of your business." I looked into his blue eyes, trying to figure out just how drunk he was. "Can you find your way back home?"

"Yeah, I'll be fine." He smiled again. Reaching up to my cheek, he pushed a red curl behind my ear. "You really do look pretty tonight."

I rolled my eyes. "Good night, Jess."

He climbed outside and stumbled before landing on both feet. I watched until he disappeared into the dark shadows of our yard. That boy really was a crazy mess sometimes.

Chapter 23

Today, 12:13 p.m.

I watch the pretty face of the beauty queen as she dabs my bare skin with the fluffy towel. She wraps it around my body and tucks it between my breasts like a toga. "I'll be back with your clothes."

I bit my lip hard, tasting the metallic blood. Alone for the first time in hours, I feel the weight crash back down on my shoulders. Maybe this was a dream. A terrible nightmare of a dream conjured up from watching a horror movie before falling into the comfort of my bed. After all, it had everything needed for it. A beauty queen and a bloody scene called *Hospital Massacre from Hell.*

She returns with a mysterious bundle of clothes. Someone had gone through the drawers in my bedroom and picked out an outfit. I put my hands on her shoulders as she slides a fresh pair of panties up my long legs. Removing the towel, I keep my eyes on the ceiling while she hooks my bra around my back.

The fresh T-shirt slides over my damp hair. I hold on to her shoulders again as she pulls the worn jeans up to my hips. My head spins a little, and I clasp a hand to my stomach, feeling the nausea. The beauty queen puts an arm around my waist as we walk back to the room.

"Do you want back on the bed or in the chair?"

"Why are you helping me?"

She hesitates and finally says, "It's my job."

"But why are you helping *me*?"

"Because I want to help you, Alex. I just want to do somethin'."

I hear footsteps. Twisting around, I see my father walk back through the door. He holds a plastic container. The smell of chicken noodle soup wafts through the room. Bile rises up in my throat. He hands the container in my direction. "Sit in the chair and try to eat this."

"I told you I'm not hungry."

"When did you last eat?"

"I…ate lunch, I guess. I had pizza."

His voice is soft. "You threw that up, Pumpkin. Hours ago."

"I…I…can't eat." I close my eyes, trying to find composure. The beauty queen leads me to the chair, and I fall into the plastic seat.

"You have to try to keep something down."

My fingers dig into the palm of my hand. "I will try to eat if you let me go. I want to talk to Dr. Mason *myself*."

"Okay." His jaw clenches a little on the words. "I'll go see what I can do. Just try to eat while I'm gone."

Chapter 24

When I was eighteen...

The days of summer swept across the meadow faster than I could blink. Graduation seemed like yesterday, but that terrifying night was two months ago. A person worthy of the academic title of valedictorian should not be subjected to giving a speech. Valedictorians are people focused on grades and tests and homework. They are not the social ones who like talking to large audiences. Despite my nervous stomach, I survived that wretched night and wished everyone the best, or so I said in my prepared speech. I could not, in good faith, wish everyone the best.

At least high school and all its dramatic pieces were finally over. I was waiting for my exit from Arlis. I waited while I spent every moment of my final summer on the ranch with Jess.

"I'm bored," I said, stretching out on my back against the grassy bank next to the pond. I was getting fidgety, wishing I'd brought my drawing pad. "The fish just don't like me today."

"They never like you. Fish can sense hostility."

"Shut up!" I said, throwing a lure from the tackle box in his direction. It didn't even come close to nicking him across the arm.

"See, hostility." Jess smirked back at me.

"I am not hostile!"

"Al, you're always wound up tight about somethin'. What was it yesterday? I listened to you complain about Mrs. Fleming and her banana split for—what?—two hours."

"That OCD bitch forced me to remake it because she said the toppings were not distributed *evenly* into thirds," I spat the words, making little drops of spit fall down on my cheeks.

"Not again, okay. You got a free split out of it."

"Which *you* ate while hiding out in Jeeter's again from Uncle Frank. You really should just say something to him."

"Are you kidding? Like he's gonna understand. He's been on my case the last month. I need the breaks."

"I think he's sad to see you go and doesn't know how to tell you."

"I'm sorry, but twenty-hour days are no way to show it. Besides, if he had 'one of those damn cell phones the government uses to track our every move,' then he could find me when he sends me to town on errands."

I giggled at his impression of Frank. "That one was pretty good. I bet, though, somewhere deep inside, he's all mush. I bet he cries every night about you leaving, maybe even more than your mother."

"I doubt it. He's hard as granite. It would probably take a diamond to cut through him, and you know what they'd find inside? A heart made of dried-up dirt and cigarette ash. At least that's what Gunther said the other day."

"You really need to stop listening to Gunther. He's turned the feedstore into the beauty shop. And most of it isn't even true, like all those stupid Skeeter stories."

"Skeeter really did get Marla to climb on top of him at The Bar. Ernie was there too. He said it was nasty watching the two of them go at it."

"Gross." I rolled my eyes. The Bar never got a real name even after Ernie added the line dancing room. It was more a country club these days, but everyone still called it The Bar.

I gazed into the cloudless sky, listening to the sounds of the meadow. Sometimes it was nice to be out here. I would miss that part of Sprayberry. It was a strange thought, considering the amount of energy I'd spent thinking about how to get my father and myself off the ranch.

"Al…what are you thinkin' 'bout?"

"Nothing," I said, leaning up on my elbow to look at him.

"I don't really believe that."

"I was just thinking this is our last summer here, and it's almost over."

"I know." He turned around, his eyes looking troubled. "You wanna leave so bad it worries me sometimes that maybe when we get there, you'll just…I don't know."

I knew our lives would not be the same once we left Sprayberry. I think he felt it too. The last couple of weeks had been different with Jess. He was clingy and often serious.

"You're gonna be so busy, you won't notice that I'm not with you all the time."

"I doubt that," he muttered.

"You don't know that. It's a big campus."

"I don't care." He frowned, making his sweet face look serious. "I'm gonna need to see you every day."

"You act like I'll be in another state. It's just Austin. Everything will be fine."

"I know," he said, not looking any calmer. "I'm just sayin' that I don't want things bein' different with us."

"We're going to be fine. It's college, which is better than this rathole. We can meet some new people who are not psychotic, for a change. Leaving Arlis will be good for us. We need to go other places."

"Do you still think about goin' to Paris?" It always sounded funny coming from his lips, like those Picante sauce commercials.

"Sometimes."

"You'll go one day even if I have to take you there myself."

"Driving me to Paris, *Texas*, doesn't count." I rolled my eyes, smiling at him.

"I'm serious, though. You'll go there one day."

"I hope so," I muttered.

"I'll go with you."

I doubt it, I thought but smiled at him anyway. He's too tied to Sprayberry for that kind of thing.

Flicking the rod, he cast toward the middle of the pond. Jess settled in, watching the line. I rolled to my back and pulled the strawhat over my face to block the glaring sun. Sometimes it felt like the ranch wrapped around us like an atomic force field from the rest of the world. It would be different in

Austin, and I would miss this time with Jess. I lied to him earlier. Our lives would not be the same; it wasn't possible.

All of us were moving on after high school one way or another. Natalie was leaving at the end of summer for Tulane. Gentry had left the week following graduation and joined the Marines. After boot camp, they were sending him someplace in Afghanistan. It was a somber thought that left a small ache inside my chest at the prospect of his dangerous future.

Gentry and I had dated for the better part of my junior year. He was perfect in every way but one. My body felt empty when he kissed me. It was good enough, but I knew it should be different.

I watched other people with their tongues crammed down each other's throats, forgetting every person in the room. The night Gentry had tried to unbutton my shirt, I thought about my calculus quiz the next day. He was sweet and caring, but something about our relationship was just off. After a long talk on my front porch, we had parted ways with the promise to stay friends. Arlis was too small of a place to stack up enemies, and I was already knee-deep in bodies.

After the fight, the rumors eventually died down in the hallways, and I was officially free of Ashley. I knew it resulted from the literal public freeze-out initiated by Jess. He made it clear to the entire school what happened when you crossed a Mason. Just like the adults in this town, they scavenged to stay on the correct side of the fence to prevent social suicide.

The rest of high school was relatively nice until it came time to figure out where I should go to college. The big decision for my future turned into a month-long battle between me, my father, Jess, and the Masons. I was accepted into the honors program at the University of Texas in Austin. Jess pulled off some form of a miracle and got admitted too. I received a small, partial scholarship, but it wasn't even close to the dollar figure for living expenses and school.

After some thought, I applied to a community college that was driving distance from Arlis. Everything seemed to fall in place. I would live at home and commute to classes while keeping a few shifts at Jeeter's. Everyone else thought I was crazy. So they fixed it.

According to my father, the Masons made a generous offer I couldn't refuse. The family would pay for everything not covered by my scholarship. They insisted I would have a comfortable life in Austin, only to worry about making good grades. I told my father, "There's no way in hell I'm letting the Masons pay for college."

The debate rolled on for weeks. Everyone had an opinion. My father said it was the best thing for my future. Dr. and Mrs. Mason said I owed it to my place as valedictorian to attend a school like the University of Texas. Jess said that I was going to Austin with him, and there would be no discussion.

One afternoon, I drove the four-wheeler out to the old, burned-up stump. It was Jess's thinking spot, and I needed some serious space to unfold my torment. I sat there for hours. Sometimes I screamed, knowing only the birds and the bugs could hear me. I knew the answer the moment it was suggested, but I needed time to process. I returned to Mason Manor and walked through the door to find Jess and his parents eating dinner. I gritted my jaw with a fake smile and said, "Thank you for sending me to Austin."

I went home and added the nasty entry to that wretched Mason List. Just like everything in my life, I took ten steps back just to go forward with my future. I needed the education to receive a degree that would garner a job, to earn a living, and the means to return everything to this family. The thought still haunted me even months later.

Hearing a splash from the pond, I removed the strawhat and rolled over on my side, propping my head up on my elbow. I watched Jess reel the line to shore. He tugged it, making the muscles in his arms tighten. Jess had caught two carp earlier in the afternoon, only to let them go. We rarely kept the fish. Occasionally, I brought a few back for my father and Caroline. She could make just about anything taste good battered and deep-fried.

My instincts had been correct. A few months ago, Caroline finally convinced my father to stop by for one of her southern-fried, double-heart-attack dinners. "Love at first bite," I had teased him when he came home with a dopey smile. For the first time since my mother, he seemed happy. Everything got brighter in the Tanner house with Caroline in his life. It made leaving him at the end of summer a little easier.

Jess tossed the lure back out to the murky water. Through the white fitted T-shirt, his body moved with the throwback motion. His long fingers settled the rod in place. Jess rested a dark elbow on his propped-up knee. The faded jeans stretched tight across his thigh.

I wasn't oblivious to the fact Jess was an attractive guy. He was probably the cutest guy in our high school. Most of the time, I just didn't give it a second thought because it wasn't relevant to our friendship. Despite being the object of every Arlis girl's fantasy, he'd never dated anyone after Ashley. I teased him about a few of them, but Jess said he wouldn't float that crazy creek again until he was far out of Palo Pinto County.

Once we got to Austin, it wouldn't take long for that grin and baby blues to snag a new girl. That's when things would get different between us. I would focus on my career goals, and he would find other interesting people to fill his time.

Sitting up, I grabbed another a can from the cooler. It was just Dr Pepper and A&W root beer today. After a couple of swigs of DP, I eyed the large bag of Skittles propped up against the side. I swear Jess bought a sack big enough for an industrial-sized candy bucket that would feed all the trick-or-treaters in a tri-city area.

My lips pursed in contemplation, and I shot Jess a glance out of the corner of my eye. Boredom brought out the pester-y side of me. I tipped the red bag and got a big handful. With a quick toss forward, multicolored splatters filled the pond with small ripples. I giggled before he even had time to react. I knew it would piss him off, which was the whole point.

"Alex, stop that!"

He reached over to take away the bag just as I fired off another fistful. Jess tossed the rod to the ground. I pulled my elbow sharp to the right to keep the candy out of his reach. Before I knew it, my arm knocked his phone off the tackle box into the depths of the murky pond water. The small, black square made a solid plop, then disappeared from sight.

Oh, shit! I was dead.

With the bag still clenched in my hand, I scampered to my feet and sprinted out into the meadow. The soles of my gray shoes pounded in no particular direction through the grass. I had a head start, but his long arm circled around my waist, taking me down in a rolling tackle.

A rainbow of candy rained down from the sky, pelting my face. As Jess pinned me down on my back, I felt the meadow grass poking through my shirt. I struggled to get free, but his hands held my arms down on each side of my head. His legs trapped my lower torso to the ground.

Jess smirked at me. "Why do you always have to be such a pain in my ass?"

"Let me go!"

"If you're so bored, I should haul you right back over there and toss you in the pond. Let you dig 'till you find my phone."

"You wouldn't!" I spat, feeling a little panicked. He *would* do something that crazy, thinking it was so damn funny. I tried to pull a leg free, only to have it pinned down by his thigh. I looked back up and tried to reason. "Besides, it's not like it's still gonna work."

"I might do it anyway, just to watch you in that nasty water." He smiled an evil grin, his eyebrows arched over his eyes.

I stopped struggling since it was pointless to fight one of his vice grips. Instead, I mustered up a pathetic, sad look to plead for some mercy.

"Jess, I'm really sorry. It was an accident."

"An accident?" He leaned a little closer with his ornery smile. Jess was enjoying the fact that he could still torment me.

"Yes, please…I'm sorry."

Jess leaned a little closer, then in the space of a nanosecond, ten years of friendship changed forever. The grin disappeared as I felt his pink lips. They pressed softly against mine. As quickly as they touched, he pulled back.

I could barely breathe. Jess remained still; his face displayed a hesitant, uncertain look. His black hair fell slightly over one eye, but he didn't move to brush it away. I knew he was waiting for my reaction to this sudden event that petrified us both.

My mind screamed at my lips to say something. I needed to stop this before it became something it could never be for us. Yet, I froze. My arms didn't push back. My mind didn't stop the thoughts that tumbled from a dark, hidden place. No, instead I stayed completely still as my non-reaction gave Jess the answer to his nervous, unspoken question.

Slowly he leaned down, never taking his blue eyes off mine. His bottom lip touched first, and my eyes closed. Jess kissed me slowly. His lips were soft and warm and tasted sweet. I stopped breathing altogether as he pushed my mouth open with his tongue. I forgot I was in the meadow. I forgot the sun burned down from the sky.

His kisses trailed over my cheek and down my neck. The soft lips touched my bare skin in the neckline of my tank top. My heart pounded in my chest as I tried to catch my breath. Leaning up, Jess looked at me again. The blue eyes seemed darker and a little nervous. He didn't get that way very often. He ran his hand over my stomach and hesitated before he touched my breast. My cheeks were already red, or I would have turned deep crimson. Jess leaned in, kissing me softly before slipping his tongue back in my mouth.

He moved his hand under my gray tank top and across my bare stomach. I got all warm and tingly as his fingers skimmed the lace trim of my bra. I wanted him to take it off. I wanted his mouth to kiss me there too. My heart beat under the palm of his hand as he touched me through the fabric. His hand slipped around to my back and fumbled with the clasp.

Jess will see me naked. The thought flashed from somewhere in my subconscious. *What am I doing?* The remnants of sanity pulled themselves out of the ditch. I needed to stop this. My palms touched each side of his cheeks, pulling his face from my body.

"We really can't do this," I whispered, our faces only an inch apart.

"It's okay." His voice was a little deeper than usual. "We don't have to do anythin' right now. I don't want to have sex with you. No…I mean I do want to have sex, but that's not what I'm tryin' to do right now. Shit, I'm screwin' this all up."

"No, it's not that…it's just…we can't do this…this…you and me."

"What are you sayin', Al?"

I still had my hands on his cheeks as I stared into his sweet face. Leaning forward, his lips brushed mine again. He pulled back just enough to look in my eyes.

"We have to talk, Jess."

"I don't wanna talk." He kissed me harder that time, and I let him. I let myself feel his lips again for just a few minutes, and then I pulled his face back up. His eyes were a deep, dark blue as he gazed back at me. Jess rolled off of me and stretched out on the meadow grass. Reaching over, he grabbed my hand, playing with my fingers. I couldn't think straight. The intensity of his last kiss had left me breathless.

"Al, I know this is….I know it's complicated."

"It's more than complicated. I grew up here…and your family…this can't happen between us. It's…*me*. You…you don't even know what you're doing."

He let out a deep breath. "That's not true. I've felt this way for a while."

"You've felt this way for a while? How long?"

"I don't know. Maybe since we were fourteen."

Fourteen? My heart might have actually skipped a beat. This wasn't good.

"I think that's 'bout the time I realized you had boobs."

"You can't be serious."

"I'm serious. And to be honest, it started before then. I just didn't understand what I felt for you."

"But you dated Ashley…you *had sex* with Ashley."

Jess rubbed his forehead, which I knew meant he was stressed. "You want the truth? I dated Ashley as more of a distraction. I didn't know what to do with how I felt 'bout you. I was a stupid kid. It's not like I could talk to you. I wanted to tell you, but honestly, I didn't know how to even bring it up. And with Gentry, I knew you'd never do anythin' with him. It killed me to see you together, but I knew it wouldn't last. So I waited."

"Waited for what exactly? For some moment to just go for it and catch me off guard?" My thoughts were jumbled. My world just changed forever with him, and I couldn't even think straight. My lips still burned from kissing him, from kissing *Jess*.

He placed my hand on his chest, right over his heart. It was beating fast under his shirt. "I'm scared too, Al."

I couldn't breathe. He felt warm under my hand. I couldn't think about anything else but touching his body again. Sitting up, I moved a little away from him. Jess watched me for a moment, and then got up next to me.

I took a few deep breaths and fought to get a grasp on the situation. He reached up and touched my face, making me look at him. "It's okay."

"No…*no*…it's not."

“I’ve thought ’bout it a lot, you know. You just look so pretty sometimes. I would watch you when you weren’t lookin’. Sometimes, I would imagine what it would be like to kiss you.” His fingers ran through my long, red strands of hair. “I think ’bout all of it, you know. You and me, being here together. It’s always been you, Alex. It’s what I’ve always wanted.”

“You can't be thinking about me,” I whispered.

“Why not?”

“Jess…you just can’t. Not like that.” I turned to look into his blue eyes, trying to reason with him. “We are just comfortable together. Familiar. I understand. It can get confusing. But that’s all it is. You don’t really *want* me.”

“No, I do want you. That’s the thing. I see you every day. I know you better than anyone else.” His index finger brushed across my cheekbone, then trailed down my neck to my shoulder.

“You see these…I’ve watched every one of these freckles form on your skin. You have ’em from all the time we spent here together. And I know in here”—his hand moved to rest lightly across the top of my left breast—“I know that you hate those freckles. And you’re afraid to cry because you see it as a weakness. And I know you look at me different than you do anyone else.”

“Jess…” I moved his hand off my chest.

“I know you feel somethin’ for me. What just happened was enough to prove it. You kissed me back, Al. You let me touch you, and I know you liked it. But I know it’s scarin’ you too.”

He stopped talking. I wasn't sure if he wanted me to argue back or wait for all his words to sink into my thoughts. I knew he would never understand why this couldn't happen. The tension in my brain suffocated me.

I was vaguely aware of how damaged I was compared to most other girls. I had years and years of mental anguish caused by the death of a parent and losing one's financial freedom. I was a homeless street urchin that became a walking, talking, bought-and-paid-for Mason charity project. My future hinged not on a romantic relationship with Jess, but a college education provided by his parents. The debt I owed this family was so big. I couldn't take the most precious thing from their lives. No matter what I felt, I would never take their son.

Turning away from him, I couldn't look in his eyes. Being with Jess meant too many things. Between his family and my past, he deserved better than me. I bit down hard on my lip, trying to squash back the sudden rush of emotions.

"Al, it's okay. I know this is a lot to process. I know how you're feelin'. I don't even have to look to know that you got that lip of yours clenched right now. It's why I've never done anythin' 'bout how I felt. I knew you'd do this. It would freak you out."

Jess pulled my chin around so he could watch my face. His finger pulled my lip out from my tightly clenched teeth. His eyebrows stayed knitted up in a look of concern. I could tell his mind was trying to pry into my confused thoughts.

"Alex, I'm not sorry for finally kissin' you. I know it scares you and sets off one of those internal arguments. I see it goin' on right now inside of your head. You need some time to think 'bout it. I understand. I'm scared too, but I know I'm right 'bout us." He smiled. "I won't kiss you again until it's your idea. I promise. I want this to be one hundred percent from you. We've got somethin' that people look for their whole lives. We just found it when we were eight. Because of that, I can wait a little bit longer."

"I don't want you waiting on me," I whispered.

"You don't really got a choice in that. Actually, I believe a little in fate."

"Fate…is just wishful thinking."

"For a girl who wishes on stars, you just don't get it. I'm tryin' to say some things are just meant to be." His fingers touched each side of my cheeks again. "Alex, I…" My hand flew up to his lips. My fingers pressed hard, stopping the words.

"No," I sputtered as the air evaporated from my lungs. I could not allow Jess to say it. My breathing got a little ragged. Jess kissed my fingers, and I yanked them off his lips. "I think we need a little space." I managed to get the words out. The nerves in my stomach kicked in, and bile trickled up in my throat.

"Okay." He nodded.

We both got up, and the awkward tension crackled through the air. I took in a quick breath in my nose and let it out slowly.

"Jess, I care about you. Please know that. You mean more to me than anyone else. But I can't promise anything. We are only eighteen. You've never even left here. You don't know what you want yet. I don't know what I want yet. Away from here, Jess. Austin is going to be so different than Arlis, and it's just the beginning for me. I may stay in Texas or I might leave. See the world. Do something on my own. I don't want to hold you to anything. It's going to be tough out there. We are going to need each other.

But as friends, Jess. Just *friends.* Anything else could jeopardize that. I don't want to lose you over it."

"You won't lose me. I promise. You're the most important person in my life. Always will be."

"Always is a long time, Jess. A lot could happen."

"Nothin' could happen that would be big enough to change it. Sometimes I feel growin' up together, there's a little piece of you that grew inside of me. I couldn't leave you if I tried."

I stared into his sweet face and saw the same one I met in the hallway all those years ago. I knew him better than anyone, and he knew me just the same. I needed that boy, and he only needed *that* girl. All this talk would fade in the shadows once he went to college and met a campus full of beautiful and *rich* girls. Jess would understand and be grateful that I stopped a potentially embarrassing accident today. He would find someone worthy of those words—a girl who wasn't his family's pet welfare project.

Jess wrapped his arms around my body. I froze, feeling his lips next to my ear. "Alex, it will happen. We are supposed to be together. One day you'll let me say those words to you." All his fingers stayed in the appropriate places, and then he let me go. My lungs released a sigh of relief.

I turned away to keep from seeing the hurt in his blue eyes. We gathered up the fishing supplies in silence. His phone stayed forgotten at the bottom of the pond. Every few moments, my eyes darted over at Jess. His jaw was clenched tight. I swallowed hard, knowing it was the way it had to be for us. Over time, he would forget these feelings.

After loading up the four-wheeler, Jess looked directly at my face. A week smile flashed before he fired up the engine. I climbed on the back, holding loosely to his shoulders as we headed toward my house, or rather, the *Masons'* farmhouse.

We bounced over ruts in the dirt trail. I grabbed his shoulders tighter to keep from falling off the back. *Jess kissed me.* The thought floated around in my head. I was scared of how it would change us. I was scared of how it made me really feel. For a moment, I closed my eyes, remembering my one and only kiss with Jess. I locked the memory away deep inside my heart.

Chapter 25

When I was eighteen...

I was leaving Arlis. It wasn't the first time I had traveled outside the city limits since we arrived in the old Bronco. I did my fair share of trips and vacations, courtesy of the Masons. Today was different. I was finally leaving—for good.

I filled my car full of boxes for the drive to Austin. I finally had four wheels of my own. The ten-year-old Ford Escape was a gift from my father and the only expense covered by a Tanner. I dubbed the old car El Chigger since it was a red hooptie the size of an insect. The passenger door was just a shade off from the body, and the windows refused to move without a swift punch to get the little motor running. I knew it had problems, but at least it had a working CD player.

As for Jess, he had left yesterday for early move-in because of his fraternity. I looked at the calendar this morning and noted the date. Six weeks and two days since he had kissed me. Six weeks and two days since his hands had touched my body.

We never talked about it after that day in the meadow. It was awkward at first, and then it was like it never happened at all. Sometimes I'm not sure it actually did, except when he looked at me and his eyes got a little dark on the edges. I knew Jess was thinking about us again, which made by body remember what it felt like to be kissed by my best friend. I tried to push those thoughts away, but lips that tasted as good as his were hard to forget.

I knew what needed to happen so I counted down the days until I moved to Austin. I silently said good-bye to Sprayberry last night. I hoped one day my father could do the same.

As thoughts of the past plagued me on the drive, an old image of my mother flashed before my eyes. She stayed tucked out of reach on most days. As the years passed, I forgot the clarity of her face or the exact floral scent of her perfume. It hurt sometimes when I realized I would never really know the person I had called *Mother*. I had been a child and only experienced the childlike aspects of our relationship.

As the last few weeks haunted me, I felt more like an adult with adult decisions. I realized what I never really had in my life. I wondered what she would have thought of Jess. What she would have said about my friendship with him? Would she even approve of my choice of college and the Masons' involvement? I shrugged off the thoughts. It was useless to scrutinize a hypothetical, alternate world, considering it was her illness and death that brought all of us together. Without those problems, the Masons would have never been forced into my life. The family and Jess only existed because of her cancer.

I navigated El Chigger through the dorm parking lot, stopping in the first space I found in the back. I felt the nervous butterflies in my stomach. Go big or go home, and I was *not* returning to Arlis.

My dad smiled through the glass, waiting for me to get out. I felt a little sad knowing he would be all alone in the farmhouse. I'm sure it was only a matter of time before the serious relationship with Caroline became permanent. We had a few talks on my feelings toward the idea. I liked her, but more than anything, I just wanted my father to be happy.

Gathering a few items, we made the first trip to the dorm room. I had little knowledge of my roommate except that her name was Sadie. The name alone divulged nothing into the character of the person who would share a space smaller than Mrs. Mason's closet. After checking in with the RA, I found our room vacant but full to the brim on the side next to the window.

The bed was covered with a puffy, white-eyelet bedspread and a pile of silver pillows in different shapes. The desk was full of photos and trinkets, indicating someone who came from a past full of exciting moments and trendy friends. I wondered why she would take potluck for a roommate. My situation was pretty obvious, but the story sitting on the desk said something else about this Sadie.

My father and Caroline carried my simple belongings up from the car while I unpacked. With every item I shoved into my closet, I glanced over at the identical door. Curiosity got the best of me. I pulled the adjacent handle and peered inside her closet.

The contents were a little intriguing. Half the closet contained an assortment of suits that resurrected the ghost of the original Jackie O. The rest was rows and rows of the same pony-embossed shirt, just in different colors. I wrinkled up my nose with confusion. Living with this Sadie would be interesting.

The door opened while I slammed the closet shut. It was just my father and Caroline with the last load. My father appeared a little lost with no more boxes to tote upstairs. It was that time. We made the last descent down to the parking lot for our official good-bye. I watched his face shift between emotions.

"Pumpkin, I guess this is it." The tears glistened in the corners but stayed in place next to the wrinkles around his eyes. I never thought much about my father's age. Today, he seemed old with tufts of gray over his ears.

"Bye, Dad." I put my arms around him for a hug. His familiar scent sparked my nose, a faint, mechanical smell that soaked into all his clothes worn to the hardware store.

"I'll be okay," I said quietly.

My throat tightened and burned. I clenched my teeth down on my lip to keep my composure. We would be apart for the first time in eighteen years. I truly loved my father. Tragedy has a way of bonding people different than a traditional relationship. My father and I were like Velcro in some ways: polar opposites stuck together, holding down the fort, even during those times our personalities clashed like oil and water. I released my grasp and backed away.

"Now, don't stay out too late and don't drive too fast. I don't want to get a phone call saying you've been in an accident."

"I won't, Dad. I promise." I nodded, thinking of a night long ago in a Jeep that never came to his knowledge.

"And don't drink and drive. No, just don't drink period," he babbled, while his boots shifted on the sidewalk in a nervous side step.

"I promise." I glanced over at Caroline, looking for a little help.

"I think it's time to let her go, Henry." She smiled, putting an arm around his back. His fingers reached down to grab her hand. Just watching the gestures eased my sadness a little. I wrapped them both in one last hug, then watched the truck drive away. Back in the dorm, I walked through the wooden door to my new home. This time, I had company.

"Alex?" A shorter girl with long, blonde hair greeted me. She had a grin as big as Julia Roberts's and a set of emerald-green eyes.

"Yeah, Alex Tanner. You're Sadie, right?" She wasn't at all what I had expected. Living in the honor's dorm, I had a mental perception of a certain type of student who occupied the halls, but this Sadie fit none of those.

"The one and only. Hope you don't mind, but I picked the bed by the window. I got here early from Richmond, the one in Virginia." The smile appeared to be stuck permanently on her face.

"No, that's fine. I'm not very picky," I said back with a shrug. It at least explained the whole random-girl-room-assignment choice. No person in her right mind left that side of the country for Texas.

"Why did you come to school in Austin?"

"I'm a legacy on my mother's side. She grew up in Dallas."

"I was from there, once."

I watched her fingers unhook the clasp on the ankle of her dress shoes that coordinated with the sundress; not the strapless type worn to the lake, but the beautiful, flowy kind, meant for a garden party. She exchanged the platform heals for a matching pair of flats.

"And now?" She looked up in interest.

"Oh, I'm from Arlis. It's outside of Fort Worth, sort of."

Sadie put the shoes away in a neat row, then turned her full attention to me. In the glow of the sun, I realized her eyes were not green, but a shade of hazel that could change with every outfit or the tone of her mood.

"I guess we are both new to Austin. It's a good school, though. Do you have a major yet?"

"I'm business for now, I guess." It seemed like the typical student answer this morning, but slightly lackluster telling Sadie.

"They have a good business program here. I'm a double major, actually. International business and accounting."

"That's impressive."

"Well, a girl needs to learn how to make the deals when running a company, and also make sure no one else is cheating her."

I looked at her again. Sadie had a presence that was undeniable. It was hard to describe. She was a classic beauty, like her Jackie-styled suits. However, it wasn't just her looks that were striking. I realized why she was living in the honor dorm. Sadie had intelligence and charisma. She would run the world one day while everyone else sat and watched.

"Oh, I almost forgot, sweetie. A really cute guy stopped by looking for you. Dark hair? Blue eyes?"

"Oh, that's Jess."

"Hmmm...boyfriend?" She hesitated on the last word, fishing for information. This would get interesting. I never had to explain our attached-at-the-hip type connection back in Arlis. Everyone just knew.

"No, we grew up together. He's a...childhood friend."

"That is one lucky childhood, sweetie."

"I guess you could say that."

Her hazel eyes lingered on my last words while her lips pursed into a bow. I think she was trying to see if I were lying. If she only knew; yet that was the cool thing about Austin—no one did know about me.

"So I came back to see if you had arrived. I'm going to the student organization fair. I thought you might like to come?"

"Okay, sure…I'm really not the club-joining type, but I don't mind going."

"It's never too early to plot the direction of your life. You need to think about your future from day one and get ahead. Everyone here was first in their class, president of five clubs, and nailed the SAT. You have to do something to stand out. I don't know you, and I have no idea what you plan to do here, but no woman runs her own company by accident. It all comes from purpose-made decisions." Her eyes studied me again.

"So you plan to do that? Own a company?"

"That I do, sweetie. I plan to run my own company, and maybe marry someone who plans on running the country."

"What?"

"Sorry, I got off on one of my Hillary moments." She rolled her eyes.

"As in, Clinton?"

"Yeah, I tend to be a little obsessed with her at times. She's a brilliant lady. I find it fascinating to watch the ambition and determination of someone like Hillary Clinton. She knows what she wants and isn't afraid to jump in and take charge." She finished with a satisfied smile.

"Wow, well, I guess lead the way."

"Great! I'm thinking debate team."

"Sure?"

I wasn't used to being around someone who was a tight, wound-up ball of ambition. In the moment, I pondered if this girl ever had fun or if college were a business plan. It didn't matter. Fun wasn't the motivation for me in college anyway. I was here on someone else's buck and for a very different purpose.

The more Sadie talked, the more I felt sucked into my new chapter in life. She could push me in the right direction. As we got in the elevator, I thought about Jess. Part of me really wanted to call him, but I knew it was time to get used to having a life outside of each other.

Chapter 26

Today, 1:33 am.

I wait impatiently for my father to return. The beauty queen watches me silently from the other side of the room. Lifting up the spoon, I struggle to swallow another bite of chicken noodle soup. I will it to stay in my stomach, knowing the importance of food right now.

My father comes through the door but says nothing. His jaw clenches as he reaches up to scratch his solid, gray head. I take another bite to show I am eating. Gagging, I force the liquid to go down my throat. His tired eyes watch me in the chair. "I think you should just rest a little longer, Pumpkin."

"Why? Just get a wheelchair and get me the hell out of this room."

"You're still not feeling very well. I…um…think you should just stay here. Try to sleep again."

"You want me to just go to sleep? No, Dad, I need to see Dr. Mason." He absently slips his eyes toward the beauty queen and then back to me. He wasn't telling me something. "You have to stop lying to me…you have to stop, Dad. Just take me to see him and then…I'll lay down again."

"I'm sorry. He's not here."

"What? Where is he?"

"Look. I think…"

"Shut up!"

My words hit my father like arrows. I hoist myself from the chair and stumble out the door. I hear his feet coming up behind me. I cut to the left and through an empty side hallway. I know the passageways better than him. I find a flight of stairs and make my way down and around a corner.

The waiting room sat empty except for a lone man in the back corner. They were gone—every last one of them. I pound on the desk with my fist. The frizzy-haired woman glances up. She freezes, seeing my face.

"Where's Dr. Mason?"

"Um, he's not here, ma'am."

"Where is he?"

"He's in Dallas, ma'am."

Fear cripples me at the ankles. I slide down the side of the counter. My father watches a few steps away. "I'm sorry, Pumpkin."

"Why are you doing this to me? You know how…how important."

I rub my raw eyes, feeling the dizziness in my head. It hurts so incredibly bad. Biting down on my lip, I feel the comfort of the sharp pain. I clench tighter and tighter to take away the raw ache inside my chest. The metallic taste of blood coats my tongue.

"I'm just trying to protect you. You are not handling this very well, and I just thought being here was better for now.

"Like you can say anything about handling things," I snarl at him. "I was there, Dad. *Remember?* I was there. You stopped existing. You stopped and…"

His face twists up in sadness before I could even get the words out. I want to blame everything on him, but I know it would make nothing better. Yelling cruel words made no difference right now.

"Your friend called back."

"What?" In my fog of misery, I fail to see the beauty queen approach in her silent nurse shoes. She sits down next to me on the floor.

"Your friend. She said her plane should get in around nine in the mornin'. It's the earliest one she could get out of Chicago."

"Sadie's coming here?"

"Yeah."

"How? I don't understand."

"Your dad had me call her."

Looking up at my sad father, I watch him swallow hard, his Adam's apple shifting in his throat. He was trying. He was trying so very hard to help me right now because he *did* know. My father was handling things for me while I could not bear to face this chapter of my life.

"You called Sadie, and she's coming?" I peer back at the beauty queen as she nods yes. "But she had…um…she…um…had the campaign dinner. It was yesterday or today or tomorrow. I don't know. She's coming?"

"She was upset about not getting one earlier, but she wants you to know that she's comin' into Dallas."

"I'll get the truck." My father mutters in a gruff voice before exiting through the revolving door.

I turn back to the girl sitting next to me, knowing our paths were about to split again as I left the hospital. Her eyes sparkle with tears. "Alex, I'm really sorry."

Never in a thousand years did I ever think I would receive an ounce of comfort from those shiny lips. She leans over and wraps her small arms around my body. I let myself relax against her warmth, clinging to her as we sit on the floor of the hospital waiting room.

I whisper against her shoulder, "Thank you, Ashley."

"If you need anythin'…when, um, you get back…maybe…I could do somethin'."

"That would be nice." I swallow hard, feeling my tears roll down in Ashley's pretty hair.

Chapter 27

When I was nineteen...

It finally happened. My diary sat exposed to an entire room of snarky critics. My eyes moved from one image to the next, seeing my gray drawings on the wall of the gallery. They all served as a reminder that my soul was charcoal, which came in the form of a pencil I used to sketch the details.

Looking across the room, I stopped on the smile of my blue-eyed boy. Tonight was essentially Jess's grand idea, one that caused a deep inner struggle. I had five drawings in Gallery 51's spring exhibition because he insisted that I enter the competition. I was the only freshman who made the cut.

Over the last year, I lived the typical college life, at least the one of an honor student. I juggled classes, attended the occasional party, and crammed for tests over boxes of late-night pizza. Sadie joined the campus debate team and convinced me to dabble in an assortment of other groups. With the help of my new roommate, my life morphed into a new one outside of Arlis, with one exception.

My friendship with Jess intrigued Sadie. She didn't believe in the concept of having a male best friend. Every time she brought it up, I swore Jess and I had known each other for so long, our relationship was far past anything romantic. I never convinced those hazel eyes it was true. Despite her persistent questions, she liked Jess and found him *quite charming*.

On most days, I actually enjoyed having Sadie as a roommate. She added a motivational drive to the atmosphere in the room. Her presence alone pushed me in directions I didn't think possible. I shared Sadie's outlook of hard work and determination and easily adapted to her purpose-driven goals for the future.

In the light of my new life, I never told Sadie the details about my past in Arlis. I enjoyed being free of the baggage. Sadie was too intelligent to believe I presented the full picture. She probed with questions, but at this point in the friendship, she never tried to dig deep into an unwanted pit. Regardless, I knew how she operated. Sadie was buying her time, waiting for the kill.

Jess got deeply involved with his fraternity. Even with our new lives and different schedules, we squeezed in an occasional dinner and random cups of coffee every few days.

On a cold afternoon in January, Jess brought an artsy flyer to wave in my face. Gallery 51 was reviewing pieces for the spring artist exhibition. The show was geared toward the indie college crowd, but it was still an actual competition at the upscale-bar-turned-retro-art-house. He had pestered and harassed until I submitted my entries. I had expected to be declined by the snooty judges. To my surprise, I made the cut for the spring show. Ten artists had received the green light, each submitting five separate pieces, making fifty entries for the showcase award tonight.

Walking over to Jess, I stood beside him as he looked at my work. He smiled like a kid in a candy store, who just found a package of Skittles the size of a garbage bag. It was the same grin I captured in my drawing of him, fishing next to a pond at Sprayberry. The gallery required each entry be available for purchase. A sale seemed outside the realm of plausible outcomes for my artwork. Nonetheless, *Flecks of Blue* had a price tag on it.

"Is it weird to think someone might have a picture of you hanging up in their house?"

His eyes absently swept down my body, looking at my party outfit put together by Sadie. "I don't mind. It's more of a landscape, anyway."

"I guess so."

"Besides, I have the original. Who cares if they get that one?"

"The original?"

"The first one you tried by the pond, remember?"

"That awful thing?" I laughed, thinking about my first attempt when I was twelve. "You still have it?"

"Are you kiddin'? How could I get rid of somethin' like that? Perfect blackmail." He smirked.

"You would."

"Actually…" He leaned in close to my ear, his lips touching my hair as he whispered. "I have all of your originals, even the ones on the napkins."

"What? How…did you?" The words stumbled in confusion. My heart beat a little faster, seeing flashes of all the times he cleared the table at Jeeter's. I assumed the napkin doodles went in the trash with the ketchup packets. My skin got warm thinking of Jess saving something so trivial. The thoughts made me want to wrap my arms around his shoulders, squeezing tight. Instead, I bit my lip, trying to focus on something else.

We kept our physical interactions to a minimum. On my part at least, it was intentional. He had kept his word and never tried to kiss me again. Tonight was hard. Even though he wasn't touching me, Jess didn't bother to hide his true feelings. They were as clear as his blue eyes. It was all very confusing because my heart wanted to thank him for always believing in me.

"You look pretty tonight," he whispered next to my cheek.

"Thank you. Sadie made me wear her clothes. The dress is too short."

"I kind of like it that way." He grinned, and my face got hot. Stepping back to his own personal space, he pointed at my last entry. "Does Uncle Frank know 'bout that one?"

"Um, no." I shook my head. I'm sure Frank would spit fire on the ground from both my drawing and the retro hipster attendees at Gallery 51. I could hear his Marlboro voice muttering, "Nothin' but a bunch of damn hippies standin' around while there's work to be done."

With his question, I reflected back across the showcase entries. *Flecks of Red* featured Jeeter's with only the outline of the neon sign and taillights in crimson. *Flecks of Green* displayed an entire wooded landscape with a single green tree. *Flecks of Blue* showcased a teenage boy fishing by a pond. *Flecks of Orange* highlighted a faded sunset over the old farmhouse and a lone, orange kitten on the porch.

Flecks of Yellow was the one in question by Jess. It featured a cowboy on a horse, standing in the yellow meadow grass. I had captured Frank's rugged face, complete with cigarette dangling from his lips, and his yellow tinted hat and handkerchief tucked into his pocket.

"I think you got a shot with the one of Frank."

"Maybe."

"I took a picture of it on my cell phone. I'm plannin' to show it to him. I can't wait to see his reaction when I make him look at it on my *devil box*."

"That's just great. You're going to torment Frank with my drawing of him." I smiled, shaking my head. "But really, you think I could actually win?"

"Yeah, I do, and I'm not just sayin' that."

"Thanks…I mean it. I would have never done this without you."

"You're beautiful and smart and insanely talented, Al." He pushed a piece of my hair back behind my ear. "I just wish you saw yourself the way I see you."

I froze. My heart beat a little faster, hearing his soft words and seeing his eyes get a little dark on the edges. The feeling happened again. I wanted to hold him tight against me. Looking away, I searched the gallery for my father, Caroline, and the Masons. They were alone somewhere in a sea of men in skinny jeans.

"We should probably go find the rest of them," I suggested.

"I guess." He let out a deep breath and smiled. "Mother is probably ready to shit some bricks."

"Pearlized ones." I laughed faintly.

"Are you Alexandra?" I turned around to find an older man in a suit with curly spirals of hair clipped closely to his skull. He stood about six inches shorter than my accelerated height.

"Yes?"

"I'm Professor Lynch. I work in the university's art department. Mind if we visit?"

"Hey, Al, I'll go find 'em." Jess excused himself.

I shifted nervously in front of the professor, wishing Sadie had not insisted I wear these damn heels for the show. They hurt, and I bobbled around like an anxious giraffe.

"Alexandra, I haven't seen you enrolled in any of the department classes."

"I'm a business major." I'd seen plenty of art teachers with eccentric quirks. Pascal Frasier, my old teacher in Fort Worth, was beyond strange. However, Professor Lynch wore a jacket and glasses and seemed relatively normal.

"But nothing in the art department?"

"I guess I never thought about it. I'm in the honors program."

"You still have the rough edges of a young amateur, but excellent potential. I see something in these." The professor looked at me closely. "I'm not sure the others see it."

"I don't understand."

"Take the one with the tree. Some would say it's a simple landscape with an off-center oak lit up like a pine on Christmas Day. Instead, I see a lone sapling that doesn't seem like it belongs with the shared dirt the tall tree was forced to grow in. The sprouting limbs seem to push out, keeping the surroundings at a distance."

My stomach dropped a little as I tried to look away. I bit down hard on my lip and focused on the knot of his tie. He seemed to pay no attention and continued to the next one.

"And in *Flecks of Red*, that's an interesting choice of color to bring to the front. I see many facets of the rainbow in the building. The letters of the store sign itself are old yellow bulbs. But you picked to highlight the red outline. Red usually means love and passion or sometimes anger and violence."

I felt sick. I didn't like this one bit. Who was this person reading my pictures like a deck of tarot cards? I hoped he stayed clear of the blue highlights surrounding the pond and the boy fishing. My insides couldn't take a breakdown of that image.

"Do I have your attention now? There's a unique style, but you have something deeper hidden beneath the simple sketches. I see emotion and vulnerability. That's a natural talent, which can't be taught. Here's my card. Stop by, and we can discuss next semester. Maybe you should look at doing both."

"Okay, I'll think about it." A pressing weight in my chest seemed to push the words out.

"That's fine. Think about it. Dream about it. Whatever it takes for you to accept it's the right decision. It would be a shame for your talent to go to waste."

"Thank you."

I left in search of the others, feeling very confused. I talked briefly to Sadie, who was engrossed in a discussion with a shaggy-haired political science major, wearing a white shirt, tie, skinny jeans, and tennis shoes. Not an odd combination for the room, but something out of the ordinary for Sadie. Yet, she never passed up a good conversation involving foreign policies. This room was prime fodder for Sadie to find a kindred spirit.

Making my way through the crowd, I located the others. Jess didn't see me approaching, but I heard the low words spoken in a heated exchange with Mrs. Mason. Pinpricks etched up my back at the implications of the conversation. I wished I'd never heard it.

Brushing past them, I made my way to the front for the showcase award. I tasted the nervous bile forming in my throat. What if I won? What if I didn't? The news came with a bittersweet ending. Maybe I wanted it more than I realized. My hopes were crushed by a portrait of used tissues, which featured painted tears that symbolized dying Ethiopian children.

"I'm sorry, Al." Jess wrapped an arm around my back for a side squeeze. It felt almost as good as the one I fought to give his body earlier in the evening.

"It's okay."

"You'll get them next time, Pumpkin." My dad patted me on the shoulder, trying to reassure me in his own way.

"Thanks, Dad." I noticed his hand was intertwined with Caroline's. The sight made me feel happy.

"I always knew you'd be a star. I framed a few and put 'em up by the register. Can't wait for you to see 'em."

"You didn't have to do that, Caroline. Thank you." I gave her a tight, sincere hug. She felt small beneath my arms, like I could crush her if I pressed too tightly.

"You have nothing to be ashamed of tonight, Alexandra." I turned my full upright attention to Mrs. Mason, who looked extremely out of place in her pale-pink silk suit. I held back a chuckle when I glanced at the pearl necklace wound tight around her elegant throat.

"Thank you, ma'am."

"You are doing an excellent job in school, and your pictures captured the ranch beautifully." The drawn-out words stabbed me in the chest. Every syllable stressed dollar signs on my conscience in direct correlation to my school performance.

"Thank you, ma'am."

My eyes flickered over to Dr. Mason, who nodded in agreement. He was always the quiet sort, very warm and patient. His kind blue eyes always reminded me of Jess's. They were outlined in dark lashes, identical to his son's.

Jess and I walked the group to the car for their drive back to Arlis. After many good-byes, I got in the truck with Jess. I plopped down in the tan leather passenger seat, putting Sadie's jewel-encrusted pumps on the dash. As we left the parking lot, I rolled down the window, feeling the cool breeze hit me in the face.

"Wanna go somewhere? It's not that late." His deep voice caught my attention as he leaned back behind the wheel, driving with his right wrist.

Jess looked good tonight. Watching him, I felt that pull again, but it was more than just the physical attraction. Jess was part of tonight in a way that was years in the making. The intensity of our history allowed a sea of emotions to surface. I needed to go back to the dorms for some distance and perspective on the evening. Instead, I opened a can of worms.

"What did you have in mind?"

"We could try the new coffee place on Sixth? Or…we could just go drivin' around for a while. Get out of here. It wouldn't take long to ditch all of this if you want?" In the background, I heard Kenny Chesney's voice in the truck. I knew Jess was itching for his favorite combination of dirt and twang, followed by parking and sitting on the tailgate of his truck.

"Maybe the coffeehouse."

"Okay, it's your night. Coffee it is."

It was a public place and incapable of the hidden dangers involved around a dark, starlit night and my guard down. I watched the flash of streetlights reflect off the window glass and felt Jess glance in my direction a few times.

"You okay?"

"Yeah."

"Are you disappointed?"

"I don't know."

"You shouldn't be. Alex, you're good. It's just the first one."

"I could draw a scribbly tornado, and you would still say that."

"That's not true, and you know it." He shot me a broody frown to emphasize his point.

"Don't give me that irritating look."

"All my looks irritate you, so I don't think there's any other option."

I rolled my eyes, leaning my head back against the seat. I tried to hide the small grin on my lips. "You exasperate me sometimes, Jessup Mason."

"Damn! Big words and both names."

"Shut up."

"So what'd that professor want?" Jess asked, never missing a beat.

"Professor Lynch was interesting."

"And?"

"I don't know." I let out a deep breath, looking back over at Jess. "He could see things in the drawings, like he understood them, I think."

"Really?"

"Yeah, I got his card. He wants me to come by his office next week to talk about getting into classes and being my mentor and shit."

"I told you, Al. You're good and you need to start realizing it. You should talk to him."

"I can't just do art. Where is that going to get me in life? And I can't do both. It would mean more classes and I would probably take more than four years. It's just going to be longer and cost more to do both."

His eyes met mine on the last words. Explaining to him the turmoil I felt was like teaching ants to march backward. The thoughts circulating through his shaggy head only had Mason dollars tied to them.

"It's okay, Al. Really. We can make it work."

We, as in, his family. The damn Masons. Jess parked the truck at the coffeehouse and looked at me. I pulled the door handle and jumped out, preventing another aggravating discussion over my bank account that got weekly Mason deposits.

I marched up the steps on the wooden patio attached to the front of the store. I caught one of Sadie's stupid heels in a crack, causing my foot to stay and my body to go flying. The impact left me facedown across the crackly boards.

"Damn it!"

"Let me help you." Jess unleashed my foot. Standing up, I pulled off the damn pumps and chunked them in the patio trash can, resulting in a satisfying thud.

"This is why I don't wear those ridiculous things. I've got a splinter in my hand too." I held up my palm as the blood oozed down to my wrist. Jess laughed right in my face. "Stop that!"

"You're a girl who hates girl things, but you freak out over a splinter."

"That's a small dagger, you jerk."

"Okay. Okay. Small dagger. Let's go inside. I'm sure they have a first-aid kit with tweezers for small hand daggers."

"I hate you right now."

"I know. Your cheeks are showin' that temper of yours even in the dark."

"Stop harassing me."

"Me, harrassin'? Oh, that's nothin' compared to what you're gonna get from Sadie. She'll be pissed at you for destroyin' her makeover project."

"Why does everyone think I need some style intervention? I have a style."

"You do?" I saw the crinkles around the corners of his eyes as he baited me with the question.

"I do. It's called Alex."

"That's the truth. It's one-of-a-kind, complete with a voice-recorded talk box of insults."

"That *magically* only comes out at you."

"Go sit at the table while I order so they don't notice your nasty feet." Jess held the glass door open.

"I have nice feet."

"For a sasquatch."

I flipped him off, then walked in the door. About a dozen students occupied the French-inspired café tonight. I plopped down at an empty table and wrapped my hand in a napkin.

Jess returned with two foamy mugs the size of soup bowls. He slid in the booth across from me, then fished something out from his pocket. "Here's the tweezers, and I got you a cappuccino with those extra shots of espresso you like."

"Thanks. You know that's my study drink. Are you trying to keep me out all night with you?"

"Maybe," his pancake syrup voice dragged out the word.

I took a sip, feeling the warm liquid slide down my throat. "That tastes perfect. I might have a new favorite place."

"You have a little right there." Jess pointed to my mouth. My tongue licked it off the corner of my lips. The color flashed on my cheeks when I realized Jess was watching me. I reached for the tweezers to work on my cut. The splinter was large and deeply imbedded under layers of skin.

"This isn't working."

"Let me try."

I slid my hand across the table. His fingers tightened around my wrist. The expression on his face changed to complete concentration. The pain of the wound faded to another part of my mind as I watched him. A piece of hair fell across his eye. He lifted my fingers up closer to his face to get a better look.

"I'm going to have to pry it open a little. You okay with that?"

"Yeah…I once let you cut my hand with a dirty knife. I think you're pretty safe with the tweezers."

"I guess that's true." Jess smirked. His fingers gripped my hand. They felt warm in every place he touched me. I watched blood trickle from the opening. I bit down on my lip, trying to calm down.

"You sure you're okay?"

"Yep."

"Well, I got it. That was one hell of a splinter. I mean, small dagger." He winked.

Grabbing a napkin from the table, Jess dabbed the blood, then pressed my hand closed to keep it in place, but he didn't let go. He touched my wrist, looking through my handmade bracelets. Jess slipped a finger under the brown band woven from the hair of BB's mane.

BB had died about a year ago. She was grazing in a small pen outside the horse barn when a sudden spring thunderstorm crept up on the ranch. She got spooked and took off across the meadow. Frank found her a few hours later, halfway down a ravine. He put a bullet through her brown skull to end her suffering. Jess used a tractor to extract BB from the jagged rocks and took her to the burned-up stump.

Before we buried her, I snipped a few pieces of her beautiful mane. I made two braided bands: the one Jess looked at on my wrist and the other matching one he wore just under the cuff of his dress shirt.

Jess let go of my wrist and picked up his mug. I saw him exhale deeply in contemplation as he looked back at me. "I can't change your mind 'bout this summer?"

"I need to do this."

"I know and I understand. It's just hard to think you're not comin' home this summer."

Sadie helped me apply for "a summer in paradise," according to the brochure for Camp Rochellas. She said, "Working with kids at a camp was like a community relations gold star on my resume."

"It's just a couple of months, Jess."

"I know. But even here, I could find you in about five minutes if I needed you. I can't do that if you're in some swamp in Louisiana."

"We can still talk. That's what these little black boxes are for, *Frank*."

"Funny, Al. But Arlis is gonna be total shit without you."

"I know, but you'll still have Frank." I winked at him.

"Yes, I'm already plannin' to take him to hang out with the has-beens at Nickel Bridge."

"You'll be okay." I patted his arm.

"I guess." He picked up my hand, holding it tight in his palm. Jess intertwined our fingers, brushing my skin with his thumb. I watched him across the booth. I watched the blue eyes get dark on the corners as I let him hold my hand.

"I heard your parents earlier, talking about Sprayberry."

My question came out and hovered in the air. I watched him across the table, his jaw clenched slightly in response. His fingers gripped my hand. "They want an answer by the end of summer."

"That soon?"

"I guess Frank's doin' okay for now, but who knows how long he can run the whole damn place. Some of the guys have been with him awhile, but he's gotten a little confused lately. Mother said she needs to work on a Plan B if I am not gonna run Sprayberry."

"What do you want to do?"

"I don't know. It's a lot of pressure. Shit, I thought Frank would outlive Moses just for spite. It's too early for this decision. I don't want to even think 'bout it. If somethin' happens to Frank, I'd have to leave school. I'm nineteen. I don't know if I want to run a cattle ranch the rest of my life."

"I know it seems like that now, but you love Sprayberry," I said quietly. "I know you do more than anything else. I think you would be happy there."

"I don't know. Maybe…if the circumstances were right, I could stay there forever."

I felt a little fidgety and suddenly hot. His eyes shifted to me with the deep meaning of those words. I knew what he really wanted—something I couldn't give him.

His fingers rubbed over the top of my hand. "And this is why I didn't want to talk 'bout it. I just want to have fun with you tonight."

"I'm having fun." I smiled sadly at him. "I'm sorry I brought it up."

"It's fine. I can't change the inevitable. But it doesn't have to all be decided tonight." He shrugged. His shoulders were heavy with the weight of his destiny. We both knew he would go back to Sprayberry; it was just a matter of *when*. Jess traced over each of my fingers, then squeezed my hand tighter. I let him hold on to me just a little longer.

We said nothing for a while. He held my hand. I drank my coffee. He watched me with his blue eyes. From an outsider's view, I'm sure they read this differently than it really was for us. I finished the last sip of the giant cappuccino and pushed the cup over in the corner.

"You ready to go?"

Jess nodded and then pulled me up from the bench, keeping a tight grip on my fingers. He tugged me through the café to the exit. *I should let go now.* My brain chanted the words as I walked barefoot behind Jess, but I couldn't bring myself to release this connection to him. We reached his truck, and Jess opened the door for me. Only then did he let go of my hand so I could climb inside.

We pulled out of the parking lot without saying anything. I reached over and turned the radio to a station playing Kings of Leon. Using the steering-wheel controls, he flipped it back to Jason Boland.

I changed it back with the console dial. At the stoplight, we stared at each other until he winked and flipped it again. I grabbed the knob and clicked it back, getting the last few notes of my song.

"Okay, fine. It's your night, Al. We can listen to crap."

I settled back against the tan leather, grinning.

Jess parked his truck in the student parking lot. I opened my door to find him standing next to it. He turned around, backing his butt up against my seat.

"What are you doing?"

"You threw your shoes in the trash, remember? I'm not listenin' to another bitch fit when you step on a broken beer bottle."

"I don't have bitch fits."

"Just get on."

I climbed onto his back with Sadie's short dress pushed up to my hips. Jess pulled my legs tight across his stomach, holding them under each knee. Clinging to his shoulders, I felt his warm body pressed against me, just the way I wanted to feel him all night.

"Ready."

"Yeah," I answered next to his ear.

"Then hold on." Jess took off running toward the dorm entrance. I clenched his waist with my thighs to keep from falling. My fingers dug into his chest as he zigzagged around parked cars and jumped over parking blocks. I laughed hard against his neck, and it felt good. I needed this with him. *I needed him.* The thought caused me to take a deep breath of the cool air.

At the entrance, I slide down his back to the ground. Jess turned and looked at me. He was so close, but yet his body didn't touch me anymore. My toes twisted around next to his ostrich boots. I took another deep breath, trying to stop what I was feeling. I wanted his warm body against me. I wanted to feel him again.

"Al…" He smiled that intense, puckered-up grin that made his whole face light up. "I like it when you laugh like that."

"Really?"

"It's your happy one. I don't hear it very often. Not like tonight."

"That's because I'm having fun tonight." I laid a hand on his chest as I said the words. His heart was beating as fast as mine. I told myself not to touch him, but I couldn't pull away.

"Good." Jess pushed a piece of my hair behind my ear, letting his thumb touch my face. He brushed down my cheek to my lips. My face flushed as he traced over the bottom one.

"You smell good tonight too. Like peaches."

"No, I don't. You just want me to smell like them because they're orange."

Jess slipped his hand around my waist, pulling me against his chest. Leaning in close to my neck, he planted a faint, warm kiss slightly just below my jaw. "You're lyin'. I smell peaches."

"Maybe," I whispered.

Jess pulled back enough to watch me. His blue eyes scanned over my face and neck. I smiled at him, feeling the warm buzz of the moment. It was slightly intoxicating being wrapped up in the shadows under the streetlight.

Jess grinned, then leaned forward, kissing me in the same spot again. His soft lips skimmed further down my neck. I closed my eyes, letting myself feel him touch my skin. He was good at this. He was good at making it seem okay.

"You think it means less if you just kiss my neck?" I whispered.

"I don't know. Does it?"

It was innocent, I told myself, except my body reacted to the sound of his low voice. It responded to his breath floating against my neck. It betrayed me almost as much as my heart beating frantically in my chest.

Leaning forward, Jess broke his promise again and kissed my chest. He let his lips sit in place, scorching my skin. Moving his fingers, he traced along the silky fabric on my back. Jess was touching me and kissing me, and I couldn't think. He made me feel things I kept locked away. My toes curled against the cement as I tried to get control of my feelings. One turn of my cheek, and I could taste his sweet lips again.

I felt his hand dip down past my waist, tracing my butt cheek through the silky fabric. I sucked in a deep breath through my nose. "What are you doing?" I whispered.

"I don't know. I wanted to touch you all night."

"So you decided to just do it."

"Yeah, I guess. Are you mad?"

"I…I don't know."

Jess moved his hand back to my waist. Looking into my eyes, he smiled sweetly, holding me against his chest. I felt the full outline of his body through my stupid, thin dress. He was messing with my head tonight—messing with my body and making it want things.

"I think I should go back to my room."

"Al, wait. We could go somewhere."

"And do what exactly?"

His sweet, blue eyes pierced into mine, holding me captive. "Go drivin'…just talk…we don't even have to get out of the truck. I just…I don't want tonight to be over yet."

Because Jess knew I wouldn't let him this close again. His eyes pleaded with me. Those damn blue eyes were my weakness. I had to be strong.

"I can't," I whispered, feeling the bittersweet punch in the gut.

His eyes got sad, and it took a moment for him to release me. Jess finally leaned forward, giving me a quick peck on the cheek. "Night, Alex."

Suddenly set free, I watched his ostrich boots head back to the truck. My heart beat in a painful acceleration, and I released the breath I'd failed to realize I was holding. Faint traces of his cologne remained in the air.

I waited, angry at myself, hoping he would turn around. I was weak. I was so weak that I would have let Jess kiss me on the lips if he had tried. My stomach tightened. I watched until his dark hair faded away into the parking lot.

Turning around, I walked barefoot into the dorms. I sat down in the hallway outside my room. I needed him, and it made me angry at myself. I needed him the same way I needed air: a little bit over and over again just to survive. It was wrong. I shouldn't feel this way about him. I *couldn't* feel this way about him. I refused to allow it.

After a good amount of mental torture, I got off the floor to face my roommate. I opened the door to find Sadie ironing her sheets before putting them on the bed—just another one of the OCD tendencies of Sadence McAllister.

"You're so strange sometimes, Sadie." I shook my head, watching her remove the imaginary wrinkles from her already-starched white sheets.

"I wouldn't go there unless you want to discuss the items hanging in your closet and don't even get me started on your pseudo-psychotic nail polish collection."

"Okay, okay. How was…"

"Charles. All tie and no plan. Complete insane and non-plausible ideas that will go nowhere. But he was cute. So I listened and played civil until I thought my brain would just self-destruct to put me out of my misery."

"Can't you just discuss normal things?"

"What's the fun in that? So where have you been?"

"That new French coffee place on Sixth."

"And how is Jess tonight?"

"Fine." I stayed clear of the telltale eyes and fell back flat against my mattress. I got myself in a real mess tonight and I didn't have the energy for her to poke holes all through it.

"Where are my shoes?"

"Long story."

"Concerning my shoes?"

"I would be more concerned someone your size has such big feet and can share shoes with me."

"*Alex*, where are my shoes?"

"Okay, okay. I'll get you some more," I muttered under my breath. "I'm sure the *Masons* can afford a pair of your fancy, designer shoes."

I didn't hear a reply. Sitting up, I found Sadie's hazel eyes scrutinizing my slumped frame. "So…" she probed.

"What?"

"This isn't about shoes."

"Let it go, Sadie."

"Let's discuss the long story. You know the one where Jess is in love with you and you pretend he isn't."

"No, it's not like that."

"Alex, that lie isn't working anymore. He stared at you all night. It was a toss-up between exorbitant pride and some broody I-want-to-take-that-dress-off stare with those blue eyes. A little cute actually, but you…"

"Sadie!"

"You can't deny it, sweetie. Not anymore. He's way too transparent with his feelings."

"I know," I whispered.

My shoulders sagged, and I collapsed back on my bed, feeling the suffocating pressure in my chest. Tonight was a train wreck. I never should have let him touch me. I never should have let him kiss me. The answer to his question was yes: his lips on the neck and skin and top of my breast was *kissing.*

"So what made you all twisted up and full of doom and gloom with your cowboy?"

"He's not *my* cowboy."

"Sure, sweetie. Why don't you tell yourself that little fake story and tell me the real one."

"I told you it was a long story."

"I'm up and you're jittery, from what I assume was a monolithic cup of espresso you had with Jess as he gazed into your eyes, which sent you into some neurotic internal fit. So start talking."

"All right, all right. If it will make you shut up, I'll tell you the truth." I walked over to flip off the light, launching the room into a safe darkness. "Don't say I didn't warn you when I said it was long."

I sat cross-legged on my bed. My heart beat fast in my chest as I told Sadie the ghastly story of my life. It was the first time I ever told anyone. I'd never had someone I trusted enough to hear all the messy details. When I finished, I waited for Sadie's reaction. I'd spent enough time in her company to know she was processing the information. She skipped right over the humiliating part, where I confessed to living in my car, and went straight to the problem.

"So you're pretty indebted to the Masons."

"Yeah."

"Well, at least you're getting a college education from it. You have to look at it that way. It defines your future. You had no choice but to say yes and let the Masons send you to school here."

"I know. I came to the same conclusion."

"Here's something you need to think about. People use other people for self-gain—even expect handouts from others. I think you are different. This family offered you a life. It wasn't something you just expected from them. So I don't think you're using them."

"It doesn't feel that way." I reached for the bottle of water sitting on my nightstand. The hour of talking left my throat dry and scratchy.

"What do you plan to do with your list?"

"I'm not sure just yet. I figured one day the answer would be standing in front of me, or maybe screaming at me. I don't know. The whole thing's a little crazy."

"I'm a planner. You knew that already. I'm not just a Type-A personality, but more like an A-plus. I understand lists. I have lists of lists. Don't roll your eyes. It's true. My future is in those lists. They only work because I have a plan. If you intend to keep your Mason List, then you need to figure out the goal. Otherwise, a list without a tangible plan or purpose will hold you back instead of moving you forward. Something that significant will only become mushed-up nonsense in your brain, distracting you from the important decisions in your life. Trust me on that one, sweetie."

"What would you do with it?"

"I wish I could help, but it's not my life that was affected. I didn't make this one. It's your life and your list. Only you know what resolution will give you a sense of absolution, a sense of peace."

"I wish this wasn't so damn complicated."

"I know. But I understand now, I think."

"You do?"

"Your friendship with Jess is…very complex. And since we are dissecting that blue-eyed cowboy, is Jess as good as I think he is?"

"Sadie! I didn't have sex with him. We're not that kind of friends."

"I wasn't implying that you did. Jess is, oh, how do you put it? That boy has intensity to his personality. He's one of those that you just know from one kiss how the rest will be. I've been on that twisty road, and the end was even better than the beginning. So was it good?"

"It doesn't matter how he makes me feel. There can never be more between us. Not with everything that happened. Jess is a Mason, and he's gonna take over the ranch soon. He will have all the power and could even kick my dad out of the farmhouse if he wanted to."

"You didn't answer my question."

"Fine." I sighed, annoyed. "It was something I can't even explain. You take everything between us. We know each other so well. When he kisses me, it's like I can't even think straight. His lips are so soft, and then his eyes get dark, and I know…what he's thinking. And I can't breathe. Like I can't breathe unless he keeps kissing me…and it takes everything in me to tell him to stop. Because I…I can't *do* this with him. I can't, Sadie. *I just can't.*"

"And that's my point. You need a plan. I'm not sure how you intend to keep this little friendship going the way it is."

"I know." I felt sick hearing her words. It would be a long night.

The next morning, I received a bouquet of tulips. Before I opened the card, I knew the orange flowers came from Jess. My heart beat frantically in my chest seeing his handwriting. We needed this summer apart if I were going to continue taking from his parents.

Beautiful flowers for my beautiful girl. Cheesy as hell, right? But I know one day you'll let me say the real words to you.

—Jess

Chapter 28

Today, 2:27 am.

My father grips the steering wheel. I sit in the passenger seat of his black Ford F150. We pass only one car on the way out of Arlis at this time of night. I'm still awake as the truck gets on the interstate. I want to be asleep, but then again, I want to be awake.

My father looks over in my direction for the hundredth time. "You should try to sleep."

"I'm not tired," I mutter the lie. I'm exhausted in both my body and mind. I rub my fingers over the blue stars inked into my wrist. As the truck whisks down the highway, I seek comfort from the same stars shining through the windows.

"Did I ever tell you about the first time I talked to your mother?"

"What?" I mutter.

"Your mother thought I was crazy." He chuckles a little to himself. "I saw her on this little bench in the park where I took my lunch breaks. She was beautiful, Alex. I'd never seen anyone like her. She had this long, red hair. It's what I noticed first, you know. Made her stand out from all the other girls."

"You liked Mom because of her hair?" The knot in my stomach grew tighter.

"Yeah, I did. It had me all crazy. She came to the park the same time I did every day. I watched her for weeks before I got up the nerve to talk to her. And you know what I did? I told her I loved her."

"The first time you talked to her?"

"I did. Then I spent the next month trying to make her think I wasn't insane. But it was true, you know. I loved your mother the first time I ever saw her. I loved her even more the first time I ever talked to her. The day we got married, and the day you were born, it just got stronger. I still love her now, Alex. It doesn't just stop because someone is gone. I want you to know that."

"What about Caroline?"

"It's complicated, you know. Your mother was the love of my life. When you feel that connected to another person, I think a part of you is just bound to them, even when they're gone. And that's okay. It's how you know the feelings you had for them were real. But what I feel for Caroline is strong, and I do love her. I give her all of what is left."

"She's okay with it?"

"Alex, my feelings for Caroline are more complicated than just a simple answer. Maybe we should save that part for another night." He reaches over and grabs my hand. "I was just trying to help you."

"I know." I swallow hard; my tongue feels like sandpaper. "I stopped thinking about it for a while at least, but it's hard…I don't know what I'm supposed to think. Or what I'm supposed to do anymore."

"Maybe you should try praying for a miracle."

"Don't start with that tonight. I need facts and…and answers."

"Sometimes we don't have concrete facts and answers. Sometimes all we have is faith and hope, and you just have to trust it."

"So I ask for one of your *miracles*. What if I don't get the one I want? What then? I get my hopes up, only to have to experience this all over again?"

"Maybe. I don't know. But you just have to accept the fact you got the miracle that needed to happen."

"What about deserve?" I yank my hand free of his tight grasp.

"I don't understand."

"Maybe I did bad things. Maybe I can't ask for something because I'll just get what I deserve."

"I don't think it really works that way. Don't give up hope, no matter how impossible it feels."

"You believe in miracles. I believe in retribution." Curling up against the window, I start to shake. I wasted so much time doing so many stupid things. I would do anything right now to get those days, months, and even years back.

My shoulders shake as my body tries to hold back a sob. I think about my stupidity. I think about how I would do things differently if given the chance. My thoughts hurt too damn much. The stars haunt me as I cry against the window.

Chapter 29

When I was nineteen...

A week after finals, I drove El Chigger to the luxurious swamp of Louisiana. My destination was just over the border in the middle of no-man's-land, about fifty or so miles east of Beaumont. I followed a long, dirt road that stopped under a sign painted in red letters, CAMP ROCHELLAS.

Hesitating on the brake, I studied the area just through the gravel driveway. I was a little nervous coming to this place alone. Sprayberry had haunted my thoughts, like a comfortable memory, the entire drive here. Part of my soul yearned for another summer on the ranch. Caroline would give me a job in a heartbeat. My father would be thrilled. Jess would be…

It's just a few months, I thought, letting my foot off the pedal. It was time to move forward and meet my new summer companions. Unloading my bags from the trunk, I walked across the worn grass path, following the signs for the staff bunks. The room held a musty scent of old wood and mothballs.

A few people smiled with a hello but talked amongst themselves. I got the impression this was not the first summer for most of the staff. My teeth bit down on my chapped bottom lip. *It's just a few months*, I reminded myself. I came to Rochellas to teach art. Therefore, I would focus on the students.

I began the first two-week rotation trapped in a room with children who preferred PlayStations over painting. The sweet and appreciative students proved to be few and far between. The majority of the kids bordered on obnoxious brats, banished away by their parents for the summer.

On the second day, while adjusting to the grueling hours of Rochellas, I met the first person who bothered to have a conversation with me. He didn't have much choice. I literally crashed into him, knocking us to the mess hall floor in a red explosion of marinara and noodles.

"Shi—" I caught my words, trying to honor the counselor rules. I looked into a set of humorous brown eyes, resting under blond, scraggly hair. "I'm so sorry. It's my fault."

"You have noodles in your hair."

"Shi—" My face turned red as I swatted at pasta hanging next to my ears. This day just grew increasingly better. I had overslept this morning and missed breakfast. Now, my lunch was on the floor, and I was covered in marinara. My afternoon class started in fifteen minutes. Those little brats were brutal. Just a splatter of sauce would turn this group into an unruly, laughing riot until their parents picked them up next Friday.

"Here, let me help you. I'm Dutch, by the way." He held out a tan hand for me to shake. My eyes followed up his brown arm that led to a cutoff shirt sleeve.

"Alex." I clasped his fingers for a moment, then let go to grab a napkin.

"Alex, huh?" Dutch took the white paper from my hand and removed the sauce from my right thigh. He wiped in slow movements. "Those are some nice legs. Way too long and sexy to belong to some Alex. You sure it's not Lexie?"

"Are you for real?" I blurted out laughing.

"How real do you want me to be?" Dutch stood up, flashing a grin that probably worked on most girls, or just life in general. Grabbing my hand, he pulled me up from the puddle of scattered food. "So what hellish activity did you get pegged with this year?"

"Art."

"That's intense, being cooped up with those rich brats in a room. You should try switching to the boats. You'll get the best tan of the summer."

"I like art."

"We'll see if you do at the end of the first session. I gotta run now. I'm a lifeguard. Poolside, not lake. See you around, Lexie."

He sauntered off barefoot from the mess hall. I noticed his blond, surfer hair had lighter streaks from the sun, or maybe he actually highlighted it. Rolling my eyes, I contemplated the only person who had bothered to notice my arrival at camp. He was pretty as in pretty hair, pretty skin, and pretty damn self-assured—a combination I assumed got the attention of most enamored females, including me as I watched his ass disappear out the door.

That evening, I arrived alone in the mess hall for dinner. I heard a girl laughing before I even approached the rusted door. My stomach grumbled as I made a beeline for the food.

"Lexie!"

I stacked a small salad on my tray and something resembling meatloaf. I grabbed a bowl of macaroni and cheese. My stomach grumbled, so I grabbed a second one.

"Lexie!"

I turned around, hearing the voice again. At a table by the window, the blond boy named Dutch waved in my direction. I walked over and hesitantly took the empty seat next to two other staff.

"Hey, you survived. I was afraid the little shitters tied you up in that hellhole."

"Oh, um…no."

"So, Lexie, this is Darcy and Brecken." I tensed at his use of my new nickname again. I wanted to correct him but held my tongue in front of his friends.

"The hot girl with the sexy name." Darcy smiled, and my face got red with her comment. She had full lips, accented with a tiny Cindy Crawford mole above the left side. "I'm just kiddin'. Well, not really. Isn't that what you called her, Dutch?"

"Don't be a bitch, Darcy." Dutch glared in her direction.

She flipped him off, then looked at me. "Don't believe the crap Dutch says about us. This is my second year at Camp *Hell-as*. Dutch and Brecken's third." Her blonde hair hung in damp waves around a cutoff yellow Rochellas T-shirt that covered her swimsuit. Looking closer, I realized it was her lacy, black bra cups poking out from the ripped neck.

"Ain't she his new Hatchet House girl?" Brecken spoke up from his sleepy trance. The pupils of his eyes waved in and out above a full face of hair.

"What's a Hatchet House?"

"Ignore my dumbass friend." Dutch elbowed Brecken. "He's a little… um…preoccupied right now."

"She wants to know about the Hatchet House, Dutch. You should go ahead and tell her. It's not like she won't find out." Darcy cackled again in that obnoxious voice.

"Shut up." The cut of his brown eyes shut her down this time. He turned his attention back to me as I chewed another bite of meatloaf. "So, Lexie, you should hang out tonight with us. We've got this little tradition out on the docks during the brats' campfire night. It's an invitation-only party. Really laid-back."

Dutch casually touched my shoulder as he talked. His fingers slid down my arm, ending with an accidental boob brush. I couldn't help but smile at the innocence he tried to project from his brown eyes.

Dutch was good at blatant flirting while shuffling it behind a slow, rugged smile, which reminded me of a California beach version of James Franco. Charisma and charm are not just acquired; people like Dutch are just born with it. So was another person I knew. I swallowed, blocking out the thought.

"So who goes to the docks?" The question came as I scooted back into my own personal space. I wondered if this were an actual party or a private invite to get me alone.

"Brecken, Darcy, and a few others."

"I don't know. I'm not much of a water person."

"Oh, we don't get in the water." Brecken perked up, his hazy smile buried beneath the brown whiskers on his face. "You have to come, Lexie. It's what makes the summer with those little shits bearable."

"He's right, you know." Dutch leaned in a little closer, resting a hand on the side of my chair. I felt the slight brush of his fingers against my bare thigh. They lingered just below the frayed denim. He smiled again, and my stare dropped to his lips.

"Okay, I'll come." I took his hand off my leg, but Dutch held onto my fingers. His arched eyebrows dared me to pull away. *Charming bastard.* I almost laughed in his face.

I knew of guys like Dutch. The type that left you saying, "What the hell just happened?" The only difference: I never had one set his sights on me. I was an average tomboy, who was cursed with red hair and freckles. I guess camp made life an even playing field; everyone took a cold shower and wallowed around in the same dirt.

Dutch let go of my fingers and rested his hand on my inner thigh. It happened so fast, I wasn't sure what to do. Darcy jumped up from the table and came around in my direction. She slapped his hand away from my leg.

"Stop touching her, you jackass. Come on! Let's get ready for the party." She stood about five inches shorter than me. Linking an arm through mine, she pulled my taller body from the chair. She gave me no choice except to follow her out the door.

Darcy pulled a pack of Virginia Slims from her shredded, ass-hugging shorts. She gestured in my direction, but I gave a quick shake, signaling *no.* In the night air, she blew out a cloud of smoke between us. She flicked the ash, with a half-interested gaze over my plain, gray T-shirt.

"Do I need to change for this party?" Not sure why I even threw out the question since each suitcase had more of the same.

"Nah. It's on the docks. You're cute, you know. In that natural way."

"Okay?"

"He likes the cutesy, fresh ones."

"Fresh?"

"Something new to catch his attention. Here's the deal, Lexie. I don't wanna get mixed up in whatever game he's runnin' with you." Pulling in another drag, she blew a ring of smoke, filling my lungs with more second-hand smoke.

"I can't tell if you like his bullshit or are just too naive to see it. Either way, Dutch is fun. Pulls you in real nice with all his little compliments and smiles, makin' you feel all hot and dazed. Then bam! Don't trust the bastard. Cute as a puppy, then he sneaks up and bites your ass."

"Thanks, I guess?"

"Should see your face." Her quips of laugher propelled white clouds from her nostrils. "He's not actually going to put teeth marks on your butt. Well…I don't know. I haven't seen him since last summer. Who the hell knows what he's into these days."

Her sharp-pitched cackles seemed out of place within the quiet campgrounds. Contemplating her warnings, I took the quips with a grain of salt. Besides, I had no intentions of having a torrid summer fling with *any* boy, let alone Dutch. My life was already a complicated mess.

"So what's this Hatchet House?"

"Oh, hell, I might as well tell you. It's a lawn shed about half a mile or so in the woods away from main grounds. It's full of equipment and shit they want to keep away from the kids. The staff uses it for quick, ass-grabbin' sex. Not much privacy in the bunks, you know. If you get asked up there, or I guess I should say *when* that bastard charms your cotton panties off. Better be damn flexible so you don't touch anythin'. That place has more STDs than a sorority bitch on spring break."

Darcy pulled in another drag, waiting for my reaction. The girl scared me a little, like an angry, fighting pit bull, latching on teeth and nails. The smoke blew out of her noise as she laughed. "I'm just messin' with you."

"People don't hook up there?"

"Nah, they do. You're just fun to talk to because I can't shock many people anymore. You get this petrified look. Kinda fun."

I trotted along beside Darcy. She took me to the back corner of the bunks. Under her bed, she pulled out a wood crate. My eyes grew wide seeing the contents inside.

"Now, Lexie, if you're plannin' to come to these things, you'll have to contribute. Can't have you moochin' on all the good stuff."

"Okay," I swallowed.

The party provided a glimpse into the darker and wilder side of camp. Rochellas was a college student's hazy summer job and the worst nightmare of a camper's parents, if they knew the morality of those who cared for their precious, undisciplined offspring.

Seven of the staff met up on the docks to partake in a tub of hard liquor and large amount of pot, consumed in joints as well as a few bongs. As it turns out, Brecken was preoccupied during our dinner in the mess hall. "High as shit in the trees" was the term Dutch used. He swore it was just a summer thing for most of them, except for Brecken.

As the newest invitee to the dock, I listened as the group swapped stories from past years. Brecken, who supervised archery, chose not to shower all summer. "If you smelled like shit, the little shitters kept their distance." He used his idea to drive the campers away so he could sip on a flask and take midday naps against a tree.

I cringed, listening to Darcy's story. Last summer the group had one party that got a little out of hand. The staff faced the next day hungover and irritable as hell. Darcy slipped the kids Benadryl, and then loaded them up on the boat for a ride out to the middle of the lake. She passed out across the steering wheel, nursing one hell of a hangover, while the kids took a nap on top of a pile of life jackets. They floated for hours, almost reaching the other side of the lakeshore.

Darcy said something regarding Dutch, but Brecken shut her down fast. Actually, he gave her a slight push that ended with one big splash in the lake. She clawed up the side, pulling his lawn chair over backward. Water sprayed up while angry words echoed from the black pool.

"That's not fair, you know. I didn't hear your worst camp story," I teased Dutch, looking into his brown eyes. He leaned forward and kissed me instead of answering. His lips tasted slightly of bitter tea. It was different than kissing Jess; the confused thoughts drifted through my mind. It was different but good. I wanted Dutch to kiss me again because it was easy with him.

The days flew by with the turnover of new campers every two weeks. I ate every meal with Dutch, Darcy, and Brecken. As a person who once survived on vending machine drivel, I never complained about the lack of gourmet food while the others ripped the shit out of the mess hall staff.

Several nights each week, my new friends held an invitation-only party on the docks. I stayed clear of the drugs even though it was tempting to fade into the smoky escape. Those nights offered a relaxing time in the summer away from our kid duties.

Darcy taught me how to play quarters, and I got pretty good at a few drinking games. Other nights, the group gambled cleaning duties by playing Texas Hold 'Em. I cleaned the toilets for days in a row until Brecken taught me how to cheat.

Sometimes we just chilled out on the dock drinking, or in the case of the others, smoking. Once in a while, we hooked up Darcy's iPod. She liked to dance all swanky and nasty in the humid air. I danced with her a few times. My father would have yanked me right off those wooden boards if he saw me. Dutch, on the other hand, liked to watch us.

I knew these people were crazy and unconventional as hell, but they were nice to me, with minimal pressure to partake in their recreational drug use. I preferred to think of it that way instead of the reality: my friends were high more often than sober, but they made me feel welcome. That's what mattered most at camp.

Everyone lived by Dutch's unwritten rule of Rochellas: "Never talk about the world outside the red arched sign because it ruins the high." I didn't know majors, hometowns, or even the colleges attended by most of the staff. I didn't know their families or even if they had siblings. The most important piece: they didn't know a single thing about Alex Tanner.

One night as I sat on the boat dock, it occurred to me that most of these people assumed I really was *Lexie.* I never bothered to correct the nicknamed dubbed by Dutch's attempt to flirt on the day we met. This summer, I *could* be someone else. The idea felt new and invigorating, like an Etch A Sketch shaken until clean.

At Rochellas, this Lexie never lost a mother to cancer. She never watched the world pick through her belongings as the sky fell all around her. This fun-filled girl was never dragged to another town, only to be homeless. She never experienced the glares, taunts, or pity from a place that survived on gossip. Most importantly, this camp never heard of a Mason and this *Lexie* owed them absolutely nothing. I was free of everything.

I spent most of that free time at the pool, laughing at Dutch. I wasn't under the delusion our friendship was exclusive. My intensions were strictly platonic, which blurred occasionally as time went on at camp.

"Friends with flirting benefits," at least that's what he called it. Every time he kissed me, I enjoyed it. Dutch was just so damn good at sucking me into his irrational thoughts, a seamless transition from laughing to flirting to being touched by a guy who was intoxicating with experience.

Deep down, I knew he didn't care about me. He just liked having fun and pulled you along for the ride. That's all I wanted too, but I made it very clear: friends with flirting benefits included absolutely no sex.

Even with that one little rule, I still had fun with Dutch, at least until my past invaded my present. Those were the days when I called Jess and my problems came right back to haunt me. We didn't talk much while I was at camp since it required a short hike to a clearing in the swampy woods to get cell phone reception.

He was always sweet on the phone, his familiar voice grabbing me right in the chest. Most of the calls were much of the same. Jess said Arlis sucked without me. The town's notorious were up to their usual. Skeeter Rawlins got drunk in the middle of a Tuesday and fell off Nickel Bridge, breaking an arm and a few ribs. My father's proposal to Caroline over Memorial Day weekend still traveled around in some circles as the latest news. The residents counted down the days to the fall wedding and the lucrative invite to a party at Sprayberry.

The grass fires north of Arlis, filled Jeeter's and the feedstore with ongoing conversations about those affected by the blaze. Jess promised he was nowhere near the area with fireworks. He ran into a few of our classmates, including Ashley. She was driving down Main Street one afternoon, and he flipped her off just because it made him feel better.

Every time we talked, the warmth of his voice and familiarity of our words became harder to bear. It was inevitable I would miss Jess, but I didn't expect it to be this difficult hearing him on the phone. I knew him too well. I knew the words that caused his eyebrows to wrinkle up. I knew that when Jess sounded frustrated, he pushed the hair off his forehead. I knew the exact way his tongue absently licked his upper lip when he talked about eating a hamburger from Jeeter's. I knew the way Jess smiled as he teased me from hundreds of miles away.

Sometimes I think it was just easier when the bars on my cell phone showed no service. I didn't have to deal with the awful pain he caused in my chest.

The weekend after the Fourth of July, I left with Dutch and a few others for a much-needed sabbatical and my first trip to New Orleans. Bourbon Street looked exactly how I imagined: fun and full of booze and sex. We hit the strip, crawling between the bars, leaving a trail of alcohol tabs for those twenty-one or in the possession of fake IDs. My plastic Texas license held a picture of twenty-three-year-old Lexie Carter from Nacogdoches. Dutch set up my new ID two weeks ago when he mailed a picture, along with my 200 bucks, to someone he knew in Houston.

As we entered a small club, I was already drunk from the shots I pounded in the last two bars. Dutch pulled me to the middle of the cramped dance floor. He smiled an intoxicating grin as we intertwined in a dirty grind.

Usher's smooth voice drifted through the bar as I pressed my back into Dutch's chest. He leaned in, kissing my neck as his fingers slid across my stomach and over my hips, pulling me hard against his body. We danced under strobe lights; it was hot and sweaty and sexy. I turned around, tasting his rum-coated lips as he slipped his tongue in my mouth. The alcohol moved through my body and the room got a little hazy, making me forget people could see us.

Dutch dipped me low to the floor, slowly grinding against my hips to a Timberlake song. "Lex, you have to stay with me," Dutch whispered in my ear.

I shook my head *no.*

"Come on, baby. It's our night. You can't leave me hangin' like this. You want it too. I can feel it."

"I'm staying with Darcy. You know that already."

"Darcy is not staying in your room tonight. She'll be tied up with whoever the hell has his hand up her shirt over there."

"Matt."

"Good for you. More than Darcy will bother to know. Come on, we shouldn't both be lonely. I could just stay in your room and talk, Lexie..." His soft, caressing use of my nickname always made me feel a little wilder. Dutch inched his hand over the back of my jeans, his fingers tracing the edge of the pocket.

"Is that what you're calling it now? I'm not *talking* with you tonight." I pulled back, watching his face turn into a pout. "Come on, let's keep dancing."

"Maybe I should find someone else who really wants to dance."

"Maybe you should. There's a whole room full of them." I let go of his body and gestured out toward the floor. "I'll find someone else to entertain me."

Turning in the opposite direction, I walked toward the counter and sat down on the wooden barstool. Brecken would be back soon, and I could just hang with him for the rest of the night. Dutch was fun, but I was not caving to his pressure. I felt a set of hands go around my waist and flatten across my stomach. His thumbs rubbed back and forth over the sides of my breasts.

"None of them dance as good as you, Lex." His lips pressed into the skin of my neck. Damn, he was persistent. I let him pull me off the barstool and back toward the floor, keeping a possessive arm around my waist. Dutch couldn't verbally convince me to change my mind, but he did his best to break the wall down with his body.

My attraction to Dutch was different than my attraction to Jess. Dutch caused something to stir in me that felt very sexual and exciting but at the same time, not fulfilling, like eating a whole tub of frosting without a single crumb of cake.

On the other hand, Jess made me feel something unexplainable. Thoughts of the dark-haired boy clouded the moment. I knew it was only a matter of time before he interrupted my weekend shenanigans. Jess wasn't here, yet he was everywhere.

A pain stabbed me right in the chest. I abruptly let go of Dutch and walked to the bar for another shot. Suddenly, the idea of his hands on my body made me feel nauseated.

In the early morning hours, Dutch and I left with a few others to wander down Bourbon Street to a tattoo parlor. I watched as the others picked out barbed designs to commemorate the drunken summer of Rochellas. They took turns getting inked as I drew on a napkin in the corner.

"Lex, you can't just sit there on your ass. We are in this sick tattoo parlor in New…Aw…lins." Dutch's loud, drunk voice drew the syllables out like a stadium announcer, sending Brecken in a high-pitch howl.

"Hells yeah!" Breck took another swig out of the tequila bottle he picked up somewhere on the street.

"Hey, let me see that." Dutch grabbed my doodle on the napkin. "Damn, girl! You are good. Nope. No backing out now. That would look cool as shit right there." He flipped over my arm, pointing at the bracelets tied on my inner wrist. "I can see it right there all twisty and hot, inked into that sweet-ass skin."

"Dutch, I can't do that. It's permanent."

"You're like this crazy, freaky-cool artist." He intertwined our hands, tracing my Luscious Pokeweed painted nails. "What better way to say, 'I've got it. I've got so much talent, I put it right here'? You have to do it."

"I don't know." I looked wide-eyed back at my doodle. It was a quick, wispy sketch, reminiscent of a Celtic design I once saw in an art book.

"Come on, Lexie. Lexie!" Dutch chanted. After a few seconds, every drunken patron of the fine establishment had joined in on his charming antics.

"Oh, screw it. But it has to be a small version of it. Breck, give me that bottle."

"Oh, yeah! That's what I'm talkin' about."

I needed some liquid courage and hoped my nervous stomach could keep it down. Dutch gave me a slap on the ass as I took a seat. The burly guy, in a Tesla rock T-shirt, grabbed the scissors to clip off the strands.

"Wait!" Reaching in the midst, I unlatched the one in memory of BB, stuffing the braided band snug in my hip pocket. My lips planted on the bottle for another swig. "Okay. Let's do it."

During the cleaning and prepping, I felt the buzzy vibe of the tequila. The artist transferred my picture to a stick on stencil. The excitement built, watching the prototype come to life.

"Shit!" I sputtered as the first needle stab hurt like a bitch.

I watched the beautiful picture develop into a four-inch-long design, with loopy edges scrawling around my wrist. It glowed in the same purple shade as my nails. When the tattoo guy finished, my eyes grew wide; I was permanently inked with my own artwork.

Stumbling back to the cheap motel, I clung to Dutch with my marked arm. I was drunk—the dizzy kind of drunk that slurred my words. Outside my room, he pushed me against the wall and leaned in for a kiss, letting his weight settle against my body. His tongue slipped over mine, blocking any protest to stop.

Rational thoughts moved at a sluggish speed, hoping everyone was asleep and not meandering back to their rooms only to catch a peep show. He slipped his fingers in the waistband of my jeans, causing ticklish tremors on my skin.

"Tickle massacre." His laughing blue eyes popped into memory, bringing back all the times Jess held me down until I screamed for mercy in hysterical laughter.

Dutch flicked the button free and inched the zipper down. He pushed his hand down inside the denim. "Mercy." The word slipped out, meaning nothing to him.

"Huh?"

"You need to let me go." I tried to step to the side, but I lost one of my shoes.

"Lexie, baby." His eyes sagged in a heavy trance. "Don't leave me hangin'. I need you so bad it hurts."

To the right, a door slammed open, catching us both off-guard. Darcy came out wearing only a tight, white T-shirt and hot-pink panties. I could see through both of them. "Get your perv-y hands off her, jackass."

She pulled me toward the room, giving Dutch no option but to back off or fall down. They exchanged a wordless conversation of angry attraction. In that moment, I was positive there was truth behind the theory that Dutch and Darcy had hooked up at some point in the dirty past of Rochellas.

"Mind your own damn business," Dutch growled in her face.

Darcy let loose a string of expletives and slammed the door. Tequila swirled around in my stomach as I collapsed on my bed. Good save, even if it came from her twisted jealousy. Darcy threw the lost shoe in my direction and stormed back out into the hallway in those pink panties, slamming the door again.

Alone in the cheap room, I contemplated the events of the evening. The dark-haired boy invaded every translucent thought circling in my tequila-filled brain. In a moment of weakness, I picked up my phone and waited for his familiar sound to float through the buzzy rings.

"Alex?" Hearing his sleepy voice, I felt like I'd slipped on my favorite sweatshirt from a bottom drawer. A warm, peaceful feeling spread from my chest through the rest of my body.

"Hey," I whispered.

"What time is it?"

"It's really late."

"Somethin' wrong?" His voice got a little more alert. In the background, I heard the rustling of sheets as he sat up in his bed. I knew they were blue sheets. He was sitting in bed, shirtless, against his blue sheets, pushing his dark hair off his forehead.

"No, I…" My nails dug into my palm. "I was just thinking about some stuff."

"Are you out in the woods this late alone?"

"No, I'm actually…I'm with Darcy." It wasn't a total lie, but I couldn't tell Jess I was in New Orleans.

"Everythin' okay?"

"Yeah, it's fine. Sorry, I know it's late. I'll let you go."

The line held a pause. I pictured those troubled eyebrows contemplating the real purpose of my call in the middle of the night. Jess would worry and stay awake, tossing around after I hung up. Stupid drunk calling. I just wanted to hear his voice, and the alcohol let my guard down.

"You can call me anytime, Al," he whispered on the other end of the phone. "I don't care how late it is."

"I know, but you have to get up early."

"I do, but I don't care. Talk to me, Al. What's wrong?"

"I'm fine. I'm just waiting on Darcy while she…um…calls someone."

"I hear it in your voice." He sounded so sweet, and it grabbed me in the chest.

"I'm just tired."

"Okay." The line was silent, and then he whispered, "I miss you, Al."

My eyes closed, hearing his voice swirl around in the darkness. "I miss the sound of your voice…your beautiful face. I miss your laugh." I forgot I was in New Orleans as I listened to his sleepy, pancake-syrup-coated words. "The way you act all mad but still smile at me. I miss the way your lips turn up a little on the right side…when you're tryin' to tease me back. Do you even know you do that?"

"No," I whispered.

"It's how I know when you're lyin' too."

"I don't lie."

"No?" He chuckled in a deep voice. "I miss this. I miss talking to you…watchin' your lips move. I miss that freckle right next to the bottom one…the way it's sorta on your skin and your lip. Makes me want to kiss it…taste it."

"Jess…" I whispered, feeling my skin burn in a way that only he could make happen.

He let out a deep breath. "I know, I'm not supposed to say that stuff. I just wish summer was over. I miss seeing you."

"I know." I swallowed hard. "Good night, Jess."

"Okay, I'll let you go. Night, Alex."

We stayed on the phone a good minute, listening to each other breathe until I finally hung up. The pounding in my chest vibrated in my ears, thanks to the alcohol. In the hazy buzz, I pictured his sweet face and blue eyes, and those pink lips that felt so good when he kissed me. I whispered out loud in the dark, empty room what I couldn't say to him on the phone.

"I miss you too."

Chapter 30

When I was nineteen...

I sat at the pool, watching Dutch pretend to monitor the kids. He took another swing out of a flask then grinned at me. After we returned to Rochellas, Dutch and I had resumed as flirting friends, but things were different. Guilt ate into every free moment, making it all feel terribly wrong. I remained confused about the past and what to do about the future. It lurked around every turn of the shadowy woods. Once again, Jess was not here; yet he was everywhere, haunting my resolve to set him free.

The gate banged closed, catching my attention. I slipped off my sunglasses, seeing Franny from the main office. "Hey, some guy named Jess called for directions off the highway. He was at the main turnoff. Should be here in, like, ten minutes."

I jumped out of my chair, knocking my sunglasses in the pool. "No! Oh, crap, no!" A violent attack of nausea kicked in my stomach.

"Who's Jess?" Dutch asked from his chair.

I struggled to get the flimsy cover over my suit. "He's…um." I couldn't even get my flip-flops on my feet. "He's…someone from high school. We grew up together."

"You're from Abilene, right?"

"No, Arlis. Um, I've gotta go."

I sprinted out the gate toward the parking lot. *Why did I call Jess?* Stupid, stupid, drunk, idiotic, phone call summed this visit to Rochellas. This was bad in so many ways.

I was out of breath and panting as I watched his white truck pull into the parking lot. Maybe I could tell him I'm too sick for visitors and then throw up in front of him. It wouldn't take much; the nausea was about to choke me. He parked in an empty spot. I gritted my fingers into my palms. *The tattoo!* I wrapped the towel around my wrist, just as he climbed out of the truck.

Jess smiled, and I felt a quick stab of pain in my chest. He looked good. Jess always got darker in the summer, and it made his blue eyes even brighter. His arms slipped around my waist in a hug, lifting my feet up from the gravel. My whole body was touching him, feeling him, until Jess placed me back down.

"So…surprise?" He grinned at me.

"I know. You should have called."

"Then it wouldn't have been a surprise." His eyes flickered over my clothes, which were virtually see-through. "You swimmin' now?"

My fingers clenched the towel draped over my left wrist. I felt nervous. "No, I just…um…sit at the pool sometimes."

"Well, you must do it a lot. You look good, Al."

"Thanks." My fingers fidgeted around again, feeling a loss for words. "Well, I guess, grab your stuff. We can drop it off, and then I'll give you the glamorous tour."

"Glamorous? I thought you said it smelled like swamp shit here."

"It does, but I guess it's better than your armpit of death after being on the tractor."

"Jerk." Jess reached over and whacked me on the arm. He grinned at me, and it almost felt normal. In the distance, I saw Dutch walking back from the pool. The spiral of apprehension returned when I realized the inevitable: they would meet, and there was nothing I could do about it.

Jess followed me down the trail to the dorms. He chattered, and I half-listened to some stupid story about Skeeter. He claimed to see Jesus that afternoon in the murky creek bed as he lay passed out from his fall. Skeeter had wandered into Main Street Church last Sunday and sat right down on the third pew, making Mrs. Ida Flemming and Mrs. Crawford scoot to the middle of the row. The ladies watched Skeeter with wide eyes, fanning themselves as they were bumped from the very spot they'd occupied for the last forty years.

"It was funny. One of the usher's dropped the offerin' plate, and it hit the wood floor." He stopped walking and looked at me. "You okay?"

"I'm fine."

"You don't seem fine. No snarky comment 'bout Skeeter. I thought it would make you laugh."

"I'm laughing." I smiled at him. "Why don't you wait here? I'm going to change, then we can eat dinner before your tour." I hoped if we went early, maybe we could avoid the rest of them.

I rushed Jess through the food line, practically throwing things on his tray. We settled at a spot in the back corner, far from my usual table I shared with Dutch, Brecken, and Darcy.

"You're not sayin' much," Jess commented, while I scanned the room again for signs of Dutch.

"It's been a long week. I'm surprised you're attempting to eat that." I gestured toward his burger.

"I know. Caroline has me spoiled. You know she's got one of the girls bringin' me food out to Sprayberry."

"What kind of tip gets that service?"

"You should know." He winked.

I scanned the room again, just in time to see Dutch walk in the side entrance. He spotted me immediately and waved in our direction. I sat frozen in place, fork in mid-bite.

"Hey, what's wrong?"

"What…um…" I muttered. I couldn't even speak as I watched Dutch get closer and closer to our table with Brecken.

"Hey, Lexie." Brecken reached for our usual high five. *Shit!* I held a palm up, keeping my eyes away from Jess. Dutch sat down next to me while Brecken pulled a chair up on the other side by Jess.

"I'm Dutch, and the guy with serial-killer beard is Brecken."

"Jess," he grunted, shaking both of their hands. So far, so good, but I knew it was just the beginning.

"You grew up with Lex?" Dutch asked as he put an arm around my shoulders, letting his hand linger a moment against the back of my neck.

"Uh, yeah, I guess." His eyes moved from me, then over to Dutch, trying to piece together something that wasn't clear yet.

"Cool. Cool." Dutch reached over with his fork to grab my discarded tomatoes from my plate. He raised the bun of his burger to mash them inside. "Sorry, man, I hate to say you picked a really dull time to visit. Lex, you should have invited him to Bourbon Street last weekend with us. Now that was some fun shit."

"You were in New Orleans. Last Saturday." The words came not as a question, but a deadpan accusation.

"Yeah…um…briefly." I wasn't sure what to do at this point. The tension inside my head felt as if it would explode, leaving bits of brain matter across the table.

"Where do you work at the camp?" Jess glared at Dutch.

"I'm a lifeguard. Poolside, not lake."

"You work at the swimmin' pool." Jess looked back at me. *He knew.*

"Best damn job here. Little work and everyone likes to hang out with you. Right, Lexie?"

I swallowed hard, not answering.

"Hey, pass me the ketchup." Dutch tapped my hand. I reached up and grabbed the bottle, forgetting about my exposed wrist.

Jess yanked my arm across the table, staring at the inked design. His jaw clenched tight. "We need to talk. *Now!*" That last word came out as a low growl. His eyes burned from just a few feet away. I'd never seen him so angry at me.

"Okay."

Getting out of my seat, I went to the door, feeling his presence right behind me. I never looked back the entire trip down the dirt path to the lake. I took a deep breath and sat down on a log, expecting him to join me. He paced around the trail.

"Why don't you sit down?" I tried to keep my voice even. This would be a fight. We both knew it, but maybe I could calm him down.

"What are you doin' here?" His voice was so deep, so angry.

"I don't understand."

"Don't play dumb. You're the smartest person I know. What are you doin'? This camp and these people. Who the hell is Lexie?"

"It's just a camp nickname, Jess. It doesn't mean anything."

"That Dutch guy not *mean* anythin' either?"

"We're friends."

"*Right.* Guys like him are not just friends. I don't like him, and he reeked of pot." The disgusted sneer on his lips broke through my reserve of trying to keep this peaceful.

"You don't know him!"

"I'm startin' to think I don't know you. It's like you created an entire new identity."

"It's not like that."

"I don't know how else you would explain it."

"It wasn't intentional. It just sort of happened." I could see that was the wrong answer to his question. Jess crossed the distance between us and yanked my arm up, shoving it close to my face.

"That tattoo just sort of happen too, or was it his idea?"

"It's just a tattoo, and I drew it. It's one of my pictures."

"I have your pictures. That's not one of 'em." He let go of my arm, throwing it out like a dirty rag.

"Jess, don't be this way." His eyes followed every curve of my body from my hair down to my gray tennis shoes. I felt a little exposed under the radar of scrutiny. Was he looking for another permanent embellishment on my body or something deeper?

"I have to know." His pushed his hair back off his forehead. "Is this what you meant last summer? When you fed me that bullshit? Is this what you really wanted? This place and these people and pretendin' to be someone else?"

"Maybe I want to forget about who I am. Just for a little bit. Being here around these people—I haven't felt like poor, pathetic Alex. It was nice."

"You can't just erase your past."

"Why can't I?"

"You just can't. Because it erases…" The realization died on his lips.

"You?"

"Yes. You can't pretend I don't exist. That we aren't us. I told you I would wait for you."

"I told you not to. You kissed me. It was nice. We decided to be just friends. End of story."

"Bullshit!"

"No, it's not."

"It's complete bullshit, and you know it!"

"You're right. It's bullshit because you haven't been some angel waiting around for me. You were with other people too."

"Other people? You mean the assigned sorority pledges for date parties? Damn it, Alex! Those were not choices. Those were not *other girls*. I haven't been with any other girl since I told you how I felt."

"You have got to be kidding me? Dutch is no different than your other girls."

"Nothin' happened with them, and you know it. Stop tryin' to make excuses. Stop tryin' to deny you've done absolutely nothin' with a guy like that. Al, come on."

"Don't *Al* me!" I jumped up and stood just a few inches from his face.

"Fine, *Lexie*, or whatever the hell your name is!" His nostrils flared as he continued to shout in my face. "We are apart for one summer, and your common sense goes down the shitter. You apparently don't seem to care 'bout what I think or feel. I thought we had an understandin' 'bout our future."

"*We* are not together. There is no *our* future."

"It's been *we* since *we* were eight!" The smell of his breath came with fine drops of spit landing on my cheeks. I didn't budge. Each syllable of his words seemed to leave a lingering echo in the trees.

"My friend. That's it." My body stayed planted right in his face as I stressed the painful words back. "That was our understanding. You can't tell me who else I can be friends with. It's none of your business."

"It's my business because you are supposed to be with me…you're mine!"

"Damn it! You don't own me, *Jessup Mason!* Not *you* or your *damn parents*. No one does."

"Shit! I didn't mean it that way."

"There's no other way to mean that." My body shook with each ragged breath. The anger consumed my emotions, causing my palms to clench tight.

"Okay, fine. I meant it that way. I'm not gonna deny it. But there's still the part of you that's my friend. I'm tryin' to look out for you, but you're makin' it damn near impossible."

"You aren't looking out for me. This is not about us being friends. You are trying to dictate what I do here."

"What exactly *are* you doin' here? Tryin' to prove some point? Is this really what you want? Someone like Dutch? Some pot-smoking asshole? You do that now too, *Lexie*? You smoke a little, then *fuck* him?"

"*Shut up!*" I yelled, cutting him off.

"What? You don't like the truth thrown in your face? Hit a nerve, *Lexie*?" he sneered. "How'd it make you feel, knowin' you were wedged right in between half the other girls he had this summer? All the pathetic morons who fell for his lies that made them feel special. Did that get rid of all those *sad* feelin's of being poor Alex and your horrible past of havin' nowhere to go so you were forced to live at Sprayberry with me?"

"Stop it!" I couldn't believe he would be so mean, bringing up the very thing that haunted me. "You're being a complete asshole. I don't even know who you are right now, Jess."

"Don't know who *I* am? Really? You are so unbelievable. You created an entire new identity to be with someone else."

"You act like I'm some commune-brainwashed druggie slut."

"Your words, not mine, but that pretty much sums it up," he spat back.

I felt so angry, even my skin hurt; my fingers balled up into fists. "You have no idea how much I hate you right now."

"Feelin' is mutual."

"No one asked you to come here."

"Well, I guess you're right on that one. I thought you would be happy to see me after you made that phone call. Now, I know it came from *New Orleans*, where you went with him. Waste of time and gas drivin' halfway across the state to see if you were okay."

"I'm sure it won't make a dent in your precious Mason trust fund."

"Really? You're stoopin' to that? Alex, you have always been snarky, but as Lexie, you're just a complete *bitch!*" He crossed the few steps to shout the insult straight into my face.

"*I'm* the bitch? *You're* the spoiled, rich asshole. Just like all the rumors in Arlis."

"You mean the same rumors that said you're a *homeless slut.* Oh, wait, I guess that's all true now."

I slapped him.

The sting radiated across my palm from the force I put into the hit. This conversation needed to end before something catastrophic happened, but I think it was already too late. I had hit Jess, and he looked like he wanted to drown me in the lake.

"We need to stop." It came out breathless as I focused on the ground to break our murderous eye contact. "Take a break."

"You want a break? That's what you really want?"

"Yes." I looked up and bit down hard on my lip.

"Then fine! You can have your damn break." Jess gave me a brief look as to say, "It's your final chance." I watched his body turn and stock off down the trail.

I'd never hated Jess in the past. He made it impossible to truly hate that sweet, smiling face. Oh, I had been mad at him plenty of times, but it was never true repulsion. Tonight was different. Hidden in my gut, I knew his accusations came not from anger but something far deeper. I was slowly breaking his heart, and the pain oozed out in dagger strikes. Even in his devastation, I didn't deserve something like this from my best friend. We were not together. Yet, he made me feel like some lying, cheating tramp.

I sat on the log by the lake for almost an hour. This was a mess, like a clusterfuck of a mess. I really hit him. How was that even possible? It was his fault. He pushed and pushed, and I broke. I took a deep breath in my nose, counted to five, and released it out across the night air. I needed to calm down and then go back. Maybe we could have a civil, adult conversation about our situation.

I returned to camp, but Jess was gone. He had packed up and left after our fight. The rage inside me grew. How dare he just leave! Our problem wasn't settled. He just drove off in the middle of the night, after showing up unannounced, spouting off hurtful and hateful words.

I should call Sadie. I snuffed the rational thought the moment it hit my brain. Instead, a switch flipped in my mind as I mulled through his terrible words over and over again, like a broken record player. I stomped through the camp, looking for my target. Dutch sat on a bench just out of sight from the mess hall. I watched him exhale a faint cloud into the hair. He had a bag of Funyuns in his hand.

"Hey."

"Hey, Lexie. You okay? Your face is—"

"I'm fine." I cut his words off with a snip. I took the joint from his fingers and stared down at the faint glow on the tip. Fumbling with it a moment, I looked back into his confused face. "I just wanted to know if you're busy. Give me twenty minutes, and I'll meet you at the Hatchet House."

"Sure?" Surprise flickered across his cheeks, then a smile formed on his lips. "Um…that sounds good."

"Okay then." I lifted the end to my lips and pulled in a long drag, only to succumb to a fit of coughing.

"You shouldn't take in so much at once. That's some pure-grade shit I don't share with those losers. Here, let me show you how—"

"I'm fine," I sputtered. Taking a step back, I recovered enough to try again. My lips clamped down, and I inhaled a small drag that bubbled out with just a small throat clear. I sucked in another puff. It was easier now, so I pulled in three or four more before I handed the joint back to Dutch.

"See you in a minute."

"Lexie?"

I heard Dutch, but I walked off toward the bunks. Damn him! Double-damn him for leaving! I was so angry, I couldn't even think straight. I went to Darcy's closet to find a dress. I wanted to feel sexy for my meeting with Dutch. I yanked dresses off the hangers, looking for the perfect one. I felt the prickly sense of someone watching and turned to see a swirly image evaporate into the darkness. I was going crazy.

Turning back around, I continued to paw through Darcy's inappropriate attire until I found a red, slinky one with spaghetti straps. I took off all my clothes and pulled the spandex fabric over my body. The sensation returned, and I spun around faster this time, catching the full image in my peripheral vision.

Against the hazy darkness, Alex appeared with a concerned look etched on her freckled face. She watched; she disapproved. I didn't care. In a blink, she disappeared again as I left the bunk wearing the scarlet fabric.

Stumbling over a few rocks, I followed the trail toward the small shed located a half mile away from camp. My gray tennis shoes made the dress a little less sexy, but the walk needed the rubber soles. The frogs seemed incredibly loud tonight, like a song of echoes through the trees. Was it a large frog, bigger than all the others?

I turned around a few times, searching for the croaking noise and watching the moonlight shine like a spotlight on the trees. An iridescent glow bounced off the leaves, reflecting back as a sparkle into the dark woods. How did I miss the intensity of the moon before tonight?

The handle of the Hatchet House required a body-pulling tug. The small room had tools lining the walls and a large mower in the corner. It was dirty and gross and smelled like gasoline. So this was the glorious building the staff used as a hook-up lounge. Dutch stood by a little worktable in the center of the room. He leaned over with a small straw as I shut the door.

"What are you doing?" The question came as he inhaled white power off the dirty table. I heard music playing somewhere in the room. I looked up to see his phone perched on a shelf, setting the mood for our little meeting. Dutch wiped the powder off the tip of his nose.

"Just a little pick-me-up before I have to spend the night with the little shitters at the campfire." He smiled, and his teeth seemed to glow beneath the single bulb hanging from the ceiling.

"Is that coke?"

"Darcy keeps a stash. I thought you knew that?"

"No." I shook my head.

"You want some more of this? It's some pretty strong shit, but you seem to handle it like a champ." He reached out with the remaining butt from his joint. I took the small piece, inhaling the last few drags from the tip. My fingers dropped it to the floor, and I twisted out the remains.

"So, Lexie, I don't know what finally changed your mind, but I'm glad you did. We're going to have some fun." His fingers rested lightly around my waist, pulling me close. "You look hotter than shit tonight in that dress."

Dutch leaned in to kiss me. Over the summer, we had exchanged passionate and desperate moments, but tonight it was none of those intense feelings. Dutch exhaled, filling my nose with the scent of Funyuns. He pressed my back against the table and then lifted me in the air to sit where he just snorted the powder. The music grew louder, and his breath seemed sweaty on my neck as his mouth trailed down the front of the dress.

Dutch pulled the straps off my shoulders. He kept pulling until the top of the dress was around my waist, exposing my naked skin. I should have felt vulnerable, but my sense of shame was masked by the drugs floating in my head. The longer I was here, the less I seemed to care.

Dutch inched the dress up over my hips, leaving my ass exposed. I had left my cotton panties back in the bunk. He stepped back and dropped his jeans, then reached for his boxers. I focused on his brown eyes. I searched the dilated pupils for something real, but only found an empty heaviness.

I saw her again. Alex watched from across the room. I closed my eyes to block her out. I really was going crazy. Dutch pulled me to the edge of the table. He had no idea what this night meant for me. Maybe he was too high or just didn't care. Either way, it was too late to change the actions set in motion in the heat of anger. In this life-defining moment, I felt nothing—an empty void of raw emotions from what I tried to forget.

Dutch released my body, and it was over just like a shot at the doctor's office—just like a needle causing a quick stab of pain, followed by a nurse throwing the capped syringe away in the plastic red trash. It was impersonal yet invasive, shooting through the living cells of one's body.

"That made the night just about damn perfect." He kissed my cheek as the music echoed in a loud crescendo, bouncing off the walls, creating an aggravating volume that pounded inside my head.

I shifted on the workbench, trying to pull down my dress. The prickly wood stabbed my bare butt cheek, impaling a splinter. I laughed at the ironic stupidity of getting a splinter impaled in my ass.

"What's so funny?" Dutch asked. I noticed he was already dressed.

How did he get dressed so fast? Time was speeding by while I sat here with a splinter in my ass. Time? How much time had passed since Jess left? He left me, and I had sex with Dutch. It really happened. Jess accused me of being an unfaithful, drug-abusing whore, and just left. Now I was exactly that person—the terrible one he accused me of becoming this summer.

Who the hell is, Lexie? I heard his voice again. *You're mine.* I'm being paranoid. *It's* we *since* we *were eight.* That mocking voice is not here. *You can have your damn break. You can have your damn break.* My hands gripped across my forehead, pinching the skin around my hairline. Jess drove away. He is not talking. You are not here! Did I chant the words out loud or just as an echo in my mind? I wasn't sure.

I dragged the tips of my fingers down my face, catching on my eyeballs. Anxiety ripped through my gut, bringing up the lingering taste of bile. My eyes darted around at the hatchets and chainsaw glaring like gnawing teeth. The sound of engines and swirling wind circled through the room. I couldn't breathe. I felt pain—a raw hurt in my chest and somewhere else I wanted to forget. I panicked.

What have you done, Alex? I don't know. Something terrible. *Are you talking to yourself?* I heard the thoughts again like they were spoken out loud. *Lexie, are you okay?* The tone sounded so deep and unlike my own.

"Lexie?" Dutch's voice pulled my attention back through a silent tunnel vacuum. I heard nothing but the sound of faint music. His eyes blinked back, looking straight into mine. The lightbulb continued to swing above our heads.

"Are you okay? You should have taken it easy on the joint." His fingers brushed my bare skin as he pulled the red straps back on my shoulders. *Shit!* Until that exact moment, I didn't realize I was still perched on the nasty table, stoned out and topless.

"You leaving?" My voice quivered a little. Dutch silenced the music on his phone, then jammed the case down in his right jeans pocket.

"You want to come? I'm on campout duty tonight, remember?"

"Oh, right. I forgot you said that earlier. Go on without me. I'll come later." Dutch looked at me a second, then came back for a light peck to the lips, giving me a kiss of Funyuns-coated nothing.

"You sure I should leave you here?"

"Yes. I'm fine."

"All right. I'm pulling the zombie-in-the-woods story out tonight. Scared the literal crap out of two of them last week. Not kidding. Shit their pants when Breck jumped out of the woods. Don't want to miss it this time. Catch you later, Lex?"

"Yeah."

The wooden door shut with a hard bang, wedging it closed. I never wanted to see Dutch again in my life. Sliding off the table, I collapsed against the dirty floor. I felt as nasty as the pieces of mud and oil that clung to my legs.

I felt sick. Sadie would kill me. Jess would…my thoughts came to a halt. Jess would hate me forever. Isn't this what I wanted to prove? The fact we could never be together? No, damn it!

My throat constricted, cutting off my air supply. I couldn't have a real relationship with Jess, so I killed the only one I did have with him. Jess no longer was my future or my friend.

"Shit!" I screamed it out loud with every ounce of energy I had remaining.

The weak muscles of my stomach gave out. I leaned over and I threw up on the floor. Lifting the edge of my dress, I wiped the hem across my lips. I threw up again, feeling the liquid splash all over my legs. I threw up again, not bothering to even lean over this time. Nasty chunks of hamburger rolled down my chest. I hated Dutch. I hated my life. I hated the Masons. I hated myself. I hated Jess for leaving.

I sat in my own vomit until two in the morning, and my head was almost clear. Covered in puke, I went back to camp. Most of the staff lay asleep in their bunks when I crept through to get my phone. I needed a shower, but what was the point? I hiked back out in the woods to a spot that guaranteed three bars of reception.

Part of me wanted to call Jess in a selfish act of needing to hear his voice. It was wrong, and I knew it. I clicked Sadie's name and listened to the buzzing rings all the way in Chicago.

"Hello?"

"Sadie. I…I'm sorry. I know it's late."

"Alex? Sweetie, what's wrong?"

"I really screwed up. I…I don't know what to do."

"Where are you?" Her voice went from groggy to action mode.

"I'm still at Rochellas. Jess came to visit. We had this fight. It was bad. We've never been so horrible to each other. He was screaming at me. All these terrible things. I slapped him, Sadie. Literally hit him, then he just left. I was so angry, like I couldn't even stand being in my own skin. I did something unforgivable. It's bad, Sadie. *Really, bad.*"

"Ok, try to calm down. Tell me what happened."

The story fell out in garbled clumps of rushed words. "I'm so stupid. What have I done? I went completely insane tonight. I swear I was having an out-of-body experience. It's like I kept seeing myself do these things. I wanted to stop it, but I couldn't."

"Did you at least use protection?"

"I might have been stupid, but I'm not a complete moronic girl." My mind swirled back through the hazy moments in the Hatchet House. "That's not exactly true. I lucked out that Dutch preferred to be safe."

"Well, that's at least something right now."

"It was terrible too. I thought it would be different."

"It usually is different, sweetie. You just experienced it with the wrong person in the wrong circumstances. Trust me."

"How could I have been this stupid, Sadie? I'll have to tell Jess."

"You two are not together. Unless your relationship status changes in the future, you don't have to ever tell him."

"But it doesn't work that way with us. It's the reason we were fighting. You didn't see the look on his face as he left. I wasn't honest with him."

"You are almost twenty years old. Bonds, promises, or whatever Booneyville pact you made will not last as adults. You are not obligated to tell him anything. What you did is none of Jess Mason's business. He may think it is, but the details of tonight are most certainly not his business. Forget about what you think he needs to know."

"I wish it was that easy to forget. I feel so nasty and slutty."

"You are not slutty. Now, Dutch? I'm sorry, but I think he's a bit of a man whore. He took advantage of someone in a very distraught state tonight. This lifeguard has been interested all summer because you're the only one who said no. He knew exactly what he was doing."

"I was just so angry and…and…"

"It was a mistake. They happen. You take the lesson learned and vow not to do it again. Even the most organized person makes them."

"You don't make mistakes."

"There's varying degrees of mistakes. The main thing, you can't let it destroy you. Take the turmoil and channel it into something else. It's called capitalizing on your mistakes."

"I don't want to capitalize on it. I want to take it back. All of it. From the moment I got here. Erase this whole damn summer."

"Can you take it back? No. Can you try to move forward? Yes. You will start by staying away from Dutch and Darcy the rest of the summer. Okay? Promise me."

"You don't have to worry. I never want to see any of them again. To be honest, I'm done. Part of me wants to just pack up and leave."

"You could leave, I guess."

"And go where? I can't move into our apartment until August, and there's no way in hell I can go to Sprayberry right now."

My head hung in despair, thinking of Jess at Sprayberry, seeing his face smiling on the meadow, then changing to the haunting look of pain I had caused in those blue eyes. Knowing Jess, he would drive all night, then ride out to the burned-up stump. He would sit for hours, watching the sunrise, contemplating how I had become a wretched bitch.

"Sweetie, why not come to Chicago?"

"Chigger won't make it that far, and I don't have the money for a plane ticket." I refused to involve a single Mason dollar in this night of stupidity. All the money I made this summer had gone to the New Orleans trip and the alcohol I had contributed to the dock parties.

"What if I got you the ticket?"

"No, I can't let you."

"Early birthday."

"Sadie, you always say that. I can't add anything else to the birthday list."

"You have a list for me too?" she asked as a joke, but I heard the question in her voice. Sadie thinks I'm insane. I pictured those concerned creases above her arched eyebrows with the cluck-cluck of disapproval.

"No, I'm not that crazy. At least, I don't think I am."

"Okay, so not Chicago. Just stay and go out of your way to be a model citizen the next few weeks."

"Staying just sounds degrading. I hate myself right now."

"You seriously need to work on this anger and self-hatred cloud that follows your every move. You have to let it go. This summer just made it worse, but don't wallow in the aftermath. What happens at camp stays at camp. If asked in the future, you never heard of something called the Hatchet House and you never inhaled."

"You and your political bull-crap cover-ups."

"I'll let that one slide tonight."

"Sorry." I let out a deep breath, feeling the waves of air floating out in the dark night. The tension of a lingering headache pierced through my temples. "What am I going to do about Jess? I mean, really. This is serious."

"We covered that part. You're not telling him."

"We can't go back to the way things were, even if he doesn't know about Dutch. We have to talk about how he feels toward me and how I don't…" I bit down on my bottom lip, trying to choke out the words. The damn thing would fall off before the end of the night. "Why can't I just say it out loud?"

"Because it's not true. Because you do love him. Because you have deep psychological issues involving anger and resentment. I am honestly not sure who you resent more: the Masons, your father, your mother, or yourself. Until you fix some of this emotional debilitating hostility, you will not be able to accept the way you really feel about Jess. Friendship or otherwise."

"It doesn't matter anyway at this point. I pretty much slammed the door in his face tonight. No, I slapped him, and then he left. Jess doesn't just leave. I think I lost everything with him. Our friendship is over."

"Well, you might need to give him some time. Let him calm down."

"I don't remember a time when I did life without him. Not even here. Jess still existed even when I tried to pretend he didn't. It's like he's the other half of me. I don't know how to live without him."

"I guess you will have to live without him. I'm sorry, sweetie."

"I know. This is really hard." I rubbed my forehead, smelling the vomit soaked into my clothes.

"Just power-step one foot in front of the other. You can do it. Keep your chin up. Show all of them you're not defeated."

"Thank you, Sadie. You're a good friend."

"I know. Can't live without me. Good night, sweetie."

Sitting on the little rock, I wondered how it would feel to just cry. Let all the ugliness out for the world to see. I remembered the last time I felt the drops run down my cheeks. In a fit of rage, I had smashed my tea set against my bedroom wall. My feet had stomped the larger pieces into shards against the carpet. I remembered the snot dripping off the tip of my nose and the haunted look on my father's face. In that moment, I vowed never to let anyone see me crack again.

The next day, a cloud covered my heart, just like a scene from *Steel Magnolias*. The small television broadcasted the only VHS tape I could find on short notice. Rochellas had electronic equipment straight out of 1985. I secretly despised that movie as much as Ouiser if she were tied to a chair and forced to watch it on repeat. I needed blood and guts. A nice *Saw* movie would serve a better purpose, but that might scare the little brats into coming over to my seat.

Covering my face with a large set of sunglasses I stole from Darcy, I blocked out the chaos in front of me and prayed for this damn headache to go away, but I knew it would stay lodged right where it belonged after what I did last night.

Unless I chose to die of starvation, the mess hall lunch qualified as a necessity. I picked the back corner out of view and tried to choke down lasagna. Dutch and Darcy walked through the side door, causing my esophagus to constrict on the large chunk of meat. They each grabbed a tray and bickered all the way over to my table.

Dutch sat down next to me and leaned in to whisper, "I've been thinking about you all morning."

I froze, in silent repulsion, feeling his warm breath float across my cheek. Darcy dropped her tray on the other side of the table with a loud thud—a harsh reminder of how she would react to her dress balled up in a plastic bag under my bunk.

"So I hear you have some hot friend visiting and decided not to tell me."

"He left."

"You teasing bitch!" She laughed. "I was getting all, you know, excited. I would have *loooved* something new around here. Everything seems just a little used up these days."

I struggled not to drop my cup and placed it slowly on the tray. Any bit of appetite vanished with the thought of Darcy's disease-infested hands touching Jess. Out of the corner of my eye, Dutch glared a nonverbal *shut-the-hell-up* in her direction, making it clear Darcy's comment hit the mark. She flipped him off. I guess everyone at Rochellas knew that Dutch finally got me to the Hatchet House.

That was the last meal I shared with either of my former summer friends. Rising thirty minutes before the rest of the staff, I raced to the mess hall each morning for a quick breakfast and packed a sandwich for lunch and dinner. I ate the rest of my meals alone by the lake.

Chapter 31

When I was nineteen...

On the fourth day at school, I walked in a mindless fog back to our apartment located a few blocks off campus. Five weeks had passed since my night of self-loathing destruction. Five weeks since I'd heard from Jess. I'd gone home to Sprayberry following the last day of camp, but we missed each other by a few hours. His move back to Austin on that particular day, at that particular time, was intentional. My best friend had no desire to see me. For the first time since I was eight, Jess Mason was completely absent from my life.

My phone vibrated in the side pocket of my backpack. Stopping on the sidewalk, I pulled out the small black box. My heart sank, seeing another message *not* from Jess. Yet, I was surprised by the sender.

Lex, get ur skinny ass online. Sent u 5 emails.

I cringed, seeing my summer name. I didn't want texts, emails, or any other contact with those people, but I went ahead and replied to Darcy.

Ok.

Sadie barely noticed when I entered our apartment. Our college home was nicer than the impoverished slums most coeds inhabited to save money for more beer. All my contributions were items bought by the Masons, which reminded me of all my problems.

In the new world of apartment living, Sadie's eccentric tendencies made Martha Stewart look like a contestant on that hoarders show—not that she ever saw an episode. Sadie despised reality television and said "the public displays of ignorance was the downfall of America." Her overzealous, annoying habits crept into my daily life, causing nothing but added strife to my current predicament. Despite her peculiar flaws, she was a good friend, a loyal friend, even in spite of my stupid actions.

I sat down next to Sadie, who was engrossed in a news article on her laptop. Dressed in a yellow sundress and curls, she looked beautiful as always, even on the days she got up early for class.

"Hey, sweetie. How was calculus?"

"Ehh." I shrugged.

"Alex, you can't flunk. Your scholarship will be revoked."

I stared into the vacant TV screen. The sarcastic laugh stayed hidden. It wasn't much of a scholarship. The Masons paid for almost everything when I looked at the grand total of going to school here.

"Alex!"

"I'm going to my classes," I muttered.

"You have to do more than just attend class and pretend to be interested. I know you're unhappy, but you can't let it destroy your future. You need to find something to motivate you. There's a lecture…"

I zoned out on the cryptic word *lecture* as she continued to speak in animated fashion. Jess should be leaving class in fifteen minutes. I knew his schedule since we planned a few spaced-out slots in the day for coffee. I should be with him right now; instead, I was getting another self-motivation talk from Sadie.

The burning pain of disappointment stung my chest. I missed him. I missed talking to him. I missed seeing him. I missed his irritating, stupid grin. I wanted to call Jess so damn bad, it was killing me. I wanted to tell him I was sorry, but I just didn't know how to say it in a way that would make him understand.

"Can I see your computer?"

"Why?" Her hazel eyes squinted at me.

"Because I'm gonna withdraw from all my classes by sending a giant FU message to my professors."

"Alex!"

"Fine. I need to check my email." I groaned. "I don't want to get up for my laptop."

Sadie rotated the computer on the coffee table in my direction. Signing into my account, I read several subject lines from Darcy and a few others from Rochellas. Each of the titles seemed to grow more urgent. Most of them referenced some website. Clicking the link, a page came into view, filling the whole screen with various female names in boxy letters. I selected the one labeled Lexie, and a video sprang to life.

I gasped, and then I choked.

Sadie pulled the computer around as I stumbled to the kitchen, trying to keep my stomach contained. Bits of roast beef sandwich exploded down the side of the cabinet before I could reach the sink. It stunk. It stunk like the rotten person that lived inside of me.

I clicked PLAY again—the fifteenth time in three hours. I studied the girl in the video. She looked like a stranger with wild red hair in someone else's dress. She had a vague, lost stare in her eyes, absent of life. The video ended, and I clicked play again for number sixteen.

I thought only celebrity bitches trying to get famous ended up with a sex tape on the Internet. Yet there I sat, like a stoned bobblehead, letting Dutch's nasty hands and lips maul my skin. He'd recorded it with his phone while I thought it just played music that night. *Damn cell phones!* Maybe Uncle Frank was right to hate them.

I clicked PLAY again for number seventeen. The video feed sprang to life, and I braced for the sound of sex noises. I had an overwhelming need to watch it over and over again as some form of sick, sadistic punishment; every loop through the video was like a lash to the skin.

At least I wasn't the only pathetic moron who made the cut. On the other hand, it made my experience feel even less significant to him. The page contained twelve different videos of seven different girls. I only had one. However, the purpose was to vote for best and worst of his *spectacular* summer at Rochellas.

I watched the two that featured Darcy. One video was filmed on the docks and the other in New Orleans wearing those hot-pink panties. I recognized a couple of the other girls in Hatchet House clips: Katelyn, who taught boating, and Sara from the mess hall staff. The slut. No wonder Dutch received double servings of tater tots.

I jumped as my bedroom door flew open, crashing into the wall. Jess stood in the doorway. He was angry. *He knew.* I turned the laptop away from his intimidating stare.

"What are you doing here?"

"Let me see it."

"No."

"Stop it, Alex. You're gonna show it to me." The tone of his words scared the literal breath from my lungs. When I didn't respond, he stormed over to the desk. He reached around my shoulder to activate to worst seven minutes of my life.

He saw me naked. He saw the things that Dutch was doing to me. I covered my face with my hands and pretended it wasn't happening. I felt his anger as he stood behind my chair. It radiated out from his body with every breath. He brushed my shoulder as he reached in front of me and clicked PLAY again.

My stomach lurched, hearing those sounds from the video. I got dizzy, and my legs broke out in clammy goose bumps. I was going to throw up again.

"I'll take care of it." I heard the icy tone behind my head. He walked out of the room before I could respond. My legs felt weak as I tried to catch up in the living room.

"No," I whispered. His back stilled in the apartment doorway and then turned around to face me.

"What options do you have?" Jess's jaw clenched. "Why couldn't you've just listened to me? Did it really matter why I was tellin' you to stay away from him?"

"Jess, please, I…"

"Stop! I don't wanna hear your excuses. I'll just take care of it. I told you I'd always have your back. I meant it, even when you do somethin' as stupid as this."

"I'm…sorry." My voice shook. "Please…I…I'm sorry." I staggered as I tried to covey something with substance and not just words that trivialized his feelings. We needed to talk. He needed to hear me. I felt panicked as the situation slipped out of control. "Please don't…please don't leave yet."

"Damn it, Alex! I gotta leave. I can't stand to look at you right now. All I see is that dress and that asshole with his hands all over you while you just sit there like some…some…shit!" His hand absently clamped his forehead, pushing the hair back tight on his scalp. "I don't know if I can ever look at you the same again!"

He hated me. He didn't have to say it. I saw it in his eyes. I had to make him listen. He couldn't leave like this again. "Just wait. Let me—"

"Explain? There's nothin' you can say that will make me understand. You knew how I felt and just threw it back in my face. You don't care 'bout us. So just let me go. I'll fix your mess, and then I don't want to see you."

His eyes watched me, cold and lifeless. I finally knew the frostbite that came from a Jess Mason freeze-out. It wasn't a superficial whisk to the skin, but a pain so deep, the flesh turned black from the inside out. The joints in my knees caved, and I slumped to the floor.

I felt something on my cheeks. The tears poured down my face followed by the first sob. *I was crying.* Losing Jess finally broke me. On my hands and knees, clutching the carpet, I stared back at him.

Jess didn't move. He stayed in the doorway, watching me fall apart. I sucked in a jagged breath that transcended into an ugly cry. He looked at me one last time and then slammed the door shut.

"I'm s-s-sorry, Jess. I…I'm so sorry." Snot dripped down my lips as I waited, knowing he wouldn't come back. Sadie put her arms around my shoulders.

"Alex, I didn't mean for this to happen. I didn't know what else to do. Someone has to make Dutch take down that horrible video."

"He ha…hates me."

"You have a bond with Jess that is different than most people. It's strong. I know it hurts, but you have to give him some time, sweetie. He's just in shock right now."

"I g-g-gave him t-time." I could barely talk, causing the words to be half-syllable gibberish. "It m-made it w-worse. All…my fault."

"Don't talk. Just let it out, okay? You need this. You need to feel your emotions for a change. Grieve, Alex. You have to at some point. Stop bottling it up until you explode. All you'll get is a catastrophic mess and more problems."

Sadie pulled me up from the floor, and I stumbled over to the couch. She covered my shaking body with a blanket. I used the stupid, red, flowered quilt, a gift from Mrs. Mason, to wipe the crud running from my nose. Somewhere during the evening, the darkness brought mercy, and I drifted off to sleep.

I stayed in bed the next day. Around two o'clock, I got a text. My feet kicked the covers up, and I scrambled to my desk. The screen displayed a simple, terse statement lacking anything familiar.

It's done.

I tear rolled down my cheek. Flicking on my laptop, I hit the page Dutch so artfully constructed as his anthology to those he literally screwed over. The white screen glowed, PAGE NOT FOUND. I quickly texted a reply.

Thank you. I'm really sorry. Please call me. We need to talk.

Sitting on the edge of my bed, I waited for Jess. The screen stayed blank. I waited. I waited until I got anxious. Five minutes turned into ten, which slowly faded into an hour. I curled into a ball under the comforter, clutching my phone. It was a cave from the rest of the world, filled with the rotten cloud of my un-brushed teeth. Three hours later, I climbed out, knowing the truth.

I smashed my phone against the wall, sending parts in every direction. I got chills hearing the sound. Grabbing the laptop off my bed, I hurled it through the air too. The HP made direct contact with the mirror above my dresser. Shards of glass exploded all over the room. The computer landed with a thud, still intact. I picked up the laptop and flung it again, this time watching the screen break into pieces as it hit the closet door.

I sank to the floor, feeling the sobs shake my body. Nothing was making it better. I noticed the tattoo on my wrist. Scratching at the design with my nails, I wished it would go away. I wished I could just scrap it off my skin. It reminded me of everything horrible. It reminded me that he was gone. If I wouldn't die in a puddle of crimson blood, I would just cut the damn thing off with a kitchen knife.

The truth hurt. I deserved every piece of this grief for what I did to my dear friend. All these months, I knew where he stood and I chose to ignore and pretend his feelings were not real. He *should* hate me. Yet, he saved me once again. Jess fulfilled his last promise before exiting from my life.

Yanking open my desk drawer, I pulled out my list and studied all the varying degrees of charity from the Mason family. The latest entry always seemed inevitable. Clenching the pen between my fingers, I wrote JESS MASON in big letters, taking up three spaces. Tears fell on the page. I shoved the old piece of notebook paper back in its hiding place.

Pulling out my iPod, I flipped through the country playlists created by Jess. I found the one in question that contained just the right amount of twangy sap. Keith Urban knew just how bad I felt tonight. His soft voice brought me no closer to the person who gave me the disc; it just made the pain worse.

I turned up the volume, knowing I deserved to hurt. Stretching out on my back across the floor, I let the shards of mirror poke and cut my skin.

Chapter 32

When I was twenty...

Today was my birthday. I waited and waited and waited. Jess didn't call or even text, let alone bring me a giant bag of sugar-coated orange slices. He had started the tradition on my tenth birthday when Mrs. Mason took him to this candy store in Dallas. The next year, they brought me to the actual place. It was a two-story building that was every kid's fantasy. Jess got me a bag of orange slices every year from that store—every year until today.

Sitting on the floor of my bedroom, I took another drink of tequila. It was only four o'clock, but I was already drunk. Pulling open my dresser drawer, I exchanged the tequila bottle for vodka. I had learned that vodka didn't make me quite as nauseated, but I'd grown to like the taste of tequila, so I usually switched midpoint.

I tipped back the bottle, feeling it trickle into my stomach and spread like fire through my veins. Tears fell down my cheeks, but the alcohol made it not hurt quite so bad. I fell back against the carpet, spilling some on the floor. My room already smelled like liquor and vomit and sweat. I lived in filth, and I really didn't care; it wasn't like it was the first time.

Sadie opened my door without knocking. She came over and yanked the bottle out of my hand. "That's enough self-pity."

"Whatever."

"Get off that disgusting floor. I got you a birthday cake."

"I don't want cake."

"Well, you are not sitting in here drinking yourself into oblivion tonight. Get up and eat the cake I bought you." She stomped her foot against the carpet.

I crawled up the side of my bed, using it as a crutch. Stumbling into the kitchen, I saw a gourmet cake with writing that said, HAPPY BIRTHDAY, ALEX. The happy letters made me want to smash it.

"You better not sing to me."

"I won't sing." She smiled as she opened some party plates.

I was dizzy. I was drunk. Reaching for the edge of the cabinet, I tried to steady myself. Instead, I accidently grabbed the side of the cake box and fell backward into the floor, bringing the beautiful creation down with me.

I laughed. Lifting my arm, I licked icing off my fingers. I laughed and I laughed. I had cake in my hair and on my face. I laughed, and I wondered if it were the one that Jess liked to hear. I laughed some more as I licked the icing off that damn tattoo. I laughed as Sadie's face exploded into a red, angry demon.

"Give it to me!" she yelled.

"Give what?"

"Damn it! Get your ass up and give me that fake ID. I'm not putting up with your self-loathing, drunken fits anymore. This stops tonight, Alex!"

I stopped laughing. Sadie never cursed. She said it was an "inappropriate crutch of someone who lacked a vocabulary." Sadie cursed, which meant she officially had enough of me. Good. I didn't deserve someone as nice as Sadie.

She left the room and came back with some book in her hand. Sadie handed it to me as I used the cake as a pillow on the floor. "That's your birthday present."

The cover mentioned something about the art of expressing your feelings in constructive ways instead of destructive outbursts. "S*uper exciting*! You got me a self-help book." I threw it across the room.

This would not make a damn bit of difference. I was alone. I was sad. Jess hated me. His parents still made weekly deposits into my bank account. My title grew from poor to homeless to charity case to angry to shitty friend to slut girl.

I missed him. He walked around on campus every day, just a few steps out of reach. I wanted to see Jess, not read some nonsense about coping. I cried again, making snot drip to the floor and all over the cake. Jess's absence made a crack in my heart—a deep, jagged hole that could only be filled by the one who created it.

Chapter 33

Today, 3:37 a.m.

I open my eyes just enough to see that my father's truck is still on the interstate. The trip to Dallas was like a never-ending roller coaster, teasing into the pit of hell.

"Alex, you awake?"

"No," I mutter.

I watch the white line on the side of the asphalt. The headlights from the truck make it sparkle. Just yesterday, I drove down the same highway to Arlis. It seemed like a million years ago. His cell phone rings, and I sit straight up in the truck. He answers, and I know immediately the caller is Caroline.

"We're about twenty minutes outside of Fort Worth." He pauses, and I hear her voice but not the words. "Okay. That's fine. Okay, bye. Love you too."

He clicks END on the screen and glances over at me. His face seems tense, so I look out the window. Something catches my attention. In the depths of the dark sky, I see a shooting star. As always, I clench my eyes tight. I say the same words I have muttered for years. Opening my lashes, I gaze into the darkness. The glittery image is gone from the night as if it never graced us with its presence.

"Alex?" My father speaks from the driver's seat.

I didn't want to know about the phone call. I didn't want to know what she said. I pretend to be asleep. I pretend to not be here. I pretend to disappear like a shooting star in the night.

Chapter 34

When I was twenty...

At the butt-crack of dawn, my alarm blared in the distance. *Wake up! It's a beautiful morning!* I pulled myself from the dark trenches of sleep, remembering I was going to Arlis today. The little voice inside the clock screamed the words once more, sending a sharp chill through my shoulders. *Wake up! It's a beautiful morning!*

I carefully disarmed the little monster. The alarm clock from hell was a gift from Sadie. She said if I smashed it, she would smash me. I chose not to cross those hazel eyes; she was evil these days and might smother me in my sleep.

Check List Item One: You must wake up on time each morning.

Reaching behind my head, I fluffed the pillow and leaned back into the feathery softness. My father was getting married to Caroline today. I was happy for him, but the trip to Arlis was another story, bordering on slasher-film level. I would rather take on Leatherface, in *Texas Chainsaw Massacre,* than what I had to face today.

Check List Item Two: You need to think before you react today.

Taking out my yellow journal, I scribbled across the pages and contemplated the start of my morning ritual. "A constant routine is everything," said the stupid self-help book. After my birthday, this so-called five-step routine had pulled me up, and then pushed my sorry ass forward when nothing else seemed to matter. The whole concept was ridiculous, but it was at least enough to make me leave the front door and go to class.

I knew this book of annoying crap would never make me truly feel better. Step two suggested setting aside twenty minutes each morning for reflection time as a way to control your thoughts for the day. It recommended that I "start at the beginning." I wasn't sure what this stupid book considered *the beginning.* So on the first day, I scribbled my last tranquil, Norman Rockwell-painted memory.

The words had poured out about a girl who sat laughing in the trees. I wrote about my garden. I wrote about Digger. I wrote about my mother. As the entries progressed, the words had changed to something more cryptic and angry until they turned into pain and remorse. One morning, I wrote "I'm sorry" until I had blisters.

I looked over this morning's entry: twenty minutes of damn reflection time complete. Ripping the pages right out of the journal, I stumbled to my bathroom with the writing clenched in my hand. I stared at myself in the mirror, barely recognizing the person I saw in the reflection.

Moving on to the next step, I pulled out my hidden book of matches. It was time for my morning routine of pyrotechnics. I touched the glowing stick against the notebook paper. Orange flames ate up the sides as I dropped the journal pages in the metal trash bucket. The fire demolished my transposed feelings into a pile of ash with a devil's tail of smoke. I pulled in a deep breath, letting it scorch my lungs. I smiled; very therapeutic, just not on the level Sadie intended, or the people in the self-help book.

Check List Item Three: You must take a shower each day.

Turning on the hot water, I crawled inside, begging the spray to melt away the knots of internal pain. The idea that a loss will get easier as time passes is complete bullshit. It doesn't get easier; you just learn to function while balancing the large burden on your shoulders. I leaned against the wall and eventually sank to the floor. I cried. It was the only time I allowed it to happen these days. For twenty minutes each morning, I let myself crack while alone in the shower. This was my *real* reflection time.

Check List Item Four: You must wear clean clothes each day.

Turning off the water, I crawled out, feeling no more refreshed than before the hot blast. I tied my hair in a messy wad on top of my head. I grabbed a decent-looking T-shirt from a hanger and pulled some faded sweats on my tall frame. The gray fabric had a gaping hole in the knee. I no longer cared if I looked like shit or a runway model; either way this day would have the same outcome.

Check List Item Five: You must eat breakfast each day.

Pulling my suitcase to the living room, I smelled a dark, sweet aroma coming from the kitchen. At least something seemed bright this morning; Sadie had already made coffee. I wished for deep, mind-blowing sludge, knowing I would get a hit of watered-down caffeine from the natural energizer bunny.

"Hey," I said, pouring a cup. I took a sniff and grumbled, "Decaf again?"

"Stop being temperamental. I know you can't taste the difference, let alone smell it." She flashed an annoyed look over her shoulder while prepping a travel mug. "You don't need to be wired today."

"It's just the principle. It's like drinking O'Doul's. What's the point?" I took a swig straight black, feeling the hot liquid slide down my throat with a slight burn.

"Well, you are most certainly not having that either."

She would never let it go, even though I had been sober since my birthday. Sadie should have left me. I wasn't a good friend or roommate to her. She should have thrown my shit on the curb. I deserved it, yet she didn't leave or kick me out.

I watched Sadie take another sip of coffee. She looked up, allowing her eyes to flicker over my attire. I saw every bad thought floating around in her head. As usual, Sadie looked beautiful today, wearing what I called The Power Suit: a dark-black pencil skirt and jacket complimented with a starched white shirt and tiny pink scarf tied in a knot around her throat. Her hair was swept in a formal twist, giving the pearl earrings perfect exposure.

"Is that what you're wearing today?" she asked with pursed lips.

"It doesn't matter what I wear."

"It matters, sweetie." She sat her cup down, I assumed to offer a lecture. "It will be fine. It's just a car ride followed by a beautiful wedding. Try to say that to yourself over and over again. It will be okay."

I bit down on my lip and swallowed hard. "It will be okay. It's not like he will hurt me. The whole thing will just be uncomfortable."

"I'm sorry I can't take you."

"It's not your problem."

"You are my friend." She came over to give me a quick hug. "Call if you need to discuss anything. I'm here for you even if I can't physically come to the wedding."

"Thank you."

"Bye, sweetie."

Her heels clicked down the apartment steps. I heard a pause, followed by a quick march back to the door. Sadie made a beeline to the kitchen and opened the dishwasher. She took the coffee spoon out and reversed it to be scoop side up in the tray.

"Much better. It would have bothered me all the way to San Antonio thinking about that dirty spoon just sitting in the tray wrong."

"You're so weird."

"Says the person wearing ripped pajamas as an outfit."

"Whatever."

"Bye, sweetie."

"Hey…um…good luck with the debate."

"You too."

The door shut again, leaving me alone with my pathetic thoughts. Chigger was dead. Jess was driving me to the wedding because Sadie had a debate competition in San Antonio. I had called my father yesterday, with selfish hopes he would suggest coming to get me. After all, Caroline and I had a mega list of items to complete before the ceremony. *She needed me*, I stressed to him.

He said it wasn't necessary to come early and wanted me to get a ride from Jess the following day. I didn't say a word. My father had known for a while something was wrong between us. He had fished around a few times, but I never said anything. I would never be able to explain why Jess was absent from my life without revealing the truth. So I finally agreed to contact him for a ride.

I knew Jess would never miss Henry and Caroline's wedding. Yet, his attendance never felt real until that very moment. Clutching the tiny black phone, I had stared at the text message for at least thirty minutes before hitting SEND.

Sorry to ask. My car is dead. Can I ride with u to Arlis tomorrow?

I had waited, feeling scared that he wouldn't answer just like last time. Instead, I got an immediate response.

Okay. Pick you up at 8.

He had said yes. Part of me had wanted to jump up and down. Jess had answered yes, but the revelation also meant I had to see him in person. Part of me had wanted to crawl under the covers and not come out. I finally had some form of communication with Jess after three horrible months. Actually, three months since he had walked out of my apartment and a little over four since he had left me at Rochellas. I was nervous. I was scared to see him.

I sat down on the couch to wait, drinking my stupid decaf coffee. I had packed my suitcase last night so he wouldn't have to wait on me this morning. Now, I was stuck waiting on *him* with only my thoughts to entertain me. I took a deep breath, counted to five, and let it out. I did it over and over again. Jess knocked a little after eight. Getting up from the couch, I went to the door. My hand shook as I turned the knob.

"Hey," I muttered.

"Hey."

He didn't smile, and neither did I. Jess wore a blue, plaid, pearl-snap shirt that fit snug against his chest. In that instance, I regretted not changing like Sadie suggested. Jess avoided my gaze and looked past me for the familiar brown suitcase. He walked through the door unannounced while my fingers clenched the knob for moral support. In one swoop, he took my bag and left the apartment.

His eyes barely noticed me as I stood in the doorway. Following him down the stairs, I knew the memories of my indiscretions were still visible in his mind. Jess could not bear to look at me. Instead of gangly Alex wearing the extra-large Black Keys T-shirt, he saw that strung-out girl in the red dress with Dutch.

I stared at the cab door for a moment before climbing inside the truck. I shut the door, feeling uncomfortable after riding hundreds of times in this seat. This was going to bad; three hours of gut-wrenching silence. I stole a few glances in his direction. He looked as bad as me with dark circles under his blues eyes. I think Jess lost some weight too. His cheekbones stuck out, and his chin was a little more cut.

We got on the interstate. I pressed my body tight against the passenger door, wishing to fade into the tan exterior. It was eerie quiet in the truck. I fell into a hypnotic trance as I watched the white line on the side of the road.

About halfway there, I looked at Jess, seeing his jaw clenched tight and his knuckles white on the steering wheel. In a brave attempt to break the silence, I spoke with a small, hesitant voice like a child asking permission. "Can I turn on the radio?"

I asked but didn't dare reach for the dial. His tense composure offered no response while his hand flipped on the stereo from the steering wheel. He let the channel stay on one of the many programmed country stations. I rested my head against the window, feeling the awkward tension suck the air from the tiny space.

My mind flashed back to all the times we had bickered over the radio station and who was in control. I felt a rush of sadness; I deserved every painful piece of this trip. Closing my eyes to keep from crying, I listened to the words filling the cab: a Brad Paisley song was better than the suffocating silence.

The ceremony was a beautiful display of fall flowers that covered the grounds of Sprayberry. My father carried a blissful look, absent since the days before Arlis. Caroline floated around with a huge smile as she talked to the guests. Their happiness radiated out to everyone, giving me an inner peace toward my father. I dabbed a small tear in the corner of my eye. His days alone in the old farmhouse ended today.

I pretended to mingle amongst the familiar faces, keeping a sharp eye out for his dark hair. My rounds eventually made it over to the Masons. Jess wasn't with them.

"I am so happy for your father, Alexandra." Mrs. Mason's diamond-glittered hand took mine as she leaned forward with her light-pink, glossed lips to kiss me on the cheek.

"Yes, ma'am."

"You also look beautiful today, dear."

"Thank you, ma'am." I had let Sadie pick out an orange-red, satin dress, the color of fall. At least this time she remembered I was about six inches taller than her short frame. My one shoulder dress ended at a very modest point on the cusp of my knee.

"We heard you had a car situation."

"Yes, ma'am."

"Don't worry, dear. We can take care of it. It's time you drove something more suitable anyway."

"Thank you, Mrs. Mason."

"You are very welcome, Alexandra."

I no longer possessed the energy to grumble at the never-ending story. I'm surprised she lasted this long; not Chigger, but the ever-so-helpful Mrs. Mason on buying me a new car.

We parted ways, and I mingled through the crowd in search of my father. Every so many feet, someone latched on for a chitchat. They must have invited the whole damn town. Plump Mrs. Landry remarked I was wasting away like a wisp of grass. Ms. Virginia Abbot, sporting a gray bun, squeezed a tight hug, and then pinched my cheeks with a piercing comment about all that food I was eating in Austin. I loved that smashing another adult's face, while criticizing, was deemed socially acceptable at a wedding.

Mrs. Crawford, who always wore three strands of pearls, seemed generally concerned I would never find a husband in that city. She clucked her tongue about wasting time because I wasn't getting any younger. Meanwhile, Ms. Sara Beth Nelson asked when Jess and I would be expecting our first child. She just couldn't wait to see little ones again at Sprayberry.

I smiled politely with a *yes, ma'am* and *thank, you ma'am* around each kind, meddling woman, never bothering to correct or appear offended. Bless their dear, old, demented hearts. Never depend on Arlis for a dose of self-confidence. I was both too thin and too fat, while gallivanting around as an old spinster at twenty, who apparently married Jess when I was sixteen.

If they only knew the truth of my actions the past few months. Those bright-red lips would spread every juicy bit of gossip about that no-good Tanner girl, who was involved in drugs and wild sex, while breaking the heart of Arlis royalty. Afterward, those women would line up with oak switches, aimed at my ass, and then they would drag me by my ear to the front pew for a heavy prayer session.

I let out a deep sigh of contemplation and then continued to search for my father and Caroline. I wanted to give one last hug before they headed to Galveston. The Masons had gifted a ten-day cruise as a wedding present.

I walked past Skeeter Rawlins, giving his new appearance a double take. He sat next to Uncle Frank, wearing a manicured beard and new haircut. His clear, green eyes smiled back in acknowledgment. *Well, I'll be damned.* Skeeter looked like a whole new person in his white button-up shirt and red tie.

"Hey, Dad." I found him enjoying a second piece of lemon-filled wedding cake.

"Hey, Pumpkin. Something wrong?"

"No, I just wanted to say good-bye now instead of later. You know how it gets when you let them have birdseed." I smiled.

"Pretty crazy." He chuckled.

"I wanted you to know. I really am happy for you."

"I know you are." He hesitated, staring into my gaunt, hollow eyes. "I'm worried. I've known something has been wrong. Whatever happened between you and Jess, you should try to fix it."

"It's not that simple. I…um…did something. It's my fault, and he doesn't want to talk to me. I don't know if it can be fixed."

"Nothing is beyond repair if you really want it bad enough. Have you apologized?"

"He won't let me. Jess doesn't want to talk to me. He doesn't want to hear it."

"If you are truly sorry, then you say it until he hears you. No matter how many times it takes. I watched that boy take just about every punishment he could for you. Don't think I didn't know." Embarrassment caused my cheeks to flush. "Just never give up, Pumpkin. Not on the important ones."

"I don't know, Dad."

"Is he still important to you?"

"Yes," I whispered, fidgeting in my ballet flats. My right hand bent the knuckles back on my left with a ripple of cracks.

"You want to tell me about it?"

"No, it's your wedding. I don't want to bother you with it."

"I don't care."

"It's okay, Dad. Really."

"Okay. Come here." Wrapping his arms around my shoulders, my father pulled me in for a tight hug. It felt good leaning on him for a moment. "You will try again with Jess. Promise?"

"Okay." I nodded into his shoulder.

Jess had left the party. I didn't actually see him leave, but I felt his sudden absence. It didn't take a fancy, physiology degree to know where he slipped off to on the ranch. Leaving the cleanup to the capable hands of the Mason-funded catering staff, I trotted the short walk to the barns.

In the tack shed, I found my old, work cowboy boots stitched in a deep orange that Jess had bought me. I shoved my feet down in the dark holes and hoped for no spiders. Digging around in the shelves, I found another item hidden away in an old spot just like my shoes.

The four-wheeler fired up on the first try. With my satin dressed bunched up around my thighs, I sped across the meadow, feeling each nauseous bump. The hill with our burned-up stump came into view. I parked beside the other four-wheeler and killed the engine, staying astride the seat. I lacked the courage for the last few steps of the spur-of-the-moment plan.

Sliding off, I smoothed down my dress and walked quietly over the grass. My palm gripped the red package I had taken from the tack room. I stopped a few feet from where Jess sat leaning back against the stump. His shirt was unbuttoned at his throat and the blue tie was draped over his knee. Off to his right, I saw our names carved into the base of the stump.

JESS + ALEX

The blue eyes looked up at me. I held out my hand in his direction with my Skittles peace offering. I could hear the old teasing voice; *It's goin' to take more than Skittles, Al.* Instead of laughing, he gave me a hard stare with troubled eyes. I took a deep breath and went for it.

"I…I…I'm sorry, Jess. For everything. I just want you to hear it. I wish I could change what happened, but I can't. Just know I regret it. I never wanted to hurt you like this. And…" I swallowed hard, trying not to cry. "I miss you, Jess. I miss you every day." My voice cracked. "Thank you for hearing me. I…I'll leave you alone."

I dropped the red package by his foot and turned around, feeling the tears run down my cheeks. *At least he heard me*, I thought to myself.

"Don't go." His gruff voice made my body stop cold. Wiping my eyes, I turned back around to face him. Jess nodded a little to his right, indicating I should take a seat. I hesitated with a nervous twitch.

"It wasn't supposed to be this way." He spoke again while I stayed glued to the spot, looking down at him. "You seemed afraid of me. You know, in the truck. You were huddled against the glass as far away as you could get from me. Like I'd reach over and hurt you or somethin'."

"I'm not afraid. I just wanted to give you space."

"Please just sit," he asked again. I walked toward the tree and slid down a few inches away from him. Jess shrugged out of his suit jacket and gestured in my direction. "Put this on. You're goin' to get cold."

"You don't have to be nice. I know you still hate me."

"I don't hate you. I never could hate you."

"But you said you couldn't look at me."

"I never stopped lookin'. It's 'bout damn impossible when your pictures are all over my walls."

"Could have taken them down."

"Well, that seemed to be somethin' I couldn't do either."

"Oh."

"Just take the jacket."

"Thank you."

I slipped the dark coat over my shoulders, smelling his scent wrap around me. All these months of inner pain melted into the warm fabric. It felt like I was finally home. I stayed quiet, afraid to utter something wrong, bringing an end to the magical peace filling every broken crevice.

"I miss you too, Al. Even when I wanted to just scream at you, I still missed you." I didn't dare look in his direction at the strained words. "You know, the worse feelin' in the world is wantin' to call your best friend and knowin' you can't because they did somethin' that hurt you. Somethin' you thought they would never do. I must have picked up the phone a hundred times. It killed me every day. I wanted to go see you so bad, but I couldn't stop thinkin' 'bout what you did. I was so angry at you. I'm still angry at you."

His words tore through my heart. I wanted to wrap my arms around his body. I wanted to hold Jess and never let go. I wanted to tell his sad face I was sorry until he believed it without a shadow of a doubt. Instead, I spoke in a low, monotone voice never looking at his face. "What do you suggest we do?"

"You hurt me and I did my best to hurt you back. It didn't make it right or better. It just made us both miserable. I saw you that day before I slammed the door. You were just lookin' at me. Cryin'. I hadn't ever seen you do that before. I'd seen you hundreds of times bitin' your lip and keepin' everythin' sealed up tight. But that day, you finally let it go and I just stood there, knowin' I was the one person who finally broke you. It haunted me. Punishin' you didn't make me feel better. It just made me feel worse. I shouldn't have walked away. I'm sorry."

"Please don't apologize to me. I don't want you to."

"If you want me to forgive you, then you have to let me say it."

"It doesn't feel right."

"Alex, I missed your birthday," he whispered. "I shut you out when somethin' bad happened to you because of how it made me feel. I shouldn't have left. You hurt me, but I shouldn't have left. It's not what we do to each other."

I missed him so much. The tears slid down one after another, creating cool marks in the breeze.

"This is different. Seein' you cry."

I turned to look at him. "Yeah, it happens a lot now."

"Oh." Jess lifted a finger up to touch my face and then yanked it back.

"I'm sorry I…I hurt you."

"I know." He exhaled deeply as he leaned against the tree. "I know you are. I'm sorry I made you cry. I'm sorry I left you."

I stayed quiet, feeling the power of the words whisking around in the breeze. The meadow sounded and smelled of fall; each tree shedding the leaves to make way for new ones in the spring, creating the circle of life on the long, lanky branches. A beautiful paradise to those granted the privilege to witness the show.

"I miss comin' out here." Jess spoke again. "Everythin' always made sense in this spot. Whatever was botherin' me. I could just sit here lookin' out across the meadow. Hearin' absolutely nothin' but my own breathin'. It was easy to forget anythin' else even existed. There wasn't nothin' that couldn't be fixed out here."

"It was easier when we were kids. All of it."

"I know."

"Al, what he did was terrible. Have you been okay? I mean, handlin' it okay?"

"I don't know. Losing you was worse. I didn't think much about the video after you didn't text me back. I just thought about you."

"Yeah, my hand was in a cast that day. I didn't do much textin' for a while."

"Jess…" Guilt ate into my shaking voice. "You got hurt? What did you do to him?"

"Bastard," he muttered and paused for a moment. "I drove to Lubbock and beat the shit out of him."

"Crap. I don't know what to say."

"I was pretty upset. Lots of um…feelin's at the time." Jess cleared the catch in his throat. "He had it comin', Al. Bad things happen to stupid people. That's all you really need to know. He's still alive. Got all his fingers and toes."

"Thank you."

"Well, don't think I didn't enjoy it."

"Is your hand okay?"

"Just a small fracture across the top. Three weeks in one of those floatin' casts, then two in a brace."

"Oh."

We sat leaning against the stump. Neither of us talked after discussing Dutch's fate. Neither of us really knew where to go next. The breeze picked up rustling the grass. Orange-painted streaks filled the west sky, casting shadows with the start of night. It was only a short time before our Texas stars appeared in the darkness.

"Jess, are we really okay?" I whispered.

"Yeah."

"Promise?"

"Yeah."

Jess slipped his fingers through mine. Like a puzzle piece finding its place, I gripped tight to his hand. I never wanted to let go again. The rational side of my subconscious wanted to question it, but my broken heart refused to listen. The warmth of his skin wove magic around the shredded pieces filling the missing gaps. I was finally whole again.

"I quit the fraternity."

"You did? When?"

Jess didn't answer for some time, but clasped my fingers a little tighter. "I moved out after the first week of school. Seth left too, and we got an apartment. I had too much goin' on here."

I didn't know what to say. Jess had an apartment, and I knew nothing about it. "Where?"

"Not far from you actually. I've seen you a few times at the grocery store."

"Oh." This felt incredibly strange. Jess had an apartment and watched me sometimes.

"I couldn't keep up with school and workin' with Frank and the fraternity stuff." He let out a deep breath. "I figured out what to do 'bout Sprayberry."

"You did?"

"Yeah, he's gettin' bad. Mother's right. She can't even get him to go to the doctor. My dad spends time with him, tryin' to secretly access him. Frank knows too. Makes him a little crazy." His thumb rubbed over my skin. "They need me here…*he* needs me here."

"But you came back to school?"

"I did. We hired Skeeter to help Frank while I'm gone, but I come back every weekend. Sometimes I come on Thursdays and don't leave until Monday. Sometimes more. I'm gonna try to keep it up until I graduate. Then I'll come back and…stay." He smiled sadly at me. "I want this, Al. This place and me just go together."

"I know it does."

"But I really want to finish school too. I'm gettin' behind pretty bad. I don't know…I might not be able to finish. I'll try, I guess."

"I'll help you. Let me do it, please." The words rushed out. I saw a way to make amends with him. "We can do study sessions and, and I'll even make you flash cards. I know you love it when I make them."

"You're gonna teach me your nerdy pants ways."

"Yes. I'll do whatever it takes to help you graduate and still come here."

"Thank you." His smile seemed incredibly sad. "I've missed you so much. You have no idea how much I wanted to talk to you 'bout all of this. I've been so torn up over what I'm doin'. Confused if it's the right decision. Not knowin' if I should just quit school altogether."

"I'm sorry, Jess."

"I know." He swallowed. "Frank even figured it out. He looked at me a couple of weeks ago and said, 'Boy, there's no use tryin' to cover up the smell of shit with the stink of an 'ol pole cat.'"

"I think I even missed your Frank jokes."

"I'm not kiddin'. Frank looked at me and said it, tryin' to shake some sense into me, I guess."

I laughed faintly. "So Skeeter really works here now?"

"I wondered how long you were gonna let that slide."

"Skeeter Rawlins works at Sprayberry."

"Yeah, he's doin' good too. The other day…"

We talked until my bones froze against the stump. Jess rubbed his thumb over the top of my hand, warming up my frigid skin. After months of hurt, the rope holding us together was growing stronger. That's what happens when something severs a tie. A new one has to be woven in place around the broken threads, making it bigger and tougher than what existed before the ripping pain.

I watched my best friend, feeling a deep warmth radiate out of my chest and into my freezing limbs. It was an intense feeling that took my breath away as my mind finally accepted what it meant; something I had felt toward Jess Mason since I was eight years old.

Chapter 35

When I was twenty-one...

Today was my birthday. Standing in front of the mirror, I curled one last piece of my long, red hair. Sadie came into my bedroom and stopped suddenly.

"You are not wearing that tonight."

"I just wanted to be comfortable," I complained, but only my reflection in the glass heard the words.

She came back in the room carrying a flowy, red skirt with a black elastic waist. "Put this on, and I guess the shirt can stay."

"That's way too short. I can't wear that."

"You have those ridiculous legs and all you do is cover them up. I'm taking you out, so put on the skirt. You only turn twenty-one once, sweetie." She shook the hanger at me. I rolled my eyes as I looked at her little black dress and shiny heals. My jeans had a hole in the leg and not the fashionable kind. It was a comfortable "I've worn these for years" kind of hole.

I dropped the jeans and pulled the skirt up. I tucked my fitted black shirt into the waistband. If I bent over to put on my shoes, my black panties would flash everyone.

"That looks better on you than it ever did on me. You should keep it."

"Sadie, I will never wear it again."

"We'll see."

Hearing a knock on the apartment door, I looked at Sadie, but she just shrugged. I went into the living room and opened the door, feeling the cool air hit my bare legs. Jess grinned back at me. My breath caught in my chest, seeing his sweet face. He was supposed to be at Sprayberry because Frank needed him this weekend. "What are you doing here?"

"I couldn't miss your birthday."

"But I thought…"

"I couldn't miss your birthday," he said softly.

"Oh."

He handed me a bag of orange slices. "Sorry, but they came from here. I didn't have a chance to get the real ones."

"I'm sure these are just as good."

His blue eyes drifted over my hair and down the rest of my body to the short skirt and excessive amount of legs. "You look pretty, Al."

"Thanks." I blushed.

Jess touched my waist and then slipped his hands around my back, pulling me tight against his chest. The words remained unspoken, but we both remembered my last birthday. I blocked out those thoughts as I buried my nose into his neck. I pulled in a deep breath, getting lost in his smell. Jess didn't let go until Sadie came into the room.

"Oh, good, you made it. I was afraid I would have to employ some catastrophic incident to stall her."

"You knew he was coming?"

"Happy birthday, sweetie." She smiled, and I knew this explained her persistence in making me wear the skirt. "Now let's go have some fun."

"Where are we going?"

"That's a surprise." Jess grinned at me.

"I'm worried."

"You'll like it. I promise."

"Jess, I am not riding a mechanical bull."

He ignored me and looked at Sadie. "Seth's gonna meet us there."

"Meet us where?"

He grinned at me again. "Stop tryin' to ruin your surprise."

"If I have to ride that thing, then I'm doing a shot tonight."

"You are not getting drunk." Sadie turned to give me an evil look with those hazel eyes.

"One shot."

"That's it, Alex."

"Maybe two," I teased her. "I'm twenty-one, and you can't stop me anymore."

"*Alex*."

I giggled, following her perfect blonde curls down the stairs. Jess bumped against me on the steps. His fingers slipped around my hand. He did that sometimes, and I let him. After my father's wedding, Jess and I never discussed the implications of our Band-Aid fix to the real problem. I think we both felt anything spoken would harm the fragile state of our truce. Our casual interactions became something I dubbed the new normal. Something without a defined future. Something we both ignored.

I let him hold me. I let him touch me. It felt so comfortable and sweet, even though it was coated in twisted guilt and unspoken issues. I lacked the strength to stop it. I was selfish. Every time I wanted to establish some clarity, all the hurtful memories of those months without Jess pelted my senses. So I was his and he was mine, at least in this selfish, twisted way.

As we reached the end of the staircase, Jess slipped his hand around my waist, pulling me to his side. I smiled at him. "I'm not riding that bull."

"Who said anythin' 'bout a bull?" He laughed at me as the lights sparkled around us in the dark parking lot. His pink lips grinned just an inch away from touching mine.

I knew if he ever kissed me, this truce would be over. I would drift away into the feel of his lips. I would let him do anything he wanted, and it terrified me. I couldn't lose Jess again. I needed him. I needed him the way I needed air: a little bit every day just to survive in this dark world.

Chapter 36

Today, 4:20 am.

I am awake. I am asleep. I am calm because I am not really awake. I am somewhere in-between. Someplace where the meadow grass blows in the breeze. Someplace I don't feel the ache in my chest. I open my eyes and look out in the early morning darkness. I was here in Dallas just yesterday when everything was sunny and the buildings glowed in happiness. I was here before this place spoke of pain.

My father pulls into the entrance. The building seems frozen in the quiet parking lot. My mind plays tricks on me, and the shadows speak of torture and pain. My nostrils fill with a rotten smell that doesn't really exist.

"Hey, Alex, you awake?" My father's hand squeezes my left thigh.

The shadows reach out and grab me around the throat so I can't speak. I turn toward my father. He is tired. His eyes show worry and concern and sadness as the lights sparkle in the dark parking lot. He leans across the console and grabs my hand.

"You ready to go inside, Alex?"

I pull my hand away from him. I'm not ready for the truth so my mind slips into this numb, empty void.

"No. Can I be alone for a while? I haven't really been alone, you know."

A void fails to sling tears. A void fails to comprehend pain. A void is easier than the truth.

"I…I guess." His hand nervously scratches the side of his jaw. "You have your phone. Call me or Caroline if you need someone to come out here."

"Okay. I may just rest for a while."

"Alex?"

"I won't do anything."

"Call me." His eyes pleaded with me.

"Okay."

The truck door shuts. Silence. My heart pounds in my chest, and it vibrates into my ears. I feel a panic attack as I sit alone with my thoughts. It spreads through my chest and down into my stomach. The rotten smell fills the cab. The stench becomes stronger. The internal rumble clenches low with each breath of the imaginary smell. I will my stomach to a calm, but eventually surrender.

Slinging the door open, I vomit a pile of soup and slinky noodles. It splatters in every direction across the cement and on the tan door of the truck. I wipe my lips across the blue stars on my wrist and shut the door. I lean back into the seat, feeling the tears fall down my cheeks.

"I should have told him," I whisper to myself. I should have told him, and now it was too late.

Chapter 37

When I was twenty-two...

I watched from the safety of my dark sunglasses, with sweat dripping down my forehead. Sadie sat next to me in the adjoining chair, her rambling words echoed faintly in my left ear while I remained immersed in the volleyball game. I just wanted to watch the boy without feeling the weight of the world.

He tossed the white ball a few feet above his head. As he jumped in the air, every muscle across his chest constricted then released, sending the serve hurling across the net. The other team missed with a face dive into the sand. Jess lifted his baseball cap, running his fingers through his sweat-soaked hair. His long eyelashes winked in my direction as he walked back for the next serve. Jess looked sexy today. My cheeks burned at the thought.

"Don't you agree?"

"Hmm?" I absently muttered.

"You are so exasperating right now. The belligerent sexual tension, filtering back and forth between you two, is worse than usual this week."

"Stop being ridiculous," I spat at Sadie. Everything about her was driving me crazy today. Her blonde curls were tucked elegantly under a large derby hat that was more appropriate for the running of the horses than a spring break volleyball game.

"Really? What did I just say?" She reached into her pink cooler that matched her magenta Ralph Lauren sundress. Pulling out a wine bottle, Sadie filled an actual crystal glass with Sauvignon Blanc.

"It started with boring blah, blah, and ended with insult, insult."

"Alex, I'm trying to be completely serious here." Her sculpted eyebrows lifted with contempt in my direction as she took a sip.

"It's spring break. Nothing is supposed to be serious. Why can't you just sit back and enjoy it for a change?" I gestured out toward a crowd lounging and drinking while Flo Rida played through the speakers.

"Just agree to at least talk to Jess about it."

"I agree that wine glass is over the top for Padre. I'm not getting in a brawl for you when someone punches you."

"I guess your *boyfriend* can defend me."

"Really? You promised to keep those little comments to yourself on the trip."

"What am I supposed to do? You can't even carry on a conversation because you're too obsessed watching Tatum Channing out there."

"It's *Channing* Tatum, and Jess looks nothing like him."

"Ok, Ben Affleck in that beach movie?" She took another sip, leaving lipstick prints on the glass. "Or that vampire guy."

"Taylor Lautner? He's not the vampire. Stop pretending you actually watch movies. It's embarrassing."

"Embarrassing? I'm not the one imagining Jess naked right now."

She said the words right as he grinned at me again from the volleyball court. He was flirting from thirty feet away and not even trying to hide it. I shook my head. "I'm not picturing anyone naked. Let it go, or I will be the one to punch you. That's your two-minute warning."

"I'm trying to warn *you*. It's impossible to escape the inevitable. You know that, Alex."

"I'm not talking about it, Sadie." Avoidance. I was good at it. I relaxed back in my chair to watch. That boy never looked better than he did today. There was only one Jess Mason, and not a single actor could ever compare.

"Fine. But don't blame me when everything explodes in your face. You both walk around in some unrequited, catastrophic ball of frustration aimed at each other. You have to be honest with him and yourself. I'm not pulling you out of some disgusting pile of your own filth when this backfires. Once was enough. Just stop staring and do something about it."

"It can't happen," I muttered. "Not at this point."

"Yes, it can, sweetie. It's called having a discussion about your future. Not everything is diabolical, relationship-killer news."

"I'm not in a relationship. Besides, it won't be your problem. You and your fancy clothes will be walking the streets of Chicago."

"Alex, stop making me sound like a hooker, and be reasonable. Jess deserves to be treated better than these passive, self-indulgent moments you give him."

"Just watch the game, Sadie." *And let me have this little moment*, I wanted to scream at her. And I wasn't self-indulgent. Everything I did was for his own good. I wish Sadie would keep her perky nose out of his life.

Three months ago, something had changed Sadie's view of my situation with Jess. It all started when she took him to a social function with the campus young Democrats. She needed a last-minute date, and Jess agreed to go with her.

The next day, neither Jess nor Sadie bothered to divulge the details, but I knew something had changed. I felt it every time they crossed paths in a room; not flirty but something else that just failed to make sense. Sadie always liked Jess. After the night of the party, she shifted into full-fledged defense mode, leaving me perplexed and just plain confused as hell. I questioned Jess a few times and never got an answer.

"Are you listening to me? If you just tell him everything, you could make this work."

I ignored her and looked at the sand. I was tired of hearing Sadie so I blocked out her voice. I just wanted to listen to Flo Rida and not think about anything but my current view of the volleyball court.

Jess glanced over at me again. My skin felt hot as he watched me, like I was the only person here and not surrounded by thousands of other spring breakers. He watched me, and my breath caught in my throat. My whole body burned, and it wasn't from the sun. Jess winked again and went back to the game.

Sadie was completely right. The pull between us was different this week. Maybe it was the fact that Jess and I never had been somewhere on spring break together. Maybe it was the fact that graduation loomed just a few weeks away. Maybe it was because I knew how things would change once he went back to Arlis for good.

Over the last couple of years, Jess didn't get much of the full college experience. This trip to Padre was unusual for him. He spent all his free time trying to learn everything he could from Frank. We all knew the days with his uncle were limited, and Jess would soon be in control of Sprayberry.

I would never forget the day Jess received the news that he would truly graduate. His face had frozen in this momentary pause of disbelief, and then he went full-on crazy. Jess scooped me up like a rag doll, shaking my body around while I laughed. The more I laughed, the more he laughed in gasps of insanity. The race was over. He won. Jess accomplished the impossible. He had worked at Sprayberry and would still graduate.

Actually, his diploma resulted from the redemption promise I made to him. I swore come hell or high water, I would pull us both across that finish line, even if that meant long stretches of no sleep. My own double major had consumed all my daylight hours. More often than not, Jess had rolled into town late in the evenings, right before a test or major homework assignment. We had spent night after night cramming and half-sleeping on the floor of my apartment. I didn't care. Every moment was worth seeing the smile on his face.

Jess received his graduation news, and we had celebrated. Mine came and I had lacked the guts to tell him. A week before spring break, I received my plans for the future. Only Sadie knew the truth, which she wanted to discuss over and over again on this trip. Avoidance. I liked to *pretend* I was good at it; except that keeping this news from Jess hurt like salt on wound. The achy feeling of dread was always there even as I watched him play volleyball.

Jess took his position, wiping sand off his forearms. He queued up the final serve, allowing me a perfect view of the blue trunks, hugging every curve of his ass. The white ball flew over the net, continuing in a volley back and forth between the teams. It floated much like my relationship with Jess: an unspoken bliss destined to crash after years of avoidance.

I had accepted the fact I liked being this connected to him. I liked the way he looked at me from across a room. I liked the flirty way we fought with each other. I liked the way he made my cheeks burn red with just a wink from his blue eyes. I liked how our thoughts passed between us without a single spoken word. I liked his sweet face. I liked the way he kissed. I liked the way I still knew how it felt even though it happened years ago.

I took my sunglasses off and rubbed my eyes. All of these feelings still lived in the shadows of his family and my very existence. However, the news I got a week ago would finally send me in a different direction. For the first time since I was eight, I would be financially free of the Masons, and I had no idea how to tell Jess.

A gasp came from the crowd in our section. The boys failed to score, giving the other team another chance to serve. Sadie lifted that annoying hat, letting the sun reflect off her curls like shiny gold. She tucked the stray pieces back under before settling into her serious pose. She really was a classic beauty—flawless peach skin without a single spot. Her life would be exactly the way she chose it to be, with every twist and turn just part of a carefully constructed plan. Her first stop after graduation was Chicago, the beginning of Sadence McAllister's world domination.

"Hey, Sadie, promise me something?"

"Sweetie, that depends. I am not making a promise without the details."

"You are going to one movie before we graduate. Just one for all those sleepy-ass lectures you made me sit through to better myself as a woman. You are going to one real movie."

"I can agree to it, but I have standards. The film can't be anything related to superheroes. And I detest violence and those disgusting, strange horror movies you adore."

"Whatever. I pick the movie, and I will let you sneak in sanitary wipes for the seats. Deal?"

"Fine."

The people around us cheered, pulling my attention back to the game. The boys won. Jess and his old fraternity brothers would play in the finals tomorrow. He sauntered up in our direction, obviously happy with himself. His white T-shirt stayed draped over one shoulder, leaving his bare chest exposed with spatters of sand and sweat.

"What'd y'all think? Good game?"

"It's settled. The voice is definitely McConaughey." Sadie lowered her glasses as she watched him.

"What's she talkin' 'bout?"

"I have no idea." I wanted to kick Sadie, but Jess stood right in front of me, bumping the front of his legs against mine. "You're getting sand on me."

As I dusted off my knees, he reached down and stole my water bottle. "We just made the finals. How 'bout a little congratulations?" Taking the sweat-soaked baseball cap off his head, Jess ground the canvas right into my clean hair.

"I hate you." I yanked it off, throwing the hat back at him.

"I know." He grabbed my hand and pulled me up from the seat. "Come on. Seth wants to go over to the concert stage."

"Who's playing?"

"Does it matter?"

"Gross." Sadie's face ripped into a horrified pout. "I don't want to be in the middle of all those nasty, sweaty people touching each other."

That was enough for me to agree. My dear old roommate needed to have fun for a change. "Get up, Sadie. It's time to party." I yanked her out of the chair and threw that ridiculous hat right back in the seat.

"No," she protested as I pulled her along beside me.

The four of us trailed through the crowd to get closer to the area with the band. I felt like I was trapped in a Kenny Chesney video. Beer splashed down like a rain shower, leaving sticky traces across my shoulder. Sadie squealed.

"Come on. It's not going to kill you."

The band's tempo picked up to a steady frenzy. The crowd changed from dancing to jumping in place, a beautiful synchronized rhythm. The buildup brought palms pointed to the sky; some were empty and others clutched brown bottles. My head dipped back in abandonment; the strands of loose hair tickled the back of my neck. My eyes closed. The world went black. The only conscious sound came from the band on stage with guitars and drums, beating into oblivion, getting wilder with every chord change.

I bumped against another sweaty body. Opening my eyes, I saw Jess watching me with a grin on his lips. He was flirting again. I rolled my eyes. He grabbed my hand in the air above my head and sent my body around in a spiral. My feet gently rotated on each jump in the sand. Jess extended his arm out, then pulled me back closer to him. We moved.

We danced. We laughed. I let the music take me back to that place—the place where everything disappeared and I felt alive.

"You havin' fun?"

"Yeah," I answered.

"I really didn't think I would ever see you like some country band." He twirled me back out and around. Lacing his fingers through each of my palms, Jess pulled me closer to gloat.

"This is not country."

"They're from Oklahoma."

"Doesn't make them country. I think you found yourself a rock band."

He shook his head *no* while I got close up to his face. Nose to nose, I nodded a snide yes. Jess pushed my knuckles back slightly, threading his fingers through mine. "Stoney's playin' tonight."

"Is he now?"

"We should come back. Maybe just us?"

I shook my head *no* as his hands slipped around my waist. We danced the rest of the song with his sweaty body pushed against me in the middle of a thousand people.

The band switched to something with a heavy guitar intro. Letting go, I moved back next to Sadie. The girl had moves; the hidden rocker kind with wild, head-banging hair. We danced next to each other and with each other. For once, Sadie seemed to be an actual, normal college student.

I wasn't the only one to notice. Seth watched my roommate. The guy had it bad for Sadie, and she wouldn't give him the time of day. Seth got close enough to slip an arm around her waist. He smiled at her, flashing those perfect white teeth. Even with that, he never would have a chance with Sadie. I pulled out my phone.

"Alex, if you take one picture—"

"Come on, Sadie."

"Absolutely not."

"You need to frame something besides all those stupid awards. I want you to have a picture of all of us in your fancy Chicago apartment." I passed my phone to a girl in a florescent-yellow bikini top and cutoffs. The four of us scooted together as she took the first shot. I yelled, "Tequila!"

"Tequila?" Sadie tried to squirm free, but Seth had one side and Jess pushed us together on the other.

"Sex, sun, and tequila," I teased.

"You are so weird, Alex."

"And you're normal?"

The girl in the bikini snapped a picture after picture of us, just the way I wanted to remember it. Before the last click, I turned and grinned at Jess. He looked back at me, nose to nose with our lips just inches apart. Jess and I had our own private moment captured in time forever.

We left the concert and went back to the volleyball court, gathering up our chairs and Sadie's stupid hat. Walking to the truck, Seth babbled about the volleyball game as if none of us had witnessed a thing. His overzealous excitement was similar to Jess's: always happy.

Seth sometimes joined in our study sessions. As business majors, we even had some classes together. I kicked his ass on the tests, although it wasn't a complete beating on my part. Seth was smart and most of it manifested as second nature.

It was too bad Sadie held such conceited ideals. Seth accepted a bank job in Dallas after graduation, a very good accomplishment right out of school. His career wasn't enough to draw a second glance from Sadie. She would only settle for someone with Roman numerals after his last name and a job in the high six-digit range.

I stopped in my tracks, almost tripping over a dark-haired guy lying face up in the sand, wearing only boxers. "Should we do something?"

"Like what?" Sadie looked disgusted, like his sweat could leap from his body and land on her ankle, spreading a terminal disease.

"His mouth is just open." I peered down at the sleeping face. His lips were open at a strange angle, leaving his pink tongue exposed. His bare chest bore remnants of puke that had dried in clumps. "Can you sunburn your tongue?"

"I'll just take him back to the house." Jess reached down and threw the unconscious body over his shoulder. He was a short guy and couldn't weigh much more than a sack of feed as he dangled in the air.

"This is absurd. You are not bringing a stranger back to the house." Sadie refused to move with crossed arms, pushing her breasts high out of her pink dress. Seth noticed, and she quickly dropped them.

"It's my house. I'll do whatever the hell I want."

And I went right back into my world owned by the Masons. We followed behind without another word. Sadie fumed. Seth hummed a faint song. The new guy stayed silent, his head bobbing against Jess's shoulder. We all walked back to his truck and loaded up, putting the beach hitchhiker in the bed.

Our house wasn't on the map with the rest of the South Padre college students. The Masons recently purchased a yellow, two-story, four-thousand-square-foot beach house with private water frontage. The house even had a pool and hot tub on the back deck. Our spring break didn't come close to the nasty motel squalor of the rest of the students. We partied in the private gated area Sadie dubbed the Texas Hamptons.

Later that night, Sadie and I stood on the deck looking at the hot tub. I wasn't in the mood to socialize and needed a break from her. "I'm going for a walk. You should get in there. Be nice to Seth for a change. He's totally into you."

"I will pretend you didn't say that." Sadie looked over the edge and turned her perky nose straight into the air.

"Stop being a snob."

"I will have more trips to the doctor from that nasty, steaming tank of bacteria than if I slept with the random guy wearing the truck me hat on the beach."

"*Truck me* hat?"

"Don't act like you have no idea what I'm talking about."

"It really said *truck me*?"

"You know what I mean." She looked annoyed, and I shrugged back in confusion. "Remember the two guys in the oversized caps that said *Dirty Daddy* and *Vagina Magician* embroidered across the top? I pointed them out during the game."

"What?"

"You are so exasperating, Alex Tanner. The two idiots who tried to pick up the girl in the leopard-print top by offering to hand-paint one of those flower bikinis on her breasts cheaper than the beer tent. The *Vagina Magician* kept repeating it. 'Come on, baby. I can paint your titties real cheap.'"

"Did Sadie McAllister just say *titties*?"

"I said it on the beach too, but I guess you were too preoccupied to notice anything else. I was afraid you might actually lick his abs out there today."

"You know, Sadie, I've beat the shit out of someone before. She just kept talking—and *bam!* Blood was everywhere."

"Stop procrastinating with empty threats. I'll get in that wretched hot tub if you tell Jess the truth."

"For real?"

"I'll even be nice to the beach hitchhiker in there with Seth."

"His name is Brandon, and he's a freshman at Western State. He's a nice guy who has some shitty pledge brothers who left him."

"So we just believe everything the hitchhiker is selling and pretend he's not going to rob or murder the entire house tonight?"

"Don't be dramatic."

"Sweetie, I didn't spend the summer at drug camp. I'm not used to this level of acceptable surprises."

"Sadie!"

"A joke. I think I'm entitled to at least one after four years."

"Bitch."

"Watch the language if you want me to pay attention to Seth."

"You know, he's the type who would let you boss him around." My eyebrows arched. "Let you tell him exactly the way you like it. He might even be good at it too."

"Sweetie, tongue is extra in the little business arrangement. You want a make-out session with Seth, then I need to hear you talk about your feelings. Use those three little words."

"I love Sadie."

"Not to me, you neurotic mess. Now get your behind over there. But, Alex?"

"What now!"

"Watch yourself. Any actions on your part that are not completely sincere are wrong."

"I thought you wanted me to do something about all of this."

"I said talk to him. Tell him the truth for a change. Sometimes you forget he has feelings. *Real feelings.* You can't be flippant about it. Don't do something moronic tonight because you feel guilty about your decision. All in or not at all."

"That sounds dirty. Make up your mind."

"Stop being defiant. If you can't bring yourself to tell Jess how you really feel, then keep your ridiculously painted nails to yourself."

"Black Locus is actually a popular color."

"Who buys nail polish named after poisonous plants?"

"Whatever. I get it. Now jump in there and be slutty with Seth, and leave me alone. Give Brandon a little peck on the lips too. Don't make him feel left out."

"That's undeniably disgusting." Unzipping her sundress, Sadie let it fall to the floor, revealing a pink bikini. She glared at me all the way to the steps.

Turning my back, I walked across the deck to Jess. He sat on top of the picnic table in a burnt-orange T-shirt and faded jeans. Taking another sip of his Bud Light, Jess gave me a sexy little grin as I approached. I hated to think it was sexy, but it came across as nothing less when he allowed his thoughts to surface in the creases around his lips. He needed to stop doing that to me.

I shot an unspoken *quit* with the slant of my eyebrows. Jess chuckled under his breath as I took a seat next to him. The butterflies in my stomach changed to flying, anxious dragonflies. I had to get this over with tonight. The guilt physically hurt.

"What's goin' on over there?" He gestured back to the hot tub. Sadie's face glowed with one hell of a fake politician smile as she sank down next to

Seth in the bubbly water. One day, people would vote for that face, and it scared the crap out of me.

"I talked her in to having a little fun."

"You must have some good blackmail on her. Ms. McAllister is now slummin' with a can of beer. Seth might just drown in there."

"Or she might drown Seth. You never know with her." I watched Sadie chug the whole can in almost one gulp and then wipe her manicured fingers across her pouty lips.

"She still pissed about Brandon?"

"Yep."

"It was worth it, just to see the look on her face when I carried him to the truck. It was even better when I put him in the room next to her. I thought she might curse at me."

"You like tormenting Sadie a little too much sometimes."

"She's like a firecracker waitin' to be lit up. It's all there—just needs a match."

"I didn't know you found Sadie that attractive."

"Seth's words, not mine. The guy's got it bad for her. He gets turned on when she's all wound up. Gets a hard-on every time she gets bitchy."

"I really didn't need to know that." I looked back at the hot tub. Sadie watched me with an evil stare, sending hazel daggers right at my head. It was time to move this little talk out of her supervising view.

"So…um…you want to go for a walk?"

"Okay. Somethin' up?"

"It's nice right now out on the beach. Everyone's partying in town or in that hot tub movie from hell." I laughed.

"You like stirin' her up as much as me."

"True, but I get roommate rights. You don't have to live with her insanity."

"She's not all that bad. You know it."

"Interesting change of opinion."

"What? You know I actually like her."

I narrowed my eyes and leaned over close to his face. "You're still not going to tell me about your date with her?"

"You could always ask Sadie if you wanna know so badly."

"I'm not asking my roommate. I'm asking my best friend."

"And I said there's nothin' to talk 'bout."

"Fine. Asshole."

"You like my ass." His eyes sparkled as he flirted with me again.

"No, I don't."

Jess slid off the table, and I jumped down. His hand touched the center of my back, letting me pass in front of him. The warmth seared through the fabric, leaving an impression long after we stepped down the path. I smelled the ocean as we walked out toward the private beach. The sand squished between my toes. It was peaceful. I was fidgety.

"I see Crater," I said, looking up at the clear sky. I started our usual game as a distraction.

"Hmmm." Jess seemed amused. "Goin' for the big ones. Sure that's the best first move?"

"It keeps you from pulling those out at the end to trump me."

"I see Bootes."

"Cancer."

We played this like a chess game. I could count on one hand the number of times I'd beaten Jess since he first introduced me to the dark, mystical world floating just out of reach from Sprayberry. Usually, Jess kicked my butt, leaving me with four wins over the years; each victory rubbed so hard in his face, it was worth his months of retaliating torture.

"Ursa Major."

"Canis Major."

We kept a slow, meandering pace. The waves brushed up every so often, then swirled back into the ocean, leaving chunks of seaweed. Peering out in the darkness, I searched for my next move. "I see Perseus."

"Liar. Wrong time of year for Perseus."

"I swear it's right there." Our feet stopped moving, and I pointed off in the distance. He shook his head and stuck his hands in his pockets, kicking sand up with his bare feet.

"I'm not lookin'."

"Come on. Please, Jess. I'm not kidding."

"I'm just gonna pretend you're not tryin' to cheat. Unless you wanna forfeit?" Coming up from behind, I slipped my hands around his cheeks to tilt his face upward. My body pressed into his back, my nose into his shoulder as I forced him to see where I pointed. "Nope. I'm not lookin'. Now stop before you end up somewhere you don't wanna be."

"Fine. The moon."

"Really? The moon?"

"Yes. The damn moon counts too, even though you say it doesn't. Beach rules, not Sprayberry."

"Fine. I see your moon and raise you a Hydra."

"Now *you're* cheating."

"You get the moon. I get Hydra." His eyebrows went up, taunting me. I stalled again, searching the sky. He had me in a virtual choke hold, and I was about to lose once again. "That's the best you got, Al? I even let you have a mulligan."

"That was completely fair. Besides, I swear you said Leo twice."

"Nah…that's not gonna work. You out?"

"Fine!"

"Fine what?"

"You win—*again*."

"So that's, like, my five hundredth win? It's 'bout time you paid up."

"Bullshit. I don't remember us betting on it."

"Bullshit is right. You pulled me out here for somethin'. So tell me what it is." We stopped walking at some point, and he stared down in my face, just inches from my nose.

"I don't know what you're talking about." I was delaying the inevitable. Maybe I shouldn't tell him after all. I wanted his smile to continue just a little longer.

"Okay, then truth or dare. You pick."

"Jess, I don't play that with you anymore."

"Dare it is."

"What? No!"

He laughed as the red spread across my cheeks. How did I get myself into this mess with him?

"Alex, I dare you to get in the ocean."

"Not happening."

"Wait, I'm not finished. I dare you to get in the ocean, and it has to be deep enough to get that hair of yours wet. None of that toe-in-the-water shit."

I stared at him, feeling backed in a corner. "I hate you."

"I know, and it's really fun to watch you squirm."

"I'm not squirming."

"Then get in."

He wanted to play. Fine. I could make him squirm too. Even though I brought a suit on the trip, the black bikini stayed in my suitcase. My underwear didn't match, but hopefully, it wouldn't get to the whole set. My stomach felt a little nervous as my fingers unbuttoned my denim shorts. I paused on the zipper, looking hard into his blue eyes. Pulling the tab, I let go, and the pair fell to my ankles. I kicked them to the side, never breaking eye contact.

"Your turn."

"What are you doin', Al?"

"Your dare. Oh, and I'm not going alone. Start stripping."

Jess watched me, trying to gauge my end game. With a quick motion, he pulled his T-shirt over his head and tossed it on the sand next to my shorts. "I believe it's your turn, Alex."

I wore a gray, plaid, flannel shirt because it was chilly with the sun gone. My fingers fumbled with the buttonholes while I kept my eyes on his face. I moved slowly to the next one, revealing a little more skin. I had his attention. The teasing smirk evaporated as he watched me undress. I swallowed hard. Jess didn't seem to notice as he stayed focused on my fingers taking my shirt off. Reaching the end, I let the fabric slide off my arms. I stood clad in only my white lace-trimmed panties and gray cotton bra. The thin fabric clung over each cold B cup.

I stood just a few steps away from Jess, close enough for him to reach out and touch. I knew he was focused on me without clothes. Wasn't that the point? Distract to get out of this dare. Distract to keep from talking. Sadie's warning came back, and I pushed it away. It was just a stupid child's game.

"Jess?"

"Hmm?"

"Your turn. Well, unless you're saying I win."

"Not a chance. You tell me why we're out here, or I guess we keep goin'."

His pestering smile returned as he watched me fidget. Jess unfastened the front of his jeans and paused to study my reaction. A surge of panic shot through my gut. I assumed he had boxers underneath those tight pants. What if, tonight, of all nights, that boy went commando? My face got red at the thought of seeing him completely naked. Jess winked, and then let the denim fall to the ground, revealing a pair of form-fitted boxers. He threw them in the growing pile of clothes on the sand.

"Your turn."

Top or bottom. I had to drop one more. Damn! Why couldn't I have worn a tank top under the shirt? Jess laughed as I struggled, my cheeks getting redder by the second.

"You don't have to do this. Just tell me what's got you so twisted up tonight."

I didn't want to tell him yet. I changed my mind. I wanted to wait until we got back. Telling him tonight would ruin the trip. Looking back into his blue eyes, I agreed to still play this game.

Slipping my fingers behind my back, I grabbed the hooks of my bra. I felt nervous even though it was nothing Jess hadn't seen in the past. My stomach clenched at the thought. I wished tonight was the first time for Jess to see me naked; his sweet face transfixed, waiting for me to show him something he had wanted all these years. Instead, I remembered the anger and pain that wrecked him as he watched that video. I wished for a do-over, but those only existed in the movies—the stupid unrealistic ones with time travel. I changed my mind and reached for my panties, inching them lower over my hips.

Jess frowned. "Wait, Al. That's enough."

He grabbed me and tossed my whole body over his shoulder. My red hair flung out in every direction as my head bobbed against his back. He walked out into the water. The tips of my hair brushed the waves. Jess pretended to drop me head-first. I let out a scream and hit his legs with my fists. He changed his grip and tipped me forward. I slid down his chest, letting out a scream from the shock of the water. My feet searched frantically for the bottom.

"I've got you. I won't let go."

"You promise?" My fingers gripped his shoulders tight.

"Trust me, okay?" I smelled the faint scent of beer on his breath. He talked softly as our noses bumped in the rippling water. "Don't be afraid. Just relax. You can stand up here. We aren't that far out."

I nodded, letting myself settle against him. I uncurled my toes and extended my feet. The bottom felt both soft and rough with fragments of seashells. The ocean frightened the crap out of me during the day; a loud, dark swirl of destruction, pulling everything in its path back to the big unknown. Tonight, Jess made it a place of calm surrender.

His blue eyes watched me, and he grinned. "Tonight's our first time." I felt startled at his words. He laughed at my reaction. "To really be in the ocean together."

"Oh." A wall of water hit me from the side, plunging burning salt in my nose and eyes.

"You have to jump."

"Okay." I let go to wipe my face, and then quickly latched my arm back to his shoulder.

"Jump!"

I pushed off from the sand. We rose up together in a tangle of limbs under the dark water before sinking to the bottom. The next wave brought us back up and slowly down, creating a beautiful underwater ballet. I smiled. He laughed. I laughed. He smiled. We jumped high into the next incoming wave.

"Wanna go deeper?"

"Isn't it too late with the tide?"

"Nah. Come on." He cupped my butt cheeks in each hand, pulling me up around his waist. My thighs dug tight into his sides in fear of floating away in the dark abyss. "Keep your feet locked. I won't drop you."

"Promise?"

"No." Jess winked, even though he held me tight against his body. He moved farther out in the dark water. "You're gonna kill me one of these days."

"What for?"

"I'll be old with a cane, tryin' to fish your stupid ass out of some pond you fell in. You yellin' 'bout not swimmin' and me drownin' 'cause of the arthritis."

"That's not even realistic."

"Maybe." His eyes glowed back at me, turning darker in the moonlight. "You remember the last time I dragged you through the water?"

"Possum Kingdom."

"Yep. You were sittin' up there on top of that cliff scared shitless. I wasn't sure what to do with you. Throw you off the top or just kiss you."

"You wanted to kiss me that day? You never told me that."

"I know."

The wave splashed, pushing us up in a weightless float. I tightened my thighs, digging into his waist. As the water rolled back, my arms clung to his neck, our noses just a fraction apart. His wet hair covered his eyes.

Letting go of his neck, I moved the dark pieces back from his forehead. My fingers traced down his skin and brushed the drops of water hanging off his long eyelashes. I followed down his cheeks to his pink lips. My fingers brushed across the bottom one. My heart beat fast in my chest. *I bet they'll taste salty if I kiss them.* My thoughts twisted around as I stared at his lips. I remembered what it felt like to kiss Jess. It had been four years since that day on the meadow, and I still knew exactly how it felt to have his tongue in my mouth; a sweet piece of erotic heaven I'd tried to block out of my memory.

"Al, what are we doin' out here?"

"Uh…what?" I swallowed hard, feeling the burn of every place his skin touched me in the cold water. His scrunched-up eyebrows came back into focus. I fought the embarrassing red stain spreading on my cheeks, and I wondered if my thoughts were that transparent.

"Okay, let's go back to the beach. It's time for you to start talkin'. Whatever has you twisted up must be pretty bad if you picked gettin' in the water over tellin' me."

"Wait. I..."

"Come on. It's gonna be fine. We just need to talk, okay?"

"Okay." I frowned at his sweet face.

Jess carried me back out of the water, right side up this time until he dropped me in a disgraceful plop on the shore. The air felt chilly after leaving the protection of the ocean. It was strange to think I felt safer in the deep, tangled seaweed than talking on the wide open beach. Jess collapsed on his back in the sand next to me. I smiled a sad grin. I missed him already.

"I'm leaving after graduation, Jess."

The only sound came from the waves hitting the shore. I tilted my head sideways when he didn't respond. The tight muscles of his jaw glinted in the silver moonlight.

"Jess, say something."

"When?"

"June. I didn't know how to tell you." My chest hurt as I spoke the words. I didn't know how to explain why I had to leave him.

"Where are you goin'?"

"Paris."

"How long you gonna be there?"

"I...I...don't know. It's not a summer thing. I'm moving there."

"I see."

He rubbed the sand off his cheeks and then pushed the damp hair off his forehead. I watched in fear that another word from my lips would just twist the knife further in his heart. "Jess?"

"I'm sorry. You shocked the crap out of me. I wasn't expectin' you to say that tonight. I guess I thought you were stayin' in Austin."

"I know. I'm still in a little shock myself."

"So you gonna tell me what you're doin' in Paris?"

"Oh, well, I got into a program with the Paris School of Art. It was my professor, Mr. Lynch's idea. He helped me put a portfolio together. I didn't even know what to do. I had to get…um…recommendations and stuff." I fumbled, remembering everything I had gathered from the show I won in Dallas and the other in Houston. Those were competitions I entered after breaking the record at Gallery 51 by winning four times in a row.

"You're just takin' a few classes then?"

"No, I got a job too. Everything just sort of fell into place. Lynch has a connection. I'm working at this little gallery not far from campus. His friend Margarette is nice. I've talked to her several times already. She helped me find an apartment."

"You already have an apartment? Does your Dad know?"

"No. I wanted to tell you first."

He turned his head to look at me. His eyes reflected the pain he felt deep inside. "I wish you'd told me before now."

"I'm sorry. I know this hurts you. I know, even though Sadie thinks I don't." I swallowed the lump in my throat. The more I talked, the more I felt like I was describing my betrayal; all the hours I put into the application process; all the hours I kept from him. In my wildest dreams, I never thought I would actually get accepted and have it completely paid for on my own merit.

"You're not hurtin' me by wantin' to go to Paris. You've wanted this for years. You bought that poster at the school book fair. Wasn't that in seventh grade? I'd never seen you that excited before. And you're the only person in the history of Arlis who took French. Mother made the school get you that fancy teacher on the video satellite just so you could learn it. You've always wanted this, Al."

"I know, but I'm scared, Jess. I'm scared of wanting something this big and actually getting it. We both know what happened the last time I left. I screwed up everything for myself and…I screwed it up with you."

"You're not the same person. And we're not the same either. It's different for us now. We'll be fine. We'll talk. You'll come home for Christmas. Probably with some French guy with a stupid name like Jean Pierre. I'll hate him, of course, but we'll be fine."

"You think I'll meet someone named Jean Pierre? Really?"

"And I'll be stuck in Arlis. Maybe I should see if Ashley's back in town. Maybe it's time we became friends again."

"Asshole!" I wacked his arm. "If you hook up with Ashley again, I'll spend every dime I have to fly back over here just to slap the crazy out of you in person."

"See?" He chuckled. "We'll be fine."

"I guess."

"Just don't get all worked up. We're gonna be okay." He reached over, taking my hand, linking our fingers together. With his thumb, Jess traced circles over my wrist that had the tattoo inked into my skin. I still hated that permanent reminder. He never would say it, but he must have hated it too.

"How will it be different?"

"Because you're not that same girl tryin' to run away from everythin'. And, well, because…I'm lettin' you go."

I was torn, hearing those words spoken out loud—the finality of the meaning. Our hands remained clutched together as we lay side by side, staring up at the dark sky. I looked over at him, but Jess didn't look back.

"I'm sorry, Jess," I whispered.

"Don't apologize for wantin' to do somethin' with your life. I'm not mad at you. I understand. I really do. So I have to let you go."

"But I know I'm hurting you. I swore I would never do it again." I fought the tears welling up.

He looked at me with sad eyes. "We grew up. It was bound to happen one day. I think I always knew you weren't comin' back to Sprayberry. I knew you'd go somewhere else without me."

"I wish it didn't have to be this way."

"Al, you'll always be my best friend." He smiled sadly. "That's the thing with us. No matter what else I might have felt for you, I'll always be here as your friend. So go have your dream. Be the girl in the poster and don't let anythin' here hold you back. Live every damn minute of it. I want you to be happy. It's all I ever really wanted."

A tear fell down my check. "Jess, I want you to be happy too."

"I will. And no matter where you go, you'll always have a home at Sprayberry. You'll see me every time you come visit your dad."

"Huh?"

"Shit! That slipped out. He wanted to wait to tell you himself."

"Who tell me what?"

"Your Dad owns the farmhouse now."

"What! How?" I dropped his hand and sat up. My mind scrambled to process what he was saying to me.

"I meant that as a good thing. Don't get mad."

"What did *they* do?"

"They? It was my idea. Crap. I shouldn't have said anythin'. Your dad was gonna tell you when we got back."

"What did *you* do?"

"He was talkin' to me back in January. He and Caroline were thinkin' 'bout gettin' their own place. The farmhouse was my idea. I don't think he could afford to buy much anyway. He's only been payin' a hundred a month since you moved in."

"No." I shook my head. "He's been paying more than that. I know he has."

"Alex, he works at a hardware store in Arlis. He had bills and debt too."

"So you just fixed it?"

"I think this should've happened a long time ago. Your dad tried to work out some payment plan, but I wouldn't let him. It just wouldn't have been right. So we signed over the house and thirty acres. I tried to get him to take more land, but your dad fought me on that one."

"How could you do something like this?"

"Well, with Frank not bein' quite right anymore, I can do just 'bout anythin' I want at Sprayberry. There was some legal shit involved, but I have control of his half and I inherit the whole place when he actually dies, anyway. So I can give—"

"No…that's not…what the hell have you done? You *gave* the farmhouse and part of Sprayberry to my father! How could you do this without saying anything to me? No one told me a damn thing about it. No one asked me!"

"Alex, please don't get upset. I thought you'd be happy."

"Oh, I'm *happy*! I'm happy everything happened just like that. So easy that it didn't need to even involve me!"

"I'm sorry. I should've let him tell you, but just think 'bout it. You don't have to worry 'bout your Dad anymore. He will be fine there. And no matter where you go, you'll always have a home. That's why I did it. I did it for both of you."

"I can't talk about this right now." Jumping up, I took my shirt and shoved my balled-up fists through the sleeves. The anger prickled my nerves as I fumbled with the buttonholes. Jess watched me, looking confused. I pulled my cutoffs over my lace-trimmed panties. I took off across the sand into the darkness.

"Alex, where're you goin'?"

"I need to be alone. Don't follow me. Just let me go."

I kept walking and never turned back to catch his answer. My swirling emotions controlled every step. My father now owned part of Sprayberry, thanks to the Masons. *Thanks to Jess!* I needed to calm down. This is why Paris was important. Any hesitation of leaving just got obliterated. I got this graduate spot and job based on my own damn abilities. I finally had a future without the Mason name lingering on everything I touched. I finally had freedom from a past I could never quite shake as long as I remained here.

I kept walking until the private beach turned into a more crowded area. I watched the students. They moved in slow motion as I sat in the darkness. They danced. They drank. They partied without a single worry in their bleached-blond heads. Looking back up into the stars, I wished for that freedom—the ability to let my problems fly away into the wind without a single consequence; no past or present eating away at my soul. I wished I could just let go of this weight I felt on my shoulders.

I sat under the moonlight until my clothes dried, and then I took my sweet old time, walking back to the elaborate beach house. Breathe in. Breathe out. The nerves settled into the familiar acceptance of my life controlled by the Masons. This had to be the last time. I said it before, but this time it had to be true.

Walking up the deck stairs, the boards fell rough under my bare feet. I found Jess sitting on a fancy patio bench. It was covered in some ugly flower fabric picked out by Mrs. Mason. He didn't hear my quiet steps, so I stayed in the shadows looking at him. Jess was slumped back, staring up into the sky. He leaned up to take a swig from the Bud Light bottle and saw me watching from a few feet away.

"Hey."

"Hey."

I walked slowly over to where he sat. Standing in front of him, he looked up at me. Pure, unguarded sadness came from his blue eyes. It broke my heart.

"I'm sorry, Jess. I shouldn't have acted that way."

"Al, I didn't mean to upset you. I just liked the idea of you always havin' a home at Sprayberry. Even if you left, part of you would still be there."

"That's a nice thought."

"Why does it all feel so final?" He put a hand on each side of my waist and pulled me closer between his knees. I rested my hands on his shoulders. "I'm gonna miss you so damn much, Al."

"I know. Me too."

His fingers tugged at the two buttons I had fastened in my anger. He moved the shirt flaps away, exposing my stomach. His hands slipped around my bare waist. His right thumb touched the raised, jagged scar on my side. Slowly, he leaned forward and placed his lips against the permanent mark. I tensed, feeling his breath against my stomach. It tickled. I felt nervous and vulnerable and weak.

"You still think about me every time you see it?"

"Yes," I whispered. He kissed the scar again and then moved his lips up my stomach, leaving a trail of faint marks all the way to the center of my bra. "What are you doing?"

"I don't know. Somethin' I shouldn't."

"I know."

"Do you? Really?" His breath floated over my skin. "Do you know how many times I've seen that stupid scar and wanted to do that? How many times I've wanted to just touch you and not have a reason to? How many times I've wanted to kiss you?"

"Are you drunk?"

"This would be so much easier if I was just drunk off my ass. I'd have the guts to just go for it and not care 'bout the consequences. But I'm not drunk. I just don't care anymore 'bout doin' the right thing because you're leavin' me."

"I thought we were okay with this? We talked about it. You said we were fine."

"We did. I said the right things. I did the right things. But right now, I just want to be a stupid guy on spring break who sees a pretty girl. All I want to do is kiss you. So look me in the eyes and tell me not to do it."

"You know you can't just kiss me, Jess."

"No, I probably can't. But I would rather kiss you good-bye and deal with the consequences than regret I never kissed you tonight."

"This is insane. It will mess us up again."

"You're leavin'. How does it get more messed up than that? You didn't even include me in your decision. You didn't even ask me how I'd feel 'bout it."

"That's not fair, Jess."

"I know. Come here."

Jess grabbed my hips and pulled me forward. I let him without a fight. The guilt of his words hit the mark, making it burn in my chest. He held onto my waist as I straddled his lap with one leg on each side of his thighs. My wrists dangled loosely around his neck. Sadie's warnings came back, and I brushed them away. I remembered her words, but it was his face I could see, pleading with his eyes. Those damn blue eyes were always my undoing.

"Okay. One kiss, and then…" I'd barely uttered my reply before he leaned in with a shocking, full-mouth kiss that sucked the words right off my tongue. Jess tasted better than every deep-rooted memory I'd stored away that afternoon four years ago. His lips moved slowly and deeply as I struggled to stay focused.

"You taste like salt," I muttered against his mouth.

"So do you."

He kissed me again, and I never even tried to stop him. The feeling consumed every piece of my conscious. I couldn't breathe. I couldn't think. It felt crazy, stupid, and wonderful. He kissed down the side of my neck as my head tilted back and my eyes closed. He kissed down to the edge of my bra. Warmth spread from my belly button and into the rest of my body. I pulled back, overwhelmed by how far this quickly spiraled out of control.

"Want me to stop?"

Looking into those haunted eyes, I saw the raw pain I'd caused my friend. He didn't think tonight could make things worse. It could get worse, but feeling his lips on my skin, I didn't care.

"Don't stop." I hesitated, watching his face. "But it's just tonight and we don't talk about it, okay?"

"Just tonight."

"Promise?"

"I promise, Al."

He linked his pinky finger with mine and gave a little wink—a tiny snapshot of the former boy before he slipped his tongue back through my lips. I trusted him more than anyone else. I felt safe, so the rules of the game lifted tonight, setting me free if only for a few hours.

I kissed him back. Tugging his shirt up, I pulled the orange fabric over his head. My fingers touched his bare skin, and I allowed myself to really feel him. Leaning forward, I pressed my lips to his chest. I knew he liked it because every touch made him breathe harder.

Putting a hand on each side of my face, Jess pulled me back to his lips. I dug my fingers into his bare shoulders as he kissed me again, full on the mouth. I tasted him over and over again as his tongue slipped back and forth inside my lips. He was so good at this. *We* were so good at this together.

"I've never seen you naked," he mumbled softly. "I want to see all of you, Al."

"But you've…" I pulled back startled. He pressed his finger against my mouth to stop me.

"No, I haven't." He said it wasn't possible to erase the past, but there he sat, offering me the impossible. His blue eyes spoke back without a hint of mockery.

Jess pushed my shirt slowly off my shoulders and down my arms. The gray plaid fell somewhere on the dark porch. I didn't know. I didn't care. It didn't matter when those lips kept moving on my skin, his hot breath touching me everywhere.

He reached behind my back and worked the hooks on my bra. As he slipped the gray straps down my shoulders, Jess looked into my eyes. I felt nervous as Jess saw me for the first time. His sweet face smiled at me. "You're really beautiful, Al."

I closed my eyes as he kissed down the front of my bare chest. I sucked in a deep breath. I needed him. I needed him like I needed air. I needed him in a way I had never needed him before.

"Stay with me tonight," he whispered into my neck. "I want to keep touchin' you. All of you. I want it so damn much. I want to know what it feels like to be inside of you. I want to see the look on your face when it happens. I want to know just once, what it feels like to be us. Really us."

I stilled at the thought. I was scared. I was scared to say it. I was scared to hear it out loud. I was scared to think about how it would change things. I looked back into his eyes. Those damn blue eyes. Our paths were officially going in separate directions. I could give Jess one night—a stolen moment during spring break.

"Yes," I whispered. He stared back at me stunned. I don't think Jess ever thought I would agree. My heart pounded in my chest. This was really happening. I bit down hard on my bottom lip, trying to calm down.

"Are you okay?"

"I'm just…" I smiled, feeling nervous as I looked at his sweet face.

“It’s okay.” Jess whispered, taking my hand and placing it on his chest. His heart beat as fast as mine. “I know I asked, but I only want this if you’re sure, Al.”

I nodded.

“Okay.” Jess grinned, looking as nervous as me. He leaned over, grabbing my shirt off the ground. I slipped my arms inside, holding it shut over my bare chest. Crawling off his lap, I followed Jess across the deck with my bra in my hand. Before opening the door, he kissed me slowly, pushing my back against the side of the house. His hands slipped under my shirt, moving across my naked skin. He pulled back and kissed me on the nose.

“You ready?”

“Yeah.”

We stumbled into the house, trying to be quiet so the other house guests would not interrupt this terrible idea. Jess opened the door to his bedroom and pulled me inside. The door shut with a tiny click of a lock. This time around, no one would see except the only person who mattered.

I woke to the sound of rugged breathing. Each exhale of warm air floated in small tingles across my neck. Pieces of silver moonlight peeked in the window, illuminating the heavy body tucked around my bare skin, so close and so familiar; he almost felt like an extension of my own limbs.

The last few hours played through my mind like flashes, bringing a smile to my swollen lips. It was like flying through a lovely dream. I remembered each touch, each breath, and each word. I blushed thinking of all the places those pink lips had touched my body. I swear that boy tried to kiss every single one of my freckles—the ones he thought were so beautiful. I would never forget a single moment of tonight. The memories would stay locked inside a piece of my soul.

Sadie was correct. The right person at the right time was nothing short of magic, but now it was time for me to turn back into that pumpkin. The clock across the room glowed 5:27. Scooting out from under his body, I knew it was important to vanish from the room before Jess woke up. We had made a promise that would never stick if I were still there when the sun flooded the room with reality. I wanted a bittersweet end to this perfect night, not a fight slinging blame over our careless actions.

Slipping on one of his T-shirts, the familiar citrus, leather scent filled my nose. I watched his sweet face as he slept. Jess made my body and heart feel things no one else would ever come close to touching. In a few hours, I would sit at the volleyball game, pretending this never happened. A single tear slipped down my cheek. This would hurt.

My fingers traced the jagged scars imbedded in his arm from the tree-house fire. Sometimes when I looked at Jess, I still saw that boy. The one who stood in the hallway. The one who always saved me. That boy deserved a better life than what I could give him.

Leaning over, I softly whispered against his dark hair, my parting words not for the night, but for our entire relationship. It was time. I couldn't be selfish anymore.

"Good-bye, Jess."

Chapter 38

When I was twenty-two...

I watched from the safety of my dark sunglasses, with sweat dripping down my forehead. Sadie sat next to me in the adjoining chair; her rambling words echoed faintly in my left ear. I just wanted to watch the sand without feeling the weight of the world, without hearing her stupid lecture.

"You had sex with Jess and promised not to talk about it? That's the most ludicrous, moronic, just plain *stupid* thing you may have ever done."

I didn't reply. We both knew this wasn't the worst thing I'd ever done, but I really didn't want to be reminded of that incident either.

"I told you to discuss this with him. Just try to put some perspective on your complicated relationship. Instead, you granted him some ultimate last wish and agreed to not speak about it so you wouldn't feel guilty about leaving him in a few months."

"It's over Sadie," I mumbled.

"It's not over. You may pretend it's over, but last night was just plain self-sabotage on your part because—"

"Shut up!"

"Alex."

"Shut up, Sadie. Just shut the hell up."

I felt sick. I couldn't even make eye contact this morning with Jess. He wasn't even focused on the game, and he never looked in my direction. I knew he was angry because I had sneaked away before he woke up. I didn't know what else to do but leave. I'm not sure what Jess expected to happen this morning. The consequences of our actions were speaking loud and clear in the middle of a thousand people.

I wish he'd never asked me. I wish I'd never agreed. I wish I never knew how it felt to have him touch me from the inside out. I wish I never knew what it felt like to really be us. The weight of our actions pulled tight around my neck like a noose. Most spring breakers brushed the usual crazy antics of the week right off their shoulders without a second thought. Ours came with a high price that twisted around my heart, over and over again, closing off my blood supply.

Wearing the dark shades, I watched the sand. I watched the slutty girl in the yellow bikini. I watched two guys spill beer on the people next to us. I watched everything but him.

The game ended. The boys lost. Jess and Seth made their way over to us on the sidelines. He pulled his T-shirt over his sweaty chest. My stomach twisted as I watched him get closer. I didn't know what to say to Jess. I didn't know how I should act. I didn't know how to pretend like last night never happened, and it scared me.

Jess stopped in front of my chair. He smiled, saying nothing. I pulled off my sunglasses. Sadie's voice drifted away with the rest of the spring breakers. His blue eyes spoke a thousand words all rolled into a heartfelt stare. They calmed the panic inside my body. In the silence between two friends, the air carried an entire conversation. His dark lashes blinked back a vow I knew he meant more than anything: *I promise this will not destroy us.*

Chapter 39

When I was twenty-two...

I pulled my suitcase out to my father's truck. The brown bag contained only personal items since I planned to buy most things once I arrived in Paris. The moment seemed surreal. After months of endless planning, preparation, and finally graduating, I was leaving. I went back and sat on the porch steps to wait. The sun beat over my head and sweat ran down my back, creating wet spots against the fabric of my T-shirt. Things I would not miss: damn fire ants and the sticky heat of a Texas summer.

"We gotta go, Pumpkin."

"I know. Just a few more minutes." I looked at my phone, seeing the screen absent of any texts or missed calls. I waited, feeling a little sick.

My father stood in front of me and put a hand on my shoulder. "We can't wait any longer."

"But…he promised."

"I'm sure he just got tied up. We need to leave, or you'll miss your flight."

I climbed in the truck, feeling panicked. We pulled out of the driveway with my face pressed against the glass, half-expecting him to come flying across the yard from somewhere out on the meadow. Jess promised to be here this morning. *He promised!*

All the way into the city, my father chatted with his words of thoughts and wisdom. The creases around his bright eyes seemed deep today. He was sad but tried every possible way to stay upbeat about the trip. He used *that* word over and over again, except this wasn't just a trip. I let my father stay in his deep-rooted denial as I stared at my phone, hoping Jess would call, but the little box remained silent the entire drive to the Dallas-Fort Worth Airport.

Checking in at the ticket counter, I glanced down once more at the phone clasp in my hand. I assumed Frank had Jess knee-deep in something far out in the depths of Sprayberry; his morning consumed with responsibilities much more important than me leaving. I did my best to understand and felt the guilt of the moment. I had no right to ask anything of him.

Over the last few months, the regret of college stupidity stabbed away, over and over again. Jess never kissed or touched me, but I felt it anyway—the electric pull even when he was all the way across a room. We were always close, but it had transcended into a different type of unspoken cement binding us together, which made this lack of a good-bye cut so deep. I needed to see him just one more time. I needed to hear his voice. I needed to feel his arms wrapped tightly around my shoulders. Instead, I just felt hollow, like a limb had been severed from my body with a dull knife and I was leaving it behind at Sprayberry.

The anxiety bubbled around inside my stomach. I pulled out my phone and placed the silent box in the security bucket. Turning around, I gave one last wave toward my father. He stood on the edge of the gated area. His hair was mostly gray these days. He wiped away a tear in the corner of his eye. I felt sad for the middle-aged man standing alone, watching his only child leave. He knew deep down, I wasn't coming back for a very long time. I wished Caroline were here to soften the blow, but she was forced to stay behind with an emergency at Jeeter's.

My father smiled one last time before turning away. Fighting the urge to run back and sling my arms around his neck, I stepped forward through the body scanner. The grinding noise generated a perfect image that violated my body straight to my scared soul.

I wanted Paris. I needed Paris. I silently chanted the words as a reminder.

The wait for the flight seemed endless. Sticking in my headphones, I slipped away into the sounds of Kings of Leon. I eventually boarded the Boeing 767 with the rest of the world travelers, all destined to new places and new adventures in cities of the unknown. Taking the window seat, I glanced at the large man squashed in the one next to me. A strange odor wafted up from around his body. Cringing, I took a deep breath through my mouth, trying not to think of the many hours to come crammed just two inches from this weird, bologna-smelling stranger.

Checking my phone one last time, I flipped the OFF switch and settled against the seat. I yearned to keep it activated but didn't want to chance crashing the plane with my desperate need to hang on to the hope of hearing his voice.

My toes fidgeted inside my gray canvas shoes. I hated flying. The sound of the engines vibrated my seat as we left the tarmac. My white knuckles dug into the thighs of my jeans, making the Poison Oak-colored nail polish glow against my skin. Deep breath in. *Bologna.* Deep breath out. Grabbing the sketchpad from my travel bag, I flipped through pencil outlines to the first blank page. Nothing calmed my nerves more than putting gray lines on the paper. My heart jolted in my chest as I saw the familiar handwriting on the page.

Alex,

Did you really think you could leave without me having the last word? Well, here it is. I know. You hate me right now. I can hear you muttering out loud the ways to kill me. You know that's just going to scare the shit out of the poor idiot trapped next to you. Better keep it together. Air marshals handcuff people for that kind of crap, you know.

But seriously, Al, I've dreaded this day for months. So much that I just couldn't make myself come to the airport. I couldn't see you. I couldn't watch you leave. It hurts too much. Maybe if I don't see you go, I can still pretend you might just walk through the door tomorrow. Crazy, I know.

So I guess this is it. I'll miss you. I'll miss us. I already do. You mean more to me than anyone else. I want to say those other words to you, but I know it won't make this any easier. Just know that you'll always be my girl. I promise.

I know you're scared right now. But you're gonna be just fine. And don't cry. This paper ain't worth any of those damn tears of yours. Be happy. Remember, this is your time, Alex. Enjoy every minute of it. I hope you find what you're looking for out there.

Send me an email or something in a few weeks after you get your shit unpacked. Don't worry about me. I'll be fine. I wish I could have done more today, but this is all you get. Cheap-ass way out. I know.

—Jess

A tear rolled down my left cheek. Touching his familiar handwriting, I traced the sentences with my finger as I read them once again. In my mind, I heard his pancake-syrup voice, slurring the words together. My chest hurt. The pain came as if a gun fired tiny bullets into my skin with each word. The tears fell in a steady stream from both eyes as I reached the end with his scribbly name.

Damn you, Jess. I clutched the book to my chest, like I could hug him through the pages. I knew a letter fared better than an ugly scene at the airport, followed by a string of constant, sad phone calls. We both knew this was the better end.

I wiped snot on my sleeve, not caring if Bologna Man saw it. My teeth found their old familiar groove in my bottom lip; an ugly cry needed to wait until later. Tucking the sketchpad back into my bag, I pulled out my headphones. I stared out the little window at the squares of fields and ranches thousands of feet below me. I fell asleep without even a glimpse of the deep blue ocean.

The congestion of the Paris airport surpassed the ever-present dysfunction of Dallas-Fort Worth. I made it through customs. The nerves of the unfamiliar circled through the blood in my body. I found my bag in the maze of people babbling in a hundred separate languages. Reaching the lobby doors, I saw a tiny little sign with my name: ALEXANDRA TANNER. The tall, elegant woman poised with a silhouette of a model. She seemed younger than I expected.

"Margarette?"

"*No. Je suis Greta. Mlle Margarette est occupe. Je vous emmene a l'appartement.*" Her heart-shaped face blinked with wide, green eyes, waiting to see if I comprehended. The city lights illuminated her chocolate hair, which was cut in a short bob around her long neck. My vast knowledge of French vaporized from my head. She smiled faintly with understanding. "You have long flight. Better tomorrow."

"Thank you. You are taking me to my apartment? *Vous me aider a l'appartement?*"

"Yes. I help. I stay in apartment too. I show you city."

"You are my roommate?"

"No. *Petite* room. *Une* room?"

"Only one room?"

"*Oui.*"

"*Vous vivez ene meme batiment?*" Greta shrugged, uncertain of my garbled words, which held a southern accent compared to her voice that sang the syllables like poetry. I followed behind to a waiting cab. "Do you live in the same building?"

"Oh. *Oui.*"

The cab driver flew down the freeway, passing cars faster than I could comprehend. Fatigue crashed my senses as I peered out the window glass. New and old buildings rose up from the ground and flashed by in a blur. We crossed a river and moved deeper into the city.

"You go to the university too?"

"*Oui.* I am second year."

"The tower?" I asked Greta, feeling the shame of knowing the question sounded like a tourist. I knew the apartment and university resided close to Champ de Mars. I needed to see the one place that would make everything feel grounded.

"*Oui.*" She turned to the driver and rambled off a sling of sentences that flowed like a beautiful song. As far as I knew, she just cursed him out with the voice of an angel. The cab whipped by pedestrians and turned corners on two wheels. Hitting the breaks, a squeal echoed as I fell forward against the back of the seat.

"You ten minutes."

"*Merci.*"

Stretching my long legs, I ran past the visitors with maps and little packs fastened around the waist. I knew the spot from years of conjured-up memories. The lone bench rested just off the sidewalk. The last few steps made my lungs constrict in breathless spasms. I sat down, feeling the hard metal beneath my legs. Staring out toward the tower, I did the one thing I always wanted but could never do with the poster in my room. I turned around to see the view from the other side of that little bench.

Chapter 40

Today, 5:36 am.

A tap on the glass causes the bruised heart in my chest to lurch right through the fabric of my shirt. I see a pair of hazel eyes smash right into the dark tint, searching for their prey. Sadie. Clicking the release button, I give my friend access to the sealed-up truck.

"What is that horrific smell?" Sadie spat as she hikes a tiny leg up into the driver's seat. Even in the middle of the night, she wore a designer pair of crisp jeans and tan high heels.

"Sorry. I threw up."

"Did you eat a decomposed carcass of some road animal? It is positively disgusting out there. And humid. Why does it feel like the steam room of Bontegia?"

"Bontegia?" I smile. My lips curve just enough on the edges. I would like to think it qualifies as a true smile.

"Oh, sweetie." Her green eyes reflect back in the same shade as her silk tank top. "We have discussed Bontegia. The holistic gym with the focus on the mind, body, and spirit. Remember? You called it a ridiculous use of my over-indulgent expense account."

"That sounds familiar." I really do smile that time. "You're early. I thought it would be close to nine?"

She reaches over and threads her fingers between mine. I wait for her to insult my chipped nail polish. "I cashed in a favor from someone I can't mention. So I arrived in *style* in my own private jet."

"Wasted that one on me?"

"Just for you, sweetie."

"Thank you."

I had asked Sadie once why she decided I was worth her time. Every moment of every second of her day came in a detailed plan, usually established weeks or months or years in advance. I asked my question before our senior year. Sadie had pursed her lips in a tiny bow before answering. "Sweetie, you seem to need a friend more than an enemy, and I am either one or the other."

"Okay. Now that I am officially in Texas, I refuse to let you stay in this dreary parking lot. No more hiding. Time to step over the vomit and march inside that ghastly place. You have to see him at some point."

"I know." The raw pain scraps in my throat. "Will you go with me?"

A brief look of fear appears on her beautiful face, and then quickly dissolves into her ever-present confidence. "Yes. I can go with you."

"Thank you."

I climb across the console to exit from the driver's side to avoid the mess by the door. We cross the parking lot to the revolving entrance. She links an arm through the crook of my elbow. I notice the enormous shoes propping up the tiny person. I notice the orange streaks as they come around the buildings. The light at the end of the tunnel, I suppose, to those looking for that sort of omen.

"I accepted the position in DC. I had every intention of calling you tomorrow. Well, I guess that is today now, isn't it? Maybe you should come for a visit. Get away for a bit. The winter will be horrendous compared to here. But you could stay indefinitely. How does that sound?"

Her green eyes cut toward my sullen face. She fails to offer a smile with the invite. I fail to acknowledge the underlying meaning to her words.

Chapter 41

When I was twenty-four...

Today was my birthday. Sitting at a table with Greta and two other students, I sipped a glass of Syrah. We chatted back and forth in easy conversation, all being in French. It was beautiful underneath the lights of the city. It was beautiful in so many different ways. I laughed at a story told by Hanna Prescott. She was another American who was in the program with me. We traveled together sometimes. Hanna and Greta were good, decent people; nothing like the Dutchs and Darcys of the world.

My phone buzzed in my pocket. Taking out the little box, I smiled at the words on the screen, feeling the warmth spread through my chest.

Happy Birthday, Alex!

I still thought about him every day. I thought about him, and it was okay. I didn't fall down in a puddle of tears and misery. I didn't drink myself into oblivion or dream of slitting my wrists.

You remembered my birthday.

I remembered.

We talked occasionally; never for very long and never about anything of much importance. Jess and I were both busy in our new lives. I think we finally reached a place of comfortable existence. We could talk, and it was okay. We could *not* talk, and still survive.

Thank you.

Are you having a party or something?

Yes.

Have fun. Good night, Alex.

I looked back up at my friends around the table, celebrating my birthday. Hanna poured more wine in my glass. Reaching forward, I clinked the crystal against the others. The sound echoed under the sparkling lights. I was here and he was there—each choosing a different fork in the road, each learning to breathe on our own, seven time zones apart.

Good morning, Jess.

Chapter 42

When I was twenty-five...

I rolled down the windows of the rented Hyundai the moment the tires touched the dirt road. They went down on all four doors as if the mere presence of Arlis willed them into submission. Feeling the air whip through my hair, I reached for the radio knob to switch stations. My hand froze in mid-stride hearing the deep voice of Jason Aldean. I smiled, imagining Jess flying down this very road listening to the twangy voice sing about some tractor. I'm sure he loved this one. I wondered if he could hear it right now, our lives parallel once more in the world.

Looking up through the front glass, I saw the vacant farmhouse under the half moon. My father and Caroline had gone to Abilene to visit her cousin. They would return in the morning, just in time for the Mason's Thanksgiving dinner spectacle.

Walking through the familiar old house, I felt like a stranger amongst items I had seen most of my life. Time never had a good way of standing still, except at Sprayberry. I was the cog out of place here as the hum of a well-oiled ranch continued to pump out the same barrels.

Opening the back hallway door, I found my room the same as when I left for college. The shelves were lined with old books and walls covered with paintings by an amateur. I paused in front of a photo of a laughing woman with red hair and a small, carrottop child—by far the one I always liked the best of my mother. She was happy in that one, and so was I. My father must have pulled it out while I was gone.

The rest of the frames chronicled a whole life with a dark-haired boy, from riding horses to the ridiculous snapshot from the night in the ER with his burn bandages. On the corner of my desk, another portrayed two smiling kids dressed in Arlis blue caps and gowns.

Feeling exhausted, I left the memories for a hot shower. The steam helped with the suffocating hold of apprehension. I would see him tomorrow. The entire flight and car drive riveted with nothing else but rambling thoughts of Jess Mason. What would I say to him? Would he be different, look different, or act different? The fear crept in around the edges. Maybe he wouldn't care to see me at all. I swallowed hard, knowing that was just plain stupid nerves.

Since I left, my days had become a life without him. The day-in and day-out of consistent mundaneness followed with splashes of the wild and extraordinary. I lived exactly as he had asked me to that night on the beach. I experienced it with nothing holding me back. I had a life with a job and classes and people who opened up endless possibilities. I had friends from countries I only heard mentioned in Discovery Channel shows. I had exactly what I desired the entire time I lived in Arlis—a life free of the Masons.

Brushing out my hair, I settled into the old desk with my trusty journal. The train might leave the station, but something always came in the baggage. Tucked in the back section of the little red book, I pulled out the Mason List. My need to mull over the contents failed to surface as often while in Paris. One foot on Sprayberry, I needed to see it. The urgency spread, catching my breath. After all these years, how could something so small and insignificant have such power?

A sharp tapping sound riveted off the glass window. The paper remained clutched in trembling fingers as I peered out into the darkness. A face pressed tight against the glass with a wicked smile. I folded the paper in half and shoved it out of view. Raising the window, I shook my head.

"Jerk! You scared the crap out of me."

"I know. Sort of the point."

"What are you doing here?"

"Figured you were already back. I wanted to see you."

"You could have seen me tomorrow. It's twelve-thirty."

"Which is tomorrow, smartass. And I haven't seen that rotten face of yours in a hell of a long time. I couldn't wait any longer."

Twenty-eight months, thirteen days, and roughly seven hours, according to the green glow on the desk—not that I was counting. Jess climbed through the frame, shutting out the cold behind him. Turning toward me, he never paused as he scooped me up in a tight hug against his chest. He squeezed the breath from my lungs as I took in the scent of Ivory soap against his neck. Every bit of reservation had left the moment I saw his face through the window. The grip of his arms relaxed, and I slid down his chest, causing my T-shirt to inch up and expose my white panty-clad butt.

Feeling self-conscious, I turned bright red in the dim shadows of my desk lamp. I tugged at the bottom of the fabric, pulling it down as his eyes cast over the front of it.

"Is that my shirt?" A large blue number, the same as his favorite cowboy Emmett Smith, graced the front over my breasts, which incidentally was the same number Jess wore on his high school football jersey.

"Maybe."

"You know that was my favorite, and you stole it."

"I didn't steal it. It's been right there in that closet. You could have taken it back anytime."

"Liar. I think it came back in your suitcase." He reached up and touched the side of my neck. His fingers ran over my skin, then down through my loose hair. His thumb stroked the soft strands at the end. I watched his face shift to that look—the one I knew very well, a desire deep in his blue eyes that said, "I want to kiss you." My breath held for a second, thinking he might just do it. "They not have any sunshine in Paris? You're like crazy pale and just all freckles."

"You jerk." I punched him slightly in the shoulder, feeling the pull of our familiar dance. I looked back into his eyes and without thinking. I slipped my arms around his neck. Jess held me tight against his chest. It felt so incredibly good to touch him after all these months. My tall frame relaxed against his body, molding into the every curve. The room went dark as my eyes closed. His right hand left my shoulder and traced lightly down my spine, coming to rest on my hip—a delicate and familiar touch coming from his hands.

While in Paris, I think my mind had done an excellent job suppressing how much I missed him, how much I wanted to feel him; excellent, until he climbed right through the window. I whispered against his shoulder, "I've really missed you, Jess."

"I know, Al. Me too."

I released my grasp and backed away. Jess held onto my hand and turned it over, exposing my wrist with blue stars inked into my skin. "What's this?"

"I drew it. You don't like it?" I wasn't sure what his reaction would be to my adding another permanent spot, once again, while I was away.

"It's really good. I get it, I think. Texas?"

"Something like that." I smiled as he released my hand. The tattoo was a simple design of four stars: a memorial to the beautiful sky I had left behind, drawn in the same color as the eyes of the person who showed it to me. Ironically, I now had both; a left hand that bore shame and a right that captured something I couldn't explain to anyone. Climbing in my bed, I covered up my freezing legs. "How you been? I mean, really."

He plopped down on the little twin bed, making the springs creak with each bounce. "Rough, but I'm hangin' in there. It has been long days and even longer nights sometimes. I swear problems around here don't come in threes. It's more like thirty-threes."

"I'm sorry I didn't come to the funeral. I wanted to. I just… I had…" My voice trailed off with little conviction.

"It's okay. Not much notice. Frank went out the way he lived around here: sneaky and inconvenient."

"That's one way of putting it. He went off like a crotchety old dog in the pasture to die alone."

"Can't say I blame him, Al. Propped up against a tree with his last thoughts bein' the meadow grass wavin' in the wind under the blue Texas sky. I guess it must have been peaceful."

"I guess so."

"I keep hearin' his cranky voice, you know. 'Boy, we don't got no time to be shootin' the shit.' I hear it every time I stop to take a break. Makes me work twice as hard. I want to do this place justice. He trusted me with it even if he had an odd way of showin' it."

He was tired. I could see every one of those lines of fatigue. His days were filled with unlimited responsibility. Most graduates took a job they would just leave for the next big thing. Jess inherited a life, a legacy.

"You're doing a good job. I know you are. It's just going to take some time with the transition."

"Thank you." He watched me for a moment with emotion tugging around his tired eyes. "Means a lot hearin' it from you. But I'm scared a little, Alex. I'm scared of failin' and detroyin' it."

"I believe in you. Besides, there's no way you could destroy something you love as much as Sprayberry."

"I just don't want to be the stupid one who ran the place into the ground. The buyers are antsy. They're worried I can't deliver the same quality. Damn Frank was doin' the job of 'bout five guys. It's a wonder he didn't fall over dead before now. It's officially mine. When Frank died, everything reverted to me legally except my parents' house and the oil. That's still tied up between all of us. But I officially own every piece of Sprayberry. All sixty-three hundred acres."

"Wow. I…I didn't know it would happen that way or that fast."

"I didn't talk 'bout it much because it scared the crap out of me. It's why they had to know if I wasn't willin' to do it. Arrangements had to be made. It's hard, but I know it was the right decision. Mother had no idea, though, on what it took for Frank to handle the place. I stayed with 'em for a while, but I had to move out. She was drivin' me crazy. I'm not livin' with 'em anymore."

"The eight-thousand-square-foot Mason Manor was just too small?" I giggled as I watched his face.

"Not funny."

"Okay. I'm sorry. So where do you live?"

"I moved into Frank's house."

"You've got to be shitting me! The spook house? We were too scared to even look at that place, and you live there?"

"Don't worry. I haven't seen any shrunken heads stuffed under the floorboards." He chuckled, rolling his eyes at my thoughts. "Just dirty old man shit."

"Like what? Never mind. Gross. I don't want to know."

"Not like that. Just nasty menthol medicine and cigarettes. The smell seeped into everythin' in that place."

"I'm gone, like, five minutes and you move in the freakin' spook house. I don't even know what to say."

"You're gonna laugh your ass off when you see it too. I can take you up there in the mornin'?"

"Okay."

"Good." His jaw clenched on the words with troubled thoughts, churning just behind the blue.

"What?"

He reached up and touched a piece of my red hair, letting the long strands pull through his fingers. "You weren't gone for just five minutes."

"I know." A jab of guilt erupted inside my chest. I had planned to come back for several visits. Despite the best intensions, I always seemed to book a ticket to someplace else—someplace new that didn't inflict pain. The thought of seeing his face and then leaving again was more than I could stand. So I just never made the emotionally riddled trip back.

Scooting closer, I rested my head against his shoulder. The pain remained, but it felt better just to touch him. "Tell me what else I've missed."

"I don't know." He picked up my wrist and rubbed his thumb over the blue stars inked into my skin. He held on and didn't let go. I wondered if he really understood what it meant. I'm sure he thought it was for Texas or Sprayberry or some constellation in the sky. Part of me wanted to tell Jess the truth. That tattoo might as well have been his name scripted in my skin; a tiny blue star for each of the letters in his name as they faded off in the distance.

"Come on." I needed to keep him talking before I said something stupid. "It's Arlis. You must have something good."

"Well, I guess Skeeter's got a girlfriend. She's a teacher from over in Mineral Wells. I think she's related to Ms. Baker. He met her at the church's Labor Day picnic. He can't stop talkin' 'bout her."

"Like, a completely normal woman? And she knows that Skeeter thinks they're dating?"

"Yep. I've had dinner with 'em." He let out a deep yawn. "And I guess the Landrys may sell. Said they're gettin' too old to keep up with it. Kids don't want it. Now that Frank's gone, they think it's time to see what else is out there before it's too late. They asked if I wanted it. I don't know. It would be another nine hundred acres. I'm still thinkin' 'bout it. I'd like to do it because of the Landrys, and it's good hay land."

"Just add it on to Sprayberry?"

He reached up, running his fingers through his soft, black hair. "I don't know. It has been Triple L as long as most can remember. I might keep it separate. It's a big decision, though. I'm already strugglin' with what I got."

I felt the stress oozing from his body. He was different than the carefree boy I'd left behind at Sprayberry. This man felt the weight of the world driving him along, pushing and pulling alongside a cliff. Lifting my head from his strong shoulder, I peered into the familiar face. "You've changed."

"I have?" The eyebrows furrowed up.

"Not in a bad way." I touched his cheek, feeling the stubble under my index finger. "I've known you for so long, I guess you just feel different. It's a good different. I know it's hard, but it makes you happy, doesn't it?"

"Yeah." His lips turned into a wry grin on the corners that faded into a little laugh. "Happy as a gambler who won a three-tit hooker."

"What?"

"Frank. Gotta love the nasty old bastard." He chuckled, letting out another yawn. His eyes seemed heavy as he leaned his head back on my wall. I nestled myself against his side. "The Bar got pool tables and some coffee shop couches. Ernie's tryin' to upscale the place, I guess. I've been there some with Buzz."

"Buzz is back?"

"I thought you'd heard. He blew out a knee his second year at West Palo. He was picked up by Tech before it happened too. Shitty luck, I guess.

He went off the grid after that and worked as a roughneck down in the Gulf. He got tired of living on the rigs and came back lookin' for a job. Buzz said he missed Arlis. Oh, and he goes by Bobby now. You'll have to see him before you leave. I hired him to work at Sprayberry."

"Buzz goes by Bobby, and he works for you?"

"Yep. Still gettin' used to usin' his real name too." He let out a big yawn, drowning out the last works. "Ashley's back too, you know. She's got a kid."

"No! She has a child? Like, she's a mother?"

"Yep. Little girl."

"She doesn't look anything like you, right?"

"You just like bein' nasty, don't you? She's not tellin' anyone who the father is. I don't think he's from here. She just showed up with the baby. She's workin' at the hospital as a nurse too."

"Wow. I just can't see her as a nurse. That would require Ashley to actually be nice."

"It has been a long time, you know. My dad says she's not too bad. I haven't seen her yet." His boots hit the wood floor as he stood up. My chest tightened. *Jess was leaving.* The clock arms turned at warp speed this visit. One blink, and I would board a plane. One blink, and he would be gone for another year or more.

"You leaving?"

"Nah." Jess pulled off his shirt. "I'm stayin'."

"Wh-what are you doing?" I tried not to look, feeling my cheeks turn red. His body had changed into a more filled-out adult version of himself, with a center patch of dark chest hair. In a few more years, Jess would be the mirror image of Dr. Mason; most considered him an attractive man stuck with the perpetual boyish face. Jess would look even better, with the smile of that ornery boy frozen in time. And as he grew older, that pair of blue eyes would still shine like sunbeams from a pile of wrinkled skin.

"I'm exhausted. I think I've been awake for 'bout thirty hours, and before that, we worked cattle for several days straight." Each boot came off, and he lined them next to my bed. "I stayed up takin' care of one last night. Prolapsed uterus and lots of blood. She pulled through."

"Guess you have learned something."

"Guess I have. I lost two the other day, though. Coyote pack took"em down." He dropped his jeans, leaving just his blue plaid boxers. He knew I was looking at him and gave me a wink. I rolled my eyes back at him, shaking my head *no*. "Come on, Al. It's not like your dad's here to kick me out this time. How old were we? Twelve or thirteen?"

"Thirteen."

"I never saw him get worked up 'bout us too many times. But that night. Damn. He looked like he was goin' to explode. He threw my duffle bag right out your window. I stood there confused as shit."

"Dad had taken me to buy tampons that day and freaked out. Then he tried to give me some kind of sex talk."

"Betcha just turned bright red."

"No, jerk." I frowned, throwing my pillow toward his head. He ducked, and the fluffy square hit my desk instead. A book fell, vibrating off the wood floor while the graduation picture teetered on the edge. Distracted, I didn't see Jess grab the pillow for a quick hit to my face, smothering me down against the bed. I screamed into the fabric as he let go, laughing so close I could smell his brushed teeth.

"So what'd he say 'bout me?"

"Nothing. He just said you couldn't stay anymore and then kicked your stupid ass out like I'm about to."

"You can't kick my ass. And you know what happens when you try." Jess climbed on the bed next to me and held the pillow up like a threat. He smiled with humorous eyes racked in fatigue. I felt a tightening in my chest as I watched my friend. I had missed him more that I could even put into words.

"Maybe I've gotten better at it while I was gone."

"Doubt it." Letting go of the pillow, Jess lifted the blanket up, exposing my bare legs sticking out from under his shirt. He reached over and pulled the hem down to cover my panties from being exposed. His face grew serious. "Tell me to go, and I will."

"Don't go." Nothing inside of me could look into that sweet face and tell him to leave. I moved to the edge, letting Jess slide between me and the wall. Under the faded purple comforter, his body fit snug against my back and curved around my butt. I reached up and turned off the lamp, bathing the room with only moonlight. I relaxed into the steady beat of his heart against my shoulder blades.

"You still smell like peaches."

"You just want me to smell like peaches." I smiled in the darkness, feeling his left hand settle in the center of my stomach over my belly button. Our feet intertwined, making the cold stiffness of my toes melt into his skin. Our bones settled and our muscles relaxed.

"I hate workin' all day and crawlin' into bed alone," he whispered into my hair. "It's a sad feelin' bein' here sometimes. It makes me miss you. It only feels right when you're here too."

"Maybe this isn't a good idea, Jess." I tried to move away, but his biceps grew tighter into a bear hug, clutching me to his chest.

"Please stay. I just want to lay next to you tonight. Feel you beside me. Hold you. I need this, Al." His heart beat faster through the fabric of my shirt. I needed to say no. Staying with him was a very bad idea.

"Okay."

He released his tight grasp, letting his fingers graze over my arms. They skimmed across my breasts and settled into a comfortable embrace back over my stomach. His breath felt warm against my neck. I fought the internal struggle and relaxed against his chest again. He felt too damn good.

"Tell me about Paris," Jess whispered in my hair.

My eyes darted to the old poster that was tacked to the wall with the yellowed tape—the one I had stared at night after night in this very bed. That picture failed to give it justice. "It's beautiful."

"More than Sprayberry?"

"Different than Sprayberry." I thought about all the days I had spent wondering around the city, all the places I had traveled. "I like the buildings.

They're so incredibly old. The history is just different when you walk down the streets. You see it and feel it in an entirely different way."

"I don't even know all the places you've been."

"Mainly Paris. I saw Marseille. I took a train down to Avignon and Nice. Italy was so incredible. I loved Florence and Rome. A few months ago, I flew over and spent a weekend in London. I took a bus out to Stonehenge. I sent you postcards."

"I know." I felt his breath settle into the folds of my hair. "I kept 'em all."

"I draw bridges now."

"What makes you do that?"

"I don't know. Something about them being so large and vacant, I guess. Even with all the people, they exist as lonely giants towering over everything." Just like me, but I kept that part out. "Parc Monceau has this little red one. I must have sketched it twenty different times, from twenty different spots." I felt his hand link through my fingers and rub over my knuckles as if he imagined the pencil clasped there in frantic motion.

"Parc dec Buttes Chaumont has this waterfall. They made it, I think, but it's still beautiful shoved in the middle of a city. A white marble gazebo looks over the water. It's not really a gazebo like the ones in Texas. They call it *Temple de la Sibylle.* There's a cement bridge sticking out of the rocks. I've never seen anything like it. So I had to put it down on paper."

"I like hearin' you talk about it. Makes me know that you're happy there. I can hear it in your voice."

With his arms wrapped around my body, his words made me feel sad, not blissfully content the way Jess imagined. The thoughts caused me to pause for a moment before continuing with the story he wanted to hear. I talked of Gustave Eiffel's suspension bridge and the one dubbed the Suicide Plunge. My voice grew faint with Montmartre Hill and Luxemburg Gardens. His breath grew shallow against my ear as I described every inch of the Louvre Museum.

Our bodies breathed the same; they breathed together, but I think they always did. Listening to Jess sleep, a peaceful feeling came over my body and whisked me away into my own dreams. A night full of haunting images flashed like snapshots from my subconscious—a colorful strobe of pictures very far from Paris.

I dreamed of the meadow full of green grass. The wind brushed my face. I heard the sound of laughter as I looked over my shoulder. A dark-haired boy tackled me to the ground. A set of blue eyes stared down at me with a wink. I smiled, feeling his lips press against my skin.

The intensity of the need for him spread through my body. I clung to the secret hidden images, never wanting them to stop. His hand teased up my leg and over my knee. His fingers spread across the smooth skin of my thighs. I wanted this. I wanted him. He pulled the hem of my shirt slowly over my head.

I was naked beneath him as he kissed me. It felt incredible. His mouth tugged at my bottom lip. He slipped his tongue over mine, leaving a sweet, minty trail. A warmth spread through my body, alerting my mind, making me more awake, more aware with each kiss that I wasn't in some dream. I blinked back into his blue eyes, watching me from my childhood bed.

"Is this real?" I whispered.

"Yeah." His lips moved over my bare skin. "You still think 'bout it, don't you?"

I was having a hard time staying focused as his mouth touched my right breast. My breath caught in my lungs. "We were supposed to forget."

He lifted his eyes and watched my face. "I never was much good at forgettin' you. I thought 'bout us every day that you were gone. I thought 'bout how this would feel."

Those words broke through the shreds of my reserve. I wanted to see Jess tonight, but I needed to feel him too. Placing a hand on each side of his cheeks, I looked into his sweet face. The sincere admission caved whatever was left of right or wrong. I kissed him. I kissed him hard, giving him everything I could in that moment.

"Alex. I just want you to know. There hasn't been anyone else," he whispered the faint words against my lips.

I had no right to feel happy, but the emotions twisted up through my chest. "Me either."

"No?" Jess seemed relieved.

"No," I whispered. Wrapping my legs around his hips, I pulled his warm body as tight as I could against my bare skin. Nothing would ever compare to the way it felt like to really be us. My nails dug into his shoulders with every movement. His warm breath spread across my neck with each gasp; a frenzy of lost time ending almost before it started. As the moonlight came through my bedroom window, the second time lingered more like the drip of sweet honey as I slipped into another beautiful and hazy memory of being completely consumed by Jess.

We kept going until he collapsed asleep, with me draped across his body. I heard the peaceful sound of his steady heart beating against my ear. In the morning, the guilt would eat away like acid into undeniable regret. Tonight, I pushed it away. Tonight, my dream was real. I drifted off to sleep, with my cheek against the soft patch of curls in the center of his chest, and his hand resting in a possessive embrace over my bare hip.

A buzzing pulled me from the warm cocoon. Using every ounce of energy in my body, I crawled from the twisted pile of limbs. I picked up my phone, trying to shut the screeching thing up before it woke Jess.

"Hmm."

"Alex?"

"Umm. Hold on."

Damn! I didn't need Sadie's dose of moral medication this morning. Pulling on my shirt, I slipped out the bedroom door, closing it quietly behind me. I caught one last glimpse of his sleeping face before it shut. At the kitchen table, I peered at the cell phone screen, trying to pull together something she wouldn't detect in my voice. I put a big smile across my bruised lips. He made me feel things—physical things that would be impossible with someone else. The smile became embarrassing real. *Shut it down, Alex.*

"Sorry, I was still asleep."

"Don't you get up with the rooster or something down there in Arlis?"

"For the last time, no roosters live at Sprayberry. Why are you calling me so early, anyway?"

"Sweetie, I can accomplish more before breakfast than most can in an entire day."

"It's six a.m. on Thanksgiving morning."

"Now that I am working on Senator Andrew's campaign, I have to look awesome and be awesome at the drop of a hat. The day and time are irrelevant."

"You are insane."

"Why are you whispering?"

"I'm not whispering."

"Sweetie, I know you. And that's denial whispering."

"I'm jet-lagged. I flew in from Paris yesterday. Remember?"

"I'm not buying it. Where are you?"

"At my dad's house."

"And where is our favorite cowboy right now?"

"At Sprayberry."

"One and the same. Very evasive, sweetie. So, what did the dysfunctional childhood friends do last night?"

Sadie could twist me a new one with the slightest wave of her hand, even from hundreds of miles away. I wondered how many other people's moral conscience wore pink lipstick and had wicked hazel eyes. Even this early in the morning, I pictured her beautiful blonde hair bouncing along with each high-heeled, perky step. Good grief, I hated her sometimes.

"Sadie, I don't want to hear it, okay? It was his idea. Not mine."

"Does it really matter who caved? Again, I might add?"

"Yes, it does."

"Fine. Keep turning in these cataclysmic circles of destroying your friendship, then putting a Band-Aid over the real issue. Two steps forward for Jess, only to have you yank that silk rug right out from under his boots when you leave for another year. Speaking of which, that's why I called. Are you still coming to Chicago on the way back?"

The air exhaled from my lungs with a hiss between my teeth. Regret. I knew it would come in the morning. I hated that evil little creature chopping away at my memories from last night, making the guilt churn in my stomach. *Thank you, Sadie. Thank you very much!*

"I'm still coming. I'll email my flight schedule."

"I am truly sorry, sweetie. I really hate putting a damper on your Thanksgiving reunion by pointing out the obvious, but you are not doing Jess any favors. His idea or yours? Still the same outcome."

"You're right. Okay."

"As always."

I rubbed my tired eyes, feeling them move around in their sockets. A migraine loomed. "So what phony Thanksgiving dinner are you attending since you stayed in Chicago?"

"We have three stops today, including a recorded segment at a soup kitchen."

"Are you having Andrew spoon-feed a bag lady for the American people to watch?"

"Alex! Be nice. It's a very nice gesture. Then tonight we have a formal gala with the governor at the annual lighting of the Christmas tree. He's endorsed Senator Andrew, you know. Game changer for us."

"Hmmm. Congratulations. Are you taking *the* Harrison Waldengrave the Fourth?"

"Why must you always say it that way?"

"What else do you call someone who sounds like an English Lord?"

"Don't be pretentious. Harrison is a normal guy. I can't wait for you to meet him."

"I'm sure he's a regular prince charming." It was time to end this call before I snapped at her well-intended interference. "Look, I'm tired. No coffee yet this morning. I'll let you go. See you in a few days."

"Good-bye. Oh, and eat a piece of turkey for me. You know I gave up antibiotic-filled protein, but I'm feeling a little remorse today. First Thanksgiving without roasted duck, but I guess your turkey will do."

"And I still take advice from you. Seems a little wrong."

"But you know I'm always right. People pay money for it now. That's an idea. I should send you an invoice. Maybe that would make that self-destructive head of yours listen for a change."

"Good-bye, Sadie."

"Bye, sweetie."

I clasped the phone in my hand, feeling the weight of the coming conversation with Jess; less than twenty-four hours on American soil, and we had already created an uncomfortable situation.

Through the kitchen window, only slivers of orange radiated out of the darkness. Morning had yet to make an appearance at Sprayberry. I could leave. I could sneak out before his dark lashes even opened. It's what I did last time, and it saved our friendship. I could do it again; pull on some pants and leave before he woke up, followed by an awkward few days of Thanksgiving, then a plane ride back to Paris.

Turning the knob, I prayed the door didn't squeak. Jess sat fully dressed on the edge of my bed with a piece of paper in his hand, reading by the bedside lamp. He looked up at me and frowned.

I froze. I froze as my heart stopped and skipped a beat. The words on that paper were more personal than any diary entry ever could be; it contained the stuffing inside my blackened soul. The pain resumed just behind my rib cage, and my arms went numb.

"Where…where…" Panic made its way out in ramblings. "Where…find…you're not supposed to see that!"

"Took some searchin', but I found it and I've seen it."

"Searching? You were trying to find it? Why? Why did you go through my stuff? You had no right, Jess. No right!"

"Sadie said you were obsessed with some list you made when we were kids. I thought—"

"Obsessed!" I shouted, cutting him off. I paced, feeling more panicked as control left every cell of my body. "Well, that makes me sound completely sane, doesn't it? Glad the two of you had a little talk. When did she call? Just now? That bitch hung up after ripping me shit this morning before I was even awake. She knew I would sit there and be pissed at myself while she had the nerve to call you and make more problems, siding against me."

"I didn't talk to Sadie today. Don't blame her. And nobody's gangin' up on you. Last night I saw you with somethin' through the window. I put it together and I wanted to know."

"It's not what it seems. Just give it to me."

"I want you to talk because it obviously means a hell of a lot to you."

"But it has nothing to do with you."

"It doesn't? Are you kiddin'? It's about my family. Shit, Alex. You have me on here."

"Give it to me, Jess." I growled the words. I needed control—to feel that paper in my shaking, sweaty palms.

"Not 'till you talk 'bout what this means to you."

"What's there to say? I hate your family. I hate Sprayberry. It's all on there in one big fat list. It says it right across the top: REASONS I HATE THE MASONS. That should explain everything. Isn't that what you want to hear?"

I expected to see some stunned expression, followed by screaming words. I knew the anger that could come from his blue eyes. Today, in the dark light of morning, he stared at me with something else I couldn't quite place. He let out a deep breath and scratched the side of his head. "Al, sit down and stop pacin' around like you're itchin' to break somethin'."

"What did you say?"

"Come on, Al. I know you better than anyone. I *know*."

"I don't break things."

"We both know you do when you get upset. So sit." He pulled me down on the mattress beside him and handed the paper to me. I quickly folded the page to cover the words. "When'd you start it?"

"I don't want to talk about it."

"Alex, you don't really hate us. When did you start writin' it? Talk to me."

"Fine." I let my eyes zone out on a spot across the room. "I was ten. It was the night of the carnival when I threw up on your boots."

"When'd it stop?"

"It hasn't, Jess. Don't you get it? I can't let go. It eats away at me. I'm twenty-five years old, but every time I open that paper, it's like I'm eight again. It makes me feel…angry…and…mad…and I want to smash things." I trailed off. Jess didn't respond. He was in deep thought. I had given him just a small sliver of the dark pieces I felt inside my soul. He wanted to know. *Damn it!*

"Jess?"

"Why didn't you talk to me 'bout it? I know you've had a hard time with this stuff but—"

"Why?" The anger surged. I jumped up and resumed to pacing. "*Why?* I hated everything about why I came to live here. I hated being at Sprayberry. From the moment I arrived, all I ever wanted to do was leave. I sat at night thinking about it. Wishing for it. I missed my home. My *real* home. I missed my life, but we couldn't leave. It was all gone. We had nothing. We had nothing except your *damn* family and their *damn* money."

I paced and paced, slinging my arms. I looked crazy. I felt crazy. I tasted the venom in each biting word—a deep, toxic bile that came from the suppression of these feelings.

"We lost everything. I'm not sure my dad even ate most of the time. We got kicked out of El Charro. The nasty *El Charro*, Jess. The black, mold-infested El Charro and the meth head who kept me up at night as he beat the shit out of his girlfriend. You know he used to watch me and my dad? Every time we walked up the stairs, he sat on the hood of his car smoking a cigarette. The guy had this tattoo that looked like a demon down the side of his neck in black ink with these red, swirly, possessed eyes. I'd try to sleep at night, but all I'd hear was his screaming. I'd dream about those blood-red dots chasing me."

I laughed a little, shaking my head. "At least we had an actual room then. That was before we got kicked out of El Charro. That's right. We couldn't even pay to live there. So we slept in our car. Bugs crawled on me at night, Jess. Did you know that? *Literal bugs*. I felt them sticking to my skin as I tried to sleep. Every time I closed my eyes, I was terrified they would bite hunks out of my arms."

"Alex."

"No, Jess. You asked why. I'm telling you *why*. I'm telling you all of it. Did you know it was in July? Almost the whole month of July we lived in there. The heat cooked our nasty sweat into the cloth seats and made them reek. It was this disgusting smell like rancid meat and dirty ass. It stuck in my nose and it took hours to shake it when I got up in the morning. It made me feel dirty. I never felt clean. When you met me? That's where I lived. That's what I smelled like. You brought more shit to the hospital every day in that damn duffle bag than I even owned."

Jess got off the mattress and tried to touch my shoulders. I slung his hands away and stared into his face. "I can't separate it, Jess. The bad stuff made me trapped in this messed-up codependency with your family. Every time I turned around, something else was thrown in my face. I couldn't leave. I couldn't stop it. I couldn't forget about it. I couldn't accept it. No matter how many times my dad tried to cram it down my throat. So I made the list. I wrote it down. Every damn piece of it. In some twisted way, it made me feel better. I planned to make it right one day. Maybe it would lift this smothering weight from my chest. Maybe I could breathe again. Maybe I could finally let go. I could look you in the face with a clear conscience and not feel like some piece of gutter trash who—"

"Alex, don't say that."

"It's the truth." A tear fell down each side of my face.

Jess touched my cheeks. I no longer had the strength to push him away. "Aren't you tired? I mean, aren't you exhausted carryin' this shit around?"

"Yes."

"Sometimes things just happen. You don't understand why. You just have to accept it was supposed to be that way so you can move on."

"You want me to just accept it? All of it, like it was supposed to happen?"

"Yes."

"She was *supposed* to die. We were *supposed* to be homeless. We were *supposed* to come to Arlis. I was *supposed* to meet you."

"Alex, whether you believe it was supposed to happen or not, it happened. Pushin' me away doesn't fix any of it."

"I know, okay. I know."

"Then how long are you gonna keep punishin' me for it?"

"I'm not punishing you. I'm just trying to do the right thing here."

"What's that exactly?"

"I don't know anymore. It all became too complicated." I was exhausted. I couldn't think or feel anymore. My knees wanted to give out; too much processing in too little time.

"I know it's complicated, but livin' here again, I see you around every corner. All the places we've been at Sprayberry. Alex, all the memories I have of this place include you too. I know you never wanted to be here, but you *were* here. And I don't wish it was any different. I just wish you saw it that way."

"I don't know if that's possible." My eyes closed, the pressure building inside. I just couldn't process it anymore. His pleading eyes felt like knives in my stomach.

"Come here, Al." His hands touched the side of my waist, pulling me closer against his chest. His boots stepped forward, one on each side of my bare feet. He was warm. I was cold. He pulled my weight against him, and I relaxed, feeling his familiar curves molding to my skin. Emotionally stripped and worn down on the inside, I let him hold me. I let him, once again, take care of me.

"I love you," Jess whispered against my head.

"Why did you have to go and say that?" My arms went slack, and I backed away, pressing myself against the wall by the closet. The air pulled through my nose in stale gasps. A tremor started in my hand. I balled my fingers in a fist to snuff it out.

"I'm sorry, but it's the truth. I know it scares you to hear it. Hell, it probably pisses you off too. But, I love you, Alex."

"Don't say things like that."

"I know all of this shit is twisted up inside of you. I understand and I hate it too. I hate that you had to live it, but it happened and you can't change it. And I can't change it."

"No, but I can stop this with your family. Being with you is like taking the ultimate thing from the Masons, and I can't do that. I can't be with you, Jess."

"Then why did you sleep with me before you left? Did you really think you could just be some random hookup? That you'd be just some random girl to me? It hurt, Alex. It hurt like hell watchin' you act like it never happened."

"We promised, Jess. No talking about it."

"I guess we aren't talkin' about last night either? I know you were just gonna leave again until you caught me with that paper. Just sneak away this mornin'. Right, Alex? You were just gonna sit across the dinner table eatin' turkey. Just gonna look me in the eye and pretend it didn't happen again. Act like I didn't spend half the night inside of you."

"Damn it, Jess. You came to see me. You started it. I didn't ask you to." I felt the anger surge with the accusation and the blame. There would be no uncomfortable and deceptive Thanksgiving dinner if he had kept his hands to himself last night. If he had just got in his truck and drove back to his own damn house.

"You sure as hell didn't stop me, and that's my point."

"I thought we had an understanding."

"An understandin'? One where you have sex with me and we pretend it didn't happen because you have a deep grudge toward my family?"

"Yes! I don't know!"

"She's right. Shit!" He laughed, shaking his head. "Sadie's right. I never thought I'd end up sayin' it. I'm the hopeless dumbass."

"Sadie?"

"How'd she put it? 'Jess, you are positively one of the last of your kind and that will lead to a very destructive downfall.'"

"What the hell did you talk about with Sadie?"

"You. We talked about how you're so jacked up. It doesn't matter what I do or how I feel." He shook his head. "You badgered me 'bout that party? It drove you crazy not knowin' what happened. But you couldn't bring yourself to ask her because you were afraid to have her rip you up. I think you already knew. Didn't you?"

"Knew what?"

"What we talked about. Sadie and I never made it to the party. We sat for hours at a restaurant. I think she planned it from the beginnin'. Get me away from you so she could hear my side of things. Sadie asked me if I just loved you or was *in love* with you. I said both. I can't really separate how I feel anymore. It's just the way it is. No end. No beginning. It just part of existin'." He shrugged.

"She felt sorry for me, Al. Sadie McAllister looked at me with those freaky shit eyes and felt sorry for me because she didn't see this workin' out the way I planned. You were too absorbed with the past, she said. You'd never let yourself actually love me. I'd never hear those words from you. I said I didn't care. It didn't matter how long it took, or where you went, or what you did. I had faith that one day you'd be ready, and I would be here at Sprayberry, waitin' for you, because that's how it's supposed to be. That's how this ends."

His breath came out in short bursts. The room felt claustrophobic. I watched him stare back at me from across the room; my body stayed pressed against the wall. This was completely insane. He really just said it; just spat that out and unleashed a whole truckload of problems. The thoughts tumbled around, spitting out the only thing I could process.

"You're not a dumbass."

"That's all you've got to say?"

"No." My hand slid across my stomach, feeling the nervous rumbling. "I get it. It's not that simple. You say it's what you want, but you don't know any different. If you met me tomorrow as some random girl in a café, you wouldn't feel the same way about me. I know you wouldn't."

"But I did meet some random girl. She was standin' in a hallway. I made her laugh. I made the random girl feel somethin' when she was broken.

I watched her face change. I've seen it a hundred times since then. Nothin' makes me happier than knowin' I'm the one that makes her feel that way."

"It's not the same. We were kids. You were eight. And it wasn't random. That hospital brought us together. That damn hospital and your damn money."

"You can't change the past, Alex. And you have no idea how bad I wish I could change it for you. But I can't. So you gotta choose to accept it or not. Accept me for who I am to you. Accept what the Masons did for you. You accept it all or walk away. It's your choice. All I have ever done is try to hold on to somethin' I thought was good. Somethin' that makes me happy. Somethin' that makes *you* happy if you'll just let it."

A beeping noise came from inside his jeans pocket. His blue eyes seemed annoyed as he fished out the little phone.

"Yep." His face looked stressed as he listened to the caller. "I'll be there in a few. You get the post-hole digger hitched up. I'll grab Reid and Bobby and see if we can head 'em off before they reach Prickets'." He nodded. "Yeah, I know. It'll be hell if they scatter in that intersection. Okay, yep. Bye." He ended the call and looked at me.

"Something wrong?"

"Yeah, that was Skeeter. Some idiot took out a chunk of fence across from the Landry's last night. We've got 'bout a hundred headed down the road." He seemed tense and already distracted with a hundred red faces. "Al, I gotta go."

"I know."

Jess stopped in front of me; the biggest conversation of our lives remained unsettled, like a basket of blood-soaked laundry dumped on the floor. His hands cupped the sides of my face; he looked troubled. Leaning forward, Jess acted like he would kiss me but changed his mind and pulled away. He left down the hallway. Not knowing what else to do, I followed him outside the house. Clinging to the post on the front porch, I felt the chill of the cold air bite into my naked legs. Jess opened the door to his truck.

"Al." He let out a deep breath. "There's no use fightin' 'bout it when you're just gonna leave in a few days, and it's just gonna hurt all over again. Let's just eat some turkey and forget 'bout it. I know it's what you really want."

"You know I'm not trying to hurt you."

"Really? Then why does it feel that way? I love you. And you're choosing not to love me back. That hurts pretty damn bad."

"Jess…don't."

"Just forget 'bout it, Al. I gotta go." Jess pulled a cowboy hat off the dash and smashed it on his dark hair. He climbed in the truck, slamming the door. A loud rumble echoed as the pipes fired up, and he was gone in a cloud of dust.

I leaned against the rail, letting the cool air numb my trembling nerves. I couldn't shake what he had said. Instead of going back in the warm house, my bare feet paced over the wooden boards—back and forth as a cold gust of wind flipped up the edge of my shirt. I stopped, feeling no relief as the anxiety built in my chest. His face and those words; I still heard them echoing in my head. I saw them floating around, almost visible in the air after being hidden for so many years.

The orange sun rose in a gradual assent in the sky, bringing light to Sprayberry. I sat my frozen thighs down on the black, wooden porch swing Caroline had my dad install the last summer. Letting my numb feet hang over the edge, a feeling of peace came over me as I saw the familiar shadows change into full color.

I forgot how beautiful Sprayberry was in the morning. Words could never describe the natural wonder and majesty of the place. Even though I was numb from the November wind, I sat swinging on the porch, watching the start of a new day as the sunbeams brushed the earth, like a magic wand, bringing the place to life.

My father and Caroline pulled up in front of the house. He got out, staring at me on the porch. "What are you doing, Alex?"

"I'm just enjoying the morning." My jaw shivered with the words. He climbed the steps and smiled at me. Leaning over, my father gave me a tight, warm hug that felt like a minute for every day I didn't return home. Jess wasn't the only person hurt by my absence.

"You're cold."

"I'm okay. You came back early."

"It's almost nine, Pumpkin."

"Oh." My joints seemed frozen in place when I let go of his shoulders.

"Let me grab you a blanket." He stepped inside the house for a moment and returned with a brown, rugged one—a present for my father that I had bought my sophomore year with Jeeter's money. I buried down beneath the soft folds. My dad took a seat next to me, causing it to swing with his weight. "So when did he leave?"

"What?" I swallowed hard.

"You two are about as predictable as the sun rising each morning."

"Oh." I twisted a string on the side of the blanket around my pinky, making it turn red. "About six-thirty, I guess. Someone ran through the fence over by the Landry's."

"I see." His feet kicked up, sending us back and then forward. "So what happened that made you sit out here, trying to freeze yourself to death?"

I pulled the string tighter, and the tip turned purple around my Foxglove-colored nail. "We had a fight."

"You want to talk about it?"

"I don't know." The thread broke, releasing my finger. "I guess he said some things I didn't want to hear."

"I see."

Caroline came out the door with two cups and a smile. "Here you both go. You need to get some coffee in you, Alex. Do you want another blanket?"

"No thank you."

"All right. I'm gonna finish making pies. We're supposed to be at the Masons' at exactly noon."

Her tiny frame disappeared back through the front door. It was times like these I was reminded of how happy I was for my father. Caroline was a blessing in his life. That man was gone; the broken one that once stood in a parking lot, needing the reassurance of an eight-year-old to survive. Somewhere along the way, the roles had reversed back to their rightful order.

Maybe it was Caroline, or the Masons, or just plain time that made us come full circle. This morning, he was the parent, and I was the child, desperate for direction and comfort.

I sipped on the coffee, feeling the vapors warm my nose. In a few hours, I would be subjected to a formal Thanksgiving at the big house as Jess and I stared across the table at each other—a stare of hurt and betrayal. I may have finally driven him mad.

"He's been having a hard time, you know." My dad took a drink, letting the black liquid settle. "The ranch stuff hasn't been easy on him. The poor boy always looks exhausted, like he could fall asleep standing up. He stops by here on his way home. He tries to make it seem random. Makes up excuses, but I know he comes here instead of home because it's the closest thing to you. It makes him feel like he still has someone to lean on."

"Does he talk to you about it?"

"Not really. Caroline gives him some supper, and he mostly just sits on the steps out here, staring out into the darkness. You've always been there for him, and now he just seems a little lost."

"You've got that switched around. He's always insisted on taking care of me."

"Nah. You two always took care of each other." He tipped back the cup, finishing the last drops. The swinging was making me dizzy. The coffee swished around in my stomach, burning up through my chest.

"Well, that about does it. I'll let you get back to thinking. Better not take too long. You don't want to cross hairs with Eva Lynn if you hold up Thanksgiving by being late."

"Yes, sir."

My dad disappeared back inside to the old farmhouse, the place he now owned, thanks to Jess. I remembered the day we moved in; sometimes it seemed like yesterday and sometimes it felt like a million years ago. I looked out in the distance, wondering if he found them all, the red faces running down the dirt road. I guess I would find out at lunch while he glared across the table, hating me.

Easing up from the swing, I went inside for a warm shower. It had been a very long morning and an even longer night; the smell of his body still lingered on my skin.

After getting ready, I spent the rest of the morning helping Caroline make pies, just like old times at Jeeter's. She made a peach one, just for Jess, and a pan of mac and cheese. My father had it all wrong: Jess stopped by in the evenings for Caroline's food, not me. It was like living at Jeeter's.

We arrived at Mason Manor with only a minute to spare. Dr. Mason hugged my tall frame. Mrs. Mason leaned in for a quick kiss on the cheek, leaving a clear print of gloss.

"It's good to have you back, Alexandra. I can't wait for you to entertain us with your stories of Paris." Mrs. Mason turned my wrist over, seeing the stars. I cringed for the inevitable reaction. A lady would never adorn herself with such items. She studied it for a moment, then looked me straight in the eyes with an odd smile. "Well, that's an interesting shade of blue, dear."

"Yes, ma'am." I almost choked on my own spit. She released my hand, and I followed her into the formal dining room that seated sixteen.

"I'm sure Jessup was excited to see you last night. I'm sorry he had to run off so early. The ranch eats into every minute of his time. I try to get him to slow down, but you know how he is, dear."

Shit! The embarrassment blasted my cheeks, leaving me feeling naked. The whole damn town probably knew his truck was parked at my house last night. It didn't matter how early he left or how late he got there; somehow the gossips just *knew* in Arlis.

Dr. and Mrs. Mason took a seat at each end of the grand table. The distant cousins from Luckenbach had made the trip this year. Mr. Buckley, my father's boss, whose wife had recently passed away, sat next to Caroline. I pulled up my usual chair beside her and looked across the table, seeing his empty seat with a fancy place setting of china, rimmed in gold. Two more with folded linen napkins held places for Skeeter and the boy formally known as Buzz.

Mrs. Mason presided over the dinner, leaving no question of her role as the matriarch of the house. After my time away, her voice felt like a strong glass of sweet ice tea. The meal carried out much like those in the past hosted at the Manor, with one exception: Jess never came to dinner. At 12:35, the main telephone jingled with an incoming call. Her lips pursed into a disapproving frown as she talked with her son.

Every click of the grandfather clock counted off the minutes of his absence. I fielded questions about Paris. Mrs. Mason's cousin Betty had gone back in 1972. She grinned while her eyes begged to share her stories. I handed the conversation over to her eager face, considering the entire platter of turkey and dressing I needed to choke down my tight throat. I ate a bite for me. I ate a bite for Sadie, the manipulative bitch. My layover in Chicago had one hell of an argument on the agenda for conspiring against me with Jess.

I looked at the empty plate across from me. I heard those words again: *I love you.* I fiddled with my mac and cheese. *I love you.* I wanted to pretend he never said it since that proved to be the only reasonable solution at this point. I wanted to pretend that I didn't hear the pain in his voice as he got in the truck. *You're choosing not to love me back.* I dreaded the moment he would come in the room. I dreaded those blue eyes. I dreaded the half smile he would flash at the others. I dreaded that angry and broken glare. I dreaded the pain he tucked away to keep the peace. *You're just gonna leave.*

All I ever wanted to do was the right thing by him. Instead, I hurt Jess over and over again, like I had a voodoo doll with his head taped in the center. I jabbed and poked until there was nothing but stuffing left. My heart just couldn't stand it anymore. How could I look Jess in the face and pretend after finally hearing the truth? The answer centered in the middle of my chest as I continued to stare at his empty plate.

The elaborate meal ended, and we returned to the farmhouse. I immediately went to my room and got out my suitcase. I shoved everything I could find inside and zipped it tight. With shaking hands, I picked up the phone and called the airline. My father watched from the doorway as I spoke to the reservation desk. This was the right decision. I knew it in my heart. I clicked END and shoved the phone in my pocket.

"You sure about this, Pumpkin?"

"Yes."

"All right. I'll help you get loaded up then."

Chapter 43

Today, 5:45 a.m.

Sadie and I walk through the hospital doors. We follow the path through the winding hallway to the waiting room designated just for the ICU patients. She stops abruptly, seeing the folds of the area bursting at the seams.

"Who are these people?"

"Arlis," I answer calmly.

We were always notorious, but we were *their* notorious, which made this scene feel comforting. I scan from one familiar face to the next, seeing the Landrys, the Crawfords, and Ms. Virginia Abbot with her son visiting from Houston. I make eye contact with Mrs. Ida Fleming as she rests in the corner with her grandson, holding a teddy bear blanket. Next to a tray of sandwiches, Sara Beth Nelson visits with the Pritchetts and Ernie from The Bar. My father's boss, Mr. Buckley, stands alone by the water fountain, dabbing red swollen eyes. I see Gunther from the feedstore, talking to Bobby while Skeeter holds the hand of a tiny blonde woman. The room is flowing with people who left their families and businesses in a caravan to Dallas to be with one of their own.

A hand pats me on the shoulder, and I turn to see Caroline. Another wraps an arm around my waist. They pull me in and crush my body in a landslide of embraces. The bodies pass me around from one person to the next as words float around my head and against my neck.

"Alexandra." I turn to the familiar voice of Mrs. Mason. The polished woman reeks of a disheveled mess. She pulls me tight against her tiny body. "You're feeling better, dear?"

"Yes, ma'am."

She leans back with a tormented smile. "Good." She holds on for a moment, clenching my hands. Her eyes float in a sea of wetness before she releases me back into the masses. Shrinking away, I press my back against the wall and observe the room. Sadie stands to my right in fascination of those around us.

"You need to go," she whispers, her hazel eyes peering into mine.

"I know."

"Want me to go with you, sweetie?"

"No." I swallow hard. I need to do this alone. Walking down the hall to the restricted area, my gray shoes squeak, announcing my arrival on the path to the inevitable. An older woman with straight blonde hair glances up from her screen. Her rosy cheeks support a set of round-lens glasses. I run my hand over my stomach, trying to steady the anxiety.

"I'm here to see Jessup Mason."

"I'm sorry, ma'am. Just like I've told the others. It's family only."

"I know." I freeze for a moment, biting my lip. I twirl the band around my finger. It feels loose, like it might slip off with a shrill ping on the hard floor. "I'm Alex Mason. I-I'm his wife."

Her eyes jump up in a brief flash of pity. "I'm sorry. Let me take you back, ma'am. I'll need to have you wash up first, though."

"Okay."

The woman with the tag that reads SHARLENE puts an arm around my waist. The motherly figure tucks me close to her side as we walk through the doors.

Chapter 44

When I was twenty-five...

The roar of the engine vibrated through the ground and rattled the inside of my chest. This was it. No turning back now as the future loomed ahead in the clear, blue sky. The weight on my shoulders appeared to be almost gone. The inside of my body could breathe, like I'd been held underwater for so long I forgot how to take in a breath of oxygen. I would finally be free.

The engine killed, leaving only the sound of the wind through the trees. The boots crunched the winter grass, getting closer to where I sat on the blanket. He stopped next to my leg. Those tired blue eyes looked down at me. The heat of the bonfire reflected on my cheeks—the one my father helped build when he dropped me off by the old stump, almost two hours ago.

"I got your note."

"Have a seat." I patted the blanket next to me. "You missed Thanksgiving."

He settled down, wincing a little from the sore muscles. His body was covered in dirt, and his right thigh was stained in blood. "How mad was she?"

"You know that line that pops up sometimes right between her perfect eyebrows?"

"That mad, huh?"

"Yeah. Everything turn out okay?"

"It was a mess. We finally got 'em all. I lost eleven. Had to shoot nine of 'em. It was awful. Some got trampled down with broken necks, and then two caused an accident over by Dobbers'."

"Everyone okay?"

"Yeah, I guess. They didn't go to the hospital. It busted up their Explorer pretty good though. It was a man and woman with a little girl, just travelin' through. I didn't know 'em. It sure wasn't the way any us wanted to spend today, but it's over now."

"I'm sorry."

Jess looked sad and just plain tired. My hands ached to pull his dark hair against my cheek, but I stayed with my fingers linked over my drawn-up knees.

"I thought you'd be gone on the first plane out of here after this mornin'." His voice was gruff as he finally asked the question that stabbed away at his heart.

"I thought about it."

"What stopped you?" He let out a deep breath, watching the bonfire.

"Here." I slid the picnic basket over to him. He glanced at me like I was crazy. "There's mac and cheese in there."

"What're you doin' out here?"

"You should take this." I pulled the folded-up piece of paper from my pocket and handed it to him. His eyebrows wrinkled. "Throw it away or burn it. I don't really give a shit. Just get rid of it."

"Alex, what's goin' on?" He shoved the paper inside his coat and continued to watch me like I'd suddenly grown two heads.

"I thought we should talk." My breath floated out in the cool air, much like the release I felt on the inside as I handed over the Mason List to Jess. The scribbled torment was finally gone. "It's much better out here than yelling at each other in my bedroom. It's calm, like it's the only place in the world that ever made sense."

"You think life makes sense in the place I almost got you burned to death?"

I ignored his jab because we both knew what this spot really meant at Sprayberry. I looked at our names carved in the old stump, and the small markers for BB and Carrot buried next to it.

While I was away, I had searched for another place that gave me this feeling. I searched all over Paris and every other city for almost two years; beautiful places with unique and ancient history, but none of them ever matched up to this spot. I finally knew in my heart, the simplest places in the world sometimes have the most complex meaning.

"After you left, I kept hearing you say those words." I looked at his sweet face, feeling the warmth spread in my cold body. "You never said it to me before, or I guess I never *let* you say it to me."

"Which part?"

"That you loved me."

"Al, you've always known that I loved you."

"Maybe, I guess. But it's strange, you know? How easy it is to ignore someone's feelings until they are spoken out loud. How easy it is to pretend they are not real. I got caught up in everything running through my head like some shitty story on repeat that I couldn't hear what you tried to tell me for so long. You finally made me hear you. Believe me. Very loud and clear. For once, I want to do the right thing, Jess."

"And what's that?"

"I think I've always known. But after hearing you? I did a lot of thinking today. You're right. I'm tired, Jess. All of this has to stop. I don't hate you. I don't even hate the Masons. Not really. I hated what happened to me. They were just an excuse that made sense when nothing else did. I hated what caused me to be here and that stupid list just kept it alive inside of me. It was a way for me to never forget, a way for me to rehash it over and over again every time I looked at it. I pretended that I made it in some plan to use for the greater good. Like I could repay everything to your family and it would somehow change what happened, and I'd feel better."

"You were tryin' to repay it?"

"Maybe. I don't know. But I do know that life doesn't work that way. You made me see that this morning. I realized that holding on to this is hurting me, and it's hurting you. That's the last thing I ever wanted to do. That's not how this gets better. You said choose to accept it or walk away. You said accept who you *really* are to me. It's not a choice." I reached over, touching his arm. My fingers trailed down his Carhartt jacket to his bare fingers. I felt his heart beating in his veins. The road to getting over the past would not be easy, but it was one worth traveling for this boy. I stayed calm in my seat. I looked straight into those blue eyes without an ounce of fear.

"Jess, you said just about everything possible this morning, but you never asked me. Ask me what you really wanted to ask me."

"Because I can't. That's not the right thing. I can't ask you to stay. It was wrong of me to even put choices out there. Maybe it will happen one day for us, but I get it. You're livin' your life there, and this one is mine."

"That's the thing, Jess. Last night, you asked me to tell you about Paris. It's all those things I said, but they are empty moments. I'm alone even in a crowded room of people. I'm alone every time I laugh because you're not there with me. It's an empty dream when the other half of me is somewhere else. I am only truly happy when I'm with you. I just always thought you deserved someone better than me."

"Al, don't say that. You've—"

"No." I placed my finger across his lips. I wanted to pull him against me, make him feel what I was trying to say, but he needed to *hear* me say it. "I have hurt you. I have hurt you in so many ways, and you *never* deserved it. I haven't been the person I should have been for you. So I will just have to do everything I can from now on to be that better person. The one you deserve to come home to every night because I want to be that person more than anything else in the world. Because I love you."

The words left my lips at the same time the last brick crumbled that sat upon my shoulders, holding me down in the dust. I floated in the air—light and free with the cool breeze, tossing me around like a crimson bird circling high above us. I was finally home. I was finally happy.

"You really said it," he whispered. For Jess, I think he had waited so long to hear those words that the reality seemed imaginary.

"I should have said it a long time ago. You are the best thing that has ever happened to me. I love you, Jessup Mason. I…love…you." Leaning forward, I kissed his stunned lips. He pulled back and studied my face.

"You really want this? All of it? Because I can't leave. Sprayberry and I are a package deal."

"I want you. And if that means Sprayberry, then I'm all in."

"What're you gonna do here?"

"I don't know. Guess I'll have to figure it out."

"You're serious?"

"As serious as my bags are sitting in Frank's bedroom." I leaned forward and touched my lips to his. Pulling back, his eyes looked confused. I assumed Jess never made it past my note on the front door.

"What 'bout your apartment?"

"Guess I'll have to figure that out too."

I kissed him again, just because I could, just because that nagging voice inside my brain was dead, and I could do whatever my heart wanted. I relaxed, falling backward on the red quilt. His body came with me, never letting go as he stretched out on top of my cold limbs. I kissed his face and eyes. Jess tasted a little like salt from working today. I didn't care because it tasted like him.

This was my future. This was my home. For the first time in my life, I felt like I was truly living. Jess and I would have a life together; just the way he always imagined and just the way I had dreamed every night when I closed my eyes.

"You're really stayin' here with me?"

"Yes, and I was thinking: we should put the porch right here."

"Porch?"

"I'm not staying in Frank's forever. I saw his bedroom. It's not that funny."

He sat up, staring out across the meadow. His dark lashes blinked as he studied the horizon. "We *could* put a house right here. Why'd I not think of that?"

"That's why you need me here, for all the important decisions."

He smiled and leaned in to kiss the tip of my nose. "I love you."

"I love you too, Jess."

He settled down beside me, putting an arm around my shoulders to tuck me next to his body. My head rested against his chest. The stars would pop out soon, giving meaning to the darkness over our new home. I felt the calm, sweet peace of sharing this once again with him.

"Does this mean you'll marry me?"

"Are you asking?"

Jess rolled on his side, looking down at me with those blue eyes. He touched my cheek, running his fingers through my hair. "Will you marry me, Alex?"

"I don't know. We've only been dating for about five minutes."

He grabbed my body, half-tickling and half-kissing me. "Yes, okay. Yes!" I laughed. "I will marry you."

Chapter 45

When I was twenty-five...

"I still can't believe you're actually at Sprayberry," I teased Sadie as we sat on my bed in the farmhouse. She had come all the way to Arlis for the biggest day of my life.

"You and me both. It's like stepping in a John Wayne time warp."

I reached over, wrapping my arms around her little body. "Thank you."

"Sweetie, I don't know if I can stomach anymore of this from you. I'm afraid you'll break out in some outlandish Glee song."

"Really, Sadie?"

"Yes, really. It's okay, though. I would rather see you bouncing off the walls with that ridiculous smile on your face than lying in a puddle of vomit. And I have seen both."

"You are a real bitch sometimes." I laughed.

"I know." She smiled with her sparkly lips. "But, sweetie, I am glad that you are happy. And I am glad it finally worked out for him too. Speaking of our favorite cowboy." She pointed at the bedroom window.

I jumped off my bed and pulled the glass up to see his sweet face. "Hey."

"Hey." He leaned his head in enough to kiss me. I would never get tired of this. Our mouths automatically responded in that familiar push-pull of our lips and tongues. His hands ran through my hair and over my neck.

"*Hello.* You have an audience, who really doesn't want to see the Jess and Alex sex tape."

I pulled away, trying to catch my breath. His blue eyes were dark on the edges as he gave me an ornery smile, never looking at her. "Ten minutes, Sadie, and then she's all yours."

"You better make it nine because it's almost midnight. You know it's considered horrific luck to see the bride on the wedding day."

I crawled through the window. Jess grabbed my hand, pulling me out of view. He kissed me again as his body pushed me against the side of the house. His lips were urgent and desperate, making me gasp for air. He pulled away and kissed me on the nose.

I was breathing hard as I smiled at him. "So why did you come over?"

"Maybe I wanted to sneak in your window one last time." He winked and then leaned in, kissing me slowly as his hands slipped under my shirt.

After I had agreed to marry him, Jess loaded up my bags and drove them right back to the farmhouse. He didn't give a damn what the town gossips said about my living at Frank's with him. It was my father's opinion that had plagued on his conscience. Henry Tanner was important to him. So I had lived the last few months in my old bedroom as we planned a wedding for the first warm day in March.

"Jess, we better…um…stop."

"I know. Fifteen more hours," he whispered.

"Fifteen more hours," I whispered back.

"Fifteen more hours, and you're mine."

"I'm already yours, Jess."

"I know, but tomorrow you'll promise to be mine forever," he whispered.

"Until you have no hair and no teeth."

"Me?" He grinned. "What 'bout you?"

"I'll stay the same."

Jess ran his fingers through my hair. "You do know that I'd love you even if it was gone."

"Me too," I whispered, looking deeply into his blue eyes. "I'll love you forever, no matter what."

"Yeah?"

I nodded, making our noses rub back and forth against each other. Sometimes when I looked at him, my feelings caused a literal pain in my chest. I loved him that much. I loved him so completely that it lacked comprehension. As we stood under moonlight, I felt that stab right behind my rib cage.

"Alex, get back in here," Sadie hissed out the window. "It's eleven fifty-nine."

"Bye, Jess." I kissed him one last time before he let me go. I crawled back in the house, feeling happier than I ever thought possible.

Chapter 46

When I was twenty-five...

I followed Jess down the fancy hallway of the hotel in Dallas. Everything was dipped in high-end, designer couture. Sadie would just faint in excitement if she saw the place. He unlocked the door and then scooped me up, not in the traditional walk over the threshold, but a slung-over-the-shoulder run with my head dangling upside down. I screamed as he dropped me down on the bed.

"You better not mess all of this up. Sadie forced me to sit for two hours to look this way. It's not happening again."

"You plan on marrin' me more than one time?" He winked, then turned to the straight-faced bellhop with our bags. Reaching for his tip, the man in the black suit kept a crisp, thin line across his lips. I wondered how obnoxious Jess and I would need to get before a grin cracked on that guy's face. He turned to leave without a word.

I fell backward on the soft bed; it cradled my tired body like a cloud. The high thread count massaged my shoulders, and every breath I pulled into my lungs even smelled expensive. The joys of being a Mason, I guess.

Holding out my hand, I saw the flat, wide band with a dusting of specks imbedded like bits of snow. The ring wasn't Texas-debutant-sized with a loathsome giant stone; my perfect present from Jess was simple and plain with just a spray of tiny diamonds. I smiled, remembering the wedding and the moment he had placed it on my finger. I had looked deeply into those blue eyes and promised never to take it off.

The ceremony had been everything the residents of Arlis waited sixteen years to see at Sprayberry. Maybe not the elaborate gala dreamed up in the minds of the society women, but a simple wedding with sparkling touches added by Mrs. Mason. I mean, Eva Lynn. She insisted I call her by her given name since I was now a Mason myself.

Mrs. Jessup Mason. Alexandra Mason. Alex Mason.

The words felt strange on my tongue. It would take time—something Jess and I seemed to have an abundance of these days. The warmth spread through my limbs as I thought of many happy, endless moments of just being in his presence. I loved being close and together without the iron claw of the past holding me back. I loved telling him exactly how I felt without my conscience hammering away. Our invisible rope grew stronger and tighter every day. I felt complete and whole knowing Jess and I had an infinite forever.

I turned to look out the picturesque suite window overlooking the Dallas skyline. The building had a beautiful view of the city. Tomorrow, Jess and I would board a plane to Paris for our honeymoon. I picked the one place I wanted him to see. The giddy bubbles of anticipation rose up through my stomach. I would get to see Paris once again, but this time Jess would experience it too. Our trip served another purpose: tie up the loose ends with my apartment and the life I had left there.

I never felt like I'd given up a single thing by staying at Sprayberry. I had made the right decision; the feeling had grown stronger every day. Once we returned from the trip, I planned to concentrate on what to do with my new life in Arlis, which seemed to be the million-dollar question. The school offered me an art instructor position two days a week this fall. In Dallas, I found a gallery curator opening, but I would need to live part-time in the city.

"You hungry?" Jess asked as he pulled off his suit jacket. "You didn't eat much at the party. Caroline packed up some cake."

I grinned at him, shaking my head.

He pulled out a container and shoved a few bits of Italian crème cake in his mouth. Caroline packed that for him, not me. I watched his tongue lick a few crumbs from his pink lips. Leaving the white shirt untucked from the black jeans, he fell into the fancy chair next to the bed. I felt a catch in my chest just watching him. He was mine forever.

Jess moved his hand to the front pocket of his jeans, then pulled away. I knew he was itching to check his phone. "Go ahead and call."

"Nah. I've got to just trust 'em. I know Skeeter and Bobby can do it. It's just hard to leave."

"I know, Jess. Try to remember a plan's in place for every kind of emergency. And it's just ten days. Then you can go back to exhausting yourself as their dictator."

"Yes, ma'am, Mrs. Mason." He gave me a sly grin from his chair, waiting for the crimson to appear on my cheeks. Jess moved from the chair and crawled on top of me. "No more hours," he whispered.

Jess kissed me hard on the mouth as I tasted the sweetness from the cake. His hands slide across the silky fabric of my dress, over my waist, and cupped my right breast.

I had fought every single person on my dress: basic, plain, and simple with no train or jewels, and no lace or tulle; and absolutely under no circumstances, a damn can-can. Eva Lynn and I never quite came to terms on her idea of a bride. During one of our trips to an elaborate dress store in

Dallas, I gave an evil, sarcastic laugh and suggested cutoffs with a white tank top since we couldn't agree on the style of dress. I thought I might need a bottle of good, old-fashioned smelling salts when she collapsed in the chair. That little comment won me this satin slip dress.

Jess rolled over on his side, pulling my body tight against him. His fingers trailed down my back and cupped the silk clinging to my rear. Heat flushed on my neck as I read his thoughts. "Are you wearin' panties under this?"

"Sadie could see the lines." I looked back into his blue eyes, knowing I was right. I think this dress was the winner, just not in the way Eva Lynn had in mind.

"So that sweet ass of yours felt like this all night, and I didn't know it?" His fingers traced deep over each butt cheek. My heart beat fast in my chest as I nodded yes to the question. The plain silk dress was definitely worth every fight. His hand continued around and around, dipping lower down each thigh. I kissed him, matching the movements of my tongue to the pace of his hand. He pulled back, his eyes almost a solid dark blue. Rolling away, Jess set up. He took a deep breath, his shoulders moving with the motion.

"I need to give you somethin' now, or it won't be until tomorrow at this rate."

My skin felt chilly without the heat of his body pressing into me. "We said no presents, remember?"

"It's not exactly a present." Reaching in the side pocket of his suitcase, Jess pulled out a packet and handed it to me. I looked at the manila envelope, feeling a surge of confusion. I'd told him that I would sign any agreement he wanted to protect his family and his money. Jess refused to even have the conversation with me. Our wedding night was an interesting time to bring it up, but if he wanted something in writing, then I would agree to it.

"I told you I would sign anything you wanted." I smiled, trying to speed this up. Quicker the ink dried, the faster we could get back to the silk dress and how much I wanted to feel his naked skin.

"Al, I've given it a lot of thought. So don't think I'm throwin' this at you lightly. Open it."

My fingers opened the top and pulled out something familiar, something very wrong. "Damn it, Jess. What are you doing?"

"Look at all the pages. It's not what you think."

"I said destroy that stupid list. Now you're giving it back to me as my wedding gift?" My fingers dug into the familiar paper as the anger festered. "What kind of twisted shit are you trying to do?"

"I know this is painful for you. I know you've worked hard at lettin' it go. Maybe you did it for me. And I'm grateful. But this was always bigger than me. That's why I didn't rip it up. If you wanted it gone, you would have done it yourself. Look at the other pages."

My fingers flipped through the stack. They appeared to be a contract and bank papers drawn up for Alexandra Mason under something called The Mason List. "I don't understand."

"I had my lawyer set it up, but I couldn't give it to you until we were married. I thought 'bout tellin' you, but I wanted it to be a surprise. Just think 'bout it, Al. I've got the money in there and some investments. It should be self-sufficient once it gets goin'. So make it happen."

"Make what happen?"

"The Mason List. It doesn't have to be a bad thing. You can make it good."

"I told you that I had wanted to pay your family back, but I realized it wouldn't make this better. So I don't understand what you are suggesting here."

"You're gonna pay it back, just not the way you thought you would. I want you to go find her, Al. The girl like you. Help her out when she has no one else. Make her *hate* the Masons as much as you did." A smile smirked on his lips. "Make her angry. Make her want somethin' better. And then, you've paid it forward, which is a hell of a lot better than givin' some rich family a check."

I skimmed over the papers feeling a pain in my gut. I remembered Sadie's words: "Only you know what resolution will give you a sense of absolution, a sense of peace." I had made the right decision that gave the absolute resolution. I let it go so I could marry Jess today. He was happy. I was happy. Since the moment I gave Jess the paper, I'd felt a sense of freedom. I slipped the pages back into the envelope and looked into his sweet face. Good intentions, not malice, came from him tonight. I knew deep in my heart, Jess never would hurt me on purpose. I wanted the happiness to continue, so I kept the peace—a fight for another day.

"I will think about it." Leaning forward, I kissed his lips.

"You promise?"

"Yes, I promise because I love you." My fingers slipped inside the collar of his shirt, feeling his warm skin. I opened the top button and leaned forward to kiss his neck. Pushing the next one free, I undressed the boy who was now my husband. The anxiety of his proposition faded away as Jess laid me back against that soft, expensive bed, letting his fingers run through the long curls of my hair.

“You’re still the most beautiful girl I’ve ever seen.” His breath felt warm on my neck. “And this might be the most amazin’ dress ever,” he whispered, running his hands over the fabric.

Jess kissed me, letting his mouth tug on my bottom lip. My breathing got heavier, feeling his fingers touch me. “Keep your eyes open, Al. I want you to look at me.” He smiled one of those sweet grins. “I never want to stop seein’ you like this.”

My heart caught in my chest as I gazed up at Jess. It still felt unbelievable. I had actually married my blue-eyed boy.

Chapter 47

When I was twenty-five...

Our vacation days sped by as I took Jess from one place to the next in Paris. We visited a few friends I still had left in the city and boxed up my belongings in the apartment. He suggested keeping it, but I said no at the idea. My heart hurt just imagining staying there without him. I once heard that being in love in Paris was different than any other place in the world. For me, that hazy, warm feeling only came when Jess pressed his lips to my skin under the meadow sky. Paris was secondary.

After the honeymoon, we returned to Sprayberry. Jess continued running the ranch. The spring cattle sold, giving credibility to his new position in the shadow of Frank. By May, our house was under construction out by the stump. I continued to search for my purpose in Arlis. The days were filled with fairs, pancake suppers, church picnics, and the slew of other activities that rotated through the town square. I even covered for Caroline at Jeeter's for a few weeks so she could take a vacation with my father.

In July, I opened my own private studio in a vacant building that became available close to the hardware store. I wanted to advertise to the surrounding counties, remembering how difficult it was taking lessons all the way in Dallas. My studio would give kids and even adults a way to learn closer to home.

Occasionally, I traveled back to Austin to meet with my old advisor. He often had a project or competition he wanted me to enter. I won a few shows and sold some of my entries. Sometimes, he would suggest an open position in another city, but I always said no. I didn't want to commute or spend time away for any type of job. I had promised to live with Jess at Sprayberry, and I wanted that more than anything else in world.

Chapter 48

When I was twenty-six...

Today was my birthday and the day the furniture *finally* arrived for our new house. I had spent the morning helping the movers setup each room. It felt good. It felt so incredibly good each time I walked through the front door, except tonight I wasn't walking.

"Jess, put me down."

"Keep your eyes closed." He clamped his arms tighter around my body as his boots stepped on the wooden porch.

"I've seen the inside of the house a hundred times. I even set up the damn furniture this morning."

"This is our first official night here, so just do this for me."

"You are impossible, Jessup Mason." I grinned into his blue eyes.

"Closed, Alex."

"Fine." I shut my eyes, snuggling closer to his chest as he opened the door. I heard his boots on the hardwood floor in the living room. I loved our new house. It wasn't over the top like the Mason Manor that sat on the other side of Sprayberry. Our home was simple and very much us. My favorite part was the porch that overlooked the stump and the beautiful view of the meadow. I even installed a porch swing.

Jess continued to walk toward the dining room. His hand let go of me, and I heard the chair pull out from the table. Tilting me down, my butt touched the seat. "Okay, you can open them."

Slowly, I lifted my eyelashes to a dark room lit with about a hundred candles; the entire table and counter were covered with glowing flames that trailed into the living room and around the fireplace and on the coffee table. In front of me were several pans of food and a small cake with the words HAPPY BIRTHDAY, ALEX in scripted letters.

We both had been so busy with the move that I just planned to do nothing for my birthday. Turning to look up at his sweet face, I felt that pain in my chest. "You didn't have to do this, Jess."

"Well, Caroline made the food. I just set it up."

"It's so beautiful. Thank you."

He knelt down beside the chair, taking my hand. I saw his eyes glisten with a few tears. "I want you to know how *happy* I am. You're here with me. We're in our house together. I've wanted this for so long, and I finally get it. I finally get to have this with you."

"This makes me happy too."

"I know you've givin' up stuff to be here with me."

"No." I leaned forward, kissing him softly. "Never think that. I am here because this is the way it's supposed to be."

"Promise?"

"Yes." I touched his cheek, feeling the stubble under my fingers.

Jess pulled me up from the chair, and I followed him into the living room as the candles twinkled around us. Falling back against our new couch, I let him take off my shirt. He pressed his lips to my bare skin, kissing down my breasts toward my stomach. He pulled my jeans slowly over my hips. Looping his fingers around my white panties, he tugged the cotton fabric down to my ankles. My heart beat fast in my chest as I watched Jess take off his clothes until he was completely naked. He crawled on top of me, slipping between my thighs.

I smiled at the intense look on his sweet face. "Our guests will never sit on this couch if they know your nasty ass was on it."

"You like my ass." He grinned before kissing my lips. His tongue brushed over the freckle on the bottom one. He kissed me harder as I locked my ankles around his waist. I drifted away under the light of a hundred candles, letting his body touch me in every way possible. I would never get tired of this with Jess. I would never get tired of how it felt to really be us.

Chapter 49

When I was twenty-six...

Two weeks after we moved into the house, I drove on the dirt road to the highway for a show in Austin. I turned the fancy satellite radio in my new Tahoe to a station I had programmed just to torment the fire out of Jess. I felt a little sad being gone, even for just a few days. He was so embedded under my skin that I felt a little nauseated being apart.

As I drove down the road, I saw the child first, not the woman, walking on the highway between Arlis and Granby. He was a dark-haired boy around four or five years old, clutching a beat-up teddy bear under his arm, following behind the broken-down woman. She had dark stains on the legs of her jeans and a dirty shirt with holes. The November air was rather chilly, and neither of them wore a coat.

I felt a catch in my throat as I drove past, seeing the pair fade in the rearview mirror. I was alone and a little afraid to pull over for strangers. This world was not a nice world anymore, but something took control like I'd never even had a decision in the matter. Clenching the steering wheel, I pulled over, making a quick U-turn. I parked on the side of the road, watching from the safety of my large truck

She was a short woman, about five feet tall. Her dirty hair was fastened in a ratty clump against her neck. She never looked in my direction, but I knew she saw me. I read the thoughts etched into her face. She didn't want some rich woman in the fancy truck interfering in their lives. She figured I was sitting inside, laughing or bored with fleeting curiosity.

The pit of my stomach shook. I wasn't bored or spoiled with unnecessary shit. I swore that I would *never* be that person when I married Jess. Opening the door, I jumped out, feeling the ground under my trusty, gray canvas shoes. I walked toward the travelers, one foot in front of the other until I stood directly in their path.

She looked at me with narrow and angry eyes. Pinpricks shot down my spine, seeing the familiar grit of her jaw. I knew this face very well. It was the same face I saw in the mirror for about sixteen years: a permanent look of hatred and pride that manifested so deep it couldn't be contained.

They needed my help. I would get a backlash of hatred. She would not willingly take my assistance. Knowing the likely outcome, I could live with it. They needed me more than I needed their gratitude.

Make her hate the Masons as much as you did. Make her angry. Make her want somethin' better.

A jolt slammed into my chest. It finally made sense. I understood why the Masons just didn't have it in them to walk the other way. Why they just couldn't leave Henry and Alex Tanner sitting in their car in the hospital parking lot. How Mrs. Eva Lynn Mason, with her proper pearl necklace, didn't give a damn what others thought of her. She didn't need my love and approval to know our move to Sprayberry was the right decision. She never cared one bit that I hated the Masons as long as my father and I had a roof over our heads.

The magnitude of the moment struck me hard and deep. I stuck out my hand, trying to play it casual, which seemed impossible considering I faced the defining moment of my life.

"Hi. I'm Alex Mason. It's getting pretty cold out here. I was just on my way to get some hot chocolate at Jeeter's. Want a ride into town?"

Her gaze shifted to me and back to the car. I saw the distain in her sneer; a wordless glare that said *I don't need pity from some rich bitch.* A small voice spoke up softly from behind. "Do they have marshmallows?"

"Anything you want. Jeeter's even has whipped cream." I saw his eyes light up when I mentioned the last part. "What's your name?"

"Eddy del Torro. And that's my momma, Vanessa."

Chapter 50

Yesterday, 11:34 am.

Sitting in the back corner, I took another bite of the gooey pizza. A piece of pepperoni stuck to the roof of my mouth. I used my tongue to pry it free. Definitely not even in the top fifty best I had ever eaten, but the food wasn't the point. I watched them—out of sight and out of mind. I preferred it that way.

Eight children, ranging from roughly seven to ten years old, ran from one loud game to another. The basketball toss seemed to be their favorite. The kids belonged to a home in the south section of Dallas. They were here today because I had sponsored the trip to Mario's Pizza Land. Well, in truth, the three full hours of semi-edible goo and arcade madness came courtesy of the Mason List.

When I officially assumed responsibility of Jess's grand idea, I intended to mark an item off the old sheet and continue to the next one. This entry for carnival tickets held three tally marks. Jess would laugh in my face when I returned to Sprayberry. My rules, so I could break them as many times as I wished.

I wiped the grease off my lips and gathered up the trash. After three days away, I felt a stab of homesickness. It was strange to think I had once left him over two years, and yet I couldn't stand to be gone a couple of days. I traveled more than I planned, but I just couldn't stop. The Mason List took on a mind of its own. The ideas came faster than I could even process.

Vanessa del Torro and her son Eddy became my first project. She was a tough one to crack; the girl had ten times the hatred and mistrust than the younger version of me. Caroline gave Vanessa a job at Jeeter's. I checked off the list *my father's hardware store job.* A few months later, I added *riding lessons* when I got Eddie a horse.

My eyes scanned the list differently these days. I felt anticipation rather than the gripping control of the past. Sometimes, I purposely sought out people, and others just stumbled up under my feet. In most cases, I preferred to be anonymous. I watched in the shadows as I paid restaurant bills for random tables. I had bought high-end Nikes for an impoverished school. I never saw the faces of the kids, but I already knew how good it felt to wiggle your toes inside a pair that actually fit. I marked off *school shoes* from the list.

One night before Christmas, I tipped a waitress $5,000 at a diner just outside of Fort Worth. Concealed in the safe darkness of my car, I had watched through the window as she approached the table. Her expression had made my chest clench. I bit down hard on my lip to fight back the tears. Her tired, old face collapsed into the red cushioned seat. Without a single word between us, I saw the relief etched in the lines around her mouth. She needed a break. She hoped for a break. She wished for a break. That tip was just enough to get her there. That night, I had crossed *Christmas present money* off the list.

One afternoon, I had waited to get my oil changed and overheard a desperate man getting the bad news on his truck. I caught a glimpse at the most pathetic piece of rusted-up metal sitting next to the curb. I left my warm seat and crossed over to the new-car side of the dealership.

Whipping out my checkbook, I pointed at the white double-cab sitting on the showroom floor. I didn't need to see any piece of the inside to know the fancy truck had the best of the best. An hour later, I sat in my Tahoe as the man drove out the showroom doors. He wiped a tear across his plaid shirt sleeve. I ducked as his wild eyes searched around the parking lot, but I made sure he never saw who or what or where the gift came from that day. Pulling out a sheet of paper, I had marked through *white diamond truck for my dad.*

I had also kept my art studio in Arlis, but I gave free lessons to anyone willing to spend the time to learn. After every new student, I put a tally mark next to *fancy lessons with Pascal.* This had been my life for over a year. I thought the little bursts of excitement would fade. If anything, it grew stronger and hit deeper. I owned that list; it no longer owned me.

This trip to Dallas had set the groundwork for my most personal endeavor to date: The Anna House. Close to my old neighborhood, I bought a Victorian-style, two-story house. It was roughly 4,000 square feet. The carpenter said the building had the potential of being divided into three living quarters. In honor of my mother, I could house three families who needed a place to stay while visiting loved ones in the hospital. Once completed, I would mark off *the farmhouse at Sprayberry.* I planned to build one in Arlis too. Dr. Mason and I had even talked about the possible linkage of the hospice ward to The Anna House.

I looked one last time at the kids playing Skee-Ball. Time to go home. Time to see Jess. My lips curled up in a smile as I thought about what I planned to tell him. I almost told him last night, but I wanted to see his blue eyes in person as I said the words. Taking out my phone, I dialed his number. It went straight to voicemail as it often did when he was out on the ranch. Stuffing the black box down in my purse, I turned up the radio and listened to Brad Paisley. I was in a good mood as I drove from Dallas back to Sprayberry.

Jess wasn't at the house when I arrived. I sat on the porch, watching the sun go down across the meadow. The sounds of crickets picked up as my feet moved back and forth with the porch swing. I called Jess again, but it went straight to voicemail.

I counted back and realized I'd called three times today without talking to him, which was not that unusual when I traveled at the same time the ranch worked cattle. I was ready for him to get home. It had been almost twenty-four hours since I'd last heard his voice.

I knew it would be a long night. The ranch could change like the wind; one minute everything was fine, and the next, an all-out crisis. Jess could be tied up indefinitely. I'm sure he was at the barn, knee-deep in something disgusting. My stomach twisted thinking of the awful smell, and I choked down a dry heave.

I heard a truck pull up on the front side of the house. I waited, hearing the footsteps against the wraparound porch. I couldn't wait to see his sweet face. My heart beat fast as I thought about telling him what I found out in Dallas.

"Hey."

"Oh, hey, Dad. I thought you were Jess."

"He probably won't be home until late. I think the boys had a rough day out there. I heard something about it at the store."

"Did Gunther get tired of spouting shit at the feedstore and move on over to you?"

"Alex!"

I laughed at his frown. "Sorry."

"You get the contractor set up?"

"Yeah. I think it will turn out good. It's about five miles from our old house."

"You go by and see it?"

"No." I shook my head. "I wanted to, but I don't know if I can."

Maybe someday I would go by and see the little house with the garden. I worried it would look different than I imagined in my mind. It might be painted pink at this point, or the old tree could be bulldozed to the ground. I hated the idea of that place being something different than the picture in my memory. The sound of my phone interrupted my thoughts. I pulled it out, expecting to see Jess's face laughing on the screen. Instead, I saw Bobby scrawled across the top. "Hey, Bobby."

"Alex…" His words disappeared in the stillness of the sun. I dropped the little box, hearing a thud on the beautiful porch overlooking our place on the meadow. I ran out past the stump. Sinking to my knees, I vomited the pizza across the grass and front legs of my jeans. *No.* This wasn't happening. *No.* A large pair of arms lifted me up from behind. *No…no…no!*

"Come on, Pumpkin. Get in the truck."

Clammy goose bumps covered my skin as I bounced around in the passenger seat. My father drove faster than I knew his truck should go over the meadow. I didn't know who else followed, nor did I care. A dark cloud scooped over my fingers and wrapped in a vice grip across my shoulders. It coated me like a black cape concealing me within its elements. I fought hard to feel Jess, but that internal connection came back empty.

We reached the side of the ravine before anyone else he called. Bobby stood next to the edge, his clothes covered with dirt. I flung open the door before the truck ever came to a stop.

Some thirty feet down, I saw a horse and what I assumed was Jess. Skeeter perched next to them in the jagged area cut out by a creek. We'd ridden past it hundreds of times through the years, but never ventured into the belly of the devil.

"Wait, Alex." Bobby tried to pull me back. I slung an elbow straight into his eye, not caring if it hurt. I slipped and rolled all the way down; blood poured from my knee, soaking my jeans. I clipped my forehead on a rock right above my eye. The gash dripped down, blocking my vision. I wiped the wetness away on my sleeve.

Coming to a stop against the flesh of a tan horse, I recognized the soft coat of Katarina's Revenge. The breeder had named her after some stupid divorce dispute. That horse had the temperament of a debutant bitch. Jess always thought she was so damn pretty with her light-tan skin the color of butterscotch. She had never listened when I had tried to ride her. I had hated every smug little noise she fired in my direction.

Skeeter reached over to help me crawl around to the other side of her silent body.

I screamed.

I screamed loud and shrill, like a dying animal howling into the sunset. My stomach twisted as I reached forward to touch him. My beautiful, blue-eyed boy no longer had a face.

"I'm sorry, ma'am. I don't know what happened. She spooked on the way back." Skeeter's voice shook on each word. "Not sure why. I think his foot got caught up in the stirrup. Flipped under from what I saw. Reigns tangled up. She wouldn't stop. They fell down in here. Thrashin' everywhere. I shot her. I was afraid to move 'im, though."

Skeeter's voice narrated the horror right before my eyes. Rocks had ripped his flesh down to his bones. The area around his right eye remained beaten to a bloody pulp; his eyeball dangled off loose to one side. Flies swarmed around the open wound. *The bugs were touching him.* I swatted them away, feeling the cool grip of panic. His right arm remained free while the left twisted back in a strange angle under his back. The rest of his pelvis and legs remained trapped under the butterscotch bitch that pulled him down into the pit of hell.

I touched his arm as tears ran down my cheeks. I touched his chest; his body felt warm. I wanted to wrap myself around it. I wanted to never let him go. The knots inside me twisted up tight with the impact of the shock.

Slipping my fingers next to his neck, I closed my eyes and waited. I blocked out the commotion at the top of the cliff. *Come on, Jess.* I focused on the sounds of the meadow, the sounds of our home. My fingers shook in the blood. His lips were blue. Jess wasn't getting any air.

"Please," I muttered, staring down at him. "Don't leave me. You can't leave me like this. You promised. Remember. You…pro…promised." I choked on the last words. Everything in my life felt irrelevant and just plain stupid as his life dripped away onto Sprayberry's dirt.

Shifting my fingers, I pressed even harder against his skin. He wasn't dead. He couldn't be dead. I would feel it in my bones. My tears dropped onto his shirt and dissolved into the bloody fabric. "Stay with me. I have to tell you something, and it's not gonna be like this."

In the stillness, I felt a small flutter. I sucked in a gulp of air with an involuntary laugh. Leaning over, I was careful not to put my weight against his broken body. I kissed the place on his neck, tasting the blood on my lips. I kissed the side of his face that remained unscathed. With every piece of my soul, I willed his heart to keep beating.

"Listen to me, Jess," I whispered in his ear. "It's you and me. Remember that. I'm here. Keep holding on. You will be all right."

Pressing my lips to his blue ones, I felt the soft trickle of air from his mouth. I blew hard, pulling from the pit of my stomach. The air returned smooth from his lips. I choked back a sob and tried it again. My limited experience with CPR came from the summer at Rochellas. The few puffs into his lungs wouldn't make a difference, but the act gave me solace. I pushed out another gulp so deep I choked. I should've pressed on his chest, but I was afraid. That stupid horse may have crushed him.

I ran my fingertips over the mangled fabric just to let his body know I was still here. "I love you so much. Don't give up. I will not let you go. You can't go. Please…please…Jess." The words turned into an incoherent babble. A pair of arms pulled me away from him.

"Let me go. Stop. No, please. He needs me. Let…me…go." I fought the person with every piece of strength left in me. He would live if I touched him. My fingers made the raw, biting pain disappear. I screamed as they hauled me back up the side of the ravine. At the top of the landing, people paced and stood in confused horror all around us.

"Alex. Stop fighting."

I collapsed on the meadow grass as my father wrapped himself around my body. "But, Daddy. I have…I have to stay with…him. He needs me. I have to stay."

"You need to let the paramedics get down there. Look. Can you see it?" He pointed off to a strange-looking sled-like thing. "They will put him in the basket and get him out of there."

"He's breathing. I could feel it. He will be okay, right, Daddy?"

His face twisted up as he nodded. I fell against his arms, knowing my father lied. Just like all the times I looked him straight in the eye and said what I knew felt comforting to the broken man. The lack of honesty ripped my heart right out of my skin. He lied because I couldn't handle the truth no more than he could all those days we struggled.

Jess would not live. He was crushed from the inside out. People don't survive this sort of accident. Panic spun around in my mind, cutting off the flow of oxygen to my brain. I couldn't breathe. My world just got swallowed up into the belly of Sprayberry as madness attacked all rationality. I scratched and kicked my father. He held on with a vice grip as I twisted around, crying in the grass. I broke. Every emotion crashed and splattered in ugly pieces for everyone to see. I didn't give a damn anymore.

They say your life flashes before your eyes right before you die. In that moment, my whole world spun around in rapid motion. The thought of Jess being dead tore a deep hole through my heart, and my body crumbled into dust. I couldn't live without him. The air would stop flowing in my lungs; I would cease to exist. He was my other half. He was *me*. We breathed the same or not at all.

Slowly, the strength left my limbs. I stopped fighting and collapsed in my father's embrace. We watched the basket lift over the side in slow motion. Jess had a mask covering his blue lips. I grasped to that small hope. For a moment longer, my blue-eyed boy lived.

Chapter 51

Today, 7:05 am.

The smell of disinfectant mixes with the crisp, sterile air. I scrub my hands in the sink; the soap burns my raw skin. The black stains are gone from my cuticles, like they never existed, except for the remaining cuts in my flesh. Sharlene wraps me in a blue protective gown and points toward the glassed room.

There's an eerie silence under the room's dim lighting. I step across the cold floor amidst the faint hiss of the machines. The frigid temperature activates painful goose bumps on my skin. Approaching the edge, I see a large tube running from his mouth while most of his body is coated in white, much like the time I dressed him as a mummy. I smiled at the memory. We had stolen rolls and rolls of gauze from the hospital. Jess had walked up and down the halls, growling in a zombie's voice while I followed behind, laughing to the point of tears.

I look at his broken body as those kids drift away in a distant memory. With the shock of the accident gone, I see him clearly. Bandages cover most of his face and scalp. He seems better, and yet he seems worse than expected. I think anything shy of his usual smile would feel unacceptable.

For the first time in his life, Jess's head gleams shiny and sleek, absent of his floppy, dark hair. He would hate it more than the scars, I think. My gut lurches, knowing the damage underneath the gauze would change him forever. But I would love him no matter how he looked to the rest of the world. He was, *is*, my Jess.

I reach forward to touch the bruised skin on his cheek. His body feels warm. I trace over his remaining eye and dip down over his jaw. Leaning close, I whisper next to his ear, "Hey."

I wait for his response. Nothing but the sound of the hospital answers back. His silent lips remain still. I touch them with my thumb, thankful they are a dry, light pink instead of the oxygen-deprived blue. "I'm here, Jess. I'm sorry for not being here sooner. I got sick, but I'm better now. Ashley washed my hair. She saw me naked too."

He should laugh. He should tease something awful about Ashley holding me hostage in restraints like Kathy Bates in the movie *Misery*. Instead, he answers with the confines of stillness. This is the part that feels like a raw, open wound. The part where I feel alone, absent from my other half. I reach down to take his free hand. The other arm is swaddled in a brick of white, just like both of his legs.

"I need to tell you something." I hold tight to the familiar hand with a slew of calluses on the palm. "This was supposed to be a happy time, you know. I was going to tell you when I got back yesterday and we would get excited or freaked out or I don't know. Now I wish I just told you on the phone so you would know. I wish I hadn't waited."

Taking his hand, I place it across my stomach. "We're having a baby, Jess."

A tear slips down, and I smile at his unmoving face. Maybe I thought hearing those words would flicker some form of recognition, an emotion or just a sign that says he could hear me babbling in the room. "I wish you could talk to me right now. I'm scared. I'm scared I won't ever hear your voice again. I'm scared to do this by myself. I'm just scared right now and I need you."

Letting out a deep breath, I swallow back the burning in my throat. "You deserve to see him grow up. He deserves to have you with him. I don't know if it's a boy. He just feels like one. He'll look like you with those big, blue eyes and silly smile. Just like you did when we met. I'll never forget it, you know. Seeing you leaning back against the wall with your hair falling down in your eyes. You were something else back then…my crazy boy. You became the love of my life that day."

Leaning over, I touch my lips against his mouth. I hover in place, next to the tube, waiting for them to move. I wait for Jess to respond in that familiar push-pull of our lips and tongues. Giving up, I lean back, feeling a wet tear drop from my eye and splatter on his neck. The tear rolls off his skin and soaks into the hospital mattress. I cling to his fingers again, pulling them up to my lips and kissing each one.

"I love you, Jessup Mason. You hear me? You are the best thing that ever happened to me. So that means you can't die. It's not the way this ends. You pr-promised. You promised me…so don't go and break it."

I choke back an ugly sob. My tongue balls into a thick clump on the roof of my mouth. The pain sears like broken glass through my skin and through my bones. He would always be my boy. My happiness. My sunshine. My forever.

Curling up in the chair next to his bed, I would wait. I would not leave. No one could pry me from this very spot. Fatigue slams into my body; after the night of restless and drug-induced fits, I drift off in a peaceful sleep absent of dreams. I sleep through the faint images of nurses coming and going. I feel the soft folds of a blanket drape over my skin.

My eyes open to see Dr. Mason looking down at me. His ever-present boyish looks seem old and fragile. A bearded shadow graces his jaw, showing off a mix of black and gray.

"How is he?"

"Holdin' in there."

"He…he's going to die, isn't he?" I whispered the haunting words I had avoided since the accident.

"He could, Alex. He should already be gone. But I don't know. He might not wake up for a few days, or he might not wake up at all. But I'm not givin' up hope. You shouldn't either. Jess got hurt real bad, but he's made it this far."

Pulling up a seat beside me, his hands shake as he tries to relax against the plastic. I reach over and take his fingers between mine. "How bad are the injuries?"

"They're about as bad as they can get. We got Jess to the hospital in Arlis to wait for the helicopter to bring him here. He was dragged by that horse. They both went down the side of that hole. She fell on him. We know that because they had to pull him out from under her. They had him on a ventilator all the way here. His chest and pelvis are crushed, and he wasn't really breathin' on his own. I wasn't sure he'd even make it to Dallas, you know. He should've died out there on the meadow."

He stifles back a cry. The strong doctor clutches my hand as he continues. "They did surgery and tried to fix him up as much as possible. He's got a lot of internal injuries and some swellin' in the brain. I thought he'd die on the table. That's what usually happens. The body can't handle that much trauma. But he didn't. He's holdin' on. He's alive. It's like a…a—"

"Miracle," I mutter, feeling the tears fall down on our clasped hands.

"Yeah." A nervous laugh comes from his lips. "I'm a doctor. But I've never seen anythin' like it before in my life. It's like a damn miracle is holdin' Jess together."

That absurd word echoes like a pulse in my life. My father believed in one side of it, and Dr. Mason believed in the other. They both embraced the idea with a full heart and equal trust; a miracle for my mother with the arrival of the Masons and another that beat in the literal heart of Jess.

My thoughts flood in twisted confusion. "You really believe that?"

"I have to, Alex. He's my son. I have to believe it until there's not a reason to anymore. And right now, he's here. He's breathin'. Every time he does, I know he shouldn't be."

"That's…that's…" The wave of emotions overtakes my words. "It's just hard for me to think about."

"It's hard. But you have to hope, Alex. You have to believe in the impossible."

I swallowed hard, nodding my head. "I…I know."

He grips my fingers tighter. "I think he already knows you're here."

"You do?"

"I do. Everythin' just seems better now that you're with him."

I glance over the side of the rail. His chest moves up and down under the white sheet. His overall presence seems more relaxed, despite all the tubes and monitors. "You're right. I think he does."

"I'll see about gettin' you somethin' better than this chair."

"Okay."

Dr. Mason returns with a small cot. It fits snuggly in the corner amidst the equipment and his bed. Lying on my back next to the railing, I watch the tiles on the ceiling. Once again, all the same players scatter across the same, terrible board of life, sitting in a hospital: Dr. Mason, a mother, a father, and a child. We all hang in limbo, waiting for the verdict in a plan much bigger than all of us.

I reach up and touch his hand through the bars. I need reassurance that his heart still pumps life through that ripped-up body. I need reassurance he is still breathing. I need the facts, but those just are not possible.

Sometimes all we have is faith and hope, and you just have to trust it.

I understand that now. Closing my eyes, I clutch his warm fingers and whisper in the darkness, asking for the impossible. I ask for a miracle. I ask for Jess to come back to me.

Chapter 52

Eight days later...

The room is cold and haunting. I drift in and out of sleep, never gone for any extended amount of time in case he wakes up. Jess improves a little more each day even though he's in a coma. The doctors are still hopeful and still perplexed at his ability to stay alive.

My father tries to convince me to leave and stay in a hotel, but I refuse. I believe with everything inside my heart that Jess will wake up, and I *will* be here when it happens. So I rinse off in the hospital bathroom each morning. I sit in the chair all day talking to Jess, like he can hear me. I sleep next to his bed each night, listening to the tubes and monitors.

I hope for him. I pray for him. I wait for him.

Chapter 53

Fifteen days later...

I rest on my back, watching the sun reflecting on the ceiling. They moved Jess out of ICU yesterday and into his own room. I don't notice the sounds of the machines anymore. They blend into the background noise of the hospital. I still talk to him each day. I tell him what Skeeter says about the ranch. I tell him about the visitors in the lobby. I tell him more about the baby. I have pretend arguments about names. I talk until my throat gets hoarse and scratchy.

Sometimes I think about his voice. Sometimes I imagine I can hear his pancake-syrup words. I can hear Jess laugh. I can hear him tease me. I can hear him say, "I love you."

Chapter 54

Nineteen days later…

The room is warm as I rest on the cot next to his bed. The doctor wants to remove the breathing tube from his lungs today. They tell me this step is considered progress, but I am afraid. I have so many thoughts and questions. I have spent too many days alone, talking to a person who never answers back. But even in my fears, I believe he will wake up. I still have hope.

Hearing a faint noise, my eyes flip open. I roll off the cot and walk over to the side of his bed. My heart beats fast, and I feel as if I'm dreaming. The single blue eye looks around frantically. *Jess is awake!*

"It's okay. Don't be scared. I'm here." Tears fall down my cheeks as he stares back as me. I clasp his fingers on the good arm. My heart breaks in a thousand pieces as I see the fear etched in his face. "You had an accident. We're in the hospital in Dallas." I swallow hard, biting my lip. "Do…do you understand what I'm saying? Do you…um…do you know who I am?"

The doctor said he could have brain issues from the swelling. I am scared in a different way now, seeing the confusion, worrying he can't recognize me.

"Jess?" I whisper.

He slowly nods his head.

"Good." I smile at him, squeezing his hand. My heart beats fast in my chest, and I want to faint with relief. I pull in a deep breath, feeling calmer.

Jess lets go of my fingers and reaches toward by stomach, placing his hand against my shirt. I swallow hard. "You…you heard me talking?"

He moves his head up and down, very faintly.

I smile through the tears rolling down my cheeks. Reaching over, I press the call button to signal the nurse. I pull the edge of my shirt up, exposing the beginning of the bump on my stomach. I hold his hand against my body, looking into the sweet face. I swallow the thick lump in my throat. The bandages cover so much of his skin. Jess didn't know the extent of his scars and injuries. He didn't know some of the damage was permanent. My heart hurts for him as we stare at each other.

"I love you," I whisper. "I love you no matter what. You know that, right?"

He nods his head as a tear falls out of his single blue eye. I lean over, placing my lips against the corner of his mouth. My own tears drip onto his cheek. I want to wrap my arms around his body and never let go. I can breathe again. My miracle came true. Jess came back to me.

Epilogue

On a hill far away, a beautiful house rises up from the ground with a wraparound porch. It reigns over the land like a beacon in the meadow. A woman stands by an old stump in the yard. The bark crumbles from years of the beating sun. Her crooked fingers trace the names carved in the blackened wood.

JESS + ALEX

They remain old and withered in the stump followed by eleven more added through the years as the children got older and the grandchildren begged to have their names carved in the wood too.

She turns and walks up the stairs; her steps slow with old age. Taking a seat on the little porch swing, she touches the short, grayish-red curls resting on the back of her neck. The sun dips down below the earth. The woman waits patiently for the show to start in the dark sky. One by one, the stars come to life. She smiles, feeling content.

"Looks like a clear one tonight."

She turns, hearing the voice of the man resting on the other side of the old swing. He grins as his single blue eye lights up as bright as the twinkling dots in the sky.

"Yeah, it does," she answers back. Her heart beats just a little stronger just like it always did at the sight of his sweet face. The one right by her side since she was eight; the one she promised to love until they had no teeth and no hair.

Reaching over with a shaky hand, her crooked fingers slip into his old, callused palm. They rock back and forth as the sounds of the meadow grow louder in the night. Sometimes if she listens closely in the breeze, a chorus of small voices echoes off the trees and the grass.

"What'd you wish for?"

"Can't tell you, or it won't come true."

"Will you tell me if it does?"

"Yeah."

"Promise?"

"Yeah, I promise."

Acknowledgements

I want to thank each and every one of you for reading the story of Jess and Alex. So many wonderful books exist out in the world, and I feel privileged that you fit *The Mason List* into your busy schedules.

I have wanted to write a novel for a very long time. Even after I started the process, it took many years to turn a concept into a full-fledged story. This book only exists because of the wonderful people who provided support along the way.

My husband John, who believed I could write a novel before I had words on paper. You would not let me quit. Each time I was discouraged, you would tell me to keep going – even after you read the first draft! Thank you for always being supportive of my eccentric, creative ideas. I know it's difficult living with a part-time Hobo, who believes piling up things is being organized. Without you, I could never write a love story. You are the love of my life – fun, fights and all.

My brother Kyle, who asked if he could wait to see the movie. Nothing is more encouraging than someone who thinks my story will be that successful. You were always supportive both vocally and financially. I appreciate all your input – including the web series idea created on speaker phone while I was driving in my car.

My parents, Darrell and Georgia, who have been supportive my whole life, even when I stayed in school an extra year or so (whose counting) to get a degree in Journalism. I have always been a story teller. As my Mom use to say – "You tell Grandma Lily stories", which means I like to include the details. I think we all knew the writer was in me, I just had to figure out how to get it on paper. Thank you for always asking about my book and being financially supportive of *The Mason List.* And most importantly, thank you for encouraging me to read as a kid. You bought me stacks and stacks of books, and took me on numerous trips to the library.

My in-laws, Billy and Gayle, who have always made me feel included in their family. You are very kind and sweet. I appreciate your support both vocally and financially. Thank you for always asking about my writing project and listening to the planning details. You have spread the word online and many of my followers are because of you. You thought my story would be wonderful without ever reading a word.

My beta readers: Kelli, Patty, Rachel, Bonnie, Beth, Brittney and John. *The Mason List* would not be the same without you. I took your suggestions and factored those into the final story. I appreciate each of you for listening to me talk for hours about plot and characters. More importantly, you read the beta copy and loved it – even when it was twenty-thousand words longer. All of the readers should send you a GIANT thank you for helping me make those changes.

My writing buddy Dan, who introduced me to the world of National Novel Writing Month (NANOWRIMO). I had wanted to write, but didn't have the platform to constructively put words on paper. Thank you for letting me babble on and on about editors, word count and writing software. I'm sure there were many times you wanted to yell, "Just publish it already!"

My book buddy Kelli, who gave encouragement to keep writing this story. You were both a beta reader and my target audience. You read original drafts out of context - sometimes even broken dialogue I created in the notes section of my phone. When I was discouraged about a chapter, your excitement over the story would always get me back on track.

My editor Anna Floit, who was tasked with the original 138,000 word final manuscript. Bless you girl! I am incredibly grateful for the many hours you put into *The Mason List.* I know this project was very difficult at times. Thank you for sticking with *The Mason List*!

My photographer Andrew Lam, who was gracious enough to take my wonderful author photos. Thank you for all your help – even when I tried to "glamour" them!

The many family members and friends, who have been so supportive and encouraging – there's just too many of you to name. Thank you for always asking about my project and sharing in the excitement. You have no idea how much it meant to have people want me to finish. Writing can be a very isolated hobby. I had doubts at times and then I would cross paths with one of you, hearing your kind words. Thank you!

And thank you God, who makes miracles possible; whether they are in the form we want, or maybe the one that needs to happen. As Alex came to understand in *The Mason List*, we will never comprehend the grand-master plan, and that's ok. "For I know the plans I have for you. Plans to prosper you and not to harm you. Plans to give you hope and a future."
Jeremiah 29:11

About the Author

SD Hendrickson received a Bachelors of Science in Journalism from Oklahoma State University. She lives in Tulsa, Oklahoma with her husband and two schnauzers. Currently, her days are spent teaching computer software to oil and gas companies as well as writing technical instructional manuals. *The Mason List* is her first novel.

Visit **www.sdhendrickson.com** for more information on upcoming projects such as *Red Dirt Claws* and *The Tunnels.*

Made in the USA
Lexington, KY
28 February 2015